What people are  The Cult of Eden

In the age-old struggle between Good and Evil – between Christianity and Satanism – there are heroes and there are villains. However, as *The Cult of Eden*, the first part of Bill Halpin's The Unrisen saga reveals, in the heat of battle it is not always clear who are the good guys and who are the bad... as black and white certainties are swept away by a tide of blood-stained grey.

Charles Christian, editor *The Grievous Angel zine*

A riveting read! Halpin takes a new spin on the creepy religious cult and amps the terror factor up to eleven! Not only is the Cult of Eden like no group you've ever seen before, but the Battese family is thrown into a bizarre and complex plan to effectively undo all of creation. This stellar freshman novel from Bill Halpin has me on the edge of my seat waiting for the next installment!

Kathleen, www.belleofthebookcase.com

The Cult of Eden is one of those books that tricks you into thinking it's going one way and then BAM! it switches gears and takes you on an even crazier journey. The things the author puts these characters through should be illegal, even in a book! I'm looking forward to seeing what else he can come up with in the future, too!

Armand Rosamilia, author of the *Dying Days zombie* series

The Cult of Eden is a stellar debut novel. A kaleidoscope of religious undertones and occult sprinklings not seen since *The Exorcist*. I'm a Bill Halpin fan!

Chuck Buda, author of *Curse of the Ancients* and *The First Cut*

The Cult
of Eden

BOOK ONE OF THE UNRISEN

The Cult
of Eden

BOOK ONE OF THE UNRISEN

Bill Halpin

COSMIC
EGG
BOOKS

Winchester, UK
Washington, USA

JOHN HUNT PUBLISHING

First published by Cosmic Egg Books, 2019
Cosmic Egg Books is an imprint of John Hunt Publishing Ltd., 3 East St., Alresford,
Hampshire SO24 9EE, UK
office@jhpbooks.com
www.johnhuntpublishing.com

For distributor details and how to order please visit the 'Ordering' section on our website.

Text copyright: Bill Halpin 2018

ISBN: 978 1 78904 062 3
978 1 78904 063 0 (ebook)
Library of Congress Control Number: 2018936100

A CIP catalogue record for this book is available from the British Library.

Design: Stuart Davies

UK: Printed and bound by CPI Group (UK) Ltd, Croydon, CR0 4YY
US: Printed and bound by Thomson-Shore, 7300 West Joy Road, Dexter, MI 48130

We operate a distinctive and ethical publishing philosophy in
all areas of our business, from our global network of authors to
production and worldwide distribution.

For my grandfather,
Edward Grismer

And as he sowed, some seeds fell by the wayside, and the birds came and devoured them.

-Matthew 13:4

State of Amazonas, Brazil

The sun was lost above the dense canopy of trees and nearly forgotten, save for a few fragments of light that managed to sneak their way through. Far below, the forest floor was in a state of almost perpetual darkness. It was a place where an outsider could easily become lost and disoriented, but to the boy named Peak, it was home.

Peak belonged to the Nacana tribe, a group that numbered just under two hundred and had inhabited this area of the Amazon for centuries. Like he did on most days, Peak explored his territory after the men left the village to hunt. He was only nine years old—too young yet to be a hunter himself, but he liked to pretend. With a small, pointed branch—resembling a spear well enough in the low light—he went on imaginary quests for great, wild beasts.

This morning, Peak had awoken to a heavy thunderstorm. They were common, almost daily occurrences and did little to interfere with his exploits. But as the unseen sky boomed, the boy sensed the beginning of another headache. For the last few months, those had become as regular as the rain. Peak had kept the headaches a secret so far. His father was the chief of the Nacana, a tribe that had survived—Peak was taught—because of its strength. Men with illnesses were not allowed to hunt or fight...and could never lead.

A trek through the forest usually distracted Peak until the throbbing above his eyes faded, but today it hadn't. It was actually intensifying, moving deeper into his head. At one point the pain became so severe that Peak lost his balance and fell face first into the soggy earth. It was time to seek help. The village shaman had always been fond of Peak; the boy could think of no better person to confide in—he just hoped the treatment would be discreet. After a minute or two, Peak was able to regain his

1

posture. He pointed his nose straight up, allowing the rain to wash the mud from his face, then turned to head back home.

That was when he saw the jaguar.

Peak had never seen one so close; it was only a few body lengths away. He was told that jaguars were mighty creatures, both beautiful and fearsome. This one was not. It was a baby, no more than six months old. It sat and cried out from a small clearing in the brush, but there was no sign of its mother.

Peak smiled.

The law of the village—of his father—was clear: only hunters were permitted to engage the giant cats. Peak convinced himself that this was an exception. Jaguars began learning to hunt at this age, so the spotted orange cub would be just the right match for a chief's son. Peak believed that if he could slay it, it would prove that the strength inside him was greater than the sickness.

Peak hurled his makeshift spear at the cub, but his excitement made him careless. The throw was rushed, his technique all wrong. The branch spun wildly and landed far short of its target. The cub, startled by the noise, darted further into the jungle. Determined not to fail, Peak snatched up his weapon and raced after the prize.

The boy knew his rainforest well, but thunderstorms could create new obstacles. Unlike the sunshine, the rain made its way through the canopy to the ground with ease. As the raindrops descended through the trees, they merged to form vertical rivers in ever-changing locations. The shifting waterfalls obscured Peak's vision, threw off his sense of direction, and slowed down his hunt. All the while, the misery in his head continued to grow.

Peak approached a small, unfamiliar stream that could only have been formed minutes ago by the downpour. The cub tried to run through it, but stumbled and fell onto the opposite side. Wheezing with exhaustion, it remained sprawled out on its belly. Peak leapt over the stream without incident, landing right in front of the animal. He raised his weapon and readied the killing blow.

At that moment, Peak heard a terrible roar.

Tremors ran through his body as he turned to face what he knew was the cub's mother. Just a few paces away, the adult jaguar stood, its black eyes boring into Peak's. The beast snarled, displaying its sharp, curved incisors. Peak looked down at the branch in his hand. It seemed thinner now and duller than it was at the start of the chase. It shook along with Peak's arms.

The mother jaguar roared again, loud enough for Peak to feel the sound vibrations in his chest. Peak dropped his stick. The jaguar watched it fall, then brought its attention back to the boy. It crouched aggressively, its lean muscles tightened, clearly ready to pounce. Peak closed his eyes.

There was a shriek of pain, but it was not his own. Peak's eyes shot back open. The grown jaguar lay twitching in the stream with a spear through its neck. A *real* spear. As the animal lay dying, it streaked the flowing water with ribbons of blood. Peak looked around in disbelief until he saw his father emerge from the brush.

Peak ran over to give him a hug, but the chief did not accept it. He held the boy's shoulders at arm's length and stared intently into his eyes. The moment seemed to last forever, but finally his father smiled and touched his forehead to Peak's. Though meant to be affectionate, the impact was enough to renew the pain in Peak's skull. Peak gritted his teeth until his father pulled away.

"Tell me what happened," the chief commanded.

Peak told the story as best he could, but the words came out with unusual difficulty. He even found himself slurring at times.

"Why do you speak like that?" his father asked.

Peak knew it was because of the headaches, but was not ready to admit it. "I don't know," he lied, then tried to change the subject. "Will I be punished?"

"Yes," his father answered. "You disobeyed me."

"I needed to show you that I am strong, that I can defeat a

jaguar."

"It is not yet a jaguar. It is only a child, like you."

"But it will grow."

"Not without its mother."

The chief walked over to the dead animal. It was now being prodded by the cub. The chief reached down, grabbed it with both hands, and broke its neck. He then picked up the two carcasses, laying the mother's over his shoulder while holding the cub's by the nape of its neck.

He turned to Peak and called out over the rain. "Together, we will burn them. To honor their spirits. They should not have died today."

Peak understood that he had caused the deaths of these animals and the shame was immense. He became dizzy, then the agony in his head intensified to levels he had never experienced. It felt as if the entire tribe had plunged their spears into his skull. He saw the jungle spin, then turn on its side. Peak hit the ground hard. It was cold and wet. His whole body began to shake uncontrollably, splashing in the mud as the rain bombarded his face.

Peak managed to turn in the direction of his father and tried to call out, but could not find his voice. He saw his father drop the jaguars and run towards him, then Peak's vision faded completely. In a darkness deeper than the rainforest's, Peak felt his own mind escaping, forcing him into a sleep that he did not want.

Will 1:1

Will Battese hated New York City, but not around his wife.

In her presence, he was only allowed to "dislike it with a passion." That was because Shannon O'Cleary, the woman he sank to one skinny knee for—who said yes, but refused to surrender her last name—believed "hate" was too ugly a word and forbade him from using it to describe even one facet of the five boroughs. Will questioned the fairness to that rule, especially since his wife so often spoke the kind of language that forced movies into R ratings, but Shannon never wavered. According to her, hating New York meant that Will hated his new life there—a life that Shannon's career forced them to have and her unexpected pregnancy forced them to keep.

While his wife's extrapolation was completely incorrect— Will loved her and adored their baby boy, Gideon—it just wasn't worth the fight to change her mind. Will learned early in marriage that he could be right or he could be happy, so he consented to Shannon's watered-down alternative.

At least until the first piece of cinderblock crashed through the window.

But even as Will trudged to work on that day, unaware of the attack to come, he couldn't imagine a place more deserving of the "H-word" than the Big Apple. It was early morning, early March, and the first Friday of Lent. A time that should have been heralding the coming of Easter was instead nothing more than a bitter winter overstaying its welcome.

The wind blew in fierce spurts that stabbed at Will's freshly-shaven face. His teeth chattered almost relentlessly while a growing number of snow flurries danced around him. Dirty slush and black ice covered the sidewalks, ready to cripple the already uncoordinated twenty-five year old if he misjudged a step.

Beyond the weather, there was ugliness for all the senses. Unwashed taxi cabs congested the streets and charged fares that never fit into Will's budget. He breathed in their exhaust fumes and listened to their horns screech all the way through his morning commute. But the worst was the trash. Piled up to three bags high along the curb, Manhattan's garbage was more than just a visual blight; Will found it symbolic of the city's repulsiveness altogether.

Lake Placid had been different.

Nestled in the Adirondack Mountains of upstate New York, Will's home town had enchanting winters, full of fresh air, majestic wildlife, and vast landscapes adorned by snow. Real snow—fleecy, white, and pure. Not the gray abomination that now clung to his boots.

The city lacked other things, too. Will no longer had access to Grandpa Griff's perfect cup of Irish coffee. There was no Sunday mass that he could attend and see his father, Richard, serve as deacon. Worst of all, Will was without Danny, his kid brother and the only other person to know what it felt like to lose their mother.

"I hate this," Will said to his housemate, Kavi, who was walking beside him.

Kavi Minhas was half a head shorter than Will, but twice as fit and sported a winter coat that cost at least twice as much as his friend's. "You're not supposed to say that," Kavi said. Sharing a home with the married couple, Kavi was well aware of Will's feelings towards the city and Shannon's prohibition of them. "Watch out for spousal lightning."

Before Will could respond to the joke, he and Kavi were separated by a gray-haired man speaking into a Bluetooth earpiece who shoved his way between them. "Asshole!" Kavi yelled after the guy, but the man ignored him and kept walking.

"Well, that guy was a jerk," said Will, working his way back to Kavi. "It's hard to contain my...passionate disliking when stuff like that happens all the time."

"You just gotta make it through the day," Kavi continued. "Try to focus on the good."

"Focus on the—I can't *find* the good, man." Will dropped his head slightly and frowned, uncomfortable with his own negativity, then forced a small laugh. "You know what I saw yesterday?"

Kavi continued to face forward. "What?" he asked.

"A blue jay."

"Yeah?"

"First one of the season," said Will, with a deliberate lack of enthusiasm in his voice.

Kavi picked up on it. "And? No beauty in that?"

"Might have been," Will answered, "until it started drinking from a puddle of somebody's *vomit*." Will shook his head. "I'm not kidding, the bird was eating from a half-frozen puddle of green sludge filled with like...rice...and hot dog bits."

"Heh," Kavi chuckled. "Complain again and I'll tell Mr. DiSantos to put it on the menu. The Blue Jay Special," he said, waving an outstretched hand up and across the air as if his newly created entrée was written upon a flashy marquee sign.

"Hey, if it saves our boss some money, you better tell him you got the idea from me. It might help me get back in his good graces."

"Yeah...I doubt it."

So did Will, unfortunately. He and Kavi were both cooks at the Cosmic Ocean, a low-end Italian restaurant in Manhattan's meat packing district. It was owned by a morbidly obese man named Anthony DiSantos—a man whose face sat undisputedly at the top of the list of things Will so passionately disliked. It was a large, pockmarked face, and one permanently squished into an expression of contempt. From within it came a hoarse voice that did little more than insult and bark orders.

As a business owner, Mr. DiSantos focused solely and

shamelessly on profits. The food in his kitchen was never fresh and his menu void of originality and complexity, with small portions and minimal ingredients. It also wasn't above Mr. DiSantos to assign waiters to kitchen duty so that he could serve tables himself and keep all of the tips (which Will could only imagine amounted to diddly-squat since Mr. DiSantos moved slowly, rarely smiled, and swore in front of children).

Kavi often referred to Mr. DiSantos as a "vile thundercunt," which could always make Will laugh, despite being unsure of what exactly the phrase meant. Will preferred a simpler metaphor: a noose, strangling out any joy Will might have found at work.

The only positive attribute Will could find in his boss was predictability. Mr. DiSantos was always rotten so Will always knew what to expect. A deep breath and a quick prayer before walking through the door allowed Will to grin and bear the worst his boss threw at him. It kept his feelings towards Mr. DiSantos on the "dislike" scale. For months, Will held it there—for Shannon's sake—but then something happened that shot the needle all the way to the right.

Will 1:2

It had been Will's fault, in a way.

He couldn't just blame Skidmark or The Stink. Will was the one who had taken food from the kitchen and given it to the two homeless men. He could blame them for the destruction that came after, but not for what went down in the alley.

Will first encountered the duo shortly after New Year's Day. Their nicknames—courtesy of Kavi—were as mean as they were accurate. Skidmark was an African American man in his late fifties who wore a tattered pair of skinny jeans with a dark brown stain in one very conspicuous place. The Stink was a Russian immigrant who earned his title by somehow managing to smell worse than Skidmark.

Finishing up an evening shift, Will was taking some bags of trash out through the narrow alley behind the Ocean when he heard footsteps behind him. He spun around to see two hunched men shuffle out from the shadows. Will became paralyzed, having no doubt that he was about to get mugged.

Skidmark approached first, his hands together with straight fingers pressed into a gesture of prayer. It was an effective act of humility. "Would it be possible to have one of those garbage bags?" he asked, his voice was gruff, but kind. "My friend and I haven't eaten much today."

"We'd clean up any mess we make when we were done," The Stink added in his thick accent. He didn't appear much older than Will.

Goosebumps sprang up on Will's arms as if they were physical manifestations of the guilt he felt for his initial presumption. "Hold tight," Will said. "I have something better."

A few minutes later, Will presented the best medley of customer leftovers he could put together. The two men received clean plates, forks, and knives, along with a pitcher of tap water.

Skidmark and The Stink sat cross-legged on the cold ground as they ate their platters of day-old bread and partial portions of ziti, salmon, and chicken parmesan. The smiles on their faces were as big as if they were guests at a king's feast. When they were done, they returned the dishes to Will with a degree of gratefulness that he found near impossible to convey when later recounting the story to Shannon and Kavi.

Will continued serving these backdoor suppers to Skidmark and The Stink anytime they came around—which turned into almost anytime Will closed the kitchen. The only rule Will imposed (at Kavi's insistence) was that the homeless men not tell anyone else about their arrangement. There was no way Mr. DiSantos would appreciate the Cosmic Ocean doubling as a homeless kitchen.

Skidmark and The Stink agreed to Will's terms and stuck to their word. It was Will who got sloppy. Normally, he would only feed the men when Mr. DiSantos had left for the day or otherwise had Kavi to stand as lookout. Two days ago, however, Mr. DiSantos had taken a prolonged break to attend mass for Ash Wednesday. He left in the middle of an especially busy dinner service and Will had become swamped in the kitchen, losing track of time. When Will finally got a minute to serve the leftovers to the homeless men, Mr. DiSantos returned and caught him in the act.

While it was common for Mr. DiSantos to lose his temper, Will had never seen him that furious. His boss's face burned red as he spit curses towards Will, the homeless men, and all three of their mothers. With a dusty cross fading from his forehead, he assured Will that he would be fired, sued, and sharing a jail cell with his bum friends before the night was over. The Stink stood watching, his expression numb and his eyes glazed over. *This isn't the first time someone spoke to him that way*, Will thought. Skidmark gathered the two plates and reached out to return them, but Mr. DiSantos smacked the dishes out of his hands and they shattered on the uneven pavement.

"Clean it up!" Mr. DiSantos screamed at Will, who didn't actually end up fired, sued, or arrested. Mr. DiSantos loathed the hiring process (which he dealt with often enough from the steady number of employees that quit over the years) and avoided it at all costs. Still, he attributed his change of heart to an "act of mercy" and made sure Will thanked him for it by working overtime for the next three months.

Will's punishment, in addition to witnessing Mr. DiSantos's vulgar hypocrisy in shunning the homeless, might have otherwise been enough for Will to throw in the towel and hop on the next Greyhound to Lake Placid, but that would have been a dumb decision. In less than two days' time, his entire family was visiting. Will knew that if he could just be patient, he'd be rewarded with a much overdue reunion and the start of a very good weekend.

He was wrong.

Will 1:3

It was known as Convergence Day.

Kavi had created the phrase, of course. According to him, it was "a once in a lifetime event, when two worlds, separated by time and space, are brought together by fate to form an unshakeable era of emotional prosperity." Outside of the blatant exaggeration, Will believed the definition was accurate: his family wasn't just coming for a visit, they were moving to New York City for good.

After his father finalized the arrangements and gave Will the exact date, Will raced to mark it on an *Evil Dead* calendar Shannon had pinned to the wall beside the refrigerator. Will began "X-ing" out each passing day like a '90s teenager counting down to prom night, until there were no more white squares left to fill in. This day in March wasn't just the first Friday of Lent, it was Convergence Day. Richard, Griff, and Danny would be arriving that very evening.

Before celebrations could begin, however, Will had to make it through the work day. That's when things turned to blood, rage, and shattered glass.

In the warm months, the Cosmic Ocean actually looked quite welcoming. The building itself was adorned with handsome, blue Corinthian columns that separated a series of floor-to-ceiling windows with a glass door entrance on the right-hand side. In front of the windows was a cobblestone patio area that was kept semi-private by waist-high shrubbery. Around mid-April, the patio began to fill with customers and on particularly pleasant days, a line would form outside, sometimes reaching upwards of twenty bodies, all willing to wait for a table in the sun.

This time of year, though, the patio was closed, the hedges were no more than brittle, brown skeletons, and the patrons that crammed inside the Ocean had nothing to look at through the tall windows save for a dormant construction site on the opposite side of a one-way street. Above the Cosmic Ocean's windows, its grandiose name was spelled out in two foot tall, gold, acrylic letters, though the lack of winter maintenance turned them brown and grimy.

Still, the Ocean managed to bring in a steady flow of patrons—consisting mostly of those whom Kavi called "one-timers." They were tourists drawn in by the low prices, but who had not taken the time to read any online reviews. If they had, they'd have seen an average rating of one out of five stars. Reviewers unanimously agreed that the food was below average, the wait times above so, and the large, hairy, foul-mouthed owner made them a bit too uncomfortable.

When Will and Kavi arrived at the Ocean the morning of Convergence Day, they were greeted in the alley by Loyola Haynes, a fellow employee and pseudo slave of Mr. DiSantos.

"Gentlemen!" Haynes called out, waving and walking towards them. "I see you have survived the cold, but I am afraid we have bigger problems inside." Haynes, as he liked to be called, was a few years older than Will and had worked at the Ocean longer than any other employee, past or present. Originally from Spain, Haynes learned English as a second language yet now spoke it confidently and more articulately than any American Will knew. He had a solid work ethic and a tan, charismatic face that sported a meticulously groomed chinstrap goatee. Will respected the former and was jealous of the latter (he had tried to grow a beard once, but the hairs pricked Shannon's face every time they kissed so she forced him to shave it). Normally in a cheerful mood, Haynes sounded upset.

"What happened, man?" asked Kavi.

"It is what *did not* happen," Haynes replied. He was dressed in a long, white apron that went down to his thighs. Peeking out from underneath was the Windsor Knot of a skinny red tie along

a Jackson Pollock joke.

Will was still surveying the scene when he bumped into one of the overflowing wastebaskets. It fell over and there were sounds of breaking glass and muffled squeaks. Will counted three rats scatter from the toppled garbage and disappear through a large crack in the wall.

"Damn," said Kavi, summing it all up nicely. "Mr. DiSantos must've flipped his shit."

"You bet I flipped it." Mr. DiSantos appeared in the doorway to his office, which was perilously close to being flooded. "I made it do fucking cartwheels in the air!" He emphasized his claim by making large, circular gestures with his arms, and his face quickly turned as red as the kitchen's canned tomato sauce.

"What happened with Gustavo and Pia?" Will asked, trying to ignore his boss's antics.

"I'd sure as hell like to know," Mr. DiSantos responded. "Those immigrants fucking screwed me!"

"Just you?" Will asked. He was unable to recall a time when the couple hadn't shown up for cleaning. "They do a couple restaurants every night. I wonder if they got caught up somewhere else. Last time I checked, they do an Indian place down on 17th after us—I can't remember the name, though."

Mr. DiSantos looked at Kavi. "What about you?"

Kavi scoffed. "Because I'm Indian?"

"It's called Bombay, I think," Haynes said, stepping forward.

Mr. DiSantos nodded. "OK. I'm going to call there and see if they got ditched, too. As for you three, have fun. I want everything cleaned before we open. This first!" He pointed to the edge of the pool just outside his office. "What a fucking joke," he mumbled to himself, heading into his office. Inside, he plopped himself down behind a cluttered desk and retrieved a family-sized blue bag of Doritos from the bottom drawer. Will checked his watch: 7:30 a.m. "Close the door," Mr. DiSantos yelled, and Will obeyed. The faint sounds of Doritos crunching could be heard through the thin wood. Everyone outside the office chuckled softly.

Will was the first to stop laughing as he once again took in the mess in front of him. *This is going to take a long time*, he thought. "I guess I'll start with the mopping," he said, looking at the pool of water and trying to think of a clever enough nickname to make Kavi laugh. *Cool Ranch Lake could be funny*, he thought, but before he told Kavi he noticed a spattering of something on the floor beside the mop bucket: dull, red droplets the size of nickels and dimes. Will didn't recognize the sauce so he squatted down for a closer look.

Blood, Will thought, but quickly dismissed it. He knew it could be any one of a hundred culinary surprises—though the little puddles *were* curiously far away from the stovetop and the rest of the stains. Will saw that there was a bigger clump of the mystery substance on the edge of the counter above. This spot had a few strands of hair stuck in it, long and black—*like Pia's*.

Blood, blood, blood.

Will recoiled from the counter. "Guys," he said. "I think someone got hurt."

Kavi walked over, frowning. He knelt down and performed his own amateur investigation of congealed stains: bringing his nose close to them and taking a sniff. Haynes stood behind him and watched. After staring at the stains for a few more seconds, Kavi nodded. "Yeah, I guess it could be blood."

"Are you *fucking* kidding me?" Mr. DiSantos said, his office door open again. "One of those wetbacks cut themselves and decided it was OK to skip out on their duty? Inconsiderate pricks! None of you touch it, you hear? You're not suing me if you get hepatitis."

"Did you get a hold of the other restaurant?" Will asked.

Mr. DiSantos nodded. "They didn't show up there either."

"Well, now we know they *were* here," Haynes said. "Pia hit her head. Hard, it seems. They could've left in an ambulance."

"No note or phone call?" asked Mr. DiSantos. "Just leave us with our thumbs up our asses and a fucking mess to clean?"

A mess you made, Will thought, disgusted at Mr. DiSantos's selfishness. He couldn't stand to look at his boss, so he wandered around the kitchen some more. The stoves and the dishwashing station were in disarray, but it hadn't truly hit Will just how much destruction there was in the rest of the kitchen. On the floor behind the pass, there were broken plates, a displaced shelving unit, and a toppled dessert cart.

"Mr. DiSantos," said Will. "I...I think there was a struggle here. Look." He pointed at his evidence. "Alone, in the middle of the night, they could've been attacked. Robbed."

"I thought only your grandpa was a detective, Battese?" snorted Mr. DiSantos.

"Will's right," said Kavi. "You didn't leave the place like this, did you, boss?"

"Of course I didn't. *Jesus.*"

"Everyone! Come here please," Haynes called, and everyone followed his voice into the dining room. The restaurant sat about fifty people through a combination of red-cushioned booths attached to the back wall and flimsy wooden tables squeezed along the front windows.

Haynes was standing at one of the back booths beneath a painting of a vague country landscape. "Look," he said. "Pia forgot her purse. She must have placed it here before she started cleaning."

"What the hell?" said Kavi. Will wondered the same thing. Even Mr. DiSantos was quieting down, the red in his face had faded into a more normal skin complexion.

The four of them gathered around Pia's purse, staring at it as if it were a crystal ball. When it did not reveal any answers, Will reached in to search for one himself. His coworkers watched as he dug through the bag's contents. "This is definitely Pia's," Will said. "This is her ID—I bet it's fake though, the way the edges are fraying. My grandpa taught me that."

"Anything else?" Kavi asked.

Will dug some more. "A little cash. Here's a cell phone—and her *MetroCard*. She's not getting anywhere without this stuff. Mr. DiSantos, I think we should call the police. I'll do it if you want."

"You're right, son, but no, I'll do it." Mr. DiSantos looked up from the purse with a distant gaze. "You guys put a sign out front, we're closing up till the cops get here."

Will stared at his boss, trying to figure out how his mind worked, at which point in his life he had begun to view others as guilty until proven innocent, how it took him so long to be concerned for the friendly and hardworking couple he had hired. But Mr. DiSantos didn't remain solemn for very long. Suddenly, his face contorted back into anger.

"You sons of *bitches*!" Mr. DiSantos yelled. Will didn't know what he had done to infuriate his boss again, but then realized that Mr. DiSantos wasn't looking at him, or any of the Ocean's crew, but behind them towards the entrance.

"What's wro—" Will tried to ask, but couldn't finish the question. He heard glass shatter and then something the size of his head flew past him and splintered the painting on the wall. He spun toward the front of the store. One of the windows lay in glass fragments over the floor and flurries of snow were already spilling inside.

Kavi turned, too, but just as he did, he caught a second, smaller projectile to the knee. He cried out and toppled over. Beside him was some kind of stone, then Will recognized it as a piece of cinderblock. It had torn Kavi's jeans and skin, deep enough for blood to flow.

Will looked outside the window and froze. Skidmark and The Stink stood in the street. They were screaming back all the vicious things Mr. DiSantos had said to them in the alley two days prior. "Cocksucker! Motherfucker!" They yelled so hard their voices cracked with each curse. Stink grabbed another

19

chunk of cinderblock from a backpack Skidmark was wearing and threw it towards the Ocean.

"Watch out!" Haynes shouted and pushed Will to the side. The cinderblock struck Haynes in the lower back; he turned into it with a wince, the way a baseball player took a bad pitch.

Will looked at Haynes, then back out into the street. The Stink was loading up another projectile. "Stop it!" Will shouted towards him. "What are you doing, Stin—" He cut himself off, realizing he did not remember The Stink's real name. "Just stop!"

The homeless man did not respond. He got off two more throws, bringing down the final two windows of the restaurant. After that, both men threw up their middle fingers in unison and fled down the street.

Mr. DiSantos appeared, holding a broom like a broadsword and lumbered after them. Haynes grabbed a piece of splintered chair and followed his boss. Will considered running out, too, but decided to stay with Kavi, who had propped himself up against the wall and was cradling his knee. It looked as though the bleeding had stopped.

"Are you OK?" Will asked, crouching beside him.

"It's fine, I'm good," said Kavi. "What the hell just happened?"

"Skidmark and The Stink," said Will. "They were...enraged."

"*Shit*."

"Why would they do that?" asked Will.

Kavi tilted his head to the side and furrowed his brows. "What do you mean *why*? DiSantos cut off their food supply."

"No, man. I was more upset than them when it happened. They said they were sorry and walked away. Something else had to have set them off."

"Well, when they catch the smelly fucks, you can ask them," Kavi said. "Can you check what's going on out there?"

Will nodded. He stood up and stepped carefully over the shards of glass and into the empty patio. A crowd had formed across the street from the Ocean; a few of the onlookers held up their phones, filming off in the direction that Haynes and Mr. DiSantos chased the fleeing homeless men. Some of the witnesses were laughing, some were shaking their heads, but none came over to help. Will began to walk along the sidewalk in the direction the crowd was facing, but no one seemed to pay him any mind.

Except one man.

Will noticed him standing on the edge of the crowd. He was Caucasian, tall and lean, and looked to be in his early 40s. He wore a tight, black, crewneck sweater that looked too light for the snowfall. *Perhaps he ran outside without his coat,* Will thought, though the man did not shiver or cradle himself for warmth. More peculiar, however, was that despite the thick, gray clouds that darkened the sky, this man wore a pair of sunglasses with mirrored red tint. It was impossible to tell where the man's hidden eyes were looking, but Will couldn't shake the feeling that they were fixated on him, like the sensation of being watched by a ghostly portrait inside a haunted house. The wave of dread that hit him was as palpable as any gust of wind. Will suddenly wanted to be somewhere, anywhere, far away.

At some point—Will didn't know when—Haynes had returned from his chase. He began waving his hand in front of Will's face. Will lost sight of the man across the street—a sensation as unnerving as a spider disappearing inside your bedsheets.

Haynes stopped waving and turned to follow Will's gaze. "What in the—?" Will heard him say.

The man was still there. *Did Haynes notice him too?* Will wondered.

As if to answer the question, Haynes walked hurriedly across the street, directly towards the man. Will felt himself wanting to cry out, to tell Haynes to stop, but couldn't. Instead, he watched Haynes approach the man and begin talking with him. They exchanged a few words before Haynes raised his voice and balled his hands into fists. The stranger remained calm, his body unmoving, his head turned ambiguously in Will's direction. When the man responded to Haynes, his mouth was the only thing that moved. Haynes hesitated for a few moments, then nodded. At that, the stranger finally walked away. Will watched the man until he became lost in the crowd, which had already begun to lose interest in the events that had taken place.

Haynes crossed the street in a hurry, cutting in front of a bus that thanked him by blaring its horn. The earsplitting sound snapped Will back to life. He felt his tunnel vision clearing and a sense of calm returning.

"Who *was* that?" Will asked. His voice came out shaky. He wondered if Haynes noticed.

"He is my landlord," Haynes replied curtly. "I have been a little behind on rent and he, I suppose, thought he could intimidate me by showing up here. I…did not expect him to do that."

"What a jerk," Will said. "I don't like him."

"It isn't the worst thing to happen today," Haynes replied, then gave Will a closed mouth smile that politely declared the conversation over. Will knew it wasn't any of his business. He and Shannon had been close to eviction a few times and more than understood the embarrassment.

"How's your back?" Will asked.

"It will be fine. Just slowed me down in the chase. I could not catch…the Stinkmarks was it?"

Will shook his head but did not correct him.

"You should not have fed them," Haynes said.

"Do you think they'll be back?"

"Why?" Haynes asked, pointing at the storefront. "What is left to break?"

At that, they walked back inside the Ocean. Kavi had found the first aid kit and had bandaged his knee. He said the police were on their way, then asked what had happened outside.

Haynes recounted again how he had lost the homeless men, but left out the part about his landlord. Will saw no need to mention it now, though he planned to tell Shannon about it when he had the chance.

Mr. DiSantos returned a few minutes later, shambling through the permanently opened door. He rested on the frame and gasped for air. Haynes asked if someone should take him to the hospital, but Mr. DiSantos grunted in a way that meant no.

"Just help me," he wheezed. "To my office. Then bring me. Some soda."

"You're getting water," Kavi said, limping back into the kitchen.

Mr. DiSantos coughed and nodded.

Haynes did the best he could to assist DiSantos to the back. Kavi followed after them.

Alone in the dining room, Will walked over to the rock that had damaged the back booth. He went to pick it up, but it was so heavy he had to use both hands. *Geez*, Will thought, *how the heck did those guys throw this from across the street?*

Shannon 1:1

Shannon O'Cleary let out a deep sigh when she saw her husband's name flash up on the caller ID. Her cellphone vibrated atop her desk, running through the entire loop of its Daft Punk ringtone as she debated whether to answer it.

For the last two weeks, Will had been calling her at work with a never-ending list of questions and concerns about his rapidly approaching Convergence Day. It had a way of sapping her productivity and she didn't need any more interruptions at the moment—she was already behind schedule. To make matters worse, the Thai food delivery boy forgot to pack any utensils, and Shannon didn't realize it until after she tipped him. His mistake cost Shannon three valuable minutes of her lunch break as she searched her office for something—anything—that could be used to shovel the Beef Pad Thai into her mouth. She was about to try using two ballpoint pens as chopsticks when she came across an unwrapped plastic spork in the back of a filing cabinet drawer. *Jackpot*, she thought, then wiped the dusty relic on her green knee-length skirt.

With the necessary tool in hand, Shannon plopped down at her desk. It was cluttered with binders, furniture catalogs, and art gallery pamphlets, but she pushed them all aside to clear space for her meal. In the process, she knocked over a free standing Celtic cross—a birthday gift from her father-in-law—and it tumbled off somewhere behind the desk. *Sorry Richard*, Shannon thought. *I'll find it later*.

Shannon slid off a hairband from her freckled wrist and used it to tie her long, red hair up into a messy bun. Then, with eagerness, Shannon opened the plastic container of Pad Thai. The delectable scents of egg, peanuts, and seasoned beef filled the room.

That was when Will called. In the end, Shannon gave in and

answered, gambling that Will only had a quick question for her.

"I have a story to tell you," Will said.

Shannon sighed again. The weary tone of her husband's voice told her that this wasn't some last-minute Convergence Day detail, this was the beginning of an anti-New York City rant.

"And what do you hate today?" Shannon asked.

"Nothing," Will said, as he began to rehash the events of his morning. Shannon wedged the phone between her shoulder and ear and ate without saying a word. It didn't take long before she was barely listening. As she chewed absentmindedly on a piece of beef, Shannon found herself fantasizing about tossing her cell phone out of the window. She imagined Will's voice fading away as it fell eleven stories down and her phone cracking open the head of the delivery boy just as he stepped outside of the building.

Returning from her daydream, Shannon was dismayed that Will's story was still going. Two illegals had gotten mugged in the middle of the night, but Will made it sound like they were some kind of martyrs. *This is New York City*, Shannon thought. *Wandering alone at night with a job like that...what did they expect to happen? They should have stayed in school. Did they even go to school?* But Shannon didn't say any of that out loud. She knew her thoughts were harsh and tried to be thankful instead that she didn't have to work in that kind of dangerous environment. She reminded herself that not everyone landed their dream job—let alone right out of college like she did.

Technically, it had started out as an internship, but at Judah Décor, one of Manhattan's top interior design firms, that was just as coveted. Shannon competed with hundreds of other applicants for the position, but wasn't surprised when she got it.

Shannon had a penchant for high-end decorating that began in high school thanks to a series of rich, older, Los Angeles boyfriends. It was impossible not to fall in love with the luxury those men surrounded themselves in. Shannon would wander through their penthouses in nothing but the expensive lingerie that they had bought her, running her fingers across a statue, or a painting, or a loveseat—none of which her foster parents could afford even if they saved up for a year. She knew that was the world she wanted to immerse herself in.

Now, as an adult, she was able to channel that state of teenage wonderment into her designs, resulting in fresh, unique ideas in the industry. Combining that with her smile (secretly practiced and perfected in front of the mirror) Shannon was able to impose her lavish taste on Judah's clientele, not only convincing them to take out their checkbooks, but making them eager to do so.

It wasn't long before her bosses took notice. Only six months into her internship (just halfway through the initial agreed upon length) Judah Décor offered Shannon a full-time job. It was entry-level and low paying, but still the fastest intern promotion in the company's history. In her second year her list of clients grew, as well as her respect throughout the company. Her efforts earned her the small office in which she was now eating her Thai food. The position's pay wasn't where she wanted it yet, and her window could have had a better view of downtown Manhattan—not just the backside of a bland, brick building—but she had no doubt that she was heading in the right direction. Not once did she have to rely on skimpy skirts or excessive flirting, though she had originally been prepared for that strategy had it been necessary. Shannon was happy that it never had been. It meant she was leaving her high school self further behind.

Judah Décor didn't come without stresses, however. Shannon had to keep up with near-impossible deadlines and continually reject the horny coworkers and clientele who would hit on her despite her professionalism and the small diamond on her finger. But she would never trade it for what Will was doing. She considered putting down her spork and asking her husband why someone as talented as him was still wasting their time at that awful excuse for a restaurant. *Because I made us move down here and I let Will get me pregnant and we can't afford culinary school. Yeah, I better not bring that up,* she decided. So instead of lecturing him about switching jobs, Shannon engulfed the final mouthful of Pad Thai, sucking in the last straggling noodle with a loud slurp.

The other women in the office never finished their entire takeout order in one sitting the way Shannon did, and they made sure to point it out on a regular basis. Shannon was unsure to what degree their comments were innocent banter versus true envy, but they were annoying nonetheless. It was why she avoided the breakroom. She could understand their jealousy, though. She never cared about what she ate—she never had to. Her twenty-six year old body seemed to stay at a trim and tight 120 pounds no matter how much greasy food or Guinness beer she put in it. Even giving birth to Giddy didn't seem to affect her metabolism. She had gained weight during the pregnancy, sure, but a three-mile jog every morning shed it all within a matter of months.

Shannon finished her Pad Thai just as Will reached the point in his story when the Ocean was bombarded by the homeless men. She perked up in her chair as things became more exciting, but as Will continued, frustration crept back into the mix. She hadn't liked those two men since the first time Will had fed them in the alley. Now, they had put her husband out of work until the restaurant got fixed. What bothered Shannon the most was how surprised Will seemed about the whole situation.

"I'm telling you, babe," Will explained. "These weren't the same people I gave food to. They wanted to hurt us."

"Uh...duh!" said Shannon. "It's like the zoo—there's a reason you don't feed the animals. They attack."

"Well, that isn't why," Will corrected. "Human food can hurt them or make them sick."

"The homeless *are* sick! Schizophrenic. Just plain psycho. Different people every day of the week."

in the kitchen, he had a soft spot for familiar chains, so she figured some Big Macs would grant her forgiveness for being late and for her earlier remarks on the phone. It was essentially an artery-clogging bribe, but it was successful; Will was smiling from ear to ear. He leaned in to give her a kiss. Shannon took it, then handed over the bag.

At that point, Kavi hobbled out from the kitchen. She had a burger for him, too.

"Thought you two deserved a treat after your crazy morning," Shannon said as she hugged Kavi.

"Shannon, are these *all* burgers?" asked Will, looking up from the bag.

"Yeah. I'm the best, right?"

Will frowned. "It's Lent. We can't eat meat on Friday."

"We can't?" replied Shannon. *Shit*, she thought. *I completely forgot.* "You're telling me the one unforgivable sin in this world is having a sandwich?"

"Come on, babe. No. Just, you know, rules are rules." He turned to Kavi for support.

"Don't look at me," he said. "I ain't Catholic. I'll eat yours if you don't want it."

Will began to hand the bag over.

"No," she commanded. "You're eating it. It's not going to kill you."

Will hesitated. "They do smell good," he said.

"And remember," Kavi added. "There are starving bums in Africa. Probably in alleyways around here, too."

Will let out a little chuckle, then paused and looked towards the floor, obviously weighing the decision in his head. "Fine," he said. "Lent's almost over, I guess."

Shannon smiled. "And what do you say?" she asked.

"Thank you, Shannon," Will and Kavi said in slow unison.

"You're welcome," she said, and a cold breeze swept through the restaurant. "But let's eat somewhere else." Neither Will nor

Kavi objected.

They ended up four doors down at a coffee shop. The baristas glared at Shannon's group as they brought in the outside food and sat at a table after only buying bottles of water. Will was too busy saying grace to notice, but Shannon did. She glared back until they looked away.

"I want to know what happened with the police?" Shannon asked when everyone started eating their burgers.

"They came," answered Will. "But not much could be done. All the persons of interest are off the radar. We found some of Pia's things, like I said, but her ID is fake. Can't be sure it's even her real name. The cops said they'd check nearby hospitals, but Pia might have been afraid to go there if she didn't have insurance. One forensics guy actually showed up, took some blood samples and fingerprints. The cops aren't sure anything will come of it. Said it'll be more likely they just contact Mr. DiSantos to get their job back."

"Ha, I'd like to listen to that conversation," Kavi chimed.

"And your cinderblock friends?" asked Shannon, referring to the homeless.

"Same thing, even worse. None of us have *any* idea who they are. We gave descriptions—best we could—but the cops said it's not much to go on."

"I told the cops the nicknames I created," said Kavi. "Then I said it might be possible to find them by triangulating their smell." He took a sip of his water. "They didn't seem amused."

Shannon giggled. "I would have laughed—obviously." Then, an idea hit her. She hunched over the table with a smirk. "Hey, what if the two situations were connected? What if the Stinks *hurt* the Mexicans? That would be something, huh?"

"Finally! Somebody else on my wavelength," said Kavi. "I thought the same thing. Brought it up with the cops, too. They said they'd look into it, but didn't seem to take me too seriously. It was *after* the smell joke." He looked at Will. "You didn't back

31

me up though."

"Because I didn't agree with you," replied Will.

"Why not?" asked Shannon.

"Well, they always *did* smell bad. Truly. I figured if they'd set foot in that small, confined kitchen last night, our noses would have started to bleed as soon as we walked in this morning."

Shannon covered her mouth, giggling louder.

"But seriously," Will continued. "It wouldn't make sense. Why *start off* with a serious assault on two people? Not robbery — mind you, Pia's purse was still there. There was money in it."

"OK, but it was in the dining room," Kavi pointed out. "They might have not realized it was there."

"Fine. But it's the sequence that's wrong. If they did hurt Pia and Gustavo, that came first. Why come back hours later just to vandalize the building? It's such a lesser crime. Why not smash up the restaurant at night when they're already there?"

"I don't know," Shannon shrugged. "They're insane?"

"And why attack Gustavo and Pia in the first place? What did they ever do? It was Mr. DiSantos that took the food away. And he's *never* there overnight. The homeless would've known that."

"What if," said Shannon, playing devil's advocate, "they came to wreck the place. To stick it to DiSantos. They wait until no one is there to do it, but *oh shit*, it's the night the Mexicans show up. The bums are surprised. They have to take out the cleaners. No witnesses, you know? There's a struggle but the bums knock 'em out, then drag them off to kill them, and dispose of the bodies by slicing them up and eating them!"

"Shannon!" Will said, not without a small grin.

Shannon smiled. "Stay with me. So after the bums finish their late night snack, they realize they still haven't messed up the place like they originally wanted to. But they're full now, in a food coma. So they come back in the morning. Makes sense to me," she said mischievously.

"No, it doesn't," said Will, shaking his head. "You want to get revenge on Mr. DiSantos? You kill or—*God*—eat his employees, that's pretty good revenge. Why come back and bring all that attention to yourself? In front of fifty people. We probably wouldn't have even associated the cleaners' disappearance with Skidmark and Stink if they hadn't shown up just to throw stones."

"Why didn't you say all this to the cops?" asked Kavi.

"I think I'm right about it," Will said, "but I could be wrong. I figured if the police were more motivated to find Pia because they thought the homeless attacked them, then I wasn't going to say otherwise."

"Yeah, fine," said Shannon. "I really don't care about any of them that much. Or DiSantos. He really should be paying you until the repairs are done."

"How'd those hobos even miss that fat fuck anyway?" asked Kavi. "I could hit Mr. DiSantos if I was throwing in the opposite direction. I got hit by a brick, Haynes got hit by a brick, but you're telling me that somehow all of them passed through his orbit?"

"Oh, Shannon. That reminds me," Will said, wiping the crumbs off the table with his napkin, "speaking of Haynes, I invited him to dinner tonight. I figured he could use a home cooked meal, too, after being nailed in the back with a cinderblock and all."

"That's fine," Shannon replied. "That'll make…seven, right? Wait. Kavi, is Leigha coming?"

"Yep," Kavi answered. "I'm gonna meet her in Astoria first, then we'll head over."

"OK," she said, "so your girlfriend makes eight."

"Plus Gideon," Will added.

"Right," Shannon said. "Sounds good. You bought way too much food anyway." She stood up from the table. "It'll be a party to remember, because we won't be able to afford this amount of groceries again, now that I have a deadbeat husband." Shannon bent over and kissed the top of Will's head. "You guys ready to head out?"

Shannon 1:2

Outside the coffee shop, the snow had started up again. Shannon, Will, and Kavi hurried to the nearest subway entrance and descended into New York City's underbelly to begin their complex commute home. Starting with the C train, they'd ride uptown to Port Authority Bus Terminal, then walk underground to Times Square so that they could transfer over to the 7 train. That would take them under the East River, then above ground into Queens, and further on until they reached their final station: 61st Street, Woodside, Queens. If they were able to catch a 7 Express train (and there were no delays) the entire trip would take about an hour. If not, the 7 Local tacked on another fifteen minutes.

When they reached the Times Square station, Kavi split off from the group; he had to take the N train to meet up with Leigha in Astoria. Shannon did not enjoy traveling alone with Will through Times Square—it was by far his least favorite subway stop and he almost always grumbled about it. She could understand his dislike, the station's corridors were labyrinthic and packed with all types of undesirables: peddlers, pickpockets, lost tourists, public urinators, aggressive Scientologists, and Will's newest nemesis, the homeless. Fortunately for Shannon, there were no noteworthy encounters with anyone on the aforementioned list of unsavory characters and Will kept quiet the entire time.

Her lucky streak continued onto the platform as there was a 7 Express train sitting in the station, nearly empty of passengers. Shannon and Will took a seat next to each other by the doors. He grabbed her gloved hand and held it in his lap and together they watched as more and more passengers filed in: a construction worker with a tool belt strapped underneath his beer belly, a large family of Hassidic Jews, a group of teenage Japanese girls, people in suits, people in torn, hand-me-down coats, some people wearing Yankees gear, and some people wearing Mets gear, but nobody paid each other any mind.

The car continued to fill with commuters and before long, all available seating had disappeared. When an elderly couple shuffled arm-in-arm onto the train, Will let go of Shannon's hand and clapped her on the thigh—an unspoken understanding to offer their seats to the wrinkly lovebirds.

"I want to sit," Shannon said.

"We should really let them have it," Will insisted.

Shannon looked him dead in the eye. "Will, I'm pregnant again."

Will's eyes widened in pure shock.

"I'm kidding!" Shannon laughed. "God, I'm kidding! I just really don't want to stand."

"You're unbelievable," Will said, but then exhaled loudly. "Fine, if you want your seat that bad, keep it." He stood and gestured for the old lady to take his place. She accepted with a shy smile.

Shannon's new seatmate had quite a bit more girth than Will and essentially had to wedge her way in between Shannon and the seat's railing on the other side. Shannon huffed. She would have much preferred sitting next to her husband rather than this thick, slightly off-smelling stranger, but didn't feel right scolding Will for his chivalry. He was standing over Shannon now and smiled when she made eye contact. Shannon reached over the portfolio on her lap and hooked each of her index fingers through a separate belt loop on Will's jeans, holding him in place. Will began gently scratching her head which made her smile back.

Two stops later, at Grand Central Station, more passengers entered the subway car and it went from standing room only to everybody-in-everybody's-business crowded. The ones already on board were pushed inwards and forced to squish together in the middle of the car—Will included. Shannon had to let go of his pants. From her seat, she reached out to him in mock despair. When Will saw, he stuck one of his fingers in his belt loop and used his other hand to scratch his own head, imitating their previous configuration as best he could.

Shannon laughed just as the train chimed, signaling that it was ready to disembark. A polite automated voice called for passengers to stand clear of the closing doors. The ones next to Shannon shut, but immediately bounced back open. It was something that happened regularly, usually from somebody in one of the cars blocking or holding open a door. Shannon sighed at the delay. When the doors closed and reopened a second time, a live MTA conductor came on the intercom, his voice rapid and annoyed. "Do not hold the doors. Do not hold the doors. Stand clear of the closing doors." It was enough to do the trick, however. The third time the doors closed, they stayed shut.

The subway started with a jerk that was strong and sudden enough to send Shannon's portfolio flying off her lap and onto the black boot of a man standing nearby. She mumbled an apology and reached for it, but the boot-owner's hand got there first.

"Here you are, Ms. O'Cleary," said the man, handing it back to her.

When Shannon heard her name, she wondered who had recognized her. *A coworker? A client?* She wasn't in the mood for small talk, but forced a smile and went to make eye contact with the man.

All she saw was a warped reflection of herself in the dark-red lens of his sunglasses.

"Ms…" she said softly, with a raised pitched, hinting at the question in her mind.

"How is it that I know your name? Quite unnerving, isn't it?" The man's mouth formed a grin that lasted only a split second. "Well, it is right here on your folder."

"Yeah, I know," said Shannon. In truth, she had forgotten that her name was embroidered on the leather, but that wasn't what unsettled her. It was the man himself, though she didn't know why. It wasn't her first time seeing someone wearing shades on the subway and the man did nothing to threaten her—he even looked like a decent enough commuter. He was in his late thirties or early forties with a strong, shaven face and chiseled jaw. He was pale, but not sickly, the way one could get between summers. The man's head was completely bald—he wore no earmuffs or winter hat—and his scalp looked so smooth it was as if he had run a hot razor across it moments before stepping onto the train.

He was still holding out her portfolio, his wrist close enough to Shannon's face that she could smell his cologne. It was smoky and woody, but not quite pleasant, like a dying campfire on the beach. Shannon took the portfolio from him, but she felt increasingly uneasy. The man said nothing as he let go of her property. He just smiled at her, his teeth straight and white and handsome. Shannon didn't return it. Her dread was growing. It felt foreign—uncanny even—as if it was being forced inside of her.

Then it hit: this was the landlord from Will's story.

Shannon suddenly wanted her husband next to her again. She turned her head in his direction. "Will," she called out, but it was too weak for him to hear. She could see him staring down at his phone. He was only ten feet away, but to Shannon he might as well have been on the other side of Long Island. She felt her face flush with anger. She did not want to be anywhere near the man that stood over her, but Will—her husband and sworn protector—was oblivious to her anxiety. Then, just as quickly, she became angry at herself. *Why do I need protection? I'm in no danger. What am I afraid he's going to do? Why am I panicking?* She clenched her hands in knowingly unwarranted frustration, digging her French-manicured nails into her palms.

"Is something the matter?" the man asked, then followed her

gaze down the subway car. He spoke with a soft prestige—a voice that may have been soothing, like a concerned therapist's, if not for all the other menacing feelings he somehow conveyed.

"No, I'm OK," Shannon lied. "I just need to show my husband something." She called out again. "Will!" This time, she had mustered up enough volume for him to hear. He glanced over. When he saw her, his eyebrows arched and his lips parted slightly in a look of concern. Then, his eyes landed on the man standing over her. She watched Will's face turn pale, confirming what she already knew.

Somewhere far away, Shannon heard the conductor's voice announce their arrival to Vernon Boulevard/Jackson Avenue. She felt the train slow to a stop and heard the subway doors open. People shuffled in and out, but the man above her did not move. *I can escape,* Shannon told herself. *All I have to do is stand up and make a beeline for the platform.* But another part of her, much more logical, fought the temptation. *You're being fucking ridiculous. This man has done nothing to you. We're on a packed subway with like a hundred witnesses.* She found the strength to remain still and from her seat, stared at the doors. When they closed this time, they only closed once.

"Hey!" said a familiar voice. Shannon looked up. "Excuse me, excuse me." It was Will. He was wedging his way through the passengers towards her, but his eyes were fixated on the man in the red glasses. "Hey," Will said again when he got to him. "You're Haynes's landlord." Shannon thought he spoke bravely, considering he was talking to the same man whose mere presence had paralyzed him that morning. *Bravely,* Shannon thought, *or Will just beat me to the conclusion that this guy posed only an imaginary threat.*

"Loyola Haynes is my tenant, yes," the man replied, appearing not at all bothered by being identified.

Shannon had met Haynes a few times and had always thought Haynes was his first name. Tonight, she was taking him into her home, with her baby, and she literally didn't know the first thing about him. She couldn't worry about that right now though, she was too transfixed by the conversation in front of her.

"I am Victor Degas," the landlord continued. He gave Will a small grin. "Have we met?"

"I saw you today. I...I know Haynes—Loyola. Well, I work with him...at his work, Cah-Cosmic Ocean," Will stammered. His confidence was fading, but Shannon didn't feel pity. She was mad all over again. If Will backed away now, there would be no one left to save her. *Save me from what!* She screamed at herself. *I'm in no danger!* But for some reason she could not be convinced.

Neither Degas nor Will seemed aware of Shannon's internal struggle as they continued their conversation.

"Yes, I do remember seeing you," Degas said, nodding at Will. "It seemed that I arrived just in time to witness a set of particularly unhappy patrons. Which one of you got their order wrong?" He slipped a quick smile.

"None of us," Will answered, as if it had been a serious question. "But you know, that was enough stress for us. And for Haynes. You shouldn't have...um, you know, hounded him like that. He knows he's behind on rent. He'll get it. He's a...he's a real standup guy."

"Is he now?" Degas's grin flashed once again. "What if I told you he's *months* behind? How much time should I give him for good character alone? At what length does my generosity instead become foolishness?"

Will was silent.

A shout further down the train interrupted the tension between them.

"Give us some room, nigger!"

The harshness of the command snapped Shannon out of her trance. The shout had come from the construction worker with the big belly that had boarded at Times Square. He was yelling at a muscular but gray-haired black man wearing studio headphones and an oversized, tan jacket. Big Belly was accusing Headphones of blocking an area of the train, forcing Big Belly and others to be more bunched up than necessary.

Headphones removed his namesake from his ears and let them sit around his neck. "I know you didn't just call me that!" he yelled back and pointed a finger into Big Belly's chest. "I oughta whoop your God-damned ass!" Before he could carry out his threat, Big Belly gave him a strong push that sent Headphones crashing against the end of the car.

Stunned only for a moment, Headphones lunged back at his aggressor and threw a punch that landed solidly on Big Belly's nose. There was a nasty cracking sound. Big Belly spun from the force of the hit, sending a sprinkling of blood and spit onto a number of bystanders. There were groans of disgust and cries of panic as people tried to distance themselves from the fight. Shannon brought her legs together and lifted her knees up to her chest so that no one stepped on her.

Will was pushed to the side by the frightened crowd, as was Degas, who was struck by a heavyset Hassidic man. Degas's sunglasses were knocked off from the impact. Despite the fight breaking out to one side, Shannon found herself cocking her neck to the other, in order to see Degas's face that had been hidden under those red lenses, but she couldn't get a good view of it through the dispersing crowd. She turned her attention back to the fight.

"Good one, good one," Big Belly said nasally, still a bit dazed from the punch. He was hunched over, facing away from Headphones, but towards Shannon. This time, she had a very clear view, and what she saw horrified her.

"Jesus Christ," she cried. The construction worker was sliding out his hammer from the holster on his belt. Blood continued to drip from his face, trickling onto the floor. With the hammer firmly gripped, he spun around and sneered.

"Here you go, you fuck!" He raised the weapon over his head

and stepped towards Headphones.

"Enough! You're fucking done!" A young but brawny police officer emerged from the crowd, rushing up from behind Big Belly and grabbing his wrist. He twisted it behind the construction worker's back, kicked in his leg, and maneuvered him to the sludge-covered floor. Big Belly lost his grip on the hammer and it slid out of reach. Big Belly screamed in rage, but the cop positioned himself on top of him and jammed his knee into Big Belly's shoulder, pinning him down. "Don't fucking move!" Then, the cop looked up at Headphones. "You! Get back against the wall, now!"

"That was self-defense," Headphones snapped. "Everybody saw. Shit! I ain't staying for this!" He turned and ran into the neighboring car.

The cop, unable to go after Headphones, cursed under his breath. The construction worker was still squirming, but weaker now, seeming to lose energy from the officer's effective restraint. The cop was able to get the cuffs on him then pressed his face against his shoulder radio. "10-13. Hunter's Point 7," he said, just as the train stopped at the next station. There, Big Belly was forcefully escorted out of the train. Through the window, Shannon saw two additional officers run up to him and the young cop. Big Belly dropped to his knees, his mouth twisted in a large frown with thin strips of blood running through the gaps of his teeth. "I'm sorry!" he cried out, his cheeks flushed red from the strain.

That was the last Shannon saw of him.

The train had begun to move on, but she continued to stare out through the window. The view outside alternated between thick subway pillars and two-second snapshots of people walking or waiting along the platform. As the car picked up speed, their faces flashed rapidly, ever-changing, like an incohesive flipbook. Then, without warning, the train moved beyond the station and Shannon saw only sky.

At that point, Shannon remembered Degas. Her sense of panic returned instantly and her anxious green eyes darted from passenger to passenger in an attempt to locate him—but she couldn't. *Did he get off?* She wondered. *Did he step through to another car?* She had no way of knowing, but she was pretty sure he wasn't in *her* car. She exhaled deeply. Adrenaline was still coursing through her veins and her heart rate was still elevated, but she could feel her fear subsiding.

The tension amongst the rest of the passengers lessened as well, and they began making nervous remarks about what they had just seen. A lady passed around a Tide pen to those with blood spatter on their shirts. Another squirted drops of hand sanitizer into the palms of everyone who wanted it. A teenage boy in an orange Dunkin' Donuts polo exclaimed his excitement about getting the fight on video and showed it to the group of Japanese girls who circled around him and giggled as they watched.

"Look at this," Will said, standing back over Shannon. "All it takes for New Yorkers to be friendly to each other is to almost witness a murder."

Shannon surprised herself by laughing. "I guess so," she replied. "But I don't know what was worse, the fight or talking to that landlord."

Will nodded, but looked away. "Yeah. I…I'm glad he's gone. Are you OK?"

Shannon stood up and hugged her husband tight. His jacket was still damp from melting snow, but it didn't bother her. She spoke into his ear. "Yes, but if I see that Degas again, I just might let you take me back to Lake Placid."

When Will didn't respond, she worried he might actually consider tracking the landlord down. She backed out of the hug and grabbed her husband's face with both hands, looking him directly in the eyes. "Do *not* let that happen."

"Trust me," Will replied. "It wouldn't be worth it."

Shannon 1:3

It was a quiet ride the rest of the way to Woodside. Neither Shannon nor Will had talked any more about what they had just experienced.

As Shannon stepped off the train and made her way to the station's exit, she found herself glancing back intermittently — just to make sure Degas wasn't following behind. If he was still somewhere on the train, he didn't get off at this stop. Will noticed her doing it, but said nothing. She was able to see on his face that they were on the same page: *Let's just get our baby and go home.*

They had about a fifteen minute walk ahead of them now, away from Manhattan's skyline. In this direction, everything became relatively more residential. There was less traffic and people strolled on the sidewalk as opposed to the hurried pace of their metropolitan counterparts. There were more trees, the homes had bigger yards, and Will seemed relatively more at ease.

Abe and Sara Bentera lived three blocks over from Will and Shannon. They were a couple in their mid-sixties whom Shannon had met while cooling down after a morning jog, not long after she and Will moved in. Shannon had often seen her working in the front garden, but this time Sara waved her down to say hello. Shannon almost pretended not to notice, but decided that wouldn't be a healthy start for her new life and waved back.

Sara was the kookiest woman Shannon had ever met. She spoke in a high-pitched, excited voice that better belonged to a first grader and rocked shoulder-length gray hair with one section streaked bright pink. Half the time, Sara wore clothes of her own creation: tie-dyed or ironed-on picture shirts during the summer and cartoony, knitted sweaters in the winter. Apparently, she sold her creations online as a post-retirement side project, but who would ever buy them Shannon had no clue.

From time to time, the Benteras had Shannon and Will over

for dinner, which was tolerable, despite the two couples' age difference, thanks to Sara's neighborhood gossip and Abe's uncensored stories from his two tours in Vietnam.

In the end, being neighborly paid off. Sara used to be a nanny. She no longer practiced, but kept herself certified into retirement. Over a year later, with Shannon's pregnancy beginning to show, Sara almost begged to be the one to babysit. Despite Sara's sometimes overwhelming eccentricity, all of her references checked out and she was willing to watch Giddy for cheap. Shannon couldn't say no.

†

When Shannon and Will arrived at the Benteras' residence, Will rang the bell. After a few moments, a familiar series of clicks could be heard from inside the home. Sara swung open the door with Giddy in her arms.

"Look, Gideon! Your parents are here early!" she said. "Come in, you two, come in."

Will stepped aside to let Shannon by—his "ladies first" mentality that he stuck to religiously—but the Benteras' front porch entranceway was so narrow that Will had to awkwardly flatten himself against the side of the house in order for Shannon to pass ahead of him. She huffed as she squeezed by, wishing his chivalry came with some sense.

"What a surprise!" Sara continued inside, smiling wide enough to expose both rows of straight white teeth and a large chunk of her upper gums. "Easy day at work I take it?"

Will looked over at Shannon.

"Uh...yep," Shannon answered for the two of them.

"Well, Gideon is so glad you're here!" Sara exclaimed. "He barely napped at all today, waiting for his mother and father, I bet!" Shannon looked at her son, who didn't seem to care one bit that his parents had arrived. Cradled in Sara's free arm (her other arm was preoccupied with re-bolting the five locks on the door) Giddy dug his face into the armpit of her homemade sweater—this one sported a couple of slightly deformed rabbits holding eggs under a rainbow. In the past, Sara had offered to teach Shannon how to knit and sew, claiming how easy it was to make sweaters just like hers. *I'd rather be thrown in front of a bus*, Shannon thought, but smiled and swore she'd try it sometime.

Abe sat in his recliner across the room. The fireplace beside him burned brightly, its flames reflecting off his bifocal glasses. He was a U.S. Marine veteran; pictures of his uniformed days sat squarely in frames nailed to the living room walls. He was a fit, good-looking man in the photographs, but time and a mostly sedentary lifestyle had taken his physique away. He was always nice to Shannon, but a shrapnel scar that stretched from his right cheek to the corner of his mouth made his jaw click whenever he talked and that weirded her out a little. He looked up from his paperback novel and waved hello. Will and Shannon waved back, then Abe's eyes returned to his book. Shannon couldn't make out the title, but saw *STEPHEN KING* in huge letters along the top. She didn't ask about it—she didn't need any more horror today.

Shannon turned back to Sara and reached out for her baby. "I hope you were a good *wittle* boy today, Giddy," she said.

"Always, always, my dear," replied Sara, handing Giddy over. "But I've been meaning to mention, you should start speaking normally to him. Experts say talking like a baby can inhibit his intellectual growth."

"But he *is* a baby," said Shannon and gave Giddy a few kisses on the lips. "My *bai-beeee*."

"The earlier you speak to him as an adult, the more mature he'll develop," continued Sara.

"I heard you," said Shannon.

"I'm just trying to help." Sara raised her arm and brushed Giddy's fuzzy head. As she did, the sleeve of her sweater slid back to reveal a red rose tattooed on her wrist.

"Hey," Will said to Sara, "I never knew you had a tattoo. That's pretty cool."

Shannon had seen it before and thought Will had, too. Then, she realized it was Will's way of breaking up her and Sara's subtle altercation before it progressed into anything worse.

"Thank you, Will!" said Sara, the distraction appearing successful. She pulled the sleeve down further to reveal a thorny stem that led to a second rose blossom midway up her forearm. "This piece of art, I designed on the night of our tenth anniversary. It serves as a reminder that whatever problems Abe and I face in our marriage, we'll make it to the end together, and it will be just as joyous as the beginning."

"It's beautiful," Will said.

"You're too sweet. Just like my Abe. Being the romantic that he is, he got one, too."

Abe, with his eyes remaining fixed on the page, lifted his arm to show a duplicate image inked onto it. "She made me get a tat of a goddamn flower," he said, jaw clicking. "Shows how much I love her."

"Did I say beautiful, Mr. Bentera?" asked Will. "I meant very handsome."

"Hah! Too late, young man," Abe replied.

"Well," Shannon said to Sara, "we should head out, before your husband beats up my husband. Our family will be here soon."

"Yes," said Sara, walking them to the door, "and congratulations again. It'll be wonderful to have family so close. I can't wait to meet them." Sara grabbed Gideon's hands. "Let me know the next time you need me to take this little guy."

†

Shannon lived with her husband, son, and Kavi in a rented two-story townhouse. It was modestly-sized and served its purpose as a starter home but was nothing she'd ever brag about. The front exterior of the building was a dingy, cream-colored brick veneer that overlooked an underwhelming little patio. The three steps leading up to the front door were made of red bricks, half of them cracked or slanted and in need of repair. Beside that was their narrow, private driveway, though it remained unused as neither Shannon, Will, nor Kavi owned a car.

Kavi lived on the second floor—it was his only request upon signing the lease. It had the bedroom with a private bath and the bigger closet. It also sported a distant view of Manhattan's skyline, which is probably why Will agreed to give it to him before running it by Shannon (and why Shannon eventually convinced Kavi that he should be paying half of the entire rent).

Ultimately, their home was the best size, the best quality, and as close to Manhattan as they could afford without cramming everyone into an apartment the size of their bathroom. It did come with a washer and dryer, which Shannon loved, although they were inconveniently installed in a small room adjacent to the kitchen and downstairs bedroom instead of in the basement. It was a regular chore for the three adults to coordinate wash cycles with times when Giddy wasn't down for a nap.

"Want to get a matching tattoo with me?" Shannon asked Will as they stood over Giddy's crib—their bedroom doubling as the baby's nursery. A Winnie the Pooh mobile hung over the crib and Shannon gave it another crank. Giddy stared up, mesmerized by the chubby, yellow bear and his animal friends circling through the air. "Not something as gay as those roses," Shannon continued, "but we could think of a cool idea. I've always thought about getting one."

Will shook his head. "Nah, no thanks, babe. My body is my temple and all that. Gotta keep it pure."

"Like with all that fast food shit you eat?" Shannon asked with a half-irritated grin.

Will responded by flexing his bicep. "Don't act like you don't want this body."

"Mine's bigger," she said, and mimicked his pose. "Look."

Will stepped towards her. "Yeah right," he gripped her upper arm as she continued to hold it up. "Come on, flex," he told her.

"I am," she said.

"No, seriously."

Shannon clenched her fist and contracted her bicep as hard as she could. She felt the muscle squeeze into a tight, lean, feminine ball.

"Why aren't you flexing?" Will asked, unable to keep a straight face. Shannon realized he was teasing her.

"Oh, shut up!" Shannon punched him playfully in the shoulder. "You think you're so funny." She looked at him and then the bed. "Hey, how much time before the other Battese boys get here?"

"Danny texted me their ETA a little while ago. Should be here in about an hour and a half."

Shannon was already unfastening her blouse.

"Oh, no," Will said. "We have to clean. I still have a hundred things to do. I left work early, I don't want to waste it.

"Waste it?"

"Definitely the wrong choice of words—I just want them to feel welcome. A clean house and a shoveled driveway helps. If we have sex now, I'm going to pass out and not get anything done."

Will was right about that last part. "Fine," Shannon said. "Chores first, but let's hurry. I want to cum before we have company."

"Babe! Giddy...."

She shrugged. "He doesn't understand anything yet."

†

After about an hour, in the middle of scrubbing the kitchen

counter, Shannon heard Giddy beginning to fuss on the baby monitor—surely hungry. She set the sponge down, warmed a bottle of formula, then walked back into the bedroom. Shannon fed Giddy and he went at it for nearly twenty minutes. When he finally had his fill, she placed him back down in his crib and he fell asleep again almost instantly.

Shannon leaned over the crib and watched him sleep. She was in awe of how attached she was to this money-draining, physically and mentally exhausting sack of responsibility. She never wanted him in the first place, but having him wasn't an accident. Will believed it was, though. That was her fault. She knew he wasn't ready for a baby and wouldn't agree to it, but she needed one. When she realized that, she began locking the bathroom door every morning so she could push the small pill out through its foil packet and straight into the toilet, then flush it away.

She remembered when the two bars appeared on the pregnancy test. "Oh *shit*," she had said, with the artificial shock of someone walking into their own surprise party after seeing all of their friends' cars parked down the street. "I don't know how this could happen." She remembered Will's face when she showed him the results. His response was just as fake as hers: happiness and excitement when it was clearly fear.

She felt guilty for lying to him, at that moment more than ever. She loved Will—he was her savior in a way, though he knew little of the life he rescued her from—but she worried that love wouldn't be enough to stay. She had left plenty of men before, even the ones she thought she loved. Even the ones she let hurt her. Those were the hardest to leave.

Marriage helped. No other relationship had ever been this healthy, or this strong. The vows she made inside of that small Catholic Church gave her an accountability that she'd never had before. She held hands with Will on the altar, in front of his family, the elderly former director of her orphanage, and a handful of friends she had managed to piece together over the years—Shannon's entire world—and repeated to him the words that the priest recited: *I give you this ring as a sign of my love and fidelity. In the name of the Father, and of the Son, and of the Holy Spirit.* But as she made that oath to God, she once again worried that it wouldn't be enough. She had left Him before, too.

That's why she had needed a baby. She knew that she could never leave a baby. She could never take him away from his father, nor run away from them both and be forever marked as the woman who abandoned her child. She could never do to Giddy what had been done to her. Will may have been the vessel that helped Shannon escape her past, but Giddy was the anchor that made sure she would never drift back.

"I finished the counters for you," Will said, entering the room, unknowingly saving her again, this time from her thoughts as well as the scrubbing. "I've come to claim my reward." Shannon turned to face him as he sat back on the bed that he so meticulously made every morning. He threw his arms wide open. "Come here, baby!"

"Sssh," Shannon whispered. "Giddy's sleeping."

"Oops." He laughed.

Shannon resumed unbuttoning her blouse. "Think you can keep quiet?"

Will nodded, then shook his head "no," and then just shrugged, his gaze directed on her chest the entire time. Shannon smiled and removed her top, uncovering a lacy, black bra. The color was faded, almost gray, and it had a tear forming on the left shoulder strap. Will didn't seem to notice or care.

Shannon hiked up her skirt and climbed onto the bed, straddling Will. He sat up to greet her with soft kisses on her neck, ran his long, slender fingers up her back, then tried to unclip her bra with almost the same amount of fumbling he had displayed during their first visit to second base. When he finally unhooked it, Shannon slipped it off and let it fall somewhere beside the bed.

BEEP BEEEEEEEEEEEP! It was the sound of a truck horn.

"Fuck!" said Shannon. She peaked over her husband and out the window to see the tail of Richard's white Ford F-150 parked in the driveway. "Your dad's here, asshole."

"Keep your voice down," Will said.

"Yeah, well, keep your dick down because I'm not touching it tonight." She jumped off the bed and gathered her clothes off the floor, ignoring her son. "I *hate* getting worked up for nothing. All because you'd rather clean the damn kitchen!"

Will was still on the bed, mouth open in shock.

"What are you waiting for?" Shannon asked. "Your *cavalry* has arrived. Convergence Day is upon us. Hurray! You better go celebrate." Shannon put her bra back on, re-hooking it with barely more than a flick. Then, she caught a glimpse of herself in the mirror and didn't like what she saw. "I need to freshen up," she said. Before Will could respond, she stomped out of the bedroom and slammed the door.

Degas 1:1

Victor Degas took in a refreshing breath of the chilled, dusk air. He stood in the center of Queensbridge Park, a small field on the eastern border of Long Island City. In the warmer months, the park was host to family picnics and pick-up baseball games between motley teams of children of every background and ethnicity. Now, however, the infield diamonds were covered in snow and the park was barren of humanity, save for Degas.

The East River flowed beside him, tranquilly absorbing the falling snowflakes. Looming almost directly overhead, the majestic 59th Street Bridge spanned west over the water then melded into the Manhattan skyline. The sun continued its slow descent, slipping its way between the distant skyscrapers like sand through a giant's fingers. The array of red and orange colors in the darkening sky, juxtaposed with the steel colossi, created a view that was nothing short of awe-inspiring. Degas took off his glasses, wanting to witness the sight in its purest form, without any discoloration from the red tint of his lenses. The setting sun pierced his retinas like a dagger, yet he still managed a smile.

There was no doubt that God existed. Not to Degas. This scene embodied the precise junction between Heaven and Earth. The splendor of the sun could never come as a result of a random event and the towering pillars of industrialization would be impossible to construct—or even dream up—without minds and bodies crafted by a supreme deity.

But his awe always rotted away into frustration. The city Degas gazed upon held so many unbelievers. It was shameful, despicable even, that other men and women could stand beside him at this exact moment, sharing this exact view, and still be unconvinced that there was a God. Degas had seen cases of denial so strong that they spilled over to the unbelievers' children, and their children's children, passing it on like a genetic disease until their entire family tree decayed into a spiritual cesspool of empty beliefs.

As infuriating as it all was, Degas never blamed the particular man or woman. It was God that was responsible. God picked favorites to be saved, then locked the rest of humanity inside a prison of hardened hearts and dangled the key just beyond their reach. Instead of speaking directly to His people, God recorded His words inside an ancient book and let it sit for centuries without any update. Instead of showing His face over New York City, He chose to only hint at His existence through skyscrapers and sunsets. It may have been enough for Degas to believe in Him, but it wasn't for countless others—those whom God predestined to Hell before they were even born. Those souls never had a chance, thanks to God's self-concealment, and now they would be forever lost.

Degas was one of those lost souls, though for a different reason. He had accepted that fact long ago—accepted that his own salvation was never part of God's plan—but at this point, he didn't even want it.

What Degas wanted now was Will Battese.

Will was one of the many that God allowed to walk in ignorance. The young man was not an unbeliever (in fact, Degas knew him to be quite the devout Catholic), but rather his ignorance was in his absolute unawareness of all the horrible things Degas was going to do to him.

Sure, God gave Will instincts. Degas could almost taste the fear and anxiety that had swelled inside of Will during their encounter in front of the Cosmic Ocean and then again on the subway. It was as if Will's soul knew there was a great evil present but was unable to effectively translate that fact to its host. That was the problem with instinct—the same problem with God's existence: it lacked conviction.

If God truly cared about Will, He would have warned him of what was coming—openly, unmistakably warned him. God, in

His omnipotence, should have shouted down from the heavens in a booming voice: "Go, Will! Take your wife and your child and flee this place! Leave immediately and don't look back, for only suffering awaits you here." If Will did not listen, God could even pick the young man up in a miraculous gust of wind and carry him to safety in places never to be known to Degas.

But none of that had happened.

Will was still here. In fact, right now, he was heading home for a nice dinner, terribly ignorant of the doom at his doorstep. And for once, Degas was not angry at God for His silence.

There was only anticipation.

After what was to come this evening, Degas would depart from New York City with no promise of return. Because of this, he had been ordered to tie up all loose ends. Degas ran through the checklist in his head one final time. It was a pointless gesture; he knew it was complete, but his thoughts returned to Jason Armstrong, the man who had been the last item on the agenda.

Now, Degas felt anger—so much so that it made his body feel like it had been set ablaze. He looked down to see that the snow around him had melted, revealing a perfect circle of the dead grass below.

†

Before Degas killed him, Jason Armstrong had been a brilliant appeals lawyer, deeply committed to the separation of church and state. He had first caught Degas's attention last year, when he fought in a case against the federal government to abolish the position of military chaplains. Armstrong put up a strong argument that the existence of such religious figureheads in a government institution was unconstitutional. In the end, Armstrong lost the case, but Degas had been inspired. His mind churned with fantasies of soldiers in times of war—times when death was rampant and one's doubt about the existence of a higher power could be at its strongest—no longer having a chaplain to turn to for support, to bring them back from the edge of disbelief. Degas wondered how many soldiers would have died without faith had Armstrong's case been won.

Further research revealed that almost all of Armstrong's cases aimed to divide church and state in some way, whether it was forbidding government-funded scholarships in schools with religious affiliation, stripping Christianity programs from state prisons, or even attempting to force the Red Cross to change its logo. Armstrong's courtroom abilities were impressive enough that Degas's request for Recruitment was unanimously granted.

But abilities alone were not enough to join Degas's organization. The correct motives must also exist. Degas was given the resources and manpower to set up surveillance on Armstrong, following his daily routines, dissecting his personal life, and investigating his past. After months, Degas could discover nothing that would disqualify the lawyer from Recruitment. That meant it was time for an interview.

Armstrong lived alone in a three-story townhouse in the upper west side of Manhattan, paying nearly $24,000 a month for the elegant brownstone. Despite the value of his home, Armstrong seemed to rely primarily on the well-lit, upscale neighborhood for security. The only defenses that stood between Degas and a sleeping Armstrong were a mainstream wireless alarm system and a heavy bolt lock.

Due to the delicate information revealed in a Recruitment, meetings were private and unscheduled. Degas waited until 3:00 a.m. to infiltrate Armstrong's quarters. He easily gained access to the house using a small frequency jamming device and his set of customized steel lock picks. With the townhouse's blueprint memorized, Degas made his way softly through the entrance hall and up the staircase to Armstrong's second story master bedroom.

Armstrong was only 5'7" and 170lbs, but he slept in a king-sized bed. He began twisting restlessly under the covers as Degas crept closer. Sliding over the chair from a nearby desk, Degas sat between the bed and the doorway. A nightlight cast faint illumination into the room—dim enough that Degas felt comfortable removing his red-tinted glasses. He placed them gently on the nightstand. His face would be visible, but not every detail of it.

"Mr. Armstrong, wake up," Degas said, his voice calm but stern. When the dreaming man did not respond, Degas called again, louder this time, but with no malice. "Mr. Armstrong." The lawyer awoke with a grunt and squinted towards the sound. When he realized he was not alone, his drowsy eyes snapped open with alarm.

"Jesus Christ!" Armstrong screamed and stumbled off the opposite side of the bed. He backed up into the corner of the room, holding his arms out to guard himself. "What the *fuck!* Who the fuck are you?"

Armstrong was bald like Degas, but had a thick brown mustache that quivered in fear. He stood against the wall, wearing nothing but a pair of black boxer briefs. His body was white, frail, and without any of his thousand dollar suits, making him resemble a leukemia patient more than the intimidating attorney he was inside the courtroom. Degas's admiration did not waver, however, Armstrong's mind was the weapon he coveted.

"Mr. Armstrong, I am only here to ta—"

"I said, who the *fuck* are you?"

"Please, allow me the time to answer." Degas stood slowly. "My name is Victor Degas. I did not come to rob you or to hurt you. Look here." He gestured down to the two custom-made combat knives holstered on each side of his waist. "If I wanted to harm you, I would have while you were asleep. You see?" He pulled one of the knives from its leather sheath; it made no sound. The blade was made of 18th century Damascus steel, with teardrop-shaped blue garnets crafted into its sides. The word

56

WEEP was carved into the titanium handle with more of the rare, blue mineral. "I keep these blades in impeccable condition, Mr. Armstrong. This one could slide through your breastplate and into your heart as smoothly as though it were softened butter. You would have died before you awoke from your nightmare." Degas returned Weep to its sheath. "So, please, sit down. Know that I wish only to speak with you."

Armstrong did not sit, but his posture shifted. He took a step away from the wall, then lowered his arms and crossed them over his chest. "You break into my house in the middle of the night just to talk? Fuck!" His head shook in disbelief.

"What I am going to discuss with you—rather the invitation I am going to give to you, is nothing near suitable for an email or phone call, or even a *scheduled* face-to-face meeting. To be sure that you were alone and that I would have your complete attention, I chose this hour and this location. Perhaps my methods do not seem ideal, but this scare has made your mind most alert. That is how I want it. Now, I will not answer any more of your questions until you sit down." Degas led by example, sinking back into the chair.

"Do I have a choice?" asked Armstrong. Degas stared at him but did not respond. After a few moments, the lawyer squatted tentatively on the edge of the mattress and faced Degas.

It was then that Degas answered. "There is always a choice. There is no point to *any* of this if you lost your ability to choose."

Armstrong nodded, but seemed unconvinced. "You said there was an invitation. What did you mean?"

"I will give you that invitation towards the end of this conversation. I would first like to express my admiration." Degas leaned forward in his chair, his hands loosely clasped together. "I am *very* fond of your work. In your cases, you fight with such passion. Your tactics are innovative. Ruthless. Whether a victory or defeat, your existence continues to shatter the grip Christianity holds on this country."

"Thank you," said Armstrong. Although still unsmiling, the lawyer gave off a hint of pride from the compliment.

"Tell me," Degas asked. "Is that your intention?"

"What? To eliminate Christianity?" Armstrong acted overly appalled. "No, of course not. I never fight *against* the church, just *for* the Constitution. Protecting it. When you step back and analyze its words, it's clear that religious influence doesn't belong there. I really have nothing against any religion."

Degas smiled politely at Armstrong's lie. "But surely you do, Mr. Armstrong. This is a private discussion, so you can be candid. A keen eye can see that behind your professional actions lies a personal vendetta. You try to hide it, but I can see it is there. There's an inspiration behind your work."

"What do you know about me?" Armstrong snapped.

Degas was prepared for the question. "I know you were raised Catholic—whatever that means. Children are awoken on Sunday mornings and dragged off against their will to a row of pews where they are forced to sit still for an hour, yelled at if they talk, or move, or close their eyes. They are not Catholics. No child *is* religious, they only *bear* religion until they are old enough to make a real choice. When you reached that age, Mr. Armstrong, you never set foot in a church or spoke to your family again." Degas paused, forming the next question gently. "Might I ask, were those decisions based on your homosexuality?"

The look of shock on Armstrong's face was undeniable. "My...Jesus, how do you know about that?"

"Certainly, you deserve an explanation." Degas nodded. "The best one I can give you now is that I have resources that have allowed me to study you very closely. It puts me at quite the advantage here. You know little about me, but I know where you are from, what you have for breakfast, and every man you have slept with in the last few months. I am sorry for the sense of violation you must be feeling, but I am not here to out you or blackmail you and least of all judge you. I will be keeping all of

58

your secrets, secret. I just need to know your darkest one. What motivates your attacks against Christianity?"

Armstrong was sweating now.

Degas continued to press him. "Was it the betrayal? The ostracism? The social damnation? All stemming from your sexuality?"

He didn't look at Degas but sighed and nodded. "I try not to let anybody know that's why. I specifically avoid those types of cases: same sex marriages, gay rights, you know? I don't want that kind of attention on me."

"But contempt for the church burns inside you, doesn't it?"

"Of course it does. My family—and the friends I grew up with—want nothing to do with me now. They say I'm a sinner just because I'm gay."

"Homosexuality *is* a sin, Mr. Armstrong. They are not wrong in that. However, it is no more of a sin than committing adultery, watching pornography, or having a single, lustful thought about your neighbor's wife. Yet those sins are easily forgiven or even encouraged by the same people who despise you. What father is not delighted to know that his teenage son is having sex with the prom queen? And how extreme is that emotion reversed when the son is being willfully sodomized by the quarterback? Why does your sin sentence you to banishment while others can walk so proud in theirs?"

"I wish I knew. Their hate makes me hate them right back."

Degas watched Armstrong close his eyes, losing himself for a moment.

"So what is this?" Armstrong asked, opening his eyes. "Some type of gay man revenge club?"

Degas's face remained blank. "By no means. The scope of what we do is much, *much* larger. Homosexuality is not *my* sin, although I have many others. I need you to know that in my eyes, Mr. Armstrong, you are no better or worse than me."

"OK. Thanks? So what is the point here?"

"It is coming, I promise, but one more question. Beyond organized religion and the sad hypocrisy of men...what is your view on the existence of God?"

"Does it matter what I think?"

"In the grand scheme of things, I suppose not, but there is one answer that would make me happy. Some others wouldn't."

Armstrong's eyes returned to the knives on Degas's belt, the fear in his eyes building once again. "Do any involve using those things on me?"

"No," Degas answered. "Remember, no matter what your answers are, tonight, these will remain clean of your blood. So tell me, do you believe in God when you so effectively fight against Him?"

"I...I don't think so. There's an all-powerful entity above us and He just sits around while society squeezes Him out of their lives? Kicks Him out of schools and the military and everything else? It doesn't make sense. A few politicians, lawyers, and judges can manipulate our country's laws and *erase* God? Why would He stand for that? He should strike down people like me. So, no. I say no. He can't exist, at least not with the power He is supposed to have."

"I can understand that argument." Degas nodded. "Although I happen to believe strongly in God's existence, for my own reasons. In time, I hope to help you believe in Him as well."

"Wait. Are you witnessing to me right now?"

"Don't misunderstand me, Mr. Armstrong. I have no love for God. I believe He is a crooked being who picks favorites and leaves the rest behind. His followers claim His ways are a mystery, but there's no defense any holy man can give me that excuses God's conscious abandonment of you or I or the untold others that will be sentenced to Hell. Mr. Armstrong, here is my invitation..."

Armstrong's eyes revealed eagerness for the first time. "I'm listening."

"I am a member of an organization. We call ourselves the Edens. We would like you to join us."

"The Edens?" asked Jason, more absorbing the word than questioning it.

"Yes," Degas continued. "The name is...fun. Of course, it alludes to that great garden that existed before sin. It serves as a constant reminder that God is the one that *let* us sin. He created the serpent and set it to live among Eve, knowing the evil that it would bring her to do. He gave her a temptation that He *knew* was impossible to overcome. Then, centuries later, in His infinite desire for amusement, He sent His son to redeem us—but it can only be through Him. Why the hassle? Why not save mankind from the start? Why allow so many lives to be lost along His narrow path? I do not know, but we hope to make God regret those decisions. We live to punish Him."

"Jesus. How do you...punish God?"

Degas smiled. "By becoming one with the serpent. By taking away God's flock. Sheep by sheep until He has nothing left. We spread our hate—turn people away from Him, consciously and unconsciously, whether by law reform, promotion of Godless religions, or simply hurting those who believe in Him enough to lead them astray. You see, Mr. Armstrong, the importance of belief? You cannot truly eliminate religion unless you realize there is a real opponent to face. The Edens are not atheists. We are not agnostic. We believe God exists and we know God exists, but we hate Him. That...is what perfects our effectiveness. Hate Him, Mr. Armstrong. Hate Him for what He did to you and for what He's failed to do. Hate Him for what He *made* you."

There was silence for a time, but Degas never looked away from Armstrong's face. He studied it, searching for the slightest of tells that could reveal Armstrong's state of mind, but the lawyer was impressively unreadable.

Finally, Armstrong spoke. "I don't know if I have the motivation to become one of you. If I accept, what would you have me do?"

"At the very least, what you already do," Degas answered. "Break men away from their religion. Prevent their children from ever becoming exposed to God. The difference with us is that you will have support, resources, and camaraderie. But if you choose so, you can become more active, receive greater, more wondrous gifts, and forge greater alliances than I could ever describe to you in one night."

Neither man spoke for some time. Degas waited patiently for Armstrong to continue the conversation.

"I'm full of conflicting thoughts right now, Mr. Degas," the lawyer said, avoiding eye contact. "It is possible that I could… think about it?"

"Of course," Degas nodded. "Rarely is such a decision made immediately. We went over quite a bit. I want to give you time to digest it all."

"How much time do I have?"

"There is no set timeframe," answered Degas. He reached into his coat, but Armstrong did not flinch. Degas removed a business card. It was completely red save for a phone number in small, black font. "If you decide yes," Degas said, handing Armstrong the card, "then call this number. You will get an out of service message, but we will know when and from where you called. I will be in contact with you shortly after."

Armstrong took the card, looking over it briefly before raising his eyes back to Degas. "And what if I choose no?"

"Then do nothing. I will not speak to you again. Of course, let's keep everything you've heard here to yourself. I'm sure you understand, Mr. Armstrong. And thank you for your candidness tonight, I enjoyed our discussion." Degas stood up. "I want you with us, Jason Armstrong. Before I leave, do you have any other questions for me that will help you with your decision?"

Armstrong noticed the glasses on the nightstand. "Well, it might be unrelated, but what's with the red?"

"These lenses provide me comfort. I have a condition that makes me very light sensitive."

Armstrong opened his mouth, but hesitated for a few seconds before he spoke. "Your group, they aren't...are you...a vampire?"

Degas couldn't remember the last time he laughed so satisfyingly.

Still chuckling, Degas opened up his mouth and ran his tongue along his teeth, proving that they were all of proper proportions—no fangs. "There are no such things as vampires, Mr. Armstrong, unless you count your parents who drink the blood of Christ each Sunday morning." He saw Armstrong smile for the first time. "Yes, I am at this point one hundred percent human. These lenses are for a congenital defect known as iris coloboma. The structures that regulate how much light enters my eyes did not completely develop. Instead of being round, my pupils are shaped like keyholes. Think of them like curtains that can never close."

Armstrong squinted and leaned closer. "I see them now."

Degas put on his glasses. "Perhaps it makes me only *ninety-nine* percent human."

"I'm sorry to hear that," said Jason, sounding earnest.

Degas nodded and stood. "There are far worse predestinations for one to have."

Degas 1:2

Jason Armstrong never dialed the number on the red card.

Degas's late night conversation with the lawyer had taken place sixty-four days ago. There was a chance that Armstrong had still been undecided, but Degas believed the answer to be no. Armstrong had been given the maximum amount of time possible to respond—right up until the evening before Will Battese was to be taken. That time had run out.

Degas emerged from the subway underworld at the 72nd Street station. It was just after midnight on the first Friday of Lent. The night air was still, but bitingly cold. Degas zipped up his jacket and put on his gloves, not because he felt any chill, but because he would appear too out of place otherwise.

As he approached Armstrong's townhouse, Degas felt his body stir with resentment. He had been convinced that Armstrong would have decided to join, but he had been wrong. It was embarrassing.

Armstrong had been quiet about their encounter—every phone call, email, and text had been monitored and Armstrong himself was physically followed by a rotation of Degas's subordinates. He never spoke a word to anyone about his invitation to become an Eden. Degas found that not too many Recruits did. They were asked not to, but never specifically threatened—though most of them were highly intelligent, perhaps they just assumed that was the case. On the other hand, Degas could be led to believe that as much as the morality of the world had deteriorated, being chosen to join an organization that aims to strip believers away from God was not yet a topic that could be openly discussed or bragged about in this country. That just meant Degas's work was far from over.

Since their conversation, Armstrong had had the locks replaced and made a series of phone calls to his security system's customer service representatives. They insisted that everything was functioning properly, but ended up replacing the keypad and comping him a month of service anyway.

Breaking into his house proved no more difficult the second time around.

Once inside, Degas heard the shower running on the floor above. When he reached the dark, upstairs bedroom, its bathroom door was slightly ajar. Over the falling water, Degas could hear soft grunts and strong, wet, smacking sounds. He paused outside the door for a moment, then decided not to interrupt. Instead, he once again set his glasses on the nightstand and sat down at the foot of the bed where their first conversation took place. It would be their only conversation—Degas had not lied when he told Armstrong that they would not speak again.

Degas pulled out the custom blade from his left hip. It was forged from the same Damascus steel as its partner, though this blade's edge was deeply serrated, all the way down to its black, fiberglass handle. The name GNASH was masterfully inscribed into the fiberglass using pure, red painite. Degas ran Gnash sideways along the length of Armstrong's bed. The teeth made a quiet, soothing noise, and made fine, parallel tears in the sheet.

Soon, the grunting from the bathroom crescendoed into a magnificent groan of relief. Moments later, the shower turned off: Degas's cue to stand up. He positioned himself against the wall next to the hinges of the bathroom door. When it opened, Armstrong emerged and walked right by him with a towel wrapped around his waist.

Degas struck like a snake. He covered the lawyer's mouth with one hand and slid Gnash swiftly across his neck. Blood spewed from the wound. Degas knew that that one swipe of the serrated blade was enough to kill Armstrong, but he became lost in his attack. He continued to saw into Armstrong's flesh.

Back and forth, back and forth, back and forth.

He didn't stop until Armstrong's head hung backwards

towards the floor, only attached to the rest of its body by a few tendons. There was a weak, gurgling sound as all of Armstrong's exposed neck vessels emptied of blood.

Degas realized he must have been more upset than he originally thought. Finally, he let the body fall.

"You would have made an excellent addition," Degas said, softly and earnestly. He stepped over the body and headed for his glasses, leaving the mess and not caring who eventually found it.

"Jay?" said a voice from the bathroom.

Degas jerked around in surprise. Another man was standing in the bedroom, completely naked. He was tall with brown skin and long, wet, black hair. Degas recognized him as one of Armstrong's friends at the gym.

The naked man looked up from the body on the floor to Degas in the shadows. "Oh my God!" he screamed, and darted towards the bedroom door.

Degas was not ready for this surprise, but his reflexes were sharp. He drew Weep from his right hip and threw it forward. It lodged between the naked man's shoulder blades, barely making a sound. The man fell forward and onto his side, screaming with a disturbingly high pitch. Degas moved quickly, pinning down the victim with his knee and sinking Gnash into his heart.

When the naked man stopped breathing, Degas stood up. "Thanks for the warning," he said aloud to the room. "This isn't part of the ritual. You could have warned me someone else was here."

He went for his glasses again and gathered them without further interruption. He left both bodies on the floor, resisting the temptation to hack them up and burn the entire house down out of spite.

Killing a non-responsive Recruit was mandated in order to ensure the Edens' secrecy—there was no negotiation there—but Degas still wished everything had gone differently. His unsuccessful Recruitment had caused the crusade against religion to lose a valuable combatant. He tried to take solace in the fact that he sent Armstrong straight to Hell, at least eliminating any possibility that the lawyer could undergo a radical conversion like the Pharisee, Saul. Degas knew that Armstrong's gym lover was a self-proclaimed atheist, so it was likely that he was in Hell along with Armstrong. Those were two souls Degas was able to forever damn, but he knew that if Armstrong had joined with him there could have been slews more.

On his way out of the house, Degas slammed the door, promising himself that if anyone on the street even looked at him funny, he would cut them in half. At that thought, he recognized the rage growing inside of him and knew that he had to alleviate it before it spiraled out of control. Instead of making his way back to the B train station on 72nd, he decided to cross the western border into Central Park for a walk.

The night was clear but the park grounds were still covered in ice and snow. Trails of footprints hinted at all those who had come before Degas to walk the same winding paths and enjoy the same scenery. At this hour, however, only a few scattered dog-walkers or hand-in-hand couples could be seen finishing up their strolls before the park closed at one o'clock.

At one point, Degas heard a loud trotting sound approaching. He turned to see a horse pulling a cart up the path behind him. There were no passengers, just a driver. The words "Candy Stripe" were plastered in white on the side of the bright red carriage. When the animal saw Degas, the horse neighed and tried to veer off the path.

The driver cursed in Italian and gave Candy a strong whip. "Come on you stupid beast," the man cried. After a few more lashes, the horse obliged. As it passed by Degas, it accelerated sharply and the driver almost tumbled out of his seat.

Degas barely gave the scene any attention. He was too busy racking his brain to determine if the failure had been his fault in any way. What could he have done differently to win Armstrong over? Had he come on too strong? Or too weak? Did he reveal too much too fast?

He had not mentioned his pact with Decaar.

Degas wondered, *should I have?*

Degas 1:3

Around the next turn, Degas came across Candy again. Her cart was parked in front of a public restroom and the driver was nowhere in sight. Degas walked towards the animal. It began to breath more rapidly. Degas reached out to stroke its face. The horse tensed and jumped back, but its short rope prevented it from going far.

"You know, don't you girl?" Degas said, watching the horse now shiver in place. "You feel his presence around me. How is it that animals are more in tune with the spiritual world than humans?"

The horse stared at him with black, glistening eyes. In those eyes, Degas saw the face of Jason Armstrong, then of Will Battese, and then of Jesus Christ. "The Son of Man," Degas whispered.

His cheeks flush with renewed rage. He pulled out his blades and drove Weep into the horse's neck. Its blood spilled out onto Degas's face and jacket. The horse squealed and lunged forward, trying to bite Degas, but the mouth restraints prevented it from reaching its mark. Degas stuck Gnash in the other side of its neck. Candy broke into a violent struggle to escape, but again its restraints remained firm and the horse did nothing more than rock the cart.

Degas continued alternating blows with vicious ferocity, like a boxer on a speedbag. He continued butchering the horse, carving out pieces of muddled pulp and fur from its neck and chest, until there was no life left in the animal. Degas took a step back.

Fastened to the cart, the dead horse was unable to collapse.

Degas shuffled off the footpath without looking back. In the distance, he could see the trees dancing in the dim light of the park's lampposts, but he could not feel the wind. Wherever Degas walked, the air around him stilled and the dead branches above froze in place as if holding their breath until he passed by.

Richard 1:1

You should have stopped, he scolded himself.
You should have known what would happen.
God gave you plenty of signs and you ignored them all.

Richard Battese knew that the drive from Lake Placid to Queens would take just over five hours. Still, somehow he thought that he could complete the entire trip without stopping for a bathroom break. That turned out to be a severe underestimation of the strength of his forty-five year old bladder as he had to pull off the highway twice before even reaching Albany.

There *had* been plenty of signs—signs for other rest stops further down I-87, as well as for gas stations and restaurants up and down Palisades Interstate Parkway. Richard could have used any of those places, but instead chose to hold it in, a stubborn decision attributed to nothing more than his pride.

Now, thanks to the gridlock on the Queensboro Bridge, Richard had plenty of time to wallow in regret. Although it was less than five miles from Will's place, Richard's Ford F-150 had been idling in the same spot for close to a half hour. From his high perch in the pickup, Richard could see a cluster of emergency personnel up ahead, flooding the scene of an accident while unknowingly holding him hostage. Despite his frustration, Richard opted not to add to the symphony of horns blaring from the vehicles around him. Instead, he rolled up the sleeves of his gray button-down shirt and, with a sigh, practiced the mantra of accepting that which he could not change.

It was not an easy thing to do, given the interior of the truck. It felt spacious enough at the beginning of the trip for Richard's large, muscular frame, but became more and more confining as the minutes of inactivity ticked by. In addition to his bladder threatening to empty itself into his jeans, Richard's neck was stiff and his back ached. His long legs screamed to be straightened out of their unnatural bent position. Even gripping the steering wheel had become uncomfortable, thanks to an old boxer's fracture in his right hand.

Nearby laughter provided a welcome distraction. Richard turned and watched with innocent envy as his son, Danny, was able to stretch out completely inside of the vehicle. The little eleven-year-old was draped forward over the passenger seat, sticking a smartphone in front of his grandpa's face. A video was playing on the device and the two were cracking up.

"Sit down," said Richard, his voice loud and authoritative— one of the few parts of him that hadn't weakened over the past decade. When he spoke to his son in public, it wasn't uncommon for strangers to stop what they were doing to look over and make sure what they heard wasn't the start of an act of child abuse. Thankfully, Danny's constant smile and genuine comfort around his father was enough to ease their concern.

"Can I just finish showing Grandpa Griff something?" asked Danny. "Real quick."

"Fine," Richard said. "But are you sure he can see anything with those cataracts? Last time I took him to the eye doctor, she said they were so brown it's like looking through a glass of chocolate milk."

Danny laughed even harder.

"I see just fine, thank ya," argued Griff. "I'd be driving this truck here if you'd let me. Wouldn't be so dainty in this traffic, neither. I'd—" Griff tried to continue, but was cut short by a series of coughs. He put his fist to his mouth until the fit passed.

"I'm getting us there *alive*, Griff," Richard said, without malice. "What are you two watching anyway?"

"YouTube," Danny answered. "This morning some homeless people starting throwing bricks around, smashing everything. Happened right here in New York."

"And that's funny *why*?" Richard asked.

"Cause those are some crazy motherfuckers," said Griff.

"Yeah," said Danny. "Cause those are some crazy mother..."

"Don't," Richard cut him off.

"I wasn't gonna to say it."

"Uh huh," said Richard, unconvinced.

Even though Griff had been retired for years, he had a mind so sharp that the Lake Placid police department would still call and pick his brain every now and then. Griff would sit and consult with them, listening stoically and giving advice. Why the old man acted so immaturely around Danny was beyond Richard. He thought about scolding Griff for cursing, but held his tongue. Everyone was getting restless; Richard thought it best not to create any extra tension and just leave them to their devices.

As Richard sat listening to the sounds of shattering glass and homeless men screaming, the nagging in his legs and back became too difficult to ignore. "I have to get out and stretch guys," Richard said, but when he tried to open the door, he realized that the lanes of the bridge were too narrow—he couldn't open the door wide enough to get out without hitting the car beside him. In essence, he was trapped.

A gust of cold wind swept inside the vehicle, inciting yells from the rest of the passengers for Richard to shut the door. Just as he did, the sedan in front of them scooted ahead.

"Thank God," Richard said. He let his foot off the brake and the traffic began inching its way across the bridge. "OK, Danny," he said, "things are moving again. Sit down now and buckle up. And why don't you give the phone back to Jessi, you don't need to be watching anymore of that garbage."

Offering no resistance this time, Danny returned to the backseat. Richard adjusted the rearview and watched to make sure that his son snapped himself in. Danny did as he was told, stretching the seatbelt across his Iron Man T-shirt, the kind where the entire shirt was designed to resemble the superhero's chest plate, and fastened it into the buckle with a grunt.

"And the cell phone," Richard reminded him. Reluctantly, Danny surrendered it over to Richard's girlfriend, Jessi Reynolds.

With the angle of the rearview mirror, Richard could see Jessi's fingers interlaced in her lap. She turned one palm up and received the phone from Danny, then closed her hands back over it. Richard lingered in the mirror for a few more seconds—as it also gave him a view of Jessi's trim, crossed legs stretching out from her white dress—then raised it to a more appropriate level.

Jessi at eye level was equally tantalizing. Seven years his junior, she had yet to develop any of the creases or blemishes on her face that had crept their way onto Richard's. Hers was soft and heart-shaped, with sparkling blue eyes and just enough makeup to give her pale skin a light blush. Her curly blond hair was draped over one shoulder and bounced subtly as the truck bumped along the uneven pavement. When she caught Richard staring at her, she gave him a closed mouth smile that squinted her eyes. He couldn't help but return it, then focused his attention back on the road.

"Almost there," Richard said to no one in particular—maybe himself. It did feel good hearing it. Richard hadn't seen Will or Shannon since Christmas, the year before last. Worse yet, he only knew his grandson through photographs and video chats. If he had to pick, holding Gideon was the thing he was looking forward to the most when he arrived at Will's (besides finding the toilet).

There was no one reason why Richard hadn't seen his son; lack of money on both ends, conflicting schedules, and the difficulty of traveling with a newborn baby or a sick, old man were some of their top excuses.

But cash was the one Richard used when he offered to take over Kavi's lease. Richard was a single father juggling two jobs. The highest paying one was an independent general contractor (and it didn't pay much lately). Business was the slowest it had been in decades. It soon became a struggle to keep the lights on, let alone support Danny. More recently, Griff had been diagnosed with COPD after decades of heavy smoking. It had worsened quickly in the past few months, forcing Griff to keep an oxygen tank nearby at all times.

Though the rent for Will's building was about the same as Richard's mortgage payment in Lake Placid, having everyone in one household would help reduce costs. There would be more people available to care for Giddy and Griff. Most importantly, they would be a family again.

Will immediately took to the idea of sharing the townhouse with his father, but asked Richard why he waited so long to bring up the idea or ask for help. And what if Kavi hadn't coincidently chosen to move in with his girlfriend?

Richard replied with an uncharacteristic stammer. He told Will that he didn't want to be a burden on him and his new family, and that he thought things could turn around, and that maybe he just had too much of that stubborn pride, and lastly, that he had been waiting on his second job to allow for a transfer down to New York City.

Richard's rambling answers seemed to satisfy Will. Unfortunately, they were all lies.

Richard 1:2

The scene of the accident on the Queensboro Bridge dissolved any frustration that had built up inside Richard. A small SUV was overturned with half of its body shredded and strewn across the bridge. It appeared that two other vehicles had been involved. A taxi cab faced the wrong direction, its hood crumbled and windshield shattered. Next to it, an old model Jetta had its passenger side doors severely crushed inward. The lights from nearby emergency vehicles reflected eerily off of the ice and twisted metal, as well as a young woman's silver bangle as she stood sobbing into her hands.

As Richard inched past the chaos, he counted three body bags.

"Oh God," he heard Jessi whisper. Richard reached behind him as best he could, his shoulder joint popping in the process, and rested a hand on her knee. Jessi grabbed it and held it tight.

"A few words for them, maybe, Rich?" she asked.

Richard felt uneasy at the idea. He looked over to his father, but Griff was staring out of the opposite window, away from the crash.

"Yeah, lead us, DD," Danny said. He had climbed over Jessi to get a better look at the crash. "Looks like they could use it."

Reluctantly, Richard began reciting the prayer for the dead: "Eternal rest grant unto them, O Lord." Then, Richard stopped. There were many more lines to the prayer, but he didn't see the point. It wasn't his place anymore. "Amen," he said instead, ending the prayer prematurely.

"Amen," the other passengers echoed softly.

Richard turned on the radio, scanning it for the most upbeat music he could find.

†

Past the wreckage, the roads cleared and the ride became smooth again; Richard arrived at Will's in just under ten minutes. Pulling into the driveway and seeing his new home gave Richard a mixed sense of hope and dread.

Danny, on the other hand, seemed to be nothing but excited. Before Richard could even kill the engine, his son dove forward again between the seats.

"Can I honk the horn, DD?" Danny asked, giggling.

"I don't think so," Richard said, grabbing him in a headlock. "Not when you ask like that." Danny tried to squirm his way out, but Richard held on and dug his fingers into the side of Danny's stomach, sending him into a tickled frenzy.

"Stop, *stop!*" Danny screamed. "OK, OK, I'm *sorrrryyyy!*" Richard loosened his grip, allowing his son to pull free. "Please," Danny asked again, trying to hold a straight face, "can I honk the horn, *Dad*?"

"That's better. Yeah, knock yourself out," Richard replied, and the boy drove his head forward into the steering wheel. The horn rang out and Danny laughed some more. Richard grabbed him again, this time for a hug. "Satisfied? Now the whole city knows you're here."

"Yessa, boss. Mighty satisfied," Danny replied, then opened the driver's side door and crawled out of the truck hands-first.

"Yessa, boss?" Richard repeated, then turned to Griff. "Did *you* teach him that?"

Griff shrugged. "We watched *Huckleberry Finn* on Turner Classic the other night."

"That old black and white movie? That kept his attention?"

"The whole way through," Griff affirmed. "Now he can't stop talking like good ol' Jim."

"And you told him that he's *not* supposed to talk like that, right?" Richard asked, raising his voice.

"Not around you, I said."

"Unbelievable," Richard muttered, turning to watch Danny

76

as he skipped up to Will's front door.

There was no doubt that Danny was Richard's son. The resemblance was clear, though Danny was a thinner, shorter, more deflated version of his father. Their faces shared the same shade of icy-blue eyes and brown hair (though Richard was rapidly losing his) and had matching sturdy jawlines. But that's where the similarities stopped.

When Richard was eleven, he was already playing baseball and football. He added wrestling at puberty then boxing during senior year in high school, eventually going semi-pro until his late wife, Rita, convinced him to change career paths in order to prevent what she referred to as "mush for brains."

Richard had tried getting Danny to play sports, signing him up for a variety of leagues, but the boy never lasted more than a season in any of them. In football, Danny refused to tackle the other children. In baseball, he did little more than daydream and pick his nose out in right field. He didn't like basketball. He didn't like hockey. He didn't like soccer. Richard doubted that Danny would have enjoyed boxing, but Rita would have rolled over in her grave if he had even suggested that to their son.

It wasn't that Danny ever had a problem finding hobbies—they were just things that Richard could never have predicted, much less understood. Over the past year, Danny taught himself to play the harmonica, kept fit by ice-skating weekly at the Olympic Center, and saved up for and started an at home guppy breeding business that somehow stayed afloat despite all the fish Danny gave away to his friends for free.

Danny's most recent interest (as illustrated by his Jim impression) was slavery in the United States. The fascination started back in February, when his teacher began a Civil War module for Black History Month. That very same day, Richard got a call from Danny's principal to come pick him up.

"Apparently," the principal explained to Richard in her office, "during recess, Joey, who is somewhat of a class bully, was teasing

Darnell, one of Danny's friends. Joey threatened to purchase Darnell from his parents so that he could make Darnell his personal slave. Danny overheard…and then proceeded to throw sand in Joey's face, pull his hair, and shove him to the ground."

Richard nodded, his disappointment torn between the fact that his son started a fight and his lack of sparring technique. "What happens next?" Richard asked.

"Between you and me, Mr. Battese, I believe it was an attempt at something noble. The fact that Danny did not throw a punch and considering he has never had any disciplinary action against him before, I'm not going to suspend him. But I want you to take Danny home for the day and cool him down. Make sure it doesn't happen again."

"What am I gonna do with you, son?" Richard asked Danny later that night, both of them sitting at the foot of Danny's bed.

"Don't you know what the slaves *went through*, Dad?"

Richard pulled his son onto his lap, recognizing that there weren't many more years left for him to do that. "I do know, from what I was taught, and a lot of people felt the same way as you do. A lot of those people died fighting for the slaves' freedom."

"We learned about that. People from the north, like us. They were good people, right?"

"Yes, they were, but it was sad that it had to come to war. You're going to learn about many other wars and all the bad people that started them. It was up to the good people to stop them. That doesn't mean hurting someone is OK."

"I'm sorry, Dad."

"It's OK. I'm not mad. I'm actually proud of you in a way, for standing up for your friend. But you should never be the first to hit. Is that clear?"

"Yes, Dad."

"But, in case you *are* attacked, want to learn how to give a good right cross?" Richard swept his fist in the air with enthusiasm.

"Nah, maybe later."

Maybe later, Richard thought, recalling Danny's words. *Maybe I can tell Will the truth later.*

If only it were that easy.

Richard took the keys out of the ignition, grabbed the white strip of fabric off the dashboard, and stepped out onto Will's front lawn. He raised his brawny arms and did a few knee raises in the cold air. It felt glorious to be able to stretch and move freely again.

"Rich," Jessi called out from the opposite side of the truck. "A little help here."

"Yep," Richard said, walking around to meet Jessi on the passenger side. Together, they helped ease Griff out of his seat and down the big step of the F-150.

"God Bless you, DD," said Griff who grabbed Richard's hand and kissed it. The old man laughed and broke into a cough.

"Serves you right," said Richard, still holding on to him.

"I gotta have a little fun with you, Rich," Griff said, then turned to Jessi. "Ready to meet my other grandson, my dear?"

"Still nervous," she said quietly.

"You two need to stop worrying," said Griff. "He's always been a good boy. He'll understand this." His grip tightened on Richard's forearm and, for a rare moment, Griff's face flushed with seriousness. "He'll understand *everything*. You raised him right."

Richard nodded and squeezed Jessi's hand. She squeezed back.

"Go on and see him," Griff said to Richard. "You know I'm slow. I'll let the pretty one here escort me." Richard nodded again and walked on ahead.

"Dad!" Will cried as he emerged from the front door, carrying Danny piggyback style. Though both of his sons had huge smiles, Richard thought that Will's measured a little wider.

Will lowered Danny to the ground and hugged his father

tight. "Man, I missed you guys," Will said, looking back and forth between them like a puppy deciding between two bones.

Then he saw a third. "Grandpa! Hey!" When he saw Jessi wheeling over the oxygen tank, he turned to Richard. "Who's that? Grandpa's aid?"

Richard felt a lump in his throat. "No," he said. "It's been a while, but you remember Jessi, right? She fills in as the organist at St. Andrews sometimes."

"Yes, I do," Will replied, shaking his head like he was dusting off mental cobwebs. "You're married to Dr. Reynolds, my old pediatrician."

"I was," Jessi said with a sad smile. "Cancer took him a few months back."

"Oh," Will said. "I didn't even..."

"It's OK," Jessi said. "We tried to keep it quiet around town."

"Jessi offered to help us with the move," Richard said, changing the subject. "She's never been to New York City."

"Aw, well she didn't have to—but I mean, of course, we could use the help. It's good to see you again." He turned away, back to Richard. "How was the trip, Dad?" Danny immediately nudged him in his side. "Oh wait, I mean, how was the trip...DD?" When Danny began laughing, Will looked confused. "OK, so why did my little brother ask me to call you that?"

Richard sighed. "That's just my going nickname at this point: Daddy Deacon. He went through a few others. Let's see, there was LMD: Loud-Mouth Deacon; OMD: Old Man Deacon, and... what was it?"

"WBP," Danny said.

"Ah, yes. Wanna-be Priest. DD won out because it was the only nickname that wouldn't get Danny grounded."

Will smiled, "Well, I like it. I'm sure Kavi will too—hey, have they decided which church to transfer you to yet?"

"Not yet," said Richard.

"You have to tell me when you find out, so I can let them

know what to call you...DD."

"Wait...so who's our DD tonight?" Shannon asked, appearing in the doorway. "And more importantly, who's paying for my drinks?" She smiled and gave hugs to all of the in-laws, then Richard introduced her to Jessi.

"Am I setting another plate?" Shannon asked.

"Oh, no," said Jessi, looking to Richard. "That's a huge intrusion."

"No way," Will said. "We'd love to have you. Unless you have other plans."

"No, she doesn't," said Griff. "She's apartment sitting for an old roommate who's out of town for the whole weekend, ain't that right?"

Jessi nodded.

"Then I don't see why not," Shannon said. "You survived a road trip with these three Battese men. I'm willing to bet you need a glass of wine right about now."

Jessi's eyes were still on Richard, who felt like he had no choice but to shrug in agreement with the idea of her staying.

"OK," said Jessi, "but I might need the whole bottle."

"And top shelf whiskey for me," said Griff.

"What's that grandpa?" asked Shannon. "Did I hear you say the cheap stuff? Then, come right in."

Will held the door open for Griff, helped inside by Shannon and Jessi.

Richard and his sons were left on the front stoop. Despite the cold, he could feel beads of sweat running down the nape of his neck. He reached up and wiped them away.

Will noticed. "Hey, Dad. Where's your collar?"

"It's here," Richard replied, reaching into his pocket and pulling out his white Roman collar.

"He barely wears it anymore," said Danny.

"Why not?" asked Will.

"It's been a little tight around the neck lately."

Richard 1:3

Deacons in the Catholic Church were not permitted to hear the sacrament of Confession. That was a duty reserved for priests alone. Still, Richard was no stranger to the process. He grew up Catholic and had been a deacon for sixteen years, so he had gone through the rite too many times to count, always sitting on the opposite side of the screen from Father Monroe, the priest at St. Andrews. Until this day, however, Richard never fully appreciated the comfort that confessional offered. The dark booth provided both privacy and anonymity (or at least the veil of it in Richard's case, considering that his voice was unmistakable to Father Monroe and almost every member of the parish). The act would be different here in Queens. Admitting his transgression to Will, out in the open, was going to hurt. Worst of all, Will had no obligation to understand or forgive.

"Let's go inside," Will said, putting his arm around Richard and leading him through the front door. The entry corridor was tight and unable to accommodate the interlocked father and son, so Richard had to let go. Even walking through it single file, Richard's broad shoulders did not leave much space between the walls of the foyer. After a few feet, however, the house opened up. There was a spacious living room to the left and a steep staircase to the right leading up to the second story.

"Can I get you anything, Dad?" Will asked. "Water?"

Just hearing the word made Richard's groin flinch. "How about you point me to the restroom?"

†

The relief was immeasurable.

After almost a minute, Richard's stream of urine finally ran dry. He washed his hands then splashed his face with the excess water. In the mirror, he saw a man with bloodshot eyes that were partially covered by tired, heavy lids. It wasn't hard to believe that it was a reflection of himself. Secrets and guilt had a way of physically manifesting. He tried to decipher if this was the face of a man losing his faith or just one searching for a way to coexist with it.

Either way, Richard didn't like the way he looked — especially now that Jessi was staying for dinner. He searched the nearby drawers for any eye drops that could get the red out and found a bottle that was a few months expired. He used it anyway. Then, he noticed a face moisturizing cream on the counter. He picked it up, popped the lid, and smelled the scent to make sure it wasn't too feminine. After holding the container out to arm's length so that he could read the instructions, he applied the cream to his face and neck. There was a slight tingle that didn't feel half bad, but another inspection in the mirror did not reveal any improvement in his appearance.

Richard exited the bathroom to find Danny and Griff sprawled out over the living room furniture. Griff sat reclined in a leather La-Z-Boy chair, humming softly with its massage feature turned on. His eyes were half-closed and fixated on the big screen TV set to a local news channel. Someone had carried in his oxygen tank and the tubes were hooked up to his nose. Danny lay sideways on the end of a blue L-shaped sectional, his shoes dripping melting snow on the end cushion.

"Feet off the couch," said Richard sternly.

"Oops," said Danny. He slipped his sneakers off and slung them into a corner. Then, he attempted to dry the wet portions of the fabric with one of his socks.

"We just sat for over five hours," Richard said. "That wasn't enough? Why don't you get up and see if Shannon or your brother need any help."

"Nope, they don't. I already asked. Shannon said it's OK if I sit here with Grandpa — she didn't say it was OK for the shoes though."

"Just be careful," Richard said. "You just got here and you're already ruining their stuff. That couch looks expensive."

"It is, but don't worry about it," said Shannon, coming into the room with a bag of chips. She sat it down on the coffee table in front of Danny. "This, the couch, the chair, all the art—pretty much all the décor in this place—I get it free from work. Nothing exactly matches, but beggars can't be choosers, right?"

Richard nodded. "I guess not."

"The only thing I *will* ask is that you keep your voices down. Giddy is sleeping in the next room. I know you're dying to meet him, Rich, but he shouldn't be out too much longer."

Just then, a disturbingly loud and high-pitched sound pierced through the living room. Everyone jumped in surprise.

The screeching sound lasted only a few seconds, but its ringing echoed in Richard's ears.

"Dammit," Shannon said. "Sorry, everyone. That was our doorbell. It's all screwed up."

Will rushed out from the kitchen. "Sorry, sorry."

"Save it," Shannon snapped. "Go answer it before they ring again."

Will rushed off as he was told.

"What's wrong with the bell?" Richard asked.

"I don't know," Shannon answered, obviously still annoyed. "Something with the wiring, maybe? It's been doing that and getting worse. My husband has promised to fix it about ten times now."

"I can take a look at it tomorrow."

"Thanks," said Shannon, then cocked her head to the side. "Well, there you go, Rich," she said. "That woke him up."

Sure enough, from the bedroom Richard heard a baby's cry.

At the same time, Will returned to the living room, followed by Kavi and a young woman Richard assumed must be Leigha. She had a small, pretty face with blond hair that was a few shades darker than Jessi's. That was about all that Richard saw of her—she was bundled up in so many layers of winter clothes that she lost some range of motion in her arms and legs and marched almost like a toy soldier into the room.

"Sorry about the bell, guys! I forgot!" Leigha said with a cheery voice and charming smile, then officially introduced herself. "Man, it's getting cold out there," she said, her teeth still chattering. She pointed her arm straight to the back of the house. "We only parked around the corner, but that walk was torture."

"Somehow we persevered," said Kavi, jokingly.

Richard gave him a solid hug; Kavi was popular with the Battese family back home with how inseparable he and Will were in high school. Even Griff made the effort to stand up and shake hands.

"Do you want to go get your baby?" Shannon asked Will with an irritated tone that implied that it wasn't a question.

"You're my baby, too," Will replied, but when Shannon did nothing more than roll her eyes he hurried off into the bedroom. A few moments later, he emerged carrying Gideon and was immediately swarmed by everyone in the room, save for Griff, who didn't get up but craned his neck near fully around to get a look at the baby.

Gideon stopped crying as soon as he entered the living room. His bright blue eyes were opened wide as he seemed almost mesmerized by all the new faces around him. "Me first," Richard said, gesturing towards Will to let him hold his grandson. Will obliged.

It had been a long time since there had been a baby in the Battese family—Danny had been the last as Richard had no nieces or nephews or even younger cousins. Holding Gideon seemed to open up a locked and secured emotional bank, long forgotten, within Richard's memory. Images of Will and Danny as little children broke free from their dormant state and nearly overwhelmed Richard. He could see their eyes looking up at him with pride, love, and adoration. Then, he realized that that look was still there, especially in Will, when he greeted him outside the house just a short while ago. *Will they continue to look at me like that, when I confess?* Richard wondered. *Or was this one of the very last times they'd be proud to call me their dad?*

Richard kissed Giddy on the forehead and the baby began to cry.

"Let me take him there, Rich," Shannon said, reaching in and gently scooping Giddy away. "He's probably hungry again. He's always hungry." With that, she carried him into the kitchen.

Richard's attention was then drawn to the television, where a meteorologist gave warnings of another round of snowfall. There'd be at least another six inches accumulating overnight as the temperature in the five boroughs continued to drop.

"We should probably unload the truck," Jessi suggested. "Beat the storm."

Richard nodded. "Danny, put your shoes on. Let's do it."

"I'll help too," said Kavi.

While Shannon fed the baby, everyone else broke off into three groups. Richard, Jessi, Danny, and Kavi formed one and went outside for the heavy lifting, while Will took Leigha into the kitchen to finish preparing dinner. Griff formed the entirety of Group Three, which was put in charge of the TV's remote control.

Though the bed of the pickup was packed full, there really wasn't that much stuff compared to what Richard left behind. The majority of Will's house was already furnished, thanks to the eclectic generosity of Judah Décor. Even more convenient for the Batteses, Kavi chose to leave behind most of his bedroom furniture, which included his queen size mattress and frame, a pair of end tables, and a large oak dresser.

Richard, in turn, had sold all of his furniture for some extra cash. The biggest items Richard drove down were some shelving units and a cot for Danny until they got a new twin bed. Everything else: clothes, Danny's toys, Griff's medical equipment, and items of sentimental value like photo albums, frames, and Rita's knickknacks were packed in cardboard boxes. It made for quick work, even though they brought everything upstairs into Kavi's old room.

After Richard threw up the tailgate and locked the truck, he looked up to see the first snowflakes starting to fall.

As it turned out, Richard's team had worked so fast that they managed to finish ahead of dinner. Will said that he needed a few more minutes, plus they were waiting for one more guest, so they all plopped down on the couch.

Griff had not carried out his duties very well. He was asleep again and Richard couldn't find the remote anywhere, so everyone was stuck watching the news. The anchorman was discussing a new report that claimed autism might be on the rise in the state of New York. The east coast's leading geneticist on the subject was live via satellite to discuss the "whos," "whys," and "hows."

Richard stared blankly at the television set as the doctor gave only vague answers to the questions. Richard knew a few members of his parish were diagnosed as autistic. One teenager in particular was far along on the spectrum and was completely nonverbal. Because of his state of mind, he was not required to perform Confession. The church believed that as long as an individual is capable of having a sense of remorse for committing a sin, even if they cannot describe the sin precisely in words, that person may receive forgiveness.

It shamed him to think it, but Richard was jealous. He imagined how easy it would be to deal with his sins if he never had to confess them at all.

Richard was going to propose to Jessi.

Jessi was going to say yes.

That's where the easy part ended.

There was another major difference between priests and

deacons. Deacons could be married, but priests could not. However, in the event of a deacon outliving his wife, he was not allowed to marry again, except with the bishop's express permission. Exceptions had been made in cases where the widowed deacon was the father of a young child. With Richard being the sole provider for Danny, he did fit that criteria, but was denied nonetheless. This was because the entire community believed that Richard was having an affair with the wife of one of their most beloved pediatricians.

That was never true—at least not physically. And not at first. When Jessi's husband fell ill and was diagnosed with terminal cancer, Jessi sought the comfort of the church. One of the deacon's roles is to be a confidential counselor, so Richard, being a widower himself, made himself available to Jessi to support her through the grief.

He couldn't say exactly when he fell in love with Jessi, but it wasn't long before he looked forward to their private counseling sessions. During his sermons in mass, he began searching for her among the pews. Whenever she was in attendance, his eyes always lingered on her when he spoke. And when he gave out Communion, she always managed to appear in his line to receive the body of Christ.

Richard crossed the line when he began seeing her socially outside of St. Andrews. At first, it was only thirty minutes here and there at a coffee shop, but it soon evolved into regular dinners, arriving together for community events, and evening visits to Jessi's home after her husband lost the fight.

They never made love. They never so much as kissed, even though they both knew how badly the other wanted to. Richard refused to break his vows to the church. The problem was that no one believed them.

Father Monroe had no choice but to report the situation to the bishop, and the bishop denied Richard's request to remarry. His reasoning was that a marriage that had formed out of a forbidden relationship, whether the rumors were true or not, would do great harm to the community.

Richard understood and did not argue the decision. Even so, he could feel himself being judged by the members of the church. They either refused to make eye contact with him or delivered strong looks of contempt as he spoke. During Communion, his line became the shortest or was empty altogether. It wasn't long before his contracting business dried up—as the majority of his clientele were parishioners. There was even some talk of his dismissal from the church.

Again, Richard understood. He understood it all. He couldn't imagine the extent of damage he did to their faith—how deeply he shook it.

But he couldn't shake Jessi. He needed a fresh start. He needed it to be with Jessi.

That's why he called Will and decided to move to New York City.

There was no approval for transfer. Richard was resigning from the church.

·

Will 1:4

After all the anticipation leading up to Convergence Day dinner, Will knew it flopped. He regretted the choices that he made, one after another, until finally he wished that he could just start the whole thing over.

Of all his regrets, however, his cooking wasn't one of them. The shrimp fajitas came out beautifully. Those, along with the homemade guacamole, refried beans, rice, and cheese quesadillas, made for a homecoming feast far tastier than anything Will was allowed to prepare at the Cosmic Ocean. It was something he could be proud of. And he would have been—had he not served it cold.

Haynes never showed up, nor did he call or text Will with any update or cancellation. All the while, Will clung to the belief that his coworker wouldn't just flake on him. He tried to hold off serving dinner as long as he could. *Let's give him a little longer*, Will told whatever hungry body entered the kitchen and inquired about the hold-up. *Just a few more minutes.* By the time an out-of-patience Shannon convinced Will that everyone else should not have to suffer because of one person (and that Haynes would just be "shit out of luck" if he arrived and the food was gone) the steam from the fajitas had long since faded.

Despite the temperature of the meal, the feedback was actually still positive. As a testament to his cooking, everyone at the table remained mostly silent while they focused on consumption. The only noises interrupting the winter night were utensils scraping the plates, a lot of "Yums" and "Mmms," polite permissions to pass the dishes, and eager requests to get them back. In his highchair next to Will, even Giddy seemed to spit up less pureed vegetables than normal. The best compliment Will got was from his wife. She sent him a look from across the table: raised eyebrows and a hearty nod. "Delicious, babe," she said, and Will knew she wouldn't have said it if she hadn't meant it. Still, he could only imagine the reaction of his guests if the food had been plated on time.

But he had other regrets to focus on, including the toast.

"Cheers, everyone," Will had said, raising his glass of expensive Spanish red that Shannon charmed away from one of her clients. "Jesus had his last supper, but here's to our first back together as a family." He liked the line enough—though didn't think it was his best—but as everyone clinked glasses, Will realized that he should have thanked Kavi for all the fun and wished his soon-to-be former housemate good luck in his move. Then, Will realized that he had skipped saying grace altogether. He looked over at his father, who had always led the table in prayer, but Richard had already begun drinking his wine, not seeming to notice the omission. Richard's expression looked tired and less natural than usual, though Will would be the first to admit that being apart from his father for almost two years meant that he couldn't be sure what usual *was* for him anymore. By the time all of this went through Will's mind, he was the only one who hadn't started eating.

At one point during dinner, Griff leaned over and whispered to Danny.

A moment later, Danny yelled out, "Hey, Will," he said. "Can you pass me the salt?"

"Is that for you or for Grandpa?" Richard asked.

Danny looked over at Griff, saying nothing, but the guilt in his face revealed the truth.

"There's more than enough salt in each of these dishes, Griff," said Richard. "I'm sure you're over your limit for the day."

"Like hell," said Griff.

"It's OK," said Will. "This is salt-free salt." He winked a few times. "Right, Grandpa?"

Danny burst out laughing. "Salt-free salt!" he repeated.

Griff winked back. "Sure is, Rich. So you don't have to worry."

Richard shook his head, unable to contain his own laugh. "I don't care anymore."

This led to Will's third and biggest regret: trying to be the cool brother.

"Hey, Danny, heads up," he said, and tossed the salt shaker across the table. While Danny never had a propensity for sports, it had been far longer since Will had thrown an object in any type of competition, a fact that resulted in a toss that was way too short. The shaker knocked over Kavi's wine glass, spilling merlot onto the table and all over Danny.

"Man!" Danny cried out, stretching out his Iron Man shirt from the bottom to look at the huge stain. "This was my favorite."

"It's OK," said Will. "This wine won't stain it."

"It won't?" Danny asked.

"No way—your suit's made out of metal right?"

This time, his joke didn't land. Danny looked down at the floor, dejected.

"You don't need to tease him, Will," said Shannon.

"Danny, I'm sorry. I was just kid—"

"Come on," Shannon said, cutting him off. "Let me throw that in the washer before it dries, then I'll help you go through your wardrobe to find the sharpest looking outfit for dessert."

"But I don't even know where my clothes are," Danny said.

"Yeah," Richard chimed in. "We gave Griff the responsibility— his only responsibility while packing—to record the contents of the boxes as we sealed them. Turns out all he did was write the person's name on the box. And sometimes forgot to do even that. Can you go with them, Jessi? You were there with us. You might have a little more luck figuring out which boxes have his clothes."

"Sure, Rich," said Jessi.

After Danny and his female escorts left the room and Will cleaned up the rest of the spilled wine, it wasn't long before everyone else at the table was back in a cheery mood.

Then, the doorbell rang, and Will would learn true regret.

Will 1:5

Will winced from the doorbell's screech; even worse than the sound was the sight of Giddy spasming in his highchair, as if the faulty wiring had shocked the baby directly. After a moment's delay, Giddy let out a long, pitiable cry that only piled onto Will's guilt. *I messed up again*, he thought. He had forgotten to tell Haynes—whom he assumed had finally arrived—not to ring the bell. Will truly had meant to fix the wiring, but kept putting it off, not out of laziness, but from sheer intimidation by the fact that he literally knew nothing about how to fix wiring.

"I guess I'll get it," Kavi said, as Will gently stroked Giddy's head, trying to calm his son down. "Me, the man with the injured leg." Kavi stood and headed towards the door, exaggerating his limp.

Will kissed the top of his son's forehead, "I'll be right back, baby boy." He followed Kavi, thinking he could at least try to disconnect the doorbell. *Maybe even rip it out of the wall*, he thought, *before any other guest unknowingly reminds me of my inability to get things done.*

Ahead of him, Kavi checked the peephole. "It's Haynes," he confirmed. Will wondered about his coworker's late arrival; Haynes was always punctual. It was almost an hour past when Will said to arrive, but NYC's public transportation could cause unexpectedly long delays.

After unbolting the lock, Kavi swung the door inward and rested his forearm on the knob. "About time, man," Kavi said. "Dinner's cold."

Haynes stood with his hands behind his back. He gave a closed-mouth smile that didn't seem to convey any remorse or disappointment. The waiter was overdressed for the night, wearing a black blazer over a dark-red, button shirt complete with a black pencil tie. Will couldn't hear the wind, but saw it ripple Hayne's clothes and felt it fill the hallway with a chill. Without speaking, Haynes squinted his eyes and surveyed the foyer, his focus moving from Will to the stairs, to the hallway, and back to Kavi.

"Well, come on in, *monsieur*," said Kavi. Haynes's smile grew bigger, showing his perfectly kept teeth. Kavi turned around to Will and thrust his thumb back over his shoulder towards Haynes. "This guy and his get-up...I think he's picking you up for the prom."

Will laughed a bit uneasily at the joke and waved at Haynes, who had taken a few steps inside, standing strangely close behind Kavi. Haynes raised his arm, and at first, Will thought he was starting to wave back—but there was a hammer in his hand.

It was so out of place that Will found himself thinking: *is he going to fix the doorbell?*

Kavi was about to speak again, but before he could, Haynes swung the hammer down on the back of his head. It made a hard, empty crack. Haynes's blow landed in a way that Kavi's mouth clamped shut, severing a large bit of tongue that fell to the floor. Will watched his friend's face turn from a smile to what was best described as confusion. Although blood leaked from his gaping mouth, Kavi seemed unable to process any pain and made very little sound. Then his legs gave out and he collapsed forward.

In the kitchen, it seemed that no one had been able to calm Giddy down. Will could hear his baby crying, but it was a distant, faded sound. Likewise, the normally thunderous cycle of the washing machine swirling around Danny's shirt was dampened to the level of a stomach's growl. It was Kavi's whimpers that resonated the loudest, but as the blood quickly pooled around his face, the whimpering became gurgles.

Will took a step towards his dying friend. As he did, Haynes raised the hammer again, but his other hand flashed his palm in a stay-away gesture. "Stop," Haynes said. "That blow was fatal.

There's nothing you can do now." Will, unarmed and afraid, instinctively obeyed. Haynes stared at Will for a moment, then turned his attention back to Kavi. He got down on one knee and reversed the hammer, then plunged the spiked side into Kavi's chest. It went in deep. Blood gurgled up, black, like oil. Haynes retracted his weapon, removing red clumps of mass along with it. Kavi twitched and tried to raise a hand, but Haynes struck three more times. Kavi moved less after each blow.

Will stood there, frozen, as the hammer repeatedly entered his housemate. He knew the back side of the hammer had a name, but couldn't remember it. As a child, Will dreaded his father's do-it-yourself projects. Richard would invite Will into the shed or garage and try to explain whatever task it was that he was working on. Whether it was car engines, network cables, or woodworking, it was all boring to Will. He would daydream about comics or video games, waiting for an excuse to go back in the house. *What a disappointment I must've been*, Will thought. *If I'd listened to my dad, I could've fixed that doorbell and identified what just killed my best friend.*

Haynes stood up from Kavi's now motionless body. "OK, then," he said, nodding at it. He wiped his face, speckled with blood, with the sleeve of his blazer. The blood blended into his clothing so completely that Will wouldn't have known it was there except for the way the wet portions glistened. He looked up at Will with a gentle smile. "Is that Gideon I hear?"

The question swept away the haze covering Will's senses and the sound of Giddy crying returned, as loud as ever. *He knows my son is in the kitchen*, Will told himself. *I can't let this man get past me.* Will held up his fists in defense, with no idea how to use them against the man who only this morning was a coworker and friend. *He couldn't have transformed into this...executioner so quickly*, Will thought, *the way he so calmly killed Kavi. How could someone hide his true nature like that? How could I miss it? Do I stand a chance of stopping him?* Will's arms shook in the air, but he stood his ground, hoping that none of his fear and self-doubt was evident to Haynes.

"No, William Battese," said Haynes, and gestured softly at Kavi's body. "This fate is not for you." Somehow, Will found his voice comforting, despite the odd use of his full name. Will almost believed that he would be OK.

Then, another man entered through the open front door. He was massive. Will was 6'2", but this intruder towered over him and probably had twice the muscle mass. Unlike Haynes, however, this intruder wore a mask. It covered his entire head snugly and was made of some type of pasty white material—Will had never seen it before. It had the texture of papier-mâché, but none of its rigidity, as it seemed to expand and contract with the man's slow breaths. The only markings were a set of sharpened teeth embroidered over the mouth and black marks over the eyes which looked like keyholes.

Haynes extended his free hand towards Will, this time his palm was welcoming. "Please come with us. It will be easier without any resistance." The giant stood silent behind Haynes. Will couldn't speak, his throat muscles were clenched. He wanted to say no, but found that he had taken a step forward. *Maybe if I go*, he thought, *it will save my family.*

"Yes, that's it," urged Haynes. His eyes were the widest and brightest Will had ever seen. There was desire in them.

Suddenly, a familiar voice burst out from above. "Oh my God!"

Will looked up to see Shannon at the top of the staircase, covering her mouth in horror. At that moment, he loved her with all of his heart and forgave her for every bad thing she ever did. Will felt his strength return to him.

"Shannon! *Run!*" Will yelled, and she gave a stutter-step backwards, then took off down the hall.

"Fen, she's cornered up there," Haynes said, nodding toward the stairs. His voice was still calm. "The only way out is the bedroom window," Haynes continued, "but it's jammed." The masked man took his orders without question, but also without hurry, taking one step at a time up to the second floor.

Will wanted to tackle the masked giant in order to buy Shannon more time, but fought off the foolish urge. Still, an even sicker feeling swept over him: *was that the last time I'll ever see my wife?* Will knew he couldn't dwell on the question. He turned and ran into the kitchen to warn the rest of his family.

"Dad!" cried Will as he entered, his voice cracked from the panic. His father was already standing.

"What happened?" asked Richard. Griff and Leigha also looked to Will for answers. They were both alert—no one could have missed his screams from the hallway—but Will knew they had no real idea of the gravity of the situation.

"Haynes. My coworker..." Will gasped, finding he didn't know the best way to sum up what he had just witnessed.

"What?" Richard shouted.

"We have to get out of here! Out the back!" Will rushed for Giddy and fumbled with his highchair latch. Before Will could unfasten it, Haynes appeared. He did not enter the kitchen, but stood in the doorway, allowing Kavi's blood to drip from the hammer in his right hand. It formed a small puddle by his boot.

"The fuck?" Griff asked, forcing himself to stand as well. "Are you hurt, boy?"

"Don't worry about me." Haynes smiled. "This is another man's blood." He tapped his foot in the puddle, splashing blood onto the kitchen's white vinyl floor.

"Kavi?" Leigha asked. "Where's Kavi?" She looked at Will with pleading eyes.

What do I say? Will thought, but found no words.

Haynes answered for him. "I killed him with this hammer. His body is there, in the hallway. We did not want him and we do not want you." He raised his weapon again and slowly walked toward Leigha.

"No," said Richard stepping in front of her. "Bad idea." He raised his fists in defense. Will knew his father's voice and stance were by far more intimidating than his own.

As if to agree, Haynes paused, then took a step back. He tossed the hammer to the floor. It bounced and slid towards the refrigerator, leaving a crimson streak. "Richard, Griffin, you're coming with us. Gideon, too. You're all very important." Haynes reached behind his back and pulled out a handgun, small and gray—Will didn't know what type—and pointed it at Richard.

Then, Will heard the back door slam. He turned around and saw two more masked intruders in his kitchen. Their masks were similar to the giant's. Each had the same keyhole eyes, but the designs around their mouths varied. The smaller intruder's mask had two fangs and a forked tongue sewn into the mouth area. The other man's looked like an inverted cross, except the ends of the horizontal line curved slightly upwards, giving the impression of a subtle smile.

"What do you think of your standup guy now?" asked the man behind the smiling mask, pointing towards Haynes.

Will shivered as he recognized the voice. "Degas," he said. There was no doubt in Will's mind, but his broken voice made it sound like a question. He backed away from the intruder and against the counter.

Degas laughed with delight. "Yes! You remember me!"

"You know these people?" asked Richard.

"Yes, he does," Degas answered for him, "although not as he originally thought." Degas looked around the kitchen. "We're missing a few."

"Fen is taking care of it," said Haynes.

"OK," said Degas, pulling out a pistol of his own from behind his back. "Then we wait. I need everyone to stay where they are. And just to make sure you do..." He stepped behind Gideon, still in his highchair, and pointed the barrel of the gun at the baby's head.

"You'd kill a baby?" Will choked, feeling his eyes swell with tears.

Degas looked up at Will and the mask's smile seemed to grow. "I've done worse."

Shannon 1:4

Shannon was on her knees when she heard the doorbell ring. Its screech pierced through the floorboards up into the second story bedroom, losing none of its potency on the way.

"Fucking Will," Shannon muttered. She continued digging through the third of a series of boxes marked solely with the word "Danny." This one contained nothing but shoes and a bunch of action figures. "And fucking Griff. Didn't inventory a goddamn thing." As she closed the cardboard flaps over the mass grave of Ninja Turtles and X-men, Shannon was reminded of who else was in the room. She looked up to see Danny staring at her. "Forget I said all that, will you? But where the...*heck* are your clothes?"

Danny—who had taken off his wine-stained shirt downstairs and now sat half naked on the floor—just giggled and shrugged.

"Let's try this one," said Jessi, who tried unsuccessfully to hide a smirk. She took Will's rusty box cutter from Shannon and opened the next mystery container. It held a remote control car, the scattered pieces of a board game, a bunch of Goosebumps books, and a pair of sweatpants.

"Getting warmer," Shannon said, rising to one knee with a groan. "Keep searching, Iron Man. I'm going to say hello to Will's friend." More importantly, she had left her wine glass downstairs.

"I want to meet him," said Danny, following Shannon to the door.

"You will," Jessi said gently, "but not until we find a shirt. Remember how your father and I talked about being presentable?"

Danny nodded with a huff and went to grab another box.

Shannon exited the room, analyzing Jessi's use of the phrase "your father and I." The way Jessi grouped herself with Richard as a parental unit was a little too...*Affectionate? Obsessive a la Sara Bentera?* Shannon couldn't decide. Whatever it was, she felt Jessi was more than a friendly organist. *They don't travel all the way to New York City just to help carry some boxes. Unless it's Richard's organ she's playing.*

As Shannon headed down the hallway, she was distracted from her thoughts of scandal by a peculiar noise: a slow and steady *thunk, thunk, thunk.*

Shannon's brain, racing to recognize the sound, brought up an image of Sara planting her garden, her spade chopping through the rocky, Queens soil. *Not the same,* Shannon thought. This sounded more forceful.

But before Shannon could analyze further, the noise stopped. She heard a man speaking, but his voice was too soft to make out the words. Shannon rounded the corner and peeked over the balcony. Will was there, along with Haynes and a masked man twice the size of either of them. Kavi was on his back on the floor in the middle of the group, the center of his white undershirt ripped apart and soaked with blood. There was more pooling out from behind his head like a murky, red headdress.

"Oh my God!" Shannon said. The macabre scene hit her with such surprise and force that she just blurted it out. She put her hand over her mouth as instinctively as she had opened it, but it was too late. All three men jerked their heads up. Shannon saw the uninvited man's mask directly now. Its empty black eyes and jagged teeth were haunting, but it was Haynes that scared her the most. He stared at her, smiling. In his hand, a hammer dripped Kavi's blood on to the wooden floor.

"Shannon! *Run!*" Will yelled. Shannon was taken aback by Will's forcefulness and for a moment, stumbled. After stabilizing herself, she dashed down the hallway.

Jessi was standing in the bedroom doorway. "What's going—" she began to ask, but Shannon slid by her and yanked her inside, cutting off the question.

Though the house was old, it was built solidly, and the bedroom had a sturdy oak door. Shannon slammed it shut, then twisted the latch on the doorknob to lock them inside.

"What—" Jessi started again.

"Kavi is *dead*! There are two killers down there and *we're trapped up here*," Shannon said, her voice speeding up and cracking at the end of her sentence.

"Kavi's...dead?" Jessi echoed blankly, as if she didn't understand. She took a step back and looked over to Danny.

The boy was standing over an opened box on the far side of the room that had apparently contained some clothes, as he was now wearing a light blue, long-sleeve *Miracle on Ice* T-shirt. He was not moving except for small tremors in his hands and chin. "Jessi..." he began to say, but did not finish. He just stared at her with wide, frightened eyes.

When Jessi saw him in that state, she instantly composed herself. She straightened her posture. Her voice no longer wavered. "OK, Shannon," she said. "What do we do?"

It was a good question: Shannon wasn't sure. "Phones," she said pleadingly. It was all she could think of. "Mine's downstairs. Do you have yours?"

"No," said Jessi. "It's...Richard put it in his pocket while we unloaded the truck."

"Danny?"

The boy shook his head, apologetically. "Dad won't give me one."

"Shit," Shannon replied. "*Shit.*" She tried to process the situation and come up with a solution, but *we are fucked* was the only thing that rang clear. She found herself wishing that both Haynes and the masked giant would just go after Will. *There's a back door, Will could grab the baby and run outside, lead them away and we'd be just fine up here.*

It was then that Shannon heard the footsteps coming down the hallway. "Shit," she said again.

There was only one set of footsteps approaching. They were slow, but sounded substantial—almost like stomps. Shannon knew it was the giant. She looked back at the bedroom door and felt much less confident in its ability to hold.

"We need to barricade ourselves in," Shannon said.

The only piece of furniture in Kavi's bedroom capable of the task was his antique dresser—the one he purposely left behind because it was too heavy to move. Thankfully, it was already on the wall adjacent to the door. Shannon rushed to the opposite side of the dresser and heaved herself against it. It scooted about an inch. Without a word, Jessi—the woman Shannon met only hours ago—lined up beside her. Together they managed to slide it far enough to block the door.

The footsteps, which had been growing louder, stopped outside of the bedroom.

"Now what?" asked Jessi.

The door handle jiggled.

"I don't know—but be quiet." Shannon lowered her voice to a whisper. "The men, they only saw me. They don't know anyone else is up here."

"Then we'll hide," said Jessi.

"Hide?" Shannon asked. "Hide where?" The room was almost bare.

The door handle continued to shake, but with more intensity.

"The closet," Jessi mouthed, pointing across the room. A plantation style bi-fold door stood ajar in front of the small hideaway. "We stay in there," Jessi whispered. She picked the box cutter up and held it in front of her. "If he tries to come inside, we cut him fast and hard."

"That little knife won't work," Shannon protested.

"It will if we use it right. The eyes, the throat, the balls—we go for that."

Jessi flicked the box cutter open and a few rust flakes fell to the floor.

Shannon did not feel good about this plan. *That beast of a man is a felon or ex-military or an underground fighter. Or all of those things.* Shannon shook her head. "No. It won't be enough. He's big, Jessi."

"How big?"

"*Big.*"

The man in the hallway began to knock on the door. It was a slow and deliberate cadence, like he was taunting those inside.

"OK, OK," Jessi said, her eyes darted around the bedroom. "The window, Shannon!" she shouted, not remembering or not caring anymore about keeping quiet. Behind the stacked boxes was Kavi's little double hung window—only three feet by three feet—with its uninspiring view of the brim of Manhattan's skyline. Jessi hurried across the room to it and Shannon and Danny followed.

The back patio was twelve feet below.

"There's concrete and ice down there," Shannon said. "You think we can make the jump?"

"I do," Jessi said, nodding.

"And Danny?"

"I...I can," the boy said shakily.

"He can," Jessi confirmed. "It's not that far. If you're worried, I'll drop down first. Then you ease Danny down as far as you can. I'll catch him."

Shannon *was* worried, but didn't appreciate Jessi's decision to put her last on the list to escape. She almost objected, but it was clear that to Jessi the conversation was already over. Shannon watched her try and push open the window.

The panel didn't budge.

The knocking at the door was now so forceful that it could scarcely be considered knocking; the entire frame shook with each blow.

Jessi didn't look back, but stayed focused on the window. She pushed harder, letting out a huge, masculine grunt, but it didn't open. Danny had stepped up beside her, pushing as well. Still no movement.

Shannon saw the problem: the window was locked. "Here!" she said. "Danny move!" She shoved him out of the way harder than she meant to. The boy stumbled back but didn't fall. Shannon flipped open the window latches and Jessi pushed again. This time, the window glided open—about eight inches, then stopped. Jessi sank down into a lunge and pushed until her porcelain face flushed red. Shannon gripped underneath the bottom rail and added her strength to the effort, but the window would not open any further.

"It's jammed or something," said Shannon.

"It's OK," said Jessi, breathing heavily. "I think I can make it." Without waiting for a response, she spun around and extended her right leg back through the opening. Shannon held her up under the armpits and Danny joined in, doing his best to support Jessi's midsection so that Jessi could get her other leg through. Slowly, with their help, Jessi squirmed backwards, inching her way through the very tight opening. When she got to her butt, Danny had to smush it down with his hands in order to get it through.

But it didn't work that way with Jessi's head. Even with it turned sideways and her ears flattened against her skull, Jessi just could not make it through the gap.

A crash at the bedroom door caused Shannon to jerk her head away from the window towards the sound. A section of the door was now cracked—splintered right down the middle.

Shannon returned her attention back to the window with a sense of urgency somehow greater than she already had. She spread her palm across Jessi's forehead and pushed as hard as she could.

"Ow!" Jessi cried out. "Stop! I can't."

"You have to!" Shannon urged.

"I *can't*. Pull me back."

Shannon and Danny attempted to do just that, but found that they couldn't—they couldn't squeeze her butt through now that it was outside the window.

A new panic appeared in Jessi's eyes. It was full of the same realization that had struck Shannon at just the same time: Jessi was stuck.

"Get into the closet," Jessi whispered, tears spilling down her cheeks. "Protect Danny."

"No," said the boy. "We can get you out."

"Don't be stupid, Danny" Shannon snapped.

"She's right, Danny," said Jessi. "But you're going to be OK." She turned to Shannon. "The knife is right there on the window sill. Take it."

Shannon did and Danny began to cry.

"I'm so sorry, Jessi," said Shannon, but forbade herself from making eye contact with her any more. She grabbed Danny by the hand and quickly led him towards the closet.

They slipped inside and Shannon left the folding door slightly open, so that she could see if and when the intruder came for them. She knelt in front of Danny, between him and the door, and held the knife ready, fighting to forget her earlier insistence that the blade would be useless against the giant.

From her position, Shannon couldn't see the bedroom door, but she had a direct view of the window. Jessi hadn't given up, and she had actually made it in a little further by pushing on the wall below the window for leverage. With a little more time, Shannon wondered if they could have actually gotten her through.

Her thoughts were interrupted by another crash, followed immediately by an even larger one that shook the entire room. No doubt the dresser had crashed to the floor. A slow, scraping sound culminated in the top of the fallen dresser being pushed just into view. Heavy footsteps entered the room and then the giant appeared in front of the closet. Fortunately for Shannon, he faced away from her and towards the window. The enormous man must have been almost seven feet tall with a wide, barn door back and long, thick arms that hung by his side. The knuckles on his tan, white hands were covered with blood.

When Jessi looked up at the towering figure in the tight, gray mask she stopped trying to get back inside the room and instead froze in place. The giant took a step towards her.

"Shannon!" Jessi screamed.

Oh my God. Shut the fuck up! Shannon thought. *What the hell are you doing!? Trying to send him after me!?* She gripped the box cutter tight with both hands and held it against her sternum.

But the giant didn't so much as look in Shannon's direction. That's when she realized that Jessi wasn't shouting towards her. It was the opposite: Jessi's head was turned partway around, looking outside the window and into the darkness.

The giant drew his right arm out to his side, fist clenched.

"Shannon, *run!*" Jessi shouted. "Don't wait for me! Shannon, just ruh—"

Jessi never saw the punch coming. Her cry was cut off by a massive right hook that caught her squarely in the side of the face. The sound of the impact was all too familiar to Shannon, yet more intense than anything she had ever experienced. Jessi's upper body was thrown to the side as far as it could go then she slumped forward over the window sill.

The giant grabbed the top of her arms just under her shoulders, his sprawling hands wrapping almost completely around the tops of her arms. He gripped, and then he pulled.

Jessi was literally torn from the window, ripping against the sill and bottom rung. The force shredded lines of flesh along the front and back of her torso and legs. Jessi landed on her belly on the floor, screaming as blood flowed from the long gashes on both sides of her body.

The giant seemed unfazed by her display of agony and wasted no time in flipping her over. He began to choke Jessi with both hands.

A shadow swept beside Shannon. She was trembling, sweating, and so in shock that she didn't realize what it was until it slipped halfway through the closet door.

Shannon had time—a split second or two—to grab Danny and pull him back, but she couldn't bring herself to free either hand from the box cutter. She didn't go after him. She didn't call out to him. She just watched, with tears in her eyes, as the events unfolded.

"Jessi!" Danny yelled, emerging from the hiding place.

The giant had not seen the boy coming and turned to look just as Danny jumped onto his back. "Let her *go!*" Danny shouted, and began punching the mask. When the giant realized what was happening, he let out some sort of cross between a laugh and a growl. He reached behind him and yanked Danny off by the shirt, holding him in the air the way a mother cat carries her kitten.

"Stay still," the giant ordered, his voice deep, yet clear, but Danny flailed his body, trying to slip away. It was enough for the giant to fumble his grip on the boy.

Jessi took the opportunity to break free, using both of her hands to pry off the fingers of his one. When she got loose, she sucked in a lungful of air. Holding her neck with one hand, she used the other to begin crawling towards the closet. The dizzy, absent expression on Jessi's face made it seem like she didn't realize *where* she was going—she was just trying to get away from the giant. Nonetheless, she was about three feet away from exposing Shannon.

No, Shannon thought, willing her away. *No, please, no. Don't bring him here. Don't bring him to me.*

In the end, Jessi didn't. She never made it that far. She was less than an arm's reach away when the giant—still carrying a thrashing Danny—grabbed her hair and yanked her back up off the floor and hurled her against the wall. Jessi let out a miserable groan with the impact, then crumpled forward onto her stomach.

Shannon saw that some golden strands of hair had come loose in the giant's hand, attached to bits of scalp. She watched him toss them away.

The giant moved toward Jessi again. When he reached her, he kicked her in the side with a dark-brown, steel-toe boot, rolling her over onto her back. He bent down and pinned her to the floor with his massive knee on her chest.

Jessi wasn't done fighting. She tried clawing at the giant's mask, but he shifted his posture up, keeping her nails out of reach of his eyes. She scratched at his chest and arms, but there was almost no energy left in her defense; she didn't even tear the fabric of his shirt.

When she let her arms drop, trying weakly and in vain to push his knee off her chest, the giant punched her in the face. Shannon heard something break.

He punched Jessi again and there was no more struggle.

When she went limp, the giant stood up. He placed his boot on Jessi's face, adding more and more pressure until it caved in.

Shannon did not make a sound.

Danny was crying hard now, but it was clear he too was becoming exhausted—each outburst had less energy than the last. Shannon watched the giant lower the boy and carry him in a tight but gentle grip, cradling him across his chest. *He wants Danny alive*, Shannon realized, then wondered if that was worse.

The giant hunched over at the window, peering down towards the ground. He did not move for a few more seconds, then stood back up.

"Shit," he grumbled. "She actually got out." In his arms, Danny stared towards the closet.

Shannon prayed that the boy did not call to her for help.

Again, she got her wish.

With Danny in his arms, the giant rushed out of the bedroom. It was not until his footsteps faded down the hall that the guilt of her inaction consumed her. She fell back into the corner of the closet and pulled her legs to her chest. She closed her eyes. She closed them so tight it hurt. She wanted to seal them shut so that whether in this world or the next, she would never have to face her family again.

Richard 1:4

Long before he joined the clergy, Richard knew that Heaven existed. He knew it before the birth of his two sons, he knew it before he first made love to his wife. Those moments were glimpses into the joy he would find in an eternity with God. They served not as evidence to convince him, but reminders to strengthen the faith he already had.

Richard also knew that his belief did not guarantee a sorrowless life. Even when he stood over his wife's casket, holding her hand for the last time, Richard did not doubt God's love. Still, the questions in Richard's head drove him to agony.

Why would God take Rita the way He did?

How were there no witnesses in such a public place?

Why didn't the sheriff do his job? Why did the sheriff have to lie?

Why did I go along with it?

The answers never came. Richard didn't expect them to. God hadn't spoken directly to anyone since John the Baptist—and it wasn't to answer the saint's personal questions. *Why would God ever respond to me, someone so far from blameless?*

Despite the sting of God's silence in his life, Richard's conviction never faltered. As the man named Degas held a gun to Gideon's face, fear and anger wove new tapestries in Richard's mind, but there was not a single thread of disbelief. He only had one question for God this time: *why?*

Richard knew he'd have to find the answer himself.

A quick process of elimination ran through his head: *If they wanted to kill us, they would do it here, like they did with Kavi. They said they want to take us, but where, and for what?* He understood the idea of kidnapping infants and selling them on the black market. *But kidnapping me? Will? Griff? No one would buy us. Our organs—maybe—but not those from a sick, old man. And no one here is important enough to be worth a ransom.*

111

And just like that, Richard's mind hit a brick wall; he was all out of ideas. He feared that the answer was far worse than anything he could think up, yet felt compelled to question the source directly.

"What do you want from us?" he asked Degas, the man who was clearly in charge.

"We want many things from you, *deacon*," Degas answered. "You cannot see my face, but under this mask I am smiling brightly, thinking of them all. The first one is easy: we want everyone's cell phones."

"Give them to me," said Haynes, holstering his pistol in the back of his pants. He grabbed a serving bowl, speckled with grains of cooked rice, from the table. There was a phone sitting beside it. Haynes took it in his other hand and held it up. "Whose is this?"

"Mine," Richard lied. His was in his pocket.

Haynes clicked a button on the phone's front panel and the background lit up: a self-portrait of Shannon in front of a mirror. "It better not be," said Haynes, smirking. He tossed the phone in the bowl. "Now yours, *liar*." Richard didn't move.

After a moment, Degas pressed the pistol against Gideon's head. "Now," he demanded.

"Dad, please," Will begged.

Richard slowly and stiffly took the bowl, suppressing the temptation to strike the man in the mask. Something told him that Degas wouldn't hurt Gideon, but in this situation, Richard did not want to risk an accident. If he wanted to attack, he'd have to wait for the right time.

Richard reached into his pocket to grab his phone, but felt something else: he had Jessi's phone as well. It was a tiny, old Nokia that, with any luck, would remain undetected in his loose black slacks.

Richard quickly dropped his phone in the bowl, then passed it on to Leigha, who dropped hers in as well. Her bony arm trembled as she gave the bowl to Will, eerily reminding Richard of the offering basket at mass—an act accompanied by eager donations and upbeat hymns. This perversion proceeded in silence, with a sickness in the air.

The bowl made its way to Griff, supporting himself on a kitchen chair. "I don't carry a cell anymore," he said. Haynes searched him anyway, but found nothing. Then, Haynes took the bowl, placed it under the faucet, and filled it with water. When it overflowed, he took out his pistol once more and pointed it at Griff.

"Good," said Degas, turning to the figure in the snake mask. "Lam, kill the girl, please."

As if expecting the command, Lam was already unwrapping a thin piece of metal connected to two wooden handles. Richard recognized it; it was a cheese wire. Lam gripped it by one end, letting the other dangle, then approached the frail girl. Leigha tried to push her attacker away, but Lam swiftly countered, spinning Leigha against the wall. Lam slung the cord around her neck and pulled backward, hard. Leigha squealed, trying in vain to get her fingers in between her neck and the wire.

Suddenly there was a crash from upstairs heavy enough to rattle the wineglasses on the kitchen table. The commotion took everyone by surprise. Lam looked briefly to the ceiling and Degas dropped his gun. Richard couldn't imagine what was happening on the second floor, but it gave him the opening he needed.

Praying that he was correctly calling Degas's bluff—that Gideon wouldn't get shot—Richard lunged towards Lam.

Lam saw the attack a second too late and was slammed against the wall by Richard's blitz. One end of the cheese wire came loose from Leigha's neck. It whipped around her, freeing her, but sliced open her skin at the same. Leigha dropped to her knees, holding her neck as blood trickled through her fingers.

Will stepped forward and Degas instantly cocked his pistol and raised it back to the baby's head. Will stopped dead in his tracks. "Hold it there, William," Degas said. "Let's see how this plays out."

Richard seized the opportunity. He swung a punch at Lam, but it was too slow for a solid connection—Lam ducked and Richard's fist barely grazed the top of the mask. He swung again. This time, Lam dodged the attempt completely, deflecting Richard's fist then hooking his arms in an effective boxer's clinch. The two of them struggled against each other in a twisted dance that sent them spinning away from the wall towards the center of the kitchen.

Richard was much bigger than Lam, but his opponent's grapple was surprisingly strong. In an attempt to break free, Richard steered himself into the kitchen table, knocking it over. Dishes shattered while food and utensils were strewn all over the floor, but Lam held strong.

A small steak knife slide in front of Leigha, who was still hunched over on the floor. She saw the knife. So did Richard. Lam did not. Leigha reached for it, but when she let go of her neck, the bleeding intensified; more blood spilled down to her chest. Bravely, or perhaps unknowingly, she ignored it and managed to grab the weapon.

When she did, Richard stopped trying to break free and instead used all his weight to push Lam over to Leigha who, with surprising coordination, shot forward. It looked like she was aiming for Lam's left oblique, but Leigha's dive fell short, and instead the knife sliced the front of Lam's quadriceps.

From behind the forked tongue of the mask came a shriek that Richard never expected: Lam was a woman.

Caught so off guard by the revelation, Richard lost his grip. Lam squirmed free enough to grab his genitals, then twisted hard. Intense pain surged through his body. When his hands instinctively went to his crotch, Lam struck him in the throat with the side of her right palm. The blow sent Richard crumpling to the floor.

Lam turned her focus to Leigha. "Bitch!" she screamed, then backhanded Leigha across the face with enough force to spin her halfway around. Lam followed it up with a boot to the back of the head. Leigha fell to the floor, sprawled out on her stomach and was knocked out cold. Lam picked up the knife beside her. Now armed herself, she took unsteady steps towards the unconscious girl.

"Don't!" Will shouted. Richard hazily saw his son step in between Leigha and Lam.

"Lamia, stop!" shouted Degas, in what Richard detected as his first sense of urgency. The wounded woman took another step forward, then halted. She stood still for a few seconds—her heavy breathing fully audible under the mask—then tossed the knife into the sink.

"Are you OK?" Degas asked her.

"I just need to bandage this up," she replied. Her voice was calmer than Richard would have expected after being stabbed.

Degas turned his attention back to Richard, who was still on the floor, curled up into a partial fetal position. "You're setting a bad example for your son—I told him not to move but he couldn't help but mimic his heroic father. I don't have time now, but Gideon is going to lose a finger or two for that." He looked at Haynes. "Get the deacon under control."

Haynes pointed his gun at Richard. "I hope you're done," Haynes said. "Stand up and let's—"

This time it was Griff that seized an opening. In one swift motion, he grabbed Haynes by the wrist with one hand and the gun with the other, rolling the weapon in towards Haynes's arm. It broke Haynes's grip of the gun, allowing Griff to take the weapon into his own hand. In that moment, Griff was thirty years younger.

Before Haynes could react, Griff smashed him in the mouth with the butt of the pistol, then took two large steps backwards. He kept the gun pointed at Haynes. Griff's breathing was erratic, but his aim was steady. Then, he turned his head to Degas.

"Drop the gun, you *freak*, or this coward gets it."

"Haynes? You think he's that important to me?"

"Come on, Victor," said Haynes, spitting blood as he spoke.

"Well, I *would* be disappointed if you weren't around to see this through," Degas responded. "Very well, Officer Battese, I will comply with your demands." He dropped the gun to the floor.

"Kick it to me," Griff ordered.

And Degas did. "Now what?"

"Now," Griff said in a gravelly tone, pointing the gun at Degas's chest, "without a *baby* to threaten...you're done!"

He pulled the trigger.

Click.

Griff's right lower lid twitched. He pulled twice more.

Click, click.

Griff looked at the gun. "It's not even lo—" but before he could finish, a small cloud of mist exploded in Griff's face. Almost instantly, his arms went limp. They fell by his side and he dropped the gun to the floor. Then, he toppled backwards against the refrigerator and slid down to the floor where he stopped moving altogether.

Richard could not see him breathing.

Haynes stood in his place, holding an aerosol spray bottle in one hand and pressing the inner elbow of the other arm across his nose and mouth.

"What did you do to him?" Will shouted.

"Griff!" Richard cried out almost simultaneously. "Griff—ah, I'm going to kill you!" He tried to crawl towards Haynes but his hand slipped on blood. His arm flew out from underneath him and his head struck the tile with a loud smack. The intruders all laughed.

While on the floor, Richard looked up to see another masked man enter the room carrying an unconscious Danny under one arm.

"One of the women escaped," said the giant, his voice flat, but his words rushed.

"Away from *you*, Fen?" Degas, replied, cocking his head.

Fen did not respond.

"Hmm," said Degas. "I wonder which one it was—no, wait! Don't tell me." The inverted cross on his mask seemed to grow wider. "Who do *you* think got away, Will? Your wife or your father's girlfriend?"

A tear spilled down Will's cheek. He didn't answer.

"And if *one* got away," Degas continued, "what happened to the other?"

"Dead," said Fen. "It's not pretty."

"I'm sure it isn't. However, since someone escaped, it's certainly time to go." Degas picked the baby up. "Let's finish up here. Haynes, get Will."

"No!" Will cried out, raising his arms, but it was too late. Haynes sprayed him with the same mystery concoction as Griff. Will lost his balance and started to tip over, but Haynes caught him and lowered him gently to the floor.

Richard struggled to get up. He knew he was next.

But Degas nodded towards Leigha. "And Lam—finish with her."

Lam limped toward Leigha, who was still unconscious on her stomach. Lam knelt beside her slowly and, with both hands on Leigha's head, broke her neck as effortlessly as snapping a dead branch.

Richard felt the pain in his body vanish, numbed by anger and agony. He powered up to one knee. From where they stood, the three masked figures formed a loose circle around Richard and watched as Haynes approached, bleeding from the nose, but smiling again. *Too confident*, Richard thought. *He thinks it's four against one, but he's wrong.* Degas carried Gideon while Fen held Danny. Lam, still bleeding from her leg, was wrapping her wound with a shred of tablecloth.

As Haynes tauntingly flashed the spray bottle, Richard remembered something he'd said during one of his strongest homilies: "While it is impossible to fully know God's plan, there is always one thing that's never a mystery: what we do at any given instance." Richard knew without a doubt that it was God's will that he kill Haynes—because Richard was going to make that happen.

He rushed towards Haynes before his finger squeezed the bottle's trigger. Because Haynes wasn't wearing a mask, the surprise in his eyes was obvious. Richard felt stronger. He grabbed Haynes by both wrists, extending his arms to the side as he tackled him to the floor. The impact knocked the bottle from Haynes's grip and it slid across the floor. Richard grabbed Haynes by the neck.

"Get him *off*," ordered Degas, but his voice was drowned out in Richard's head. "Hold the baby," the distant voice continued.

Richard wasn't sure if anyone else spoke; he was now too focused on his task. Haynes's face flushed red and his eyes began to bulge. *Hurry up and die.* Haynes flailed his arms towards Richard's face, but the deacon's long arms kept him from harm. *I can do this. A few more seconds…*

But then the mist came. Richard's muscles began to disobey him. His vision blurred, the image of Haynes in front of him seemed to lose color and fade. Richard couldn't feel his hands, but he could see them: gray and ghostly and still choking Haynes. Richard swore to himself that he would kill this man before he let go. *It's God's will. It has to be God's will.*

A second mist turned Richard's gray world to black.

End of Act 1

State of Amazonas, Brazil

The days when Reverend Cara Dann could effortlessly turn heads were gone. At the age of forty-five, it took some determination—and the right lighting—but Cara could still doll herself up enough to be approached by a good-looking man.

Just not here in the Amazon. The jungle made Cara Dann ugly.

There was dirt all over her face, pit-stains that never stopped expanding, and unshaved, stubbly legs scratching against the inside of her pants. The eighty percent humidity ruined her hair. She had cut it short this time—her dark brown ponytail now barely reached her shoulders—but there was still an explosion of frizz. She couldn't see herself, as pride and experience had taught her to leave all mirrors behind, but was sure that her looks paralleled her smell quite directly.

Beads of sweat trickled down her back and into her shorts and panties, which had become heavy with the weight of the absorbed perspiration. Her belt was fastened to the tightest notch, but Cara still had to stop every few minutes to keep her pants from dropping.

Despite her frequent wardrobe adjustments, Cara was able to keep pace with Pedro, one of the hired guides. He was in his early thirties and lean-muscled with deep brown skin and a thin, spotty moustache. With him and Cara at the head of the pack were two other seasoned travelers, both doctors. The first was Michael Emmert, Cara's family physician and friend of over three decades. Ten years her elder and more than slightly overweight, the doctor had a face that was flushed red. While Dr. Michael's heavy breathing was loud enough to startle wildlife, he never fell behind and Cara never heard him complain.

"A hot one today," the doctor said, smiling proudly. Although it was technically winter in South America, the temperature in the rainforest stayed between 80 and 90°F year round. Michael had made the joke at least once every twenty-four hours since the trek began. Cara gave a courtesy laugh, the kind given to an unfunny grandfather because any other response would seem cruel. She would hear the joke again tomorrow and bear it just the same. He was a competent doctor and, except perhaps for his humor, Cara was glad that he was here.

Moving slightly ahead of Cara was Dr. Peter Reising, a linguistics professor from the University of Oxford. Physically speaking, he was the opposite of Dr. Michael: tall, lanky, and tan. His size fourteen shoes left huge prints in the mud that Cara sometimes made a game of stepping in. Although he complained constantly about the "bloody heat," his accent made his gripes charming.

Dr. Reising was not a Christian—he was a long time agnostic—but this was as much his mission as it was Cara's, if not more. It was because of Dr. Reising that she was even here. Two and a half years ago, the professor contacted her out of the blue. He explained who he was and that a new tribe in the Amazon had just been discovered. His current study was the effects of language barriers on religious ministry. He wanted to observe firsthand the process of introducing religion to a group of people to whom both the concept of Christianity and the host language were entirely foreign. He wanted Cara to help him.

Cara was flattered by the request, but not surprised. Her reputation was well known in missionary circles as the face of Indigenous People Advancement Ministry, or *IPAM*, one of the top rated Christian ministries in the world, dedicated to taking the Gospel of Jesus Christ to the world's remaining unreached peoples.

Cara had been a part of twelve missions to the Amazon alone, and this was her and Dr. Reising's second trip to the Nacana village. For everyone else, it was their first. The group consisted of Dr. Michael and six fellow missionaries from Cara's church (with the goal of spreading God's word to the Nacana) and four of Dr. Reising's staff (to watch, record, and analyze how they did it). Three Brazilian guides were also with them, hired to navigate them through the difficult jungle terrain.

The journey started off well. Cara left her base camp in the municipality of Tefé pumped up on prayer and adrenaline. As they began the two week hike, the sights and sounds of the rainforest and its exotic wildlife captivated the entire group.

Three days ago, however, the group suffered its first setback. Alan, the youngest of the group—eighteen and just out of high school—had stopped to catch his breath. Not paying attention, he rested his hand on a tree, startling the most bizarrely-colored spider Cara had ever seen. The pattern on its abdomen resembled red U.S. military camouflage but its fangs and eyes were bright turquoise. The spider struck before Cara could get out a warning. Within seconds, Alan's thumb swelled to the size of a cucumber. Dr. Michael hurried over to help, but Pedro pushed him away and pulled out his machete. The two other guides held Alan down.

Pedro severed the thumb in one swift chop.

"You will probably live now," he said.

Despite the guide's optimism, Alan went into shock. Dr. Michael took over at that point. He was able to stabilize the teen and address the wound, but did not appreciate the quality of the amputation. He insisted on real hospital care, forcing one of the guides to take a dazed Alan to base camp. Two of Cara's church members decided to turn back as well, out of fear they would succumb to a fate similar to or worse than Alan's.

As the leader, Cara knew it was up to her to keep the remaining three missionaries motivated. She gathered them into a circle.

"We were ready for this," she reminded them. "We talked about the hardships we could face. We prepared ourselves, storing mental and spiritual strength to use in times like these. Remember our goal and why we're here. Imagine the satisfaction you'll feel when we are able to witness to the furthest people from civilization. God did not forget about the Nacana, He was waiting for us to be His vessels." She took a big breath. "Let's pray."

†

As they held hands and took turns saying prayers, Cara's thoughts went back to over two years ago, to her first visit with the Nacana. While the other tribes had established dialect and local translators, the Nacana used a language that was not known to be related to any other in the world. Dr. Reising insisted that the initial encounter with the tribe was simply to make contact and build trust. No preaching. Reluctantly, Cara agreed.

In the early days of their stay with the Nacana, Cara watched Dr. Reising, one of the world's most esteemed language specialists, literally point to himself, repeating his name out loud. She soon did the same. It reminded her of high school—Spanish class in sophomore year—but here in the Amazon, there was no teacher to correct her. She did her best to identify simple objects: banana, tree, feather—but anything more complicated brought nothing but doubt and confusion. When a villager pointed to his face, Cara had to figure out whether he meant face or something more specific like cheek, skin, or brown. It was easy to become frustrated.

Dr. Reising was always there to calm her down. Over the months, words turned into sentences, and sentences into conversations. Cara marveled at the Nacana's contradicting complexity: full of nuances, like facial expressions, whistles, and tongue clicks, yet lacking certain vocabulary fundamental to Cara's work. Concepts such as sin, faith, and redemption—beliefs vital to Christianity—seemed impossible to teach because, to them, the ideas did not exist.

Cara spent eleven months in the village, but the mission did not end when she returned home. She and Dr. Reising continued to work together via video conferencing between New Jersey and England. They took everything they learned in the Amazon to create an apologetic algorithm, creating the necessary language for Cara to preach to the Nacana. It was another year's effort.

✝

Now, as she approached the Nacana village on her second visit, all Cara hoped to do was convey what she thought to be the very basic Christian message: We all sin, God punishes sin, but Jesus died so that our sins may be forgiven. The concept of the Holy Spirit was left out completely—she considered it too complicated.

"We are close, Miss Cara," said Pedro. "We have certainly been spotted by now."

"I agree," said Dr. Reising. "So why aren't they here to greet us?"

Cara shrugged and smiled at Dr. Reising, masking the worry that crept up inside her. The first time she had arrived, the whole village of two hundred had gathered. Today, however, not a single one of the Nacana was present.

"Maybe they didn't see us coming after all?" Dr. Michael suggested.

"No," said Dr. Reising. "If they're here, they know we are."

Cara nodded. "Pedro, stay with the group here at the edge of the village. Michael, Peter, come with me. Let's figure out what's going on." She led and the men followed.

The Nacana lived in a dense patch of jungle, completely hidden from the sky.

The circular perimeter was lined with about forty huts built amongst the trees. They surrounded an area cleared of brush, where the villagers once feasted and danced. It stood empty now. Then, Cara realized smoke was rising from many of the huts. *The people aren't missing,* she thought, *they're hiding.* That revelation only relieved her slightly. She approached the nearest hut and from it heard a soft, sad moaning. *Did we do something to upset them? Scare them?*

Cara continued towards the chief's home in the center of the circle. While only slightly bigger than the others, it was much more lavishly decorated with palms and was the only hut to be elevated—sitting on stilts about a foot off the ground. Two dead jaguars, one adult and one cub, were sprawled out on their bellies, one on each side of the entrance to the chief's hut. There was an assortment of brightly colored flowers lined down each of the animal's spines and thin, green palm leaves crisscrossed over their faces. Cara had not seen this before.

As Cara reached out to touch the face of the smaller jaguar, Quando emerged from the chief's home. The shaman was painted firetruck red from his fingertips to his neck. Over his face, a spiral shape was drawn in black. He had a short ponytail like Cara's—minus the frizz—but the top of his head was shaved. His ears, nose, eyebrows, and nipples were pierced with golden hoops of assorted size. A multi-colored feather headdress fell halfway off as he rushed towards Cara, speaking loudly in his native tongue. He spoke quickly and Cara, rusty from her time away, couldn't keep up. She looked impatiently to Dr. Reising.

"He is telling us to go home," Dr. Reising said.

Cara did not like Quando out of fear that he would be her greatest obstacle in converting the Nacana to Christianity. Shamans were greatly respected in the tribe, yet led the natives to believe the only spiritual forces in the world existed within the plants, trees, and animals. It was a practice none of them seemed to have questioned for centuries. Cara knew it would be a difficult obstacle to overcome, unless she could weave God through their worldly beliefs, connecting nature to a higher power.

But that was the least of Cara's worries right now. She had

never seen Quando this hostile.

"Quando," Cara said. "I know something is wrong. Tell me what's happening."

Dr. Reising continued to interpret between them. "He says the chief's son is very sick. The entire tribe is in...ill spirits. We all need to leave."

That was unacceptable to Cara. After all the effort she put into getting to the village, she would not accept immediate rejection. She knew Peak and had been fond of the boy. After giving him a *Scooby-Doo* coloring book and a box of crayons last year, he had taken quite the liking to her as well.

"Please, Quando," said Cara, "you know I am a friend to Peak. Tell your chief that we have a doctor with us." She pointed to Dr. Michael. "A healer."

Dr. Michael waved, but Quando sneered at him then spoke again.

Dr. Reising interpreted the shaman's words. "He says *he* is the healer."

Cara scoffed. Last time she was here, a tribesman was bitten by a snake. Quando spit in a bowl of mud and spread it over the wound. After hours of agony, the tribesman died. "If Quando is the healer, ask him if he has healed the boy yet," Cara said.

Dr. Reising relayed the question and Quando's face turned solemn. Then he replied.

"He says he will ask the chief. If he allows your help, then so be it."

Quando disappeared into the hut and a few minutes later called out from inside.

"He says yes," said Dr. Reising, "but, only Dr. Michael and myself." The physician took his cue and hustled into the home with his large duffle bag of instruments.

Cara sat cross-legged outside the chief's hut, clutching the small, fourteen karat gold crucifix around her neck. Looking around the village, she saw faces appear in the doorways of the huts. *Everybody is watching,* Cara thought. Suddenly, a current of excitement ran through her. *Peak's sickness could be a blessing. If we can heal the boy after Quando couldn't, surely they will recognize the power of God.*

Cara dwelled on the thought of her leading yet another group of people to Christ and how the Nacana could perhaps even spread the message to neighboring tribes. She became so lost in the fantasy that at some point she dozed off. She never heard the doctors exit the hut and jumped to her feet when Dr. Michael touched her shoulder.

The expression on the physician's face created a knot in Cara's stomach. Dr. Reising and Quando, standing further away, did not appear any less grim.

Cara waited for the bad news.

"The boy has a tumor," Dr. Michael said weakly.

"God..." Cara managed to whisper. "You're sure?"

Michael nodded. "I used an ophthalmoscope. It's a small device that allows me look into the back of Peak's eye. I found a large mass. Retinoblastoma. It's very rare in children over five, but it's there. Clear as day."

Cara couldn't find a response.

"It gets worse," Dr. Michael continued. "Based on the symptoms I got from the boy's father—difficult with the translation of course—I believe it has already metastasized." Dr. Michael tried to wipe the sweat from his brows, but his sleeve was already so saturated that it did nothing more than spread the moisture around. "It means the cancer has spread to another organ. I think it's in the brain."

"What can we do?" asked Cara, frantic now. "What can *you* do?"

"Nothing. The boy is terminal."

"It *can't* be nothing!" Cara quickly lowered her voice. "There's a reason we're here at such a crucial time. Think about it. God brought us here to save this boy."

"I'm not a neurosurgeon, Cara, and if I were, I can't just cut open his skull in the middle of the jungle. He needs a sterile operating room."

"Why the hell did you even come, then?" Cara stopped and composed herself again. "I'm sorry, Michael. I just—we can't be *useless* here. This is the opportunity of a lifetime. If we cure him, if we give these people this miracle, they'll be ours for sure!"

"Ours?" asked Dr. Michael.

"You know what I mean."

The doctor sighed and put his hand on her shoulder. "Listen, there's no miracle in my bag. That boy in there is in very bad shape, but...if we get him to a hospital in Brazil, maybe he'll have a shot."

Cara's eyes widened and she turned back around.

"That's a *huge* maybe, Cara."

But it was all she needed to hear. She turned eagerly to Dr. Reising.

"I'm sorry, Cara," Dr. Reising said, now coming forward. "I am not going to ask that question. The chief allowed you to stay here and may fancy you, but would never permit you to disappear with his child."

"If that's true," said Dr. Michael, "Peak...will not get better. Maybe we *should* give them their space."

"No," said Cara.

"Let's leave them to their customs," Dr. Reising urged.

"I said *no!*" Cara shot back. "Let me think." She clutched her crucifix again. "OK. Michael, you said he's terminal, right? Exactly how long does he have?"

"I can't say. Weeks, maybe. Months? I doubt it."

Cara smiled for the first time since she entered the village. "I have an idea." She looked over at Quando, then back to Dr. Reising. "Peter, do *not* interpret what I am about to say."

Dr. Reising gave her a hesitant nod, then said something quick to Quando. The shaman huffed and went back into the chief's hut.

Cara waved in the two doctors and the three of them huddled together.

"If this is a game," Cara said, "then we're in sudden death. *Literally*. We're playing for a young boy's soul."

"This isn't a bloody game," said Dr. Reising with a frown.

Cara knew the analogy was cold, but did not take it back. Instead, she continued. "Peak needs salvation before his time runs out. So what's the plan? Michael has a suitcase full of medicine and equipment—none of which cure cancer. But the Nacana don't *know* that. We convince the chief that the contents of that bag are the boy's best chance at survival." She looked at Dr. Michael. "I know you have some painkillers in there. A temporary reprieve from the headaches will be enough to gain us some credibility."

"Oh my God," said Dr. Michael.

Cara did not slow down. "You tell the chief you have more tricks up your sleeve—that the best medicine does not come from a pill, but from the words of *my* sermons. The chief will *drag* his son to attendance if he thinks it can save him. And Peak, he has an accepting soul, I knew it the moment I first met him. If I can get a month or two—I've converted more resistant children in less time." Cara took one of Dr. Reising's and Dr. Michael's hands in each of hers, but did not look at either of them. Instead, she closed her eyes in ecstasy. "The boy is going to die, but we'll make sure he dies a Christian!"

Act 2

Will 1:6

Will had no idea how much time had passed.

After regaining consciousness, all he could remember was an uneasy sleep with a bizarre dream. In it, Will stood in an orchard that spanned endlessly in all directions. The trees seemed to glimmer under a setting sun and its branches bloomed with the freshest apples Will had ever seen. He wanted to taste one, but the apples hung too far above him to reach. It wasn't until he approached one of the trees in order to climb it that he discovered why they sparkled: their trunks and branches were encased in razor wire. The apples were impossible to obtain.

Will ran down the rows, searching for a tree with low-hanging fruit. He passed by hundreds, but each kept its bounty as unobtainable as the last. Eventually, Will became weary and his pace slowed. On the brink of collapse, he arrived at the edge of a steep cliff. Far below, he could see another orchard, and could make out that it too was fruiting with apples. Yet in between the flecks of red was darkness and darkness was good. It meant there were no razors.

Will was determined to find a way down, but when he turned, he found a man standing behind him, shrouded in a pure white cloak. His face unseen, the mysterious figure gestured for Will to follow him and Will obeyed. The man led the way to a hidden staircase that spiraled to the base of the mountain.

They descended together, but when the man in white reached the bottom, he suddenly sprinted towards the orchard. Will watched as the man placed his palm on the trunk of the closest tree. For a moment, the bark glowed under his hand, then caught fire. The blaze spread to the entire tree and, within seconds, reduced it to ash. Without looking back, the man continued running down the row of trees, arms outstretched to his sides. His fingers grazed every tree and every tree faced the same fiery doom.

"No!" Will yelled. "Please, I need one!" But the man in white ignored him. Will chased after, but could not keep up. The fires soon merged into a wall that separated Will from the man. The wall of fire curved, encircling Will, then began to close in on him. Surrounded by flame, he had no choice but to dash through. Somehow, he emerged unharmed.

On the other side was the man, standing calmly, with his hands clasped behind his back and staring into the red sky.

"Why are you doing this?" Will asked, panting.

"Doing what, my boy?" His voice was gentle and calm, but his face remained unseen under the robe.

"Burning the apple trees."

"Hmm…it was not me."

"There's no one else here!" Will shouted.

The man glanced around calmly. "There must be."

But Will saw the evidence on his sleeves. "Your robe, it's seared along the edges."

The man pulled up his sleeve to examine it. "There must be another explanation." He shrugged.

"Stop lying!"

"Leave me alone," replied the man and turned his back to Will and continued gazing upwards.

Frustrated, Will looked down at the ground. At his feet lay a large sickle. Its silver blade caught the sun, gleaming brighter than any of the razor wire had. The cloaked man's back was still turned; Will could grab the blade and strike before he saw it coming. It was murder, but Will believed he was killing to survive. Any hesitations were wiped away by hunger, fatigue, and desperation. Will reached for the blade.

As soon as he touched it, the sun fell beyond the horizon — dropped like a picture frame off a wall. There were no stars in the night sky, only darkness.

Will remembered the attack on his family.

His eyes shot open, but the real world offered no more light than the ending of his dream. With an instinctive panic, Will tried to stand, but was pulled back down by his wrists. He landed on his butt with a splash and realized that he was up to his chest in water—cold water. He raised a shivering arm—heavier than it should have been—above the surface. He heard the harsh rattle of chains. Will was in shackles.

"Help!" he cried out in the darkness.

"Help! Help! Help!" echoed his cry off nearby walls.

"Somebody help me!" Again his voice bounced all around him, mocking him in his cell.

"Will, be quiet," commanded a familiar voice.

"Dad? Dad! I—I can't see! They blinded me!"

"No," Richard whispered harshly. "It's just very dark. This room is pitch black."

"Why are you whispering?"

"I don't want them to know we're awake. They might come for us."

Will shuddered at the thought. "Where are we?" he asked softly, following his father's lead. "Where's Giddy?"

"He's behind us. I can't see him, but I've heard his noises. They seem to come from higher up—I don't think he's in the water. Grandpa and Danny are here, too; I know the sounds they make when they sleep."

"Thank God," said Will, then paused. "Shannon?"

"I don't know where she is...or Jessi."

The room went silent. Will remembered what the giant Fen had said: that one of the women had been killed. *How do I hope for Shannon to be alive,* Will wondered, *without wishing for Jessi's death? Is my dad hoping for the exact opposite? Degas said Jessi was Dad's girlfriend. They must've been close.* Will's emotional conflict became physical pain—as if a vice were tightening around his head.

"Leigha?" Will asked.

Richard paused before responding. "She's dead."

There was silence again as Will took in what his father had said. *Leigha and Kavi...I could have done more to help you...*

After a few moments, Will spoke again. "Are *you* hurt? You were hit so hard."

"Just sore, bud. I'll be fine. What about you?"

"Freezing, but I'm OK. Except that they chained my arms."

"Mine too—all of ours probably. Your ankles should be as well."

Will moved his legs to check. There was a second of give before they, too, locked in place.

"Yeah," Will said with a sigh.

"OK, now, I want you to test something. The chains are attached to separate hubs under the water. Are any of yours loose? Is there any wiggle to them?"

"I'll check," Will choked out, embarrassed. *Why hadn't I thought of that?*

He circled his right arm around, exploring its range of motion. It wasn't much. He pulled with more strength, but didn't get any further. He tried his left arm. Same result. The shackles were solid but, oddly, the wristlocks had a thick, soft padding. It was a comfort that Will did not expect.

Next, he reached down into the water, following a chain to its base. He felt his hand brush against the hub and found that it was attached to the floor by five or six heavy bolts—too tight to unscrew without tools. Finally, he gripped the chain at the base and pulled as hard as he could.

"Ugghh!" Will strained. *Ugghh! Ugghh! Ugghh!* the room taunted back.

The restraints did not budge. Will slapped the water out of frustration. "I can't, Dad. I'm too weak."

"No, it's OK," said Richard patiently. "These people—whoever they are—aren't sloppy. We had to try though. I'll have Danny and your grandfather try, too, when they wake, just in case. In the meantime, save your strength."

Suddenly, there was a loud click and a sliver of vertical, white light appeared in the darkness. It seemed to float in the air for a moment before exploding to fill the room. So unbearably bright, Will had to bend over to hide his face in his hands. His chin bobbed in and out of the water.

"And God said...let there *be LIGHT*."

To Will, this voice was now as unmistakable as his father's. He looked up and squinted to see Degas standing in a doorway. His arms were outstretched over his head, which caused the light to cast a sinister shadow across the room. His phantom arms, stretched and distorted by the angle of the light, came to rest over Will's face. It brought relief from the brightness, but filled Will with the deepest sense of dread. Although Degas remained still, his shadow danced upon the ground. It was then Will realized that the entire room—not just his holding area— was filled with water.

Degas took a step forward over the pool, but he did not sink.

Will watched in horror as Degas appeared to walk on the surface of the water towards him.

"He *claimed* the light was good," Degas continued, "but certainly He had to know how much pain it would bring humanity. Why did He design it that way?"

Closer he came. Will's pupils were adjusting now and the silhouette of Degas began to fill with lines and colors. A white crescent appeared on his face—a smile. Degas hovered closer still, then bent over—his face was just outside Will's range of movement. The smile grew bigger.

Then Degas stood up and stomped hard with his boot. The frigid water splashed over Will, revealing the illusion: there was a raised platform that sat just under the water level. The narrow bridge began at the door and ended just beyond Will's shackled ankles.

Degas must have seen the surprise in Will's eyes. "Faithless boy!" He laughed. "Only one man I know can walk on water. You should refresh yourself on the Gospels."

"What do you want?" shouted Will, ashamed of his own gullibility.

"I want you to appreciate how beautiful the world *was*, Will, before God dipped His fingers in it." Degas stuck his middle and index finger into the pool in front of him. He twirled them around, creating a faint whirlpool. "This is our Primordial Room. It represents the Earth that existed *before* God—a time of peace. Nothing but darkness and water. Calm, safe simplicity. It existed this way for only two bible verses: Genesis 1:1, Genesis 1:2, then *SHAZAM!* God set His plans for us in motion. Plans that brought you to me—because you are here, are you not?" His face came almost nose to nose with Will's. "I want you to understand that if God had kept the world the way it was, I would never have done the things I have done nor would I do those that I am going to do." Degas paused for a breath. "Does that make sense?"

"Nothing you say makes sense," Richard answered. "If God didn't create us—"

Will heard a click, then the buzz of a distant motor.

"If He didn't create us then—" Richard stopped. He was sinking. The descent caught him mid-sentence and he took in a mouthful of water. He spit it out just before his head went completely under. Will could see the disturbance in the water from his father thrashing below the surface.

"No!" cried Will. "Let him up! Please!"

There was another click and Richard rose, just enough for his nose to appear over the water. Degas squatted in front of him.

"I have had plenty of theological discussions with your kind, deacon," said Degas. "They all regurgitate the same empty answers. I doubt that you will provide any new insights, so my curiosity lies with your son." Degas stood. "Remain calm and keep quiet, Richard, and the water will remain under your nose. If you struggle or if I decide to make waves, breathing will be very difficult."

Will knew his dad had no choice but to obey.

"Now, Will," Degas continued, "isn't there some logic behind my question? Shouldn't you resent God for making this world? For forcing you down a path that He knew would lead you in here with me?"

Degas waited patiently while Will thought hard about his answer.

"Depends if I get out or not," said Will.

"Ha. Clever," said Degas, sounding amused. "A further question: what if I lowered you into the water and allowed you to drown in the darkness? No wait—better question: what if I gathered up your family, sawed off their heads, and made you watch as I, followed by my accomplices, fucked the still bleeding holes in their necks? Lamia could use a broomstick."

Degas had issued this lewd remark with the same calmness he had displayed in the subway. It made Will gag. He could taste his dinner in his throat. *How would my dad answer?*

"I would ask God why He allowed that to happen and," Will paused, making sure he could maintain a tone of certainty, then said, "I'm sure He would have an answer."

"Yes, yes. OK, fine. I am not going to do any of those things. That would be mindless violence and violence without purpose is not how we operate. The question I'm getting at, ultimately, is this: at what point does your life reach a level of despair in which you simply cannot justify God's actions?"

"None." Will didn't hesitate this time.

Richard nodded in agreement, sending out ripples around him.

"None that you know of—yet," Degas corrected. He rolled up his sleeve and walked over to Richard. "You *don't* listen very well." He placed his hand on Richard's head and pushed it under the surface. Will watched as his father thrashed under Degas's weight.

"Degas, stop!" cried Will. "Please!"

Degas turned to Will. "I fear that I may have spoiled you for too long with the luxuries of the Primordial Room. These questions might very well come again. I will be curious to see if the answers have changed."

Finally, Degas released his grip. Richard shot up and gasped for air.

Degas left him and walked back along the platform to the doorway. "Prepare them," he said, and exited the room without looking back.

Will 1:7

"I'm proud of your answers," his father said, coughing. "No matter what happens, don't change them."

Before Will could respond, Haynes appeared in the doorway, wearing jeans and a black polo shirt. Bruises were wrapped around his neck like a scarf. Two more figures followed in behind him. Based on their builds, Will had to assume it was Fen and Lamia. They were both unmasked now, and dressed as casually as Haynes. Fen had a buzz cut and an expression that looked far wiser than Will would have expected. Lamia had bright, blond hair up in a ponytail, with a soft, oval face. Almond-shaped eyes, vividly green, sat beneath a set of eyebrows that had a slight vertical asymmetry. It made her look perpetually intrigued and—although Will was ashamed to admit it—alluring. There were no scars, no disfigurements. They just looked...normal.

Haynes and Fen both hopped off the side of the platform into the pool. Haynes went over to Griff and gently slapped his face. "Wake up, Griffin." No response. "Come on, now." He gave a few more slaps. "You'd better be alive."

"Same with you, kid," said Fen. "I gave him a heavy dose of the paralytic." He flicked Danny a few times in the forehead. Danny and Griff sputtered awake at about the same time.

"What the?" started Griff, then he realized who was in front of him. "You son of a bitch—" but Haynes didn't let him finish. He put a sack over his head and tied it loosely around his neck with some sort of ribbon. Fen did the same to Danny, then Richard, and finally to Will, sending him back into darkness.

"Listen to me," Lamia said to the Batteses. "We are going to remove your restraints and then guide you to another location. If you struggle or resist, I will dump the baby into the water and leave it there. Do you understand?"

"Fucking scumbags." Will heard Griff say.

"I'll take that as a yes," said Lamia.

Will and his family were led quite a distance away. As he walked, Will felt tile under his clammy, bare feet. The air was warm and steady, like a heated building, with a faint smell of citrus.

His captors turned him around a number of corners, so many that Will thought they might have been leading him in circles just for fun. Finally, Will was grabbed by the shoulders and steadied. Will felt something brush the back of his knees.

"Sit down, please," said Haynes. Will obeyed as he did not want his son to be hurt. The chair was very comfortable.

He could hear Danny whimpering, softly and pitifully, but there was no hint of their father or grandfather. Will wondered if they been taken somewhere else during the disorienting walk.

"Don't resist now," said Haynes, continuing with his polite instructions. If they weren't underlined with such malice, they might have calmed Will. Instead, he flinched at every movement, fearing that he would be hurt.

Will felt warm hands reach under his damp shirt as it was lifted over his head. Next, his pants and boxers were removed. Will sat naked in the chair and he felt his manhood shrivel. The feeling of helplessness drove his body to shake.

"Stay calm," said Haynes. "We are cleaning you, nothing more."

A pleasant minty scent filled the air. Will was scrubbed from head to toe with what felt like a sponge, then dried with a towel. It was warm, but impossible to enjoy because of who held it. Two of his captors helped dress him in what felt like a robe or tunic. It was soft and smooth, like the high-thread count bed sheets at home that Shannon had splurged on. Will was then dressed with pants of the same material. Still hooded, Will heard Haynes and Lamia move to the other side of the room.

"Please stop!" cried Danny. "Don't. Don't, please."

"Ack!" cried Lamia. "The boy pissed himself."

"Most kids would," replied Haynes. "Just get another pair of pants."

"It's OK, Danny," Will said, trying to sound like his father, but it came out shaky. "The wet clothes will make you sick. Let them change you."

"Will! Where's Dad?"

"He's not here, Daniel," said Haynes. "But he and your grandfather are having the same thing performed."

"They're gonna get you," said Danny.

"They already tried," said Haynes. "And failed. What has changed since then?"

"I hate all of you! I'll pee again as soon as I can. I'll pee all over you."

"Listen here, you little shit!" Lamia snarled. "If you piss one more time, I'm going to make you drink it!" The threat worked; Danny lost his defiance and stayed silent. Will again felt helpless, which in turn made him feel angry.

Eventually, Haynes took a big breath and said, "OK. Looks good." Lamia agreed and Will heard the two of them walk out. A strong thud signaled the closing of a heavy door.

"Will?" Danny asked softly. "Are you still there?"

"Yes. Right here."

"What are we—ah, I'm just glad you're with me."

It seemed that Danny had given up, knowing Will could not save him. Will wanted to give encouragement, but couldn't find the words.

The burning question still in Will's mind, however, was whether Shannon or Jessi survived. *Danny was up there, did he know who? What if neither one did and Fen was just lying? Or what if Danny fell unconscious first and doesn't know that Shannon or Jessi had died? I don't want to be the one to tell him.* In the end, Will didn't ask. He couldn't bear to hear what the answer could have been.

"Let's say a little prayer—it could do us good," Will suggested instead.

"I've *been* praying! Ever since they woke me up."

Will hadn't prayed at all. He had been so worried and scared—precisely the moments prayer was needed—but the act never crossed his mind.

"Why isn't God saving us?" Danny asked.

"He won't save us if that's not His plan," Will explained, not only to his brother, but to himself. "We're still here. That means He wants us to be here."

"I think I'll keep praying anyway."

"Good idea. I know He's listening. How about we say one together? Do you know Psalm 23?"

"Yeah..."

"Come on, let's hear it." There were a few seconds of silence before Danny sniffled and took a deep breath.

"The Lord is my shepherd; I shall not want. He makes me lie down in green pastures—say it with me, Will?"

"He leads me beside still waters," Will began, then they continued in unison: "He restores my soul." Will could hear their voices strengthen as they continued. "He leads me in the paths of righteousness for His name's sake. Though I walk through the valley of the shadow of death, I will fear no evil."

"Oh, but fear came upon me and made my bones tremble!"

Will jumped in his seat. Degas's voice had come from behind him, but Will never heard him enter. *Had he been here the whole time?*

"Evil has power that you don't fully understand," Degas continued. "Power that allows me to feel the fear inside you. It is immense! I know you are lying through your psalm, how do you think that makes God feel?"

"I am *asking* for strength, not claiming I have it," answered Will.

"Another fair answer, but has He delivered? Go ahead, finish your empty chant. Surely then you will have all the strength you need. Perhaps I can add my voice to the call, for where two or three of us are gathered in his name, He is among us. Right? Isn't that what they taught you from that *Good Book*?"

Will felt Degas's hands on his shoulders. Will must have been colder than he thought—Degas's fingertips felt like little torches. Neither Will nor Danny said anything.

"No? Very well. I think we're ready to go then."

"Where are you taking us now?" asked Will. "Why are we dressed...like this?"

"Formal attire is required," replied Degas. "You and your family are invited to the wedding."

Shannon 1:5

The bedroom closet was directly above the kitchen.

Curled up in her hideaway, Shannon was forced to listen to the sounds of the attack as they rang up through the floorboards.

"What did you do?" She heard Will shout out.

Then, Richard: "I'm going to kill you!"

It was impossible to know exactly what was happening, but the screams of her family painted only terrible pictures. She squeezed her eyes shut, trying to purge the images from her mind—to return to the darkness of her closet—but they kept flashing back, like a psychological strobe light.

She tried plugging her ears. It worked briefly—until beads of sweat began trickling down her forehead. She freed a hand to wipe them away, but in doing so, her hearing returned.

It was her husband's scream that broke her: a heart-wrenching, "No!" It was one enormous telltale heartbeat—a reminder that her inaction had left her family to suffer.

Shannon began to cry. It had been a long time since she had— the first time since her wedding day, over two years ago. Those tears were secret—even from Will—and they were different. They were tears of relief. These in the closet were not. These made her body feel foreign and heavy, anchoring her to the floor. Not as if she *wanted* to go anywhere. Despite the shame, her mind was still full of excuses: *If I tried to escape now, out the window like Jessi wanted...if I could even fit through it...I could break my legs. I could land right in front of the killers as they decide to leave out of the back. Will would want me here, safe and undetected.*

Shannon began to feel dizzy. In her self-justification, she had forgotten to breathe. She inhaled— but dangerously loud. When she caught her breath, she realized all the noises below her had stopped. *Did they hear me?* She wondered. *Or could it be over?* Shannon uncurled, then gently pressed her ear to the floor, hoping to hear nothing at all.

But there were voices. Shannon couldn't tell whose or how many—the dialogue was brief and muffled. Next came footsteps. They grew louder for a moment before fading away. Shannon held her breath again, but heard no one come up the stairs. *Why would they? Thanks to Jessi, the giant thinks I escaped.*

Shannon felt a twisted grin form on her face, but it faded as quickly as the footsteps. *Don't let your guard down yet. You have to be sure they're gone.* She inched open the closet door and scanned the bedroom. It was empty, still—except for Jessi, of course. Her body lay discarded in the center of the room, as broken and misconfigured as one of Danny's action figures. It was considerably colder now. Snow was blowing in through the broken window and had already given Jessi's collapsed skull a slight frosty glaze. Goosebumps plagued Shannon's arms as she crawled towards Jessi.

"I'm sorry," Shannon said. It was meant for Jessi, but Shannon couldn't bring herself to look at the body. She fought to stay quiet but grief overwhelmed her. "I'm *so sorry*, but I had to...or else I'd be right there beside you." There was truth in that statement, Shannon knew. Still, the words tasted sour. The thought of Jessi judging her—and not granting forgiveness—pushed Shannon to cry even harder. She wheezed, shooting a line of snot down her lip. That seemed to break her repentant trance. She wiped her nose with her sleeve then crawled around the toppled dresser and out the door.

On her hands and knees, Shannon moved down the hall to the top of the stairs. Judging from the continued silence, she decided it was safe enough to peek over the edge. She had meant to do it stealthily, but her disheveled hair draped over the stairwell. Looking down, the first things she noticed were Kavi's dead eyes, half open and staring blankly up at her.

More tears fell. One dripped off Shannon's chin and landed in the congealing pool of blood below.

Just then, the front door handle jiggled.

Instinctively, Shannon ducked back—or tried to, but something stopped her. Her hair was stuck. "Ow! Shit!" she whispered. With her head facing down in between the narrow banisters, she couldn't figure out exactly where it was caught, just—judging from the pull—somewhere on the right side of her head. She heard the door open. In complete desperation, she yanked back as hard as she could. There was a sharp pain but indescribable relief as she managed to rip free, just as someone entered the foyer.

Shannon pressed her back against the wall across from the railing. She touched the wound above her ear and winced, then saw her fingers matted with blood. She wiped them on her jeans. Looking back to the staircase, she found the cause of the injury: a loose, crooked nail on the banister. Of more concern was the fact that, hanging from it, was a sizeable chunk of red hair. It swayed softly in the draft from the open door, signaling her presence to anyone that saw it.

"Shall I help take Will?" asked Haynes from below.

"Well, that depends on how you are feeling," replied another voice. After encountering it earlier that day on the subway, Shannon would never forget it: Degas. *Will had been right to be afraid, but who could have predicted this?* She tasted sulfur in her throat, but fought the urge to vomit.

"The deacon did quite a number on you," Degas continued. "Can you carry Will without dropping him?"

"I'm a little shaky still, I suppose," Haynes admitted.

"Thank you for your honesty. And in that case, I would prefer someone else drives as well. I do not need you passing out and causing an accident on Queens Boulevard. Instead, why don't you drag out Richard while Fen—you help me with Will."

"Yes, sir," said a deep voice. "Then I'm ready to torch the place."

"Actually," said Degas. "I changed my mind on that."

"How so?" asked Haynes.

"I just cannot, in good conscience, allow us to char these beautiful bodies," Degas answered. "Fire would nullify the power of their deaths. Look here, Loyola, at this poor boy you bludgeoned." Shannon heard them gather directly below her.

"When the police come, would you rather them find a faceless burn victim or this *personal* brutality? I'm quite sure they've seen more vicious kills, but remember, you never truly know when a man or woman has reached their breaking point. Seeing a body savaged like this, it saps their humanity—for those who still value having it. Is this another chip in their armor? Or the final, *soul-shattering* straw? Impossible to tell. But while we are in the midst of some very big undertakings, we cannot forget that the little things always add up."

There was silence for a few moments and Shannon tried to make sense of what she'd just heard.

"Should we clean up, then?" asked Fen.

"Let forensics try their best to identify us. None of us are in the system and after tomorrow we'll all be long gone."

"If you're not concerned, Victor," said Fen. "Then neither am I."

"Hey," said Haynes. "What if you all leave your masks here. Hang them up somewhere for everyone to see. That should rattle them even more."

"Great idea!" Degas exclaimed. "Let's do that."

"I'm fond of mine, though," said Fen. "Lam spent a lot of time making them for us. I'd like to keep it. My *little thing* contribution is upstairs. The woman fought hard, took a lot to go down. I wasn't exaggerating earlier—it's messy...want to see?"

Shannon braced herself, but was unsure of what to do if they started up towards her.

"I certainly *would* like to see," Degas said. "But, through fate and no fault of your own, Will's wife escaped. There's nothing on the police radio yet, but we shouldn't spend any more time here as I assume it's only a matter of time. I don't want to have to kill the first cops that show up—it's the young, impressionable patrolmen who I want to live with this sight. Will you describe the kill to me on the drive?"

"Sure," Fen said, with what Shannon thought was a tone of eagerness.

Then, they continued on to the kitchen. A minute later—accompanied by the sounds of Haynes grunting and a heavy object being dragged across the floor—the three intruders headed back through the hall and out the door. Nobody appeared to have noticed Shannon's hair.

Still, she wanted to watch them leave. She crept to the end of the upstairs corridor where there was a window facing the front yard. She knew it was bold, but she pinched open the blinds ever so slightly. She saw a black van parked behind Richard's truck with the van's rear doors facing the house. Beneath its back windows, the van was detailed with the words "Johanan's Moving Company" in simple but professional-looking white print.

A moment later, Richard and Will were loaded into the back of the van. They weren't conscious, but Shannon reasoned that they had to be alive—Degas had talked about them as if they were. And Fen hadn't killed Danny. *Who else is alive?* She wondered. *Griff? Leigha?*

She saw Fen now, without his mask—but still holding it in one hand. Nothing was particularly scary about his face; which made *him* even scarier. But even that fear paled in comparison to the sight of Degas picking up a baby's car seat from beside the vehicle.

Shannon couldn't hold it back this time. She heaved. Remnants of Will's cooking, as well as her lunch, came spilling out. It splashed over her hands, but she didn't care. Her abdomen contracted so hard that it weakened her arms; she struggled not to topple forward into her own vomit. Two more rounds of puke followed, then she sat back on her knees, spitting out more chunky mouthfuls until she found the strength to return to the window.

With nobody standing behind the van, she got a clear view of the gold, New York license plate.

E-P-H-0-6-1-2.

Gotcha now, Shannon thought, reciting it in her head, but the mental repetition was halted when a woman walked into view. She was skinny, had her blond hair in a bun, and was nobody she recognized, but she carried Shannon's baby. Patting Giddy on the back, she limped over to Degas and stood beside him. They exchanged a few words while looking forward, then, for a split second, she laid her head on his shoulder. Degas carried the car seat to the passenger side door.

Giddy looked up to the window. Shannon ducked down as soon as she met her son's gaze. Under the window, Shannon found herself balled up again. Into her mind came the wish that Degas *would* take her baby so she'd never have to explain to Giddy why she let these things happen. She heard the van's engine start up and realized that if she waited any longer, her wish would come true. *No*, Shannon thought. *I can save you.*

Shannon had left her phone in the kitchen. *Get down there, grab it, and call the cops.* She bolted down the stairs, reciting the license plate sequence over and over: "E-P-H-0-6-1-2. E-P-H-0-6-1-2. E-P-H-0-6-1-2."

"E-P—whoa!". She slipped on Kavi's blood, but managed to keep herself from falling. "...H-0-6-1-2."

"E-P-H..." She flipped on the light switch. "What the fuck?" she gasped. An inverted cross of light shone across the kitchen. Shannon turned to the source: somebody had removed the lampshade from the opposite wall and over the bare bulb slung a mask. Its mouth projected the satanic image. Shannon didn't waste any time ripping the mask away.

The room's full illumination returned and Shannon saw

the aftermath of what had taken place below her. She covered her mouth at the sight of Leigha's head, twisted far beyond its natural limits.

As much as she wanted to, Shannon didn't have time to dwell on the loss of her friend. She stepped gingerly around the mess of broken dishes and blood while she searched for her phone. She soon found it in the sink—along with everyone else's—in a bowl full of rice water. She didn't bother checking if it worked.

What now?

Shannon played with ideas in her head: *I could flag down a car, there would still be plenty out, despite the weather. Or I could run to a neighbor. The townhouse behind us is vacant, up for sale; but the next door down is...no, they only speak Spanish, I think. Across the street? Fuck! I don't know who lives there. It doesn't matter, all you need is a phone to tell the cops that plate number.*

She recited it again: "E-H-P-6-0-1-2," then she stopped. It felt wrong, jumbled. *Was there an H in it?* "E-P-N. No! *Fuck!*" The sequence was gone. Instinctively she moved to go back to the window and check, praying that the van was still there, but when she stepped forward, she stumbled over Leigha's body. Unable to keep her footing this time, she fell right on top of her. It was then she heard a familiar metallic clinking.

Even before she fished Leigha's car keys out of her coat pocket, Shannon knew what to do. Calling the cops would be useless at this point. Even if she hadn't forgotten the plate number, the van would be long gone by the time the police responded and her family would be lost somewhere in the vast city.

Instead, Shannon was going to take Leigha's car, follow the van to wherever it was taking her family, *then* call the police.

It's smart and it's brave and I get to be the hero.

Shannon 1:6

Shannon charged out the kitchen door and into the backyard. Overloaded with adrenaline, her body devoured the cold night air. She had on no shoes—just socks, but her feet squished over the light layer of snow as carefree as if it was sand on a California beach. Shannon bounded across the yard then vaulted over the chain-link fence like it was a high school hurdle.

On the other side was the empty townhouse. Shannon weaved through the debris left in its backyard and around the side of the building to the street. *Leigha said that she'd parked around the corner. It's here somewhere.* Shannon pressed the unlock button on Leigha's keychain. Headlights flashed a few cars down and she sprinted towards them.

Shannon's internal clock was in disarray; she had no idea how long ago Degas had left the driveway, but there was still a chance to catch him. Degas had mentioned Queens Boulevard. If he was indeed heading there, that was south. Shannon's neighborhood, like many throughout the borough, was a convoluted grid of one-way streets. Pulling out of the driveway, Degas would be forced to go east, then north, and then west before turning south to hit the Boulevard—a big circle that, with any luck, would pass right by her.

Sure enough, just as Shannon entered Leigha's beat up Chevy Cavalier, another pair of headlights veered around the corner. She ducked as the vehicle passed by, then peeked above the dashboard. At the stop sign sat a black van with the plate number Shannon had all but forgotten: EPH0612.

†

The snowfall thickened as Shannon drove along Queens Boulevard, heading west towards the city. The poor conditions made the normally heavy and sluggish traffic move even slower. It was after 10:00 p.m. now and a river of yellow taxis flowed towards Manhattan, carrying those eager for a Friday night out despite the weather. Degas's van stood out like a beetle in a beehive.

Shannon envied the drivers and passengers around her; she pictured them all laughing as they headed to their destinations with the company of friends and family who had not been killed or kidnapped. Shannon wished it were their husbands in danger. Their sons.

The sputtering of a windshield wiper startled Shannon back from her maleficent fantasies. She could feel that her feet were completely numb now; the impromptu run through the snow had soaked her socks all the way through. The old car's heat hadn't kicked in yet—it could have even been malfunctioning—causing Shannon to wonder if permanent damage would be done to her toes.

The rest of Shannon's body jittered from the adrenaline—far worse than any caffeine overdose she could remember. Everything was still sinking in: *I'm tailing the villain—straight out of the movies*. Truly, movies gave her the only knowledge she could draw upon for this situation: *stay a few cars back, but don't lose sight of them, and don't change lanes exactly when they do*. Still, she feared making a mistake that would give herself away and complete a shameful narrative of failure.

Up ahead, Degas appeared to be in no hurry. The van proceeded steadily, stopping at red lights and obeying all the other traffic laws. A patrol car passed in the opposite direction, but Shannon never thought about reaching for her horn.

They continued west, now approaching the Queensboro Bridge. The Manhattan skyline loomed ominously overhead. Shannon feared crossing into the city, believing Degas would be harder to tail there. The streets were more congested, the traffic flow more erratic, and the jaywalkers absolutely fearless.

Shannon herself had illegally stepped in front of cars countless times to get where she was going. Her "right of way" often inspired throngs of pedestrians to follow suit behind her. If that happened now, between her and the van, she could be separated and never find it again.

But it appeared that they would not be crossing into the city after all. Just before the bridge, the van veered left onto a two-lane road. Shannon had to cut off the city bus in the lane to her left in order to make the turn. She cringed as its driver blasted an especially long horn, but Degas's party seemed to give no notice.

From there, they headed south along the river's edge. The traffic diminished and the area grew bleak. After not even five minutes, Shannon found herself in an industrial ghost town, full of dark warehouses and empty piers.

She did not want to risk exposure and fell back even more. *Would it have actually been safer in Manhattan?* she asked herself. From three blocks back, she saw the van turn onto a small street between two lifeless buildings. From the opposite direction, a dark sedan came and took the same route. Shannon reached the intersection and stopped.

"One one-thousand, two one-thousand," she whispered, continuing to five—a completely arbitrary timeframe Shannon hoped was long enough to make it safe to follow—before turning the corner.

She had to immediately start on the brakes. The sedan—a newer, red Ford Focus—was stopped in front of her. Degas's van immediately ahead of that. Together, they comprised the last three of a line of vehicles that stretched about fifty yards to a manned security gate. Whatever was beyond, Shannon knew it was where Degas was taking her family. That meant it was the end of the line for her.

"Time to get the *fuck* out," she said. The next step would be alerting the police to their location—wherever this was. Shannon shifted the car into reverse, but before she could start back, a large, gray SUV—a Suburban maybe—pulled in tightly behind her.

"Well...shit."

Moving forward was now the only option.

The only sounds Shannon could hear were the steady humming of the cars' engines. It was one of the few times she sat in New York traffic without a single horn beeping. *Every person belongs here*, she realized. *They've done this before or have been briefed. No use going to any of them for help, they'll probably gut me right here in the street.* She realized how truly in over her head this quest for heroism had gotten her. She was in more danger than she thought possible and she had no idea how to get out of it.

As the minutes crept by, so did the line of vehicles inching their way towards the gate. One driver after another greeted the security guard, then drove through. As far as she could tell, there were no IDs or documents needed to proceed, though the guard seemed to have a bit of a conversation with each of them. *This is good*, Shannon thought...*unless this gathering is small enough that the guard knows each person on sight.*

She didn't know what to do.

Run, she told herself. *No, I CAN'T*, she argued back.

Run. DON'T RUN.

Shannon's foot pumped the brake, on and off, to the rhythm of her internal debate. *You have to go. Just leave the car. BUT THEY WILL CHASE ME.* She was three cars away from the gate now. *It's OK, you're a runner, you're faster than them...you have to be. BUT I DON'T HAVE ANY SHOES.* She watched as the black van reached the gate. The guard nodded and the van rolled by without stopping.

The red Focus pulled up next and its driver stuck his head out of the window. He was a man in his forties with neatly combed brown hair and black, horn-rimmed glasses. No mask. He spoke with the guard briefly and was waved in.

Then, it was Shannon's turn.

She couldn't convince herself to run, but she had another

idea. *I'LL TELL HIM I GOT LOST*, she thought. *You think the guard will buy that? YEAH, I'LL SAY I TOOK A WRONG TURN. You expect that to work? I'LL TELL HIM I JUST WANT TO LEAVE. I'LL CRY IF I HAVE TO.*

"Another new face," the guard said before Shannon could speak. He looked young, certainly under thirty. Clean shaven and pleasant. He was dressed in dark gray slacks and a matching coat, with a golden tie peeking out from the chest. He smiled attractively enough that Shannon found herself smiling, too. "Tonight is bringing us in from all over," the guard continued, beaming with pride.

"Yes, it is."

What are you doing? Shannon scolded herself. *Are you really playing along with this?*

"Very historical," the guard continued.

"Mhmm," Shannon agreed again.

Then the guard looked more closely at her. "I hope you have everything you need to become...presentable," he said with a subtle grimace. Shannon was able to contain the shock of her shattered pride. It made sense: all the crying and vomiting she had done in such a short period of time surely took its toll on her image. Still, she couldn't remember the last time someone told her she looked unattractive. Thankfully, her head wound was not facing the guard—surely that would transform his disdain into suspicion.

"It was a long drive," was all the response Shannon could muster. The guard laughed, but it was an awkward laugh: too loud and too hearty for too poor a joke. The guard leaned out of his booth towards her. Her heart raced. He looked as if he were going to say something more, but squinted back at the trail of vehicles behind her.

"Walk blameless and righteous," the guard said to her.

"Will do," Shannon said with a nod. The guard returned it and waved her through. She let out a loud sigh as she headed left, following the only path available.

Shortly, she arrived at a large, gravel parking lot. It was dimly lit by two post lamps attached to the side of the largest building. The lamps looked newer than the structure they were mounted on, signifying a recent addition. Outside of that perimeter, the premises were dark. Shannon could only make out a few structures with wide, rectangular windows that reflected the Manhattan skyline. They all appeared abandoned. Approximately thirty vehicles were already parked in the lot—but the lineup behind her had continued to grow.

Then Shannon realized that amidst the interaction with the guard, she had lost track of the black van. She began to panic. *After all this, did I lose him? No... THERE'S NOWHERE ELSE TO GO EXCEPT BEHIND THIS BUILDING. THERE HAS TO BE A PRIVATE "UNLOADING AREA" THERE. I KNOW THIS IS THE RIGHT PLACE.*

The new plan was to park and run, but again, God was not making it easy—she wondered if He even cared about her at all. Two young men, dressed identically to the gate guard, were ushering cars to assigned spots as if they were arriving at a theme park. One of the ushers beckoned Shannon to the next available spot and she reluctantly obeyed. She knew she had to wait for the right time to escape. *If these people are as ruthless as the giant...and they catch me...*Shannon didn't allow herself to finish the thought.

The man from the red Focus passed in front of her car, walking tall, with perfect posture. Wearing jeans and a black woolen coat the same shade as his glasses, he looked like he could have been a college professor or a paralegal or a software designer. Shannon realized that he could be anything. Because of that she was afraid.

This ordinary man was also carrying a leather weekender duffel bag over his shoulder. In fact, everyone that the attendants were shepherding to the entrance had a backpack, duffel bag, or suitcase. Shannon feared walking around empty-handed would draw the kind of attention she didn't want. When none of the guards were looking, she hurried as nonchalantly as she could to the back of the car and popped the trunk, praying there was...*yes!* A gym bag. Shannon almost tore it open and shuffled through the contents. *Please, please, please...Oh thank God! She has shoes!* They were running shoes, too, and in decent shape. Shannon ditched the icy socks in the trunk then stuffed her bare feet inside the sneakers. They were about a half size too small, but it worked. Her toes applauded the warm, confining sheath.

"Welcome," said one of the attendants, just as Shannon crammed into the second sneaker. She almost fell backwards from the surprise—there had been no hint of his approach.

"Hi," she said, and flashed another smile. "So excited for tonight. Historical."

"Yes, I'm happy to be witness to this."

"Me too. This way?" Shannon gestured to the obvious entrance.

"Exactly, you'll find the vesting room inside. Just follow the line. You'll need to change into your robe before proceeding to the Nave."

The Nave? Shannon wondered, but nodded, and the man left to greet the next vehicle. It was the Suburban that had originally blocked her escape. He opened the door for the driver: a woman who must have been in her nineties. The usher reached up and grabbed her frail hand, then helped her to the ground. The old woman wrapped a golden scarf around her tiny neck and thanked the man with a smile full of unnaturally white teeth. Then, with her grin frozen in place, she pointed to the trunk. The man opened it and fished out a pink, medium-sized suitcase with wheels and a handle that the man slid out. *What the hell is happening here? What's bringing these people together? And what does my family have to do with it?* DON'T WORRY ABOUT THAT NOW, she scolded herself. THOSE QUESTIONS ARE FOR AFTER YOU GET AWAY.

Shannon moved towards the entrance but had no desire to set foot inside that building, let alone to get "vested." Fortunately, the two attendants seemed to be stretched thin from the swarm of new arrivals.

This was her chance.

Shannon darted as fast as she could out of the lighted path and into the shadows.

Her breathing intensified and she felt another smile form on her face. She looked back to the path and saw that the other guests continued to file into the main building normally, none the wiser to her escape. The gravel under the snow made for noisy footsteps, so she tiptoed until she cleared the corner.

Finally! Good fucking riddance! Shannon tossed her bag and broke into a full on sprint, ignoring the pain inside her undersized shoes. She meant to reach the river, then continue north, parallel alongside it until she found the first sign of someone whom she was certain had no involvement in this creep fest.

She ran so fast that she never saw the man until his fist collided with her face. Her upper body was thrown back from the impact, but her legs kept their momentum, flinging themselves up into the air. Shannon landed on the back of her head and saw bright flashes of light.

There were voices above her, somewhere, but they faded in and out of focus, as if the wind snatched certain words away. Shannon willed herself to get up—to continue running—but only had the strength to roll over to her side.

She spit out a mouthful of blood, but something else flew out with it. Her tongue suddenly had more space to explore. The realization hit her like a second blow: her front tooth was gone, lost amongst the gravel and snow. There was no chance to look for it as someone took hold of her ankles and dragged her across the ground.

Shannon's head spun with muddled thoughts of family, capture, and death, but one thought rang out louder than the rest:

My smile...

Song of Lamia

Josh and Debbie Richmond lived across the street from the Batteses. Despite being newlyweds around the same age as Will and Shannon, the two couples had never become friends. In fact, they did nothing more than exchange an occasional neighborly wave (which Will always initiated). The Richmonds were private, almost unsocial people, preferring to spend most evenings alone together with Fridays reserved for a home movie double feature. Debbie always chose the first—typically a romantic comedy, though tonight her selection was *Les Miserables*—and Josh the second. He had more diverse tastes, ranging from summer blockbusters to documentaries to spaghetti westerns.

This week, Josh picked the newest *Transformers*, a movie he would never actually see, because the Richmonds were the first on Lamia Malone's list. She knocked on their door and heard Jean Valjean's overture pause. There was murmuring on the other side of the door, but then it opened. Conveniently, Josh and Debbie stood there together.

Lamia shot them both in the head.

The sound of the Richmond's bodies hitting the floor was louder than the gunshots themselves, owing to the silencer that was screwed onto the muzzle of Lamia's Glock.

With the lights already off, the television frozen silent, and the couple's bodies falling straight backwards into their apartment, all Lamia had to do was shut the door.

Unlike the homes on the opposite side of the street, this one was a duplex. It had a common entrance with a lock that was incredibly easy to pick, even without Degas's expert mentoring. Inside, there was a door on the left that lead into the first apartment and a staircase on the right leading up to the other.

The second floor tenants were three pre-med students attending Colombia University: Jay Pensky, Shadi Mirza, and

Mike Schaffer (whom the other two referred to as Chappy because of the frequency of his lip balm application).

Fortunately for Shadi, he returned home to Islip every weekend to work at his father's laundromat. By the time Lamia executed his downstairs neighbors, he was already on a LIRR train car, lost in an anatomy textbook. Jay and Chappy's schedules were a bit less routine, although they often stayed in together on the weekends. Some Fridays were spent in the apartment, drinking and getting high, while other nights they bounced around local bars. Tonight was the former.

The boys rarely hosted guests, for reasons likely related to the stench that hit Lamia as she ascended the stairs: a combination of weed and stale food. However, if an unexpected guest *did* happen to arrive during the same razor-thin window of time as Lamia, she would be ready.

Jay answered after Lamia's first series of knocks, also without any inquiry from behind the door. It disappointed Lamia a bit— so far this project had presented an extreme lack of challenge. She greeted Jay with a soft blip from her silenced Glock and Jay's soul departed. Chappy witnessed it happen from the couch and dropped his beer onto his beer-stained carpet.

He managed to say "Don't, please..." before Lamia pulled the trigger.

At the neighboring duplex, on the downstairs floor, lived a man named Russell Gershaw. Russ was a fifty-year-old drunk with many excuses to be so: he was overweight, bald, divorced, single, and his kids did not speak to him. There also appeared to be no motivation to change any of those aspects of his life. Instead, he spent the majority of the disposable income earned from managing a Jamba Juice on booze.

This afternoon, he had shuffled home carrying a large brown bag with three bottlenecks peeking out from inside. Tonight, like most nights, Russ would be staying indoors. Lamia probably didn't have to kill him, for his intoxication would have by then reached a level of complete unawareness to events outside his apartment, but his life—his waste of it—was despicable in Degas's eyes.

After three knocks, a slurred, "Whosethurr?" passed through his front door.

Lamia was pleased; finally, an opportunity to use her cover story. "It's Sam from *Locks of Love*! Hi! I was wondering if you or anyone in your household would like to donate hair?" Lamia's voice was bubbly from the act. It was a silly alibi, but one of the few details that Degas allowed her to design herself. "Have fun with it," he had said.

Her own blond locks were wrapped up in a tight bun under a tan baseball cap. Lamia had sewn on the design herself: braided red hair in the shape of a heart.

"I live alone, honey," Russ answered, "and I ain't got much in the way of hair."

"Perhaps a monetary donation then?"

"Ain't got much'a that neither." He hiccupped.

"Well, even a donation as low as one dollar would get you your choice of movie tickets, air freshener, or a shot glass." There was a second of silence behind the door before Lamia heard the deadbolt sliding free.

Russ opened the door and Russ died.

At this address, Lamia didn't have to go upstairs. Gerald Jackson, the second floor tenant, was serving two months in jail after being convicted of his second shoplifting offense. Nor did Lamia have to visit Ms. Rose Weinstein's house, which once had a view of the Battese's backyard and their kitchen windows. That wasn't the case any longer, as her Cheyenne privets had matured to about six feet tall and were now bona fide "privacy shrubs."

Mrs. Weinstein's second floor still had a good view of the Batteses' house, but Rose was approaching eighty and confined by wheelchair to the bottom level of her home. She was widowed and had no visitors except a son that stopped by for an hour or two on Sundays to take her to church. She often cried at night, praying at length for God to take her.

Degas ordered her to be spared.

After Lamia closed Russ's door, her cell phone vibrated. She answered without speaking.

"Hang on in there, Lam." The voice on the line belonged to Dullahan, the fifth and final member of Degas's crew. "Will and Shannon just turned the corner onto their street. Let's let them get home." Lamia reloaded her pistol while she waited in the foyer of the duplex for the go-ahead.

Dullahan was Lamia's surveillance man, watching her back as she made her bloody circle around the neighborhood. He was disguised as a homeless man and played the part to a T due to the fact he used to be homeless—before Degas recruited him from an AA meeting. He was the oldest of their team, somewhere in his early fifties. His exact age was unknown, as he claimed to have lost count in his life as a drifter and never cared to find out. It never mattered to Degas either, whose ability to discern suitable Eden candidates was unprecedented.

After Dullahan came on board, he quickly earned his place—just as Degas had expected. For the past few months, Dullahan had studied Will's neighborhood on countless stakeouts, observing patterns of the community that made Lamia's executions as smooth as silk. He did his work willingly, enthusiastically, and without demand for extra compensation. He believed in the cause.

"OK, they're inside," Dullahan said. "Carry on."

The last home on Lamia's agenda belonged to the Mendoza family, Will's next door neighbors to the east. Scheduled for execution were Manuel and Alma, along with their two teenage children: Felipe and Marisol. Manuel was a strict and traditional head of household, keeping his family on a tight routine. Fridays under his roof consisted of an early dinner, finishing any weekend homework, then if there was time, snacks and board games.

Right now, all four of the family members were home and they would be just about done with their meal. Lamia picked the front door lock and strode into the dining room. She expected to see four people sitting at the kitchen table, but there were only three. Marisol was missing. Lamia's heart rate doubled from a sudden wave of panic. The confident mood she'd had across the street dispersed, but she did not hesitate. She shot Manuel, who fell sideways off of his seat; then Alma, who brought the entire chair back with her. Felipe, however, had impressive reflexes. He was already up from the table, running. He attempted to shout his sister's name, but only got to *"Mari—"* before Lamia shot him in the back of the head and he rag-dolled to the floor.

Marisol needed to be found—fast. Lamia walked swiftly through the lower level as she searched. The living room was clear; so were the master bedroom and bathroom. Paranoia started to seep in: *Did she see me? Did she hear her brother? If she's hiding in some closet, calling 911...If I'm the one who ruined this...*

Lamia ascended the stairs two at a time, opened up Marisol's bedroom door, and—with a huge internal sigh of relief—saw that there she was. Marisol sat peacefully at her desk with her back to Lamia. The fourteen year old was wearing large, pink, over-the-ear headphones and nodded along to her private beat.

Degas had said that the name Marisol was derived from *Maria de la Soledad*, a Spanish title given to the Virgin Mary. He also said how he despised that name, so Lamia thought she'd do something a little special.

With one hand, she grabbed the girl by the hair and yanked. The chair toppled back. Marisol screamed, but it was a hollow scream, one that was unaware of what was truly happening, as if this were just a mean prank by her older brother. It wasn't until she looked up at Lamia and the first strike from the butt of the pistol smashed her jaw that Marisol let out a true howl. Lamia quickly covered the girl's mouth, clipping the scream.

She regretted her actions now; the extravagance of the attack brought risk of being heard. Again, the thought of a mistake causing Degas's failure haunted her. Lamia improvised as best she could. She shot Marisol three times in the gut then held her down until the little girl's struggles reduced to a few minor tremors. Then she shot her again in the heart. Now that she was dead, Lamia was free to do as she pleased. She lost count of the number of times the Glock smashed the girl's face, but, in the end, Marisol no longer looked like Marisol.

Lamia dialed Dullahan. "Everything's done. *Phew!*" It came out jokingly, but there was an immense sense of relief sweeping over her.

"OK. Now, Richard hasn't shown up yet. Why don't you kill some time in there?"

"Just let me know when you're ready," she answered, then hung up the phone.

Marisol's bed was covered with an assortment of Disney Princesses, which Lamia thought was a little too immature for the teenager. There was Cinderella dressed in her formal attire, with her blond hair arranged conspicuously similar to Lamia's. Lamia took off her hat and let her own hair fall messily around her. Then, she removed Marisol's blood-spattered headphones, laid down on the comforter atop an image of Belle and her handbasket, and listened to the music—some type of merengue. She didn't understand the lyrics, but listened anyway for a few minutes until the singer began repeating the phrase *Jesús Christo*. That she recognized. She returned the headphones to their deceased owner with a careless fling and closed her eyes.

†

"It's time to wake up," Degas said softly, but Lamia already was.

She opened her eyes to see him standing in the doorway. "I felt you come in," she said. "I couldn't sleep anyway, not with this much adrenaline. I'm practically shaking. I keep reliving my neighborhood sweep. I did it!"

"And did it marvelously, I'm told." He moved closer to her then glanced down at Marisol's body. "Why so excessive?"

"I did it for you, Victor."

Degas smiled and she swooned at the sight of it, but then something else caught her attention: an abrupt bulge in his pants.

A red veil of lust fell over her vision. It didn't surprise her—it came often in his presence—but this one was practically opaque. Lamia sat up and threw her feet over the side of the bed. "Do we have time?"

"Just enough." Degas pushed her back over the bed. Without breaking eye contact, he unzipped her jeans and slid them off her body. She moaned, forcing herself to keep her eyes open and locked onto his. His colobomas contorted as his pupils dilated to their max, but Lamia felt no fear, only yearning.

He climbed onto her and her red veil turned to fire.

She gave herself to him, knowing that after tonight they would not be together for a long time. She ordered herself to not let her mind wander, to only be attuned to the present so that she'd forever be able to remember this moment. For six minutes, she lay on her back as he thrust himself inside her. Without any warning from one another, they climaxed together and soaked the teenager's covers. Degas stayed atop her when they finished, catching his breath. When he finally moved to get up, Lamia gripped her nails into his back. He smiled at her, and stayed a few minutes longer.

Richard 1:5

As Richard's fog of unconsciousness lifted, a spectacular view took shape below him. He floated high within a cathedral that was as beautiful as it was massive. Along its ornate marble walls were a series of stained-glass windows at least thirty feet tall. They shimmered with blues and greens and pinks and reds, all more vibrant than any parish décor Richard had ever seen.

On the floor, rows of theatre-style chairs arced slightly inward along red-carpeted aisles. There was subtle movement among the seats, as each one had a figure standing in front of it. The bodies stirred slightly as they socialized with others around them, a dull harmony of their indistinct words filled Richard's ears. He knew not who they were, as everyone was adorned in pure, white robes and a brightly colored cape with its own unique, almost celestial hue.

At the front of the building was a stage, atop of which was a grandiose marble altar not unlike one that could be found inside a catholic church. It held candles, countless in number, that flickered like stars underneath a huge canvas painting. Through still-focusing eyes, Richard saw an image of Jesus Christ, humbly presenting a plate of bread outwards, as if to the robed individuals gathered before Him.

So lost in awe, Richard hadn't questioned where he was or why he was floating. When his mind began to question the fantastic things he saw, it went for an easy dismissal: *you're in a dream, is all.* But as his senses awoke further, Richard could no longer convince himself that was the case. The memories of the attack began to resurface, followed by those of the Primordial Room and of Fen, undressing and bathing him. Richard had been taken to a different room than his sons. He remembered crying out for them. When he would not stop, he was hit with yet another dose of the mysterious spray that his attackers had used in the kitchen. Richard could still feel the wisps of the unknown poison burning its way through his nostrils and throat as it once again made his muscles limp and his brain surrender to darkness.

Richard had never known anything to be that fast acting and effective and he had been hit with it three times. *Could it have been a fatal dose?* he wondered. *Have I died, Lord? Is this Your temple?* The thought only made him more alert. Richard blinked quickly, trying to push away the last bit of haze from his waking senses. He had to know for sure.

God, have You brought me home? It was then that the images of the stained-glass came into focus.

Richard was struck with a resounding *NO*.

One window's red and green facets took the shape of a serpent. Its head was that of a cobra bearing its fangs, but it stood upright on green, hoofed legs. The wicked-looking beast towered over two decomposing bodies, sprawled out naked on the grass: one man and one woman. In the tableau beside it, a man in tattered clothes hung from a tree that bloomed with bright, pink flowers. At its base, shadowy figures hunched over on their knees with arms outstretched in worship.

When Richard turned back to the altar, Jesus was no longer in the canvas painting. What took His place—or more accurately, what had actually been there all along—was the face of a woman wearing a gold, jewel-encrusted crown. Her mouth was stretched open in a hideous sneer with teeth like jagged white knives. There was no loaf of bread on her platter, but a severed human head.

"Oh God..." Richard had tried to say—the culmination of all the sickness and embarrassment that he felt for seeing this building as a holy place—but he never got the words out. They had been muffled by a thick, soft cloth tied tightly around the bottom half of his face—nose included—and into his mouth. He was able to breathe, but it took effort.

Immediately, he tried to pull the cloth away, but his hands did not obey the command. Richard looked down to see his wrists and ankles strapped securely to a high-back wooden chair. The restraints were padded with a cushy fabric, just like in the Primordial Room. Richard also saw that he was wearing a loose, white robe over matching pajama-like pants. The floor was a smooth, red carpet that was not the least bit cold on his bare feet. Though none of it made him physically uncomfortable, he was flooded with intense mental anguish as soon as he turned his head to the right.

He saw his sons. No more than three feet away, Will sat dressed and restrained in exactly the same way as Richard. Beyond Will was Danny, confined identically, albeit to a smaller chair. Both of Richard's sons faced him and spoke frantically from behind their gags, but Richard could not make out what they were saying.

It wasn't until Will pointed his pleading eyes to the opposite side of Richard that he thought to turn his head left. He saw his father. Though tied up like the rest of them, there was little energy left in Griff. His eyes were open only a sliver as he stared blankly towards the floor. He barely moved, save for his chest putting out shallow, fragmented breaths. Griff was not attached to his oxygen tank.

Richard scanned the floor around his father to see if the canister was at least somewhere nearby. It wasn't, but that suddenly became less important to Richard. On the floor beside Griff was a white, wooden cradle. Through its bars Richard could see little pink toes kicking gently into the air.

Richard shook furiously in an attempt to break free from his chair, to run over and scoop up his grandson, and to lead his family's exodus from this unholy place. But he could do none of those things; the restraints were just too tight.

Richard groaned from underneath the cloth. He hadn't even come close to loosening any of the straps. Again, he felt the shadow of his years cast over him. He felt puny—worse even that he was failing in front of his sons. Richard knew that their eyes were on him, perhaps naively believing that their father would be strong enough to rip away his bindings. Little did they know he couldn't even find the strength to look back at them.

In fact, Richard didn't feel comfortable being in the same room with his family. It wasn't because of his shaken pride, but having all five of them together felt ominous, not joyous.

It's no surprise that Gideon is safe, Richard told himself. *I knew Degas wasn't going to hurt him. They aren't going to hurt any of us yet. They would have done it by now. They're using threats to make us obey and only using nonlethal tactics if we don't.*

But that doesn't mean what they have planned for us is good.

Richard took as deep of a breath as he could from behind his gag, then began to more closely survey the room. It was small, just a circular balcony that overlooked the auditorium. The front was all glass-enclosed, meaning that the exit could only be behind him; Richard just couldn't turn his head far enough around to locate it.

Judging by his position, Richard guessed that he must be at least twenty feet above the ground floor. His eyes were again drawn to the stained-glass windows and he realized that they were fully illuminated from behind. *Could it be morning already,* he wondered? *Or even later in the day? How long was I unconscious?*

The window's images were no less disturbing the second time around, so Richard quickly shifted his eyes away and to the center of room. He began studying the assembly of robed figures that he had mistakenly believed were angels, but there wasn't much to see. There was still little movement among them. Occasionally, one would turn to face another, making brief conversation, but it was impossible to make out anything that was said. They wore no masks, but they were just too far away for Richard to make out any details.

Richard recalled the last piece of information that he had

been told when Fen stripped and bathed him: *you're coming to a wedding*. There was no doubt that those below were here for that, though Richard could see nothing to decipher whose it was—or why such great lengths were taken to force his family to be there.

Again, he knew the answers weren't good. Richard desperately wished to speak with his father, curious to know if Griff had been told any more information while Richard had been passed out. *If only I could pick that brain of his*, Richard thought, believing Griff could have an insight or observation that Richard had overlooked—something that could lead to their family's escape.

But the old man just gazed off in the opposite direction. All of Griff's efforts seemed to be spent just trying to breathe.

That meant that Richard was on his own for now, and any insight would have to come from the dark recesses of his frightened mind.

Richard thought of Degas and the inverted cross on his mask. He recalled Degas's unapologetic questions to Will about God— his pointed, passionate taunting. There was the chilling imagery of the stained-glass that Richard knew, try as he might, he would never unsee. Being brought up in the Catholic Church, Richard's dealings with the occult were limited. Still, in his mind, the evidence could not be clearer: *this was a Godless place.*

Richard shivered, but his mind was steady. It continued to chisel its way through the rest of the uncertainty: *why are we here? What are we being used for? Could we be some type of gift? Some type of sacrifice?*

Nothing good, he answered himself.

So what am I going to do?

Nothing now. You can barely move.

But I can keep my guard up. I can seize an opportunity—

That won't happen easily. Degas won't let it. There's an evil inside that man like you have never known, but there is just as much intelligence, composure, and foresight. He won't just give you an opportunity to escape—you will have to make one.

The sounds of his father coughing derailed Richard's thoughts. *And what about Griff? He might not be able to keep up. What if we left him? He would understand, right?* Richard believed so. *But would my sons? Would they have the strength to abandon him?*

Would I?

Before Richard could give himself an honest answer, another question presented itself: *If somehow it came to it, would I be able to let myself stay behind?*

That question was the easiest of them all. *Without a doubt.*

The idea of giving up his life to save his family seemed like a justifiable penance.

Less than twenty-four hours ago, Richard had been convinced that he was going to abandon the clergy, turn his back on his community, and break his vows to God by marrying Jessi. Now, he didn't even know if Jessi was alive. *There couldn't be a more fitting punishment*, Richard thought, though he knew that God didn't work that way, that he didn't cast an entire family into such a nightmare because of one person's sins.

The worst of it was that Richard was so close to knowing Jessi's fate. Danny had been upstairs with her during the attack. Danny would know the truth concerning Jessi and Shannon: which one had lived and which one had died. All Richard had to do was ask the boy, except God put them both in gags and, in turn, held hostage the closure Richard needed. *No*, Richard corrected himself. *This is not of God's doing. It was Degas.*

Richard pondered that for a moment, then wasn't so sure. *Maybe it is God. Maybe this is for the best. Who am I to force Danny to relive whatever horror he experienced in the bedroom? Maybe God knows that I couldn't even handle the answer. Would I let myself fall behind if I knew that Jessi was out there somewhere looking for me? The thought of seeing her again could cause me to hesitate just a moment too long.*

But Richard was getting ahead of himself. Eagerness to

sacrifice himself did not guarantee that he would ever get a chance to do so.

Richard faced forward, staring at the portrait hanging over the altar and into the eyes of the sneering queen. Without looking away, he sought patience—and purpose—from the book of Matthew, reciting the specific verse in his head: *you must be vigilant, because you do not know the day or the hour.* Richard thought again about Degas's competence, then amended the passage.

Or the minute, or the second.

Richard 1:6

The deacon broke eye contact with the queen when he heard a door open behind him. Stepping around the white cradle and in front of the window came Degas, followed by Haynes and Fen. Degas stopped in front of Will and stood with his hands behind his back, while his two accomplices took positions on either side of him.

Haynes and Fen were dressed in garments similar to those in the audience below. Haynes's cape was a bright, plum robe with a small, white, cloth belt while Fen's was a darker navy-blue with a wider gold belt. They both wore thin, white gloves like those of a museum curator. Despite Fen's loose outfit, it did nothing to conceal his muscular physique, casting doubt that Richard would be able to stand toe to toe with him if he ever got the chance.

Degas was dressed differently. His outfit was form-fitting, with long sleeves and pants, entirely black, save for a familiar symbol expertly sewn into the center of his chest. It was of a life-sized human heart wrapped in thorns. The left chamber of the heart was pierced by the head of a lance and was bleeding from the wound. Richard recognized the emblem as the Sacred Heart of Jesus, a common symbol in the Catholic Church. The damage inflicted on the heart alluded to the manner of Jesus's death. Richard had always seen the Sacred Heart either surrounded or crowned with flames, representing God's power and love, but that component was missing here.

"This room is much drier than the first, is it not?" Degas asked, his voice was steady, but laced with cheer. "It is dry of any deeper symbolism as well, I'm afraid. Simply put, this sealed balcony was designed for anonymous viewings and secret assessments. From this vantage point, you will be able to see and hear what presides below without being seen or heard in return—I do not want the audience distracted. That was the original intention anyway. Even though the room is soundproof, I decided to stuff fine linen in between your teeth because I wanted no empty reassurances spouted off by the deacon here."

With his hands still behind his back, Degas bent over towards Richard. Degas's face was bare, as in the Primordial Room, and close enough now for Richard to see Degas's pupils. The misshapen voids seemed to shatter the cold, blue irides around them. Richard felt older than he ever had before.

Degas spoke softly now. "I can only imagine what thoughts were spiraling inside your mind, deacon, as you woke and took it all in. When you are unable to communicate in such a high stress environment, the display of emotion on one's face is remarkable—watching it all really helped me unwind. Right from there, see?" Degas pointed up to the corner of the ceiling, where Richard spotted a small security camera covered in a plastic dome.

"But not to worry," Degas continued, standing back up and looking down the row of prisoners. "Soon, all eyes and ears will be upon you, and the screams you are surely suppressing will be allowed to emerge."

Griff suddenly began to breathe more rapidly.

"Hold on a little longer, Griffin," Degas said, putting a hand on his shoulder. "You must be a part of this."

"Maybe we should let him have his oxygen after all," Haynes suggested.

After a moment, Degas nodded and Haynes hurried out of sight.

Degas went ahead and unclogged Griff's mouth. As soon as the gag was removed, Griff's empty gaze focused into an angry energy. He raised his chin and spat at Degas, but the phlegm was weak. It flew only as far as Degas's sleeve. Degas only smiled. "Cancel the ceremony! My outfit has been soiled!" Fen laughed while Degas wiped up the spit with his index and middle fingers. Then, Degas came nose to nose with Griff and smeared the spit on the old man's cheek. Griff lunged forward, snarling at Degas in an attempt to bite him, but Degas effortlessly dodged the attack.

"*That's* energy I need! Now, let me give you a gift in return." On that cue, Haynes wheeled over Griff's oxygen tank and reinserted the tubes around Griff's ears and into his nose. Griff thrashed in his chair the whole time.

"Take your fill," said Degas. "As for us, it's time to take our seats."

With that, the three men exited, with Degas ruffling Will's hair on the way out.

†

Before Richard could fully process what just happened, the bright stained-glass windows dimmed, like the lights at a theatre when the show was about to begin. It confused him for a moment, before it registered that the windows must have been backlit with bulbs rather than glowing from the sun. It also meant Richard truly had no idea what time it was.

Responding to the cue, those still standing took their seats and the muffled voices of the congregation soon quieted. After a few minutes, a very old man shuffled to the altar from the center aisle. He wore a long, scarlet cassock and a matching square hat—an outfit nearly identical to that of a Catholic Cardinal. *Stop*, Richard ordered himself. *Stop comparing whatever this debauchery is to the church.* But he couldn't resist; the similarities were impossible to ignore.

Eventually, the man in red stopped at a podium that resembled a pulpit, the place where Richard had stood countless times to speak to his parishioners.

Without clearing his throat, the old man spoke. "Greetings, Edens!" His voice thundered through the balcony room. Richard looked around his holding cell. He did not see any speakers. *That can't be that man's actual voice,* Richard thought. *Can it? He's projecting louder than me.*

"May the lord be with you," the old man said as he raised his arms towards the crowd.

"And also with your spirit," they chanted in reply. There was no similarity here—this was the exact same greeting of a Sunday mass.

"May you walk blameless and righteous."

"Yet speak lies to the heart," came the audience's response. *Well, that one was new.*

"Please be seated," the man in red asked the audience. Once they obeyed, he continued. "Thank you all for coming. For the many of you traveling from an outside parish, I am Archbishop Missek and I am pleased to welcome you to the historic St. Herodias Cathedral, where tonight, for the first time in twenty years, we will witness a *bar yetzer hara!*"

The crowd cheered, but Richard did not recognize the phrase. He wondered if it referred to the wedding. What he did recognize was the name of the cathedral. Herodias was the queen that orchestrated the beheading of John the Baptist. Richard was convinced that the painting that hung over the stage was of her.

"This monumental event," Missek continued, "centers around St. Herodias's very own Victor Degas. No truer vessel could have been chosen." There was applause and Missek paused to allow it to finish. Then, he held up his long, bent, index finger. "But first, we have a marriage ceremony. I have allowed it to take place—after Degas's insistence—here tonight, prior to the *bar yetzer hara.* These two spouses-to-be have wished to honor Degas by performing their ceremony beforehand and who was I to say no? Two most sacred events in the same night! Wonderful! And if you thought things couldn't get any better, this is a themed wedding. Biana and Pavel have chosen the theme of Santa Semana! I say, what a great choice!"

The crowd responded approvingly.

"In fact, let's have everyone put on their capirotes."

Without hesitation, all members of the audience bent forward, picked up large, conical hats that matched the color of their individual capes, and placed them on their heads. Not only did the hats stand at least three feet tall, each ending in a sharp point, they covered the faces of their wearers as well. There was a striking similarity to the dress of the Ku Klux Klan, although none of the hats were white.

"Breathtaking," said Missek. "It is like I am back on the streets of Spain. Now, one more thing before we begin, we must also give thanks—and a rather strong thanks at that—to one Loyola Haynes." Missek looked among the crowd. "Loyola, come up here, my boy."

A man in the front row, dressed in plum and white, stepped forward.

"Loyola," Missek continued, "has proven to be one of the most efficient Wayside Scouts I have seen in all my time as archbishop. His ability to perceive one's true character has brought us the ideal subjects required for both our wedding *and* the *bar yetzer hara*. I am very proud of him, as you all should be." The two shook hands and Haynes winced, favoring his arm.

"Oh, my apologies," said Missek. "Still sore, I see. Get back to your seat before this old man hurts you." The crowd laughed, as well as Haynes, as he obeyed.

"Well then," Missek said. "Let us begin."

Richard 1:7

It began with the single taps of an unseen snare drum. The lone percussion continued, slow and purposeful in its solemn march as the heads of the congregation turned towards the rear of the auditorium. An explosion of trumpets joined the cadence of the drum and they themselves formed two lines of melody: one articulate like the beat of the snare and the other with long, mournful cries. Richard watched a lone man descend the far aisle in a slow, stiff stride.

Unlike the other cult members, this man simply wore a black suit and black pants. While it was impossible to tell for sure, Richard thought him to be in his early thirties, despite a full head of gray hair, combed neatly and parted from the side. Richard then noticed that not everyone watched the gray-haired man proceed down the aisle. In fact, almost half were turned in the opposite direction. Richard followed their gaze and saw that on the other side of the auditorium, a woman was approaching the altar, walking in step with the man. A sleek, black dress clung to her thin body and a white beaded rope hung from her right clenched fist. The rope was so long that it dragged behind her on the carpet. Richard saw a crucifix attached to the ends. It was a rosary.

The woman also wore a lacy, black headdress. It sat atop red hair that was packed tightly into an almost perfect sphere on the back of her head. A tendril of paranoia gripped Richard's heart as he saw Shannon making her way down the aisle. Richard's jaw clenched as he was instantly flooded with betrayal and anger. Stronger than those emotions, however, was a feeling of resentment—not towards Shannon, but towards Will. Here, before Richard was the answer to the question of what had happened in the upstairs bedroom. His son's lover had survived; Richard's had not.

No, Richard realized, *that's not Shannon*. His eyes had again deceived him. The woman with the rosary stood at least a foot shorter than Richard's daughter-in-law and her hair was too fiery a red. He shook his head hard, as if to erase the shameful thoughts he had just had about his family, but like handwriting's faint indention on the deeper sheets on a notebook, Richard could not remove them completely.

Down below, the gray-haired man and the woman with the rosary reached the front of the auditorium. There, they converged at the center aisle, locked arms, and ascended the altar steps together, finally coming to a stop in front of Missek and directly beneath Herodias's smile. Then, the music stopped.

The scene triggered memories of the marriage ceremonies that Richard had witnessed throughout his life with the church, including his own. Compared to most, however, this procession was quite bare, and if he had not already been told that this was a wedding, he may not have recognized it as one. There were no bridesmaids, nor did anyone escort the bride to the altar. There was no ring bearer or flower girl. In fact, Richard saw no children at all in attendance—except his own.

"Ladies and gentlemen," Missek began, raising his arms to the audience. His hands were as steady as a surgeon's. "We are gathered here today to witness the joining of Biana Baryshev and Pavel Mechoso into a lasting partnership.

"In the book which our dark lord abhors, marriage unites two persons into what it claims is a unity, an *equality*, yet it has always demanded polarizing roles. The husband is to be the provider and the protector. He is tasked to love his wife with all of his heart. Yet even the most revered animals in history, such as Caleb, Father Abraham, or King David himself, could never find gratification with just one woman. They had affairs! They had concubines! They practiced polygamy without reproach! And yet God made them leaders and kings. He immortalized their names and their writings as sources of inspiration for Christians to this very day! *Hypocrisy.*" The old man almost spat out the last word.

"Then, there is the woman—the *beloved*. Whose duty it is to obey and to submit to her husband. King Solomon, in his God-given, unrivaled wisdom, considered women no more than a material possession—a *crown* to rest sanctimonious upon their man's head. And if that wasn't candid enough, the great Saint Peter, in his very first letter to the world, labels women as the 'weaker vessel.'"

Missek lowered his hands and placed them on the couple's shoulders. "Biana. Pavel. I ask you two today: are these the roles you are willing to accept?"

"They are not, Archbishop," they replied in unison. "We denounce them."

"Do you wish that the relationship between you be nothing more than that of a farmer and his sow?"

"We do not," they answered again.

"Do you seek to enter into a covenant with each other that serves to deny this faulty architecture of God?"

"We do."

"Then tell me, Biana, what is your role?"

"My role is his partner," she answered without pause, like a rehearsed vow. "I am equal to this man beside me. I love him, but I will never serve him. I choose willingly to join Pavel as his wife. I come to the altar alone; no one exists with the power to give me away. We will serve as one Eden and succeed where separate we would fail."

"You are correct, my dear," Missek said, then turned to the groom. "Pavel, what is your role?"

"My role is her partner. I am equal to this woman beside me. Physical strength does not tip the scale in my favor. I love her as she loves me. I will be her protector, but she will also be mine. We will serve as one Eden and succeed where separate we would fail."

"Then it is time," Missek said, then turned and looked offstage to somewhere out of Richard's view. "Bring us the Unity Spouses!"

Immediately, from that direction, two Edens rolled out an oversized dolly carrying something at least six feet tall and covered in a red tarp, under which there appeared to be movement.

The Edens parked the large item behind Missek. When the Archbishop nodded to them, they pulled away the tarp, revealing an older man and woman dressed in dirty shirts and pants. The two were tied back to back on a stake and gagged, resembling captives from a Salem witch-hunt, except there was a broadsword hanging from the stake between them. Even from his vantage point, Richard could see its golden handle encrusted with jewels and gemstones that shimmered in the spotlight. Richard had no way of knowing for sure if the decorations were real, but it only added to the growing question: *where did the Edens get their money?*

At that point, Missek made a grand gesture towards the prisoners. "Here," he spoke, "we have one of society's uninspiring couples, wed to one another under the defective Catholic faith: Gustavo and Pia Gutiérrez."

Richard heard a squeal beside him. He turned to see Will try and shout out from behind his gag. *Does he recognize them?* Richard wondered.

Richard looked beyond Will, to Danny, who had his eyes closed. Richard knew his youngest son's innate curiosity better than anyone. Left unchecked, it would eventually compel the boy to watch the horrors below. *Keep your eyes closed*, Richard longed to say. *And don't open until I say you can.*

And you, Will. You keep it together. Your reactions have consequences. Panic from one rubs off on us all, especially your brother. Will made eye contact with Richard, and as if sensing his father's internal commands, began to regain his composure; his only sounds now were long, deep breaths.

Back on stage, Gustavo and Pia struggled fruitlessly at the stake. Missek moved closer and stopped to examine them. After a few moments, he stroked Pia's cheek. When she turned away, Missek gave her a hard slap.

"God's marriages are weak," Missek spoke to her calmly. "They mean *nothing*. They are based on a core belief that is eroding. No one honors their vows. Divorce and infidelity amongst the Christians is as common and as *ignored* as the rats in the streets above us."

That comment made Richard sit up a little straighter in his chair. *In the streets above us*, he reflected. *We are underground. That's something to know. When it's time to escape, we need to remember to run* up *to get out.*

Richard kept his attention on Missek, who turned to face the crowd once more. "Even Paul the Apostle, in his letter to the Corinthians, states that it is *good* to stay unmarried. Perhaps this God-fearing couple should have listened. Perhaps they placed their fear in the *wrong* entity."

In the air, Missek waved an outstretched hand. His fingers glided widely, once from right to left, then from his chest up above his head, and then he spoke again.

"The Abhorrent Book claims that the man is the head of the woman, that Jesus Christ is the head of man, and that finally *God* is the head of Christ. But look around you. Does anyone see Him?" Missek's voice turned grim as he looked at Pia and Gustavo. "No, because God is not present here, nor His son. Your *heads* have abandoned you.

"It is *our* marriages that contain truth. It is *our* marriages that are stronger. *Our* marriages have always held till death since the time when the first angel fell to embrace us! *Our* marriages end God's!"

The crowd's applause began to drown out Missek's voice, but he only spoke louder.

"Pavel and Biana, are you ready to prove your superiority over Christianity's pathetic sacrament?"

"Yes, Archbishop!" They said together, and the crowd fell silent once more.

"Who will be taking the sword?" Missek asked.

"I will," said Biana.

Missek nodded and stepped aside. Biana went and removed the broadsword from its mount, then positioned herself in front of Pia. She lowered into a split leg squat and held the sword out, ready to strike. She wielded it with such ease that Richard wasn't sure if the sword was fake or if she was simply proficient enough to bear its full weight.

On the other side of the stake, Pavel removed Gustavo's gag.

"Please," Gustavo begged immediately. "We've done nothing to you, to any of you. Let us go, please."

"Is that enough conviction for you, Pavel?" Missek asked. "Is that ample strength to protect his wife?"

"It is not," Pavel answered, then turned to Biana. "Release her, my love."

Biana used the tip of her sword to slice the rope that held up Pia. The prisoner dropped to the floor, landing hard on her knees.

"Run, Pia! *Corre!*" Gustavo screamed, but Pia only stood and removed the cloth from her mouth.

"No, *mi amor*." She rushed to him instead. "I will stay." As if understanding the impossibility of escape, Pia did not try and untie her husband, but hugged him, wrapping her arms around both him and the pole. She even had a brief moment to rest her head on his chest.

"He tells her to run but the wife does not obey!" Biana shouted, her voice shrill now. "You disobey your God." She drove her black high heel into the back of Pia's knee. Pia yelped and crumbled to the floor.

As if on cue, Pavel rushed forward. He grabbed Pia's hair

then spun the long, black strands around his wrist, locking in his grip. Then, as if reining a horse, he pulled her upright and onto her knees. Pia shrieked again in pain.

"End it now," Missek commanded.

Biana held the sword on Pia's neckline, then lifted it above her head. Pia did not resist.

"No!" Gustavo screamed, convulsing in his restraints.

Then, in one swift action, Biana spun around towards the stake and swung the sword into Gustavo's neck.

Gustavo's head thudded on the floor.

Biana removed her hands from the sword but the blade held, lodged in the wood. Sounds of excitement escaped the audience. A few of them even cheered.

"No!" Pia screamed. She fought to crawl to her husband's body and Pavel allowed it, but did not let go of her hair. He was walking her like a dog. "I thought it was me! I thought it was me." She wept there at his feet.

Richard wept along with her.

At that point, Missek spoke again. "Biana and Pavel. Go claim what is yours."

Right away, Pavel let go of Pia's hair, pushed her down on her stomach, and planted his knee on her spine. One hand gripped the back of her neck while the other pulled her left arm out from under her. He extended it out and pressed it against the floor.

Biana removed the sword from the stake, then swung it again. Pia's hand separated from her wrist.

Pia's scream was hair-raising. Danny could have closed his eyes all he wanted, but there was no way to plug his ears. Richard heard the boy finally start to cry.

It's OK, Danny, Richard said to himself. *It's just about over. It has to be. Please, God just let it be.*

But against his own advice, Richard kept watching. He watched as Biana removed the diamond ring from Pia's severed hand and then turned to the audience and performed a slight curtsy. He watched it all with a burning anger and disbelief.

At that point, Missek stepped up to the still screaming Pia. "Can someone stop the bleeding?" he asked.

"No!" Pia screamed, as the two assistants returned to the stage and immediately began applying a tourniquet to her arm. Pia struggled against their help. "No!" she cried again, and managed to squirm hard enough to break free from the men. She fell back onto her stomach and crawled across the floor, making her way towards Biana and leaving a sinusoidal trail of blood in her left wake. "Please, no more!" Pia shouted at the woman who had dismembered her. "Please, just kill me!"

Biana simply stood with the sword at her side. "What pride is there in killing the weak?" she asked.

The response was enough to freeze Pia in place and the guards quickly regained their hold on her. They dragged Pia off the stage as she continued to plead for Biana to take her life. Biana, meanwhile, turned and hung the sword back on its mount.

Pavel walked stiffly to Gustavo's beheaded corpse and slipped off the matching wedding band from the left ring finger. He stepped nonchalantly over the severed head and returned to Biana's side in front of Missek.

"Well done, my children," Missek said to the couple. "Now, it is time to exchange the rings." Biana and Pavel slid Pia and Gustavo's wedding bands onto each other's fingers.

Then, Missek touched their shoulders again. "Through you as his vessels, Satan has proven his strength. He is fully gratified. I can *feel* his satisfaction. The sacrament is complete. I now pronounce you husband and wife."

The applause rang throughout the temple.

"Let's have us a kiss!" Missek cheered and the newlyweds obeyed.

The kiss was slow and tender.

Shannon 1:7

Somehow, she was able to make it to her hands and knees. Small, cold indentations in her palms told Shannon that she was still on snow-covered gravel. The right side of her mouth felt like she had been chewing on cement and, from the intensity of the pain in the back of her skull, Shannon worried that there was a fracture.

Her instinct was to get back to her feet, but her arms shook like plucked guitar strings, signaling that they would not be able to support her for much longer. As it turned out, they didn't have to. Shannon was kicked in the stomach with enough force to flip her flat onto her back.

Two figures stood over Shannon while the snow continued to fall. They wore tightfitting, black body armor—something she'd imagine the military would wear on stealth missions—and they each had a matching face wrap that covered all but their nose and eyes.

"Who are you, bitch?" asked a harsh, male voice that seemed to circle in the clouds. Before she could answer, a boot stomped down on her chest. More blood escaped through the new and unwelcomed gap in her teeth. She was kicked again, this time in her side. The impact made Shannon crumple into a fetal position. Sharp pain circulated her body in a cycle that repeated with each heartbeat. All she could do now was moan.

"Gregos said she drove in alone," said a second male voice. Shannon thought she heard an Irish accent, though it could have been another pain-induced hallucination, like the bright flashes of light she saw in what should have been a black night sky.

"Just to park her car and run?" the first man asked. He too had an accent. It was different, thicker, and maybe some type of African—she didn't have the brainpower to decipher it. "I'm not ready to interrupt Missek," the maybe-African man continued, "not after his warning. Go lock her up for now—but take her through the back entrance."

"What are you going to do?" the Irishman asked.

"Investigate the perimeter—out this way, where she was headed. Make sure no one is waiting for her."

"Grand," the Irishman said, then yanked Shannon up by her hair. "Get moving," he ordered, and Shannon tried, but it took all of her focus just to stay standing. The man shoved her forward and she stumbled, but managed to stay upright. The push actually seemed to jumpstart her lower body's engine and she found herself able to move forward, albeit resembling the worst of her many drunken stumbles home.

The man giving the orders walked ahead of Shannon, while the Irishman stayed behind her. He was close enough to grab her arm and help her keep her balance—but he committed no such gentlemanly act. Unfortunately, even with her unsteady pace and slightly zigzagging path, she was already approaching the back corner of the building. Shannon did not like the idea of being locked up to await a verdict from the one they called Missek, so she knew she had to think of something fast.

While her two attackers had done a number on her upper body, they had left her legs alone. If she could catch her breath and ignore the pain (as well as keep her balance) Shannon thought there was a chance she could still outrun them.

They were three feet from the bend. *Now or never*, she thought.

Shannon planted her feet and snapped her elbow back with a primitive grunt that sounded like that of a professional tennis server. Her bone collided perfectly with the Irishman's nose and he cried out in pain, but Shannon stood in her satisfaction for just a moment too long. When she tried to dart away, the Irishman caught her by the hair and slammed her back to the ground. Her head hit the gravel again and it had no trouble intensifying the already existing pain.

She looked up to see the two men standing over her—but

suddenly, there were four. Shannon felt the pull of her misaligned eyes, yet she could not keep the double vision from occurring.

"She's not gonna fucking listen," said the Irish twins, cupping their noses.

The two maybe-Africans nodded. "Yes, just kill her."

Before the Irishmen could follow the order, however, two pairs of hands grabbed their heads. Their necks twisted in unison and Shannon heard the clear pop of them snapping.

Shannon used all of her remaining energy to roll to the side, but the maybe-African man didn't seem to notice. His attention was on a third cloaked figure who stood over the dead Irishman.

Shannon tried to stand, but only had the strength to make it halfway up before stumbling against the side of the building and sliding back down to the ground, exhausted. She sat there, propped up against the wall, as her world fused back to one image.

"Traitor," shouted the maybe-African. "Why would you do this?"

"I'm doing this for me, Kokayi," the other man replied. This one had an American accent. "Are you ready?"

The man named Kokayi pulled down his face wrap, revealing dark, perspiring skin. "You are lucky Degas ordered us to shelve our knives."

"I've never been lucky."

At that, Kokayi charged towards the man and tackled him to the ground. Their arms wrapped around each other and it looked as if they were hugging while they rolled around in the snow. Neither seemed to be winning until Kokayi landed a head-butt into his opponent's face, buying enough time to free his hands and clasp them around the other man's neck.

Shannon watched as her savior struggled, letting out a series of sickening gulps. She realized that she couldn't sit this one out any longer. *As soon as Kokayi kills this guy, he's coming right back for me.*

Finding an untapped ounce of energy, Shannon wedged herself up the wall, still unsure how she could contribute. When she got upright, she felt a piercing sting at the top of her head. She looked up to find the cause: a row of long icicles from the roof's overhang. One had grown down far enough to graze her scalp, but its tip broke on impact.

Struggling to her tip toes, she stretched to reach the next highest one. The range of motion raked pain across her chest, but she succeeded in snapping the ice free. Just as she did, she lost her balance and found herself on the ground once again.

"Here!" she yelled and tossed the severed icicle. It landed in a pile of snow close to the suffocating man. He shot his left arm out. It bounced in stiff, jerky movements in the powdery snow until it landed on its target. As soon as it did, Shannon's savior swung his arm up and drove the icicle into Kokayi's neck. Kokayi's eyes became as wide and white as cue balls and his mouth began to bubble up blood, then he fell over to the side.

Shannon's savior stood up and nursed his neck while he hobbled over to the dying Kokayi. Without words, the man knelt and covered Kokayi's mouth then waited there until his suffering came to an end. When it was over, he wiped the blood off his glove in the snow beside him.

The victorious man turned towards Shannon and pulled away the cloth that covered the rest of his face and head, revealing wild, black hair that was twisted in sweat. He stepped towards Shannon, lumbering like a zombie, close enough for her to see the dark, gray circles under his bloodshot eyes. His face was a confliction of ages: too many wrinkles and crow's feet for someone who may not have been much older than Shannon. If he hadn't just come to her rescue, she would have been frightened enough to attempt running again.

"I think you saved my life," he said wearily, almost like he wished she hadn't.

"I guess I did," Shannon replied.

The man wasted no more time on the matter. "Why are you here?" he asked, with a tone somewhere between irritation and paranoia.

Shannon hesitated, searching for any answer that might appease him.

"You're not here by accident," the man continued, but his voice had become a tense whisper. He leaned towards her. "I know I haven't checked in for a while, but if Sham sent you, you need to go. Look at me, *see*?" He threw his arms up. "I'm OK."

Shannon again just stared at him.

"You'll ruin what we've worked for," he continued. "It's happening tonight! The *bar yetzer hara*."

"I'm not here...for that," Shannon said finally, without wanting to know what *that* was.

"Then *why*?"

"My husband," she answered, although it came out more like *husth*-band, thanks to her missing tooth and swollen jaw. "And our baby. His whole family—*my* whole family. They were kidnapped by you people. I couldn't stop them so I followed them here."

The man's eyes widened. "You survived an Eden attack? Tell me how."

"It doesn't fucking matter how. I need to *schtop* wasting time and help them."

Shannon noticed a glistening quality to the man's eyes. "There's nothing you can do," he replied. "They're dead."

Shannon's stomach churned. "How do you know?" she shouted. "You don't *fucking* know!"

The man shushed her. She felt the temptation to scream—just to spite him, but kept herself under control. "My family isn't dead," she argued—willing it to be so. "They just got here, not even ten minutes ago."

"Then they're as good as dead. You can't get to them. *I* can't get to them, not that I would try. Accept that quick enough and you'll be able to get out of here alive. No one else knows you're—ah, dammit, that's not true. I need you to stay quiet for a second." He tapped his sides, then rushed over to a small radio on the ground near Kokayi's body. He picked it up and held it to his mouth. "Gregos, this is Salome Three."

"Go ahead, Sal Three," the voice on radio responded.

"We found your lamb in question. Tell me the problem again."

"She completely botched the greeting at the front gate. She didn't know what the hell I was talking about."

"Yeah, it seems like she was just caught up in the excitement."

There was a pause before Gregos responded. "No excuses, Sal Three. Especially—hi there, another new face—especially tonight. Do you want to be the one to tell Degas or Missek that we didn't follow protocol? This girl needs to be immediately incarcerated until we figure things out."

"You're right. Consider it done," the man in front of Shannon said, but immediately mouthed the words *"don't worry"* to her. Shannon had no choice but to trust him.

"Where are you, by the way?" Gregos asked. "I'm searching for a visual but it seems a few of the cameras are down—yes, walk blameless and righteous—you want me to send someone to the control room to take a look?"

"That's OK, Gregos, we're aware of the problem. The feed will be back up shortly. You keep your focus on everyone else that's arriving. Good catch by the way with this one."

"You got it. And thanks," said Gregos.

With that, Shannon's savior reclipped the radio to his belt, then looked back at her. "There you have it. I bought you some time. You need to use that time *to leave*." He held his arm up, pointing. "If you follow this pathway along the river—"

"No, please, help me get my family back."

"I said get the hell out of here!" he shouted. His anger seemed to startle himself more than Shannon; he looked over his shoulder as if someone could have heard.

"OK, fine. *Assch*-hole," Shannon replied. "I was leaving to get the police anyway. I'll just be on my way."

"No, dammit!" He stepped close enough for her to inhale his condensed breath, but didn't touch her. "I can't let you do that."

"What am I gonna do then?"

He shook his head in frustration. "Listen to me, I know it makes sense for you to tell the police, to bring them here—I get it. But there are bigger things at play." He gave a defeated sigh. "I'm undercover."

Shannon's perked up.

"*Not* with the cops," he clarified, sensing what she had been thinking. "But I need to see this thing through; I have to witness what happens in there and there can't be any interruption."

"What's your name?" Shannon asked.

"Bass," he replied.

"Bass? Like the fish?" *The fissch*. The man didn't respond. "Tell me your real name. Your first and last name. Consider it a trust thing."

"Bass is all you get," he said, then pinched his nose in an almost comical gesture of contemplation.

He held his pose for so long that Shannon arrived at the answer first. "Make me undercover with you."

"No way. These people are more dangerous than you can imagine. Each person inside that building would rip your heart out and smile while they do it."

"But they won't *know* to! I saw the people coming in. They don't all know each other. And your little face wraps cover up almost everything. No one will suspect that I'm not one of them."

"A disguise can only get you so far. It's your complete ignorance to our procedures that will get us both caught. Like at the gate, the guard asked for the code phrase. You answered it wrong—you were probably oblivious to the fact that he was even *asking* for it. It's the reason you got that beating—and inside you'll get worse."

"But you protected me," Shannon said, "and you can protect me in there as well."

"I only killed these men because I thought you were someone else." Once again, he sounded regretful.

Shannon looked back to the bodies. "Were they your friends?"

"No!" he shot back. "But I've known them a long time. I don't regret killing them, I regret the risk that killing them has put on me. The events set to take place tonight need to happen. If the people in charge find out—about this or about you—it's over. Everything I've worked for would be for nothing."

"Events to take place," Shannon repeated back to him. "What's with all this vague *bullshit*? What's happening in there tonight? Does it have to do with my family?"

"I don't know—I think so, but I don't know how exactly they fit in."

"Then I'm going inside. I'm taking the clothes off that Irish asshole, putting them on, then I'm walking through the front door. You can come with me and feed me your code words when I need them or you can bury me out here in the snow—but if you try that option I'll scream bloody murder the whole time and hopefully that will be enough to spook your boss into cancelling his plans."

Shannon thought it was impossible that her threat would come off as intimidating after she whistled all of her S's, but Bass seemed to be either convinced or cornered.

"Alright," he said with a frown.

A part of Shannon was taken aback by his answer—and the effort she put in to earn it. *I had the opportunity to run away*, she thought. *Since when don't I take that?*

"I said *alright*," Bass repeated. "So get dressed."

Shannon moved towards the Irishman's body, then looked back at Bass. "It'll be quicker with some help."

Bass did not respond, but went on to assist Shannon in removing the guard's body armor and pants. They fit a little baggy over Shannon's tank top and jeans, but Bass adjusted them enough to be functional. The boots were about two sizes too big, but after Leigha's tight-fitting and thin sneakers, Shannon's feet welcomed the newfound space and warmth. *Let's just hope I don't have to run in these,* she thought.

Once she was fully dressed in the guard's attire, Shannon and Bass dragged the two bodies under the overhang of the building.

"They'll find them soon," Bass said. "But hopefully not tonight." He took a moment to look Shannon up and down. "We need to go in the back entrance. The less people you encounter, the better."

Shannon nodded, then took one more look at the bodies before leaving them beneath a thickening blanket of snow.

Bass led her around the rear corner of the building to a single, paint-chipped metal door. When he opened it and revealed the hallway inside, Shannon thought her head was acting up again. She was staring at a hallway that could double as a Renaissance architect's mecca. A domed ceiling stretched down a corridor mounted with large, golden candelabra and thick, Corinthian columns. The floors were checkered Cosmati tiles, a design that used glass mosaics in combination with marble. The technique began in medieval Rome, maybe—Shannon couldn't quite remember, but one thing she knew for sure was that each square foot was insanely expensive.

A few feet inside, Shannon found herself drawn to the nearest of many fresco mural paintings that adorned the walls in between some of the columns. She lingered there, staring at the picture. In it, a young teenage girl wore a flowing red dress that left her belly exposed. She was twirling, dancing in front of an old man on a throne. The image made Shannon uncomfortable, but she could not peel her eyes away from it.

Bass did not wait for her, but continued down the hallway without even calling back. Shannon hurried after him, running clumsily in her boots. The echoing of her heavy stomps made

Shannon notice one more thing about their surroundings: they were completely alone.

"Where is everyone?" she asked after catching up with Bass.

"Most of the arrivals are changing and gathering for a little... meet and greet. This structure is a lot bigger than it looks, there are four stories below us. By now, everyone should be downstairs.

"Should we really be roaming the hallways, then?"

"We'll be OK. Believe it or not, security was ordered down to a skeleton crew. The man in charge apparently wants as many as possible to be in attendance for the ceremony: the *bar yetzer hara*—what I rambled to you about out there. I'm not about to go into the details, but it's a big deal. It should require *much* more security. There's the guard you met at the front gate, me, and the two men I killed outside. I don't understand that decision, but I don't question it either." Then, Bass came to a halt in front of the only thing that looked out of place in the building so far: a modern-looking security door made of polished steel.

"Here." Bass pulled out a thick key ring with about twenty identical keys. He flipped one up from the middle of the bunch and it slid right into the keyhole. Inside was a sophisticated surveillance room, containing among it a series of server towers and three computer monitoring stations.

"Go to that central computer," Bass instructed. "I want you to cycle through the cameras until you can locate your family."

Shannon rushed with enthusiasm towards the task. The interface was intuitive and she clicked through one screen after another. There were shots of bare hallways, the front gate, and the parking lot. She saw a few stragglers leaving their cars, walking quickly towards the front doors. She soon arrived at more haunting images: an assembly hall full of robed men and women with martini glasses in their hands, then a series of muddy, cavernous chambers that held men, women, and children in tattered clothing. She quickly clicked through. *Not my family*, she reminded herself.

A few of the camera screens came up dark and scrambled, stamped with the word "DENIED." This began to worry Shannon, who panicked that one of the screens she couldn't see would be the one that pointed to the location of her family. But then, after a few more clicks, there they were. All five of them together. Alive.

"Here!" Shannon exclaimed, grinning into the monitor. "They're in a big...pool of water? Where—" she spun around just in time to see Bass holding a knife to a collection of wires in a wall panel.

The lights went out and all the electronics followed, making the room pitch black. Shannon heard the door slam and the sound of keys jingling on the other side.

She knew she was locked in, but she screamed anyway. Alone and in the dark, she realized that Bass had never asked her name.

Will 1:8

They came for him as the newlyweds took their final bows. The last thing Will saw before the hood slipped over his head was Biana's black dress shimmering through his tear-glazed eyes.

For a moment, Will welcomed the darkness that the hood provided, but quickly discovered that it offered little reprieve. The images of murder and dismemberment he had just witnessed were burned into his retinas, replaying over and over again without becoming any less disturbing.

Until today, Will would have sworn he could stomach the worst violence—and he had become proud of that fact. Over the last few years, Will had seen more than his share of gory movies, thanks to Shannon who couldn't get enough of them.

Most movie nights consisted of the newest bootleg horror film Shannon could find on Canal Street. Zombies, monsters, slashers, cannibal tribes, torture porn—she loved them all. Will didn't really mind, the pirated films cost only a few dollars, and he got ninety uninterrupted minutes—at least before Giddy was born—of cuddling with his wife. It was easy enough to avoid watching the gory stuff; Will would just divert or close his eyes.

Until the night Shannon caught him doing it.

"Pussy," she called him, as he turned his head away from a young man getting his head skewered on a drilling lathe.

It wasn't the first time she'd called him that, but this time it hit home. Will told himself that watching a scary movie wasn't the same as trying to open a pickle jar, keep down a shot of tequila, or standing up to Mr. DiSantos. Keeping his eyes open was something that should take no effort: just sit there and stare. Will made a vow to himself from that point on to watch everything that Shannon did.

Through sheer determination, Will's aversion to gore was soon reduced to slight fidgets on the sofa. As his desensitization grew, Will found that he began to look forward to the more gruesome kills, just so he could beat Shannon to the punch with a "cool" or an "oh yeah" comment. Together they would laugh as the characters on screen bled and died.

One night, Will found himself combing through online forums to find the grittiest films he could, just to impress his wife—maybe even one-up her. He bought a copy of *A Serbian Film* after it came highly recommended on a "sickest horror movies ever" thread. Will wrapped it up as an early Christmas present. Halfway through, during an unedited scene in which a man rapes a newborn baby, Shannon turned off the TV.

"Why the fuck are you showing me this shit?" she had asked. "We just had a kid. What's wrong with you?"

"I thought you'd like it."

"The trash goes out tomorrow—that movie better fucking be in it."

Will nodded.

"Good," said Shannon. "Ready for bed?"

Will certainly wasn't. He stood over Giddy's crib for a long time that night and prayed for forgiveness for ever subjecting himself to that filth. Still, it didn't stop him from watching horror movies after that night. Together with Shannon, it only got easier, becoming a routine that was as mindless for the two of them as their daily subway commute.

But routine was never the right word, Will realized. *It was an addiction.*

Up on the temple's balcony, Degas never forced Will to watch the wedding; there was no heinous contraption implanted to wedge his eyes open. *I chose to watch it, God*, Will confessed. *I wanted to see what was going to happen. What kind of person does that make me?*

An image of Shannon arose in the darkness. Will was looking up at her while she stood over the staircase back in their townhouse. "Pussy," she called down to him. Then behind her,

Degas appeared. He grabbed her by the hair and she was pulled down the hallway. "Why did I ever marry a pussy?"

Will did not want to be in the dark any longer. He thrashed in his chair, flinging his head back and forth, trying to shake off the hood. He wanted to go back to watching the wedding on stage, back to the views of Biana in her dress. He wished that she would twirl and dance with her husband for hours because as long as it was still her time in the limelight, Will would not be taken away.

But there was nothing more to be seen. It was Will's turn.

"Hold him steady," he heard Haynes say, then felt two colossal hands secure his head like a vice.

"Easy now," said Fen, but Will couldn't have moved his head if he had wanted to. After a few moments the giant's hands withdrew and Will began to move. Still tied in his chair, Will had the sensation of being wheeled down various corridors. By the sounds of it, the same was being done with the rest of his family—all being rolled in their chairs in single file to places unknown.

Giddy hadn't been fastened to a chair like the others, so Will worried that his son had been taken somewhere different until he heard the baby cry.

"He doesn't like you, Lam," Haynes said. "Here, switch spots and give him to me."

Will still couldn't believe Haynes was ever part of this. He had so many questions for the man he once respected. *All the time they'd spent together at the restaurant—were we ever really friends? Did Degas threaten you or force you into betraying me? Or were you on this evil mission all along?* But as long as he was gagged, he could never ask.

The caravan came to a halt for a few moments before the floor began to lower—some type of industrial elevator, large enough to fit everyone. After the elevator reached its destination, its doors opened with a peaceful chime. Will was then briefly back on the move. When he stopped again, multiple pairs of hands untied and rearranged him. They took his arms and raised them up and over his head, then tied them again. At that point, they released him from the rest of the straps that bound him to the chair. Before he could struggle, the whirl of a mechanical device started up and Will was slowly pulled into the air by his wrists.

When the machine stopped, the balls of Will's feet just grazed the floor. He pretty much had to stand on his tiptoes because if he tried to come down any further, the pain in his shoulders became unbearable. Hanging there, Will heard the process repeat three times.

Then, finally, the hood came off.

The four Batteses were all strung up along a large canvas, the ropes from their arms each entering separate holes in the wall behind them. Giddy was hanging from the wall too, though not by his arms. He was gently secured in a pouch like a baby kangaroo. The baby was awake now, looking around with an almost mature curiosity, making no noise whatsoever. In front of them all was a giant theater curtain. Within seconds of Will's hood being removed, the curtain began to rise.

The lights from the auditorium bombarded the stage.

Missek stood on the other side of the curtain, no more than an arm's length away from Will. The man was not just old, he was decrepit. Liver spots and branching skin tags littered his pale face, which itself seemed to almost slough off his skull. Gravity stretched his jowls down like deflated balloons and did the same to his lower eyelids, exposing bumpy, red tissue underneath that was almost the same shade as his garments.

"Immortality!" Missek shouted, directed at Will, who was close enough to taste the decay of the old man's breath. Will couldn't help but gag. His reaction made Missek smile, revealing a layer of black grime along the gumline of ghoulishly thin teeth. The audience cheered until Missek turned towards them and swiftly raised his right hand. They fell silent.

Dear God, Will pleaded. *Please save us.*

"Immortality," Missek repeated. "It is God's ultimate reward and He is very proud of it. So proud in fact that He spends the majority of the Bible bragging all about it. 'For I so loved the world, I gave you my son, my grace, my glory, blah, blah, blah, so that you may have eternal life.' It might even seem like a pretty sweet deal—if it wasn't full of stipulations! Before we receive this gift—a gift that *we did not ask for*—we must endure a lifetime of temptations. Those temptations relentlessly peck at us like birds after seeds on the wayside. Peck, peck, peck." Missek used his fingers and thumb to gesture the snapping of a bird's beak. "And if we succumb to those temptations so that we are lifted *up and away* from His righteous path, we do not receive His gift. We receive instead His most severe punishment...and can you guess what that is?"

"Immortality!" The audience shouted.

"Indeed! Forever in Heaven, to kiss the feet of the God that made us to suffer, or eternal damnation in Hell where there is weeping and gnashing of teeth and plenty of time to curse the God who knew from *before time* which ones of us would end up there." Missek paused and sassily bent his wrists on hips. "Damned if we do. Damned if we don't.

"Never once do we get the option to return to the nothingness from whence we came, from whence he *dragged* us into existence the way a parent drags a child out of their slumber. What if we just *liked* nothingness? What if we just want to go back to it? Nope! Not an option! Not on His watch. He'd rather bring us into this temporary existence known as life, show us Eternity Door Number One and Eternity Door Number Two, then force us to choose between those very different, but equally undesirable forevers. *That* is God's glory."

"His glory is false," the crowd chanted in unison.

"Yes," Missek continued, "but fortunately for us, we are not the only beings to share that resentment. There are beings that

200

were born straight into immortality, bypassing this insulting human phase altogether. They are the angels. They are older than us, stronger than us, wiser than us, and began more faithful than us. Yet they were not spared from God's false glory. Despite the angel's majesty, God went on to create us, not them, in His image. Despite humanity's sinful nature, God will allow the 'righteous' to judge and rule over the angels. No wonder why so many of them have defected."

Will couldn't figure out where Missek was going, but a growing part of him didn't care. His arms burned, his back spasmed, and the heat from the stage lights made him sweat profusely. With no way to wipe his face, the salty beads of perspiration stung his eyes.

Please save us, God. We've heard enough. Please shut him up and save us.

But Missek continued. "From the beginning, we Edens have put our faith in the first fallen angel. We find security in the fact that we are not the only ones that detest our hypocritical creator. They know that God designed them to fall, but unlike us, they can use immortality to their advantage. Already created to be beyond humans in wisdom, they grow wiser still through the centuries. They forever evolve, growing their understanding of our behavior and perfecting their ability to deceive the righteous among us. The fallen angels use God's gift of immortality," he twirled his crooked pointer fingers around in the air, "against Him. And one by one, they lead God's chosen people astray by identifying the weak-minded and plucking them away like little gray hairs.

"I'm not talking about us, of course. We are the opposite of the weak-minded. We are the enlightened, and the demons need us. They are superior and they are immortal, but they have limitations. They can only reach humanity as whispers, as shadows, as misfortunes. Scents that linger in the hearts of man, scents for the birds of temptation to descend upon. They cannot exist fully in our realm, but can only seep through the divide like smoke that crawls under the doors inside of a burning house. But we can open up those doors and let the fire flood in!

"Human-demon kinship. It has been around since biblical times, mostly in the form of possession. Demons force themselves into the souls of their unwitting human hosts. Not every man or woman is susceptible. It is only the weakest-minded: the children, the depressed, the psychotic, or the mentally handicapped. But whether the host is deceived or manipulated to accept the demon inside them, the deepest core of their humanity knows that this foreign spirit does not belong. Possessions therefore wear away their hosts. Their mind deteriorates. Their body deteriorates, rejecting the demon the way it would reject a faulty organ transplant. The erosion continues ultimately until death or exorcism, after which the demon returns to its immortal realm.

"However, once in a great while there comes a human host so special, so committed to rejecting God that their mind and body accept the demon in all its glory and all its causes. If the demon also accepts this human, it is no longer a possession, it is a fusion, a permanent unification. The two become one and the things that they can accomplish are beyond anything that can be done alone. This is known as the ritual of the *bar yetzer hara*!"

The crowd erupted, standing and cheering.

"And tonight," Missek continued, "you will witness it in all its majesty! In the air with us is Decaar himself, have you felt him yet? Decaar is the demon of unrestrained emotion! The demon of instigation and exaggeration! His whispers once united the men of the earth into constructing Babel's Tower and he is thirsty to unite God's people against Him once more. He has chosen Victor Degas to be his champion!"

At that, the crowd roared.

"And as you know, Decaar's decision does not come lightly. In return for a host that allows him to fully exist in this world, the demon sacrifices its own immortality. Though it will outlive all of us, it will eventually die along with its human shell and return to the nothingness from whence it came. But do not despair, the demons who elect to perform the *bar yetzer hara* always make their time amongst us worthwhile. They eat their fill of the wayside seeds.

"And I suppose that is enough talk from an old man like me," Missek said, stepping aside. "Here is the man you want. Degas, the temple is yours."

When Degas ascended the stage, the audience gave him a standing ovation. Degas was not dressed the same as before. Though he still wore the all black outfit with the sacred heart emblem, sitting atop it was a blood-red cloak topped with ceremonial shoulder pads. Three-inch black spikes protruding from them on each side, resembling a hawk's talons.

There's still time to save us, God.

When the cheering subsided, Degas spoke.

"Thank you all," he said to the crowd. "Allow me to be brief. Decaar's immortality is not something to give up lightly, so my choice in honoring him for the *bar yetzer hara* is to sacrifice it as well.

"Allow me to explain. A family's bloodline does not easily die. Generation after generation it is passed on—it is its own kind of immortality. Hanging behind me are five generations of the surname Battese. They come to you by way of Lake Placid, New York, but we traced their ancestry to Ireland and even into western Europe as far back as the 18th century—at least three hundred years of devoted Christian lineage."

Will heard a muffled shouting and saw that his father was thrashing at his post.

Despite the outburst, Degas ignored Richard and continued. "The Batteses have come a long way, but here before you are the only surviving men of their bloodline. Their family tree is withering, but tonight, it shall be uprooted and scorched! That is my offer to you, Decaar!"

Degas lifted his left hand in the air, palm towards the audience and fingers spread wide. Suddenly, Will saw lines of blood running down Degas's arm. Will couldn't see where he was cut.

The cheers of the crowd were deafening.

Haynes came forward and presented Degas with a large dagger. Will glared at his former friend, trying to bury him in guilt, but Haynes did not so much as glance back. His eyes were fixated on Degas and seemed to gleam with admiration.

We're not getting out of here, are we God?

"Weep has been sharpened and polished, Victor."

Degas bowed slightly and took the dagger in his right hand— the one that had not started bleeding. He held the blade up and admired it. Then, he turned and approached Griff.

If you are going to kill us, God. Please make it quick.

"Griffin Matthew Battese," he said, putting the dagger to Griff's neck. "As the oldest living Battese, you would have naturally been the first to go. Look at you."

He tapped him lightly on the cheek, but there was little response. Griff's state was worse than in the balcony; his eyes were closed and Will could not even tell if he was breathing.

"Griff is barely with us now, but that is OK. There is no shame. He did his duty in producing the next generation. Griffin, your time here has ended."

Degas swiped his dagger deep across Griff's neck.

Will watched in horror as his grandfather's blood dribbled out of the gash and into the white fabric of the robe underneath. Griff's eyes fluttered back, but besides a few weak spasms, there was no struggle.

Will screamed under his gag, twisting and turning and pulling as hard as he could on his ropes. Tears spilled from his eyes. He pressed his feet against the backdrop and pushed forward until his arms felt like they were going to pop out of their sockets. Degas watched Will intensely—unsmiling—and even took a step towards him before Will's legs dropped back to the floor from exhaustion.

Too little, too late, Will thought. *Could I have prevented this if I fought harder in the hallway? In the kitchen? A little more in the primordial room? Could I have done more to save my family?*

Then, Degas turned towards Richard, who, like Will, shook and pulled and tested his restraints. Richard had not tired yet, his angry energy still not spent, but Will knew it wasn't going to matter.

I'm sorry, Dad. I'm so sorry I didn't fight.

"Richard Jonathan Battese," Degas recited. "You are the son of Griffin, father of William and Daniel, and grandfather of Gideon." Richard thrashed on the canvas, screaming behind his gag. Degas was forced to speak louder over him. "Your youth has departed and your remaining strength is fleeting as you approach the last stage of your life. There is—"

Richard shouted even louder, but Will thought now it almost sounded like laughing.

Even Degas stopped and cocked his head slightly. Richard began nodding his head furiously while starting to shout what sounded like the two same words over and over again.

"It looks like you have something to say," Degas finally responded. "Very well. Decaar would love to hear your pleas. There were too few from Griffin."

Degas ripped the gag from Richard's mouth. Richard's face burned red and his tears mixed with saliva as he spat out the two words he was shouting from behind the gag.

"You idiot!" cried Richard, almost choking. "You *idiot*! You don't know a damn thing!"

Degas was unflinching. "My knowledge is about to surpass human limits," he replied, sheathing his dagger on his belt. Degas glanced to the auditorium, then back to Richard. "What could you possibly know that I don't?"

"I know your ritual has failed! It was failed from the

beginning, you bum! You stupid chump!"

"What are you talking about?" Degas asked, now beginning to look concerned.

The lights in the auditorium flickered.

Richard continued to yell in between his gasping sobs. "It's all wrong! It's all horribly wrong! You didn't do any research! Griffin Matthew *Battese*," he shouted mockingly, "was my stepfather! There is no Battese blood in me. Not in *any of us* up here, you moron!"

"No," said Degas, almost in a whisper. Will watched his eyes—they contained so much panic that even his colobomas seemed to shiver. It was the first time Will looked at them without fear. He felt satisfaction.

"What a way to honor your little demon, tough guy!" Richard continued. "Kill an old man? So brave! Do what God was going to do in another six months? Whoop dee doo!"

"Stop!" Degas rushed over to Richard and began choking him with both hands, the blood on Degas's palm spreading to Richard's neck. "The research was done! I had my best team on it!" Then, Degas let go of Richard and turned around. "Loyola, why would he say all this?"

Haynes walked back onto the stage, head down. "I...I didn't think it mattered, Victor."

"What?" Degas shouted.

"I...I thought the generations were *figurative*. You were putting so much pressure on me, looking for people so *specifically*...Will and his family were the closest thing I could find."

Then, for the first time, the crowd lost discipline. There was murmuring. Will heard bits and pieces: "...came all this way... it's over... imagine the sentencing."

Missek raised up his hands to the audience, but this time they did not quiet.

Richard was full on laughing now. "You've fucked everything up, Degas! You hear that crowd? You failed! You idiot! You moron! You idiot! You moron!"

"Shut up!" Degas screamed and replaced the gag on Richard.

Suddenly, Will felt a draft that was as hot as if it had just come out of an oven. The flames of the candles along the walls all bent in unison. Will heard a high-pitched cry that filled the theatre and made the audience grow quiet once again. He turned instantly to Gideon, but the baby looked completely at ease.

Will had no idea what had caused the mysterious sound, but returned his attention to Degas.

"You ruined me, Loyola!" Degas screamed. He lunged towards Haynes and tackled him to the floor. Holding down his opponent, Degas drew the blade from his sheath.

"Stop!" Missek thundered. "Let him up!" Degas hesitated briefly, letting his dagger hang over Haynes for a couple moments longer, but ultimately obeyed.

"You shall not blame this boy, Victor," Missek continued. "With a task so infinitely important, how could you not verify the facts yourself? How could you not? There is *no one* to blame but yourself."

"I...I agree," Degas said, regaining his composure although still breathing heavily. "What happens now?"

"You know that I do not yet know. Even if the church forgives you, Decaar may not. You embarrassed him and that is its own price to pay. For now, this night is over." Missek turned to the crowd. "The rest of you, on behalf of St. Herodias, I cannot apologize enough for this disappointment. There is nothing more to say. Go home, all of you. You, too, Loyola. *Get out.*"

Will watched as the Edens shuffled out, slow and deflated. When only Missek and Degas remained, they turned their attention on the remaining family members.

"These leftovers are still your responsibility," Missek said. "Take care of them, then meet me in The Library." Degas nodded quietly then Missek exited the stage.

At that point, Degas turned to Will. Despite all that had just happened, Will thought he saw a hint of a smile on the man's face.

Before Degas could say anything, however, he was approached by two Edens, still in their capirotes.

"Pardon our intrusion," said the shorter of the two, an older woman, judging by the sound of her voice.

Degas turned. "I am the one to be pardoned."

The woman stepped forward and knelt slowly and with great effort in front of Degas. Will could not see her face, but there was something familiar about her. Gray hair with streaks of pink ran out from under her mask.

"What can I do for you, sister?" Degas asked.

The woman reached up and grabbed Degas's hand. As she did, her sleeve came down to reveal a tattoo: a rose with a stem that climbed up the rest of her arm.

No, it can't be, Will thought.

"We are sorry fate fell the way it did," the woman said, "but my husband and I believe that we have served you well. While befriending the Batteses took quite an effort, we did grow quite fond of the baby. We ask that—unless you already have plans for him—you allow us to take him, to raise him as our own. In the life of an Eden."

"No!" Will shouted under his gag, thrashing again in his restraints. "No!"

Degas's full smile returned as he watched Will's reaction. "I suppose I see no harm in that. A loyal believer brought up among us, perhaps one day he could succeed where I did not. I imagine he would have been disposed of otherwise, ground up like coffee beans and poured into the river. My answer is yes, Sister Sara. You and Abe may take him."

"Thank you!" the masked woman shouted. "Oh, thank you!" She almost jumped back to her feet and raced to remove Gideon from his pouch.

"No! Please!" Will shouted. He tried again to break free, using every ounce of strength he had, but could not.

Degas stood and waited for Will's struggle to stop—long after Giddy was carried away.

"Will Battese," he finally spoke. "I was *so* close. Did you feel him? Decaar? Surely you did. I was minutes away from draining the life from you, the penultimate moment of months of observation and planning. Now...I don't know what I'm going to do with you. I want to blame you for this. I want to punish you by killing what's left of your family. Every friend you ever had, every worshipper that sat among you in church, the mailman that delivered your birthday cards, the doctor that delivered you in the hospital. I want to find them all and turn their insides out while you watch, then burn your beloved hometown to the ground. And I wish your mother was alive, so that I could be the one to snap her neck." He sighed. "Then, I recognize that none of this is your fault and I weigh the option of killing you swiftly. I need to think on this, so I will be back shortly."

Degas headed off the stage.

If he had stayed a moment longer, and listened very closely, he might have heard what Will was saying under his gag.

"I will kill you all."

End of Act 2

State of Amazonas, Brazil

Cara Dann jerked awake. A handful of fat and aggressive red ants had found their way onto her feet. She crushed them, one at a time, between her thumb and forefinger.

"You let me sleep, Peter," she said.

On the other side of the half-built house, Dr. Reising was lying atop his sleeping bag, dressed in khaki shorts and a faded green *Berghaus* t-shirt. Hands clasped behind his head, the lanky professor continued to stare at the thatched roof. "You needed it," he replied unapologetically.

"I did *not* need to piss away hours of our brainstorming session," she said, genuinely annoyed. The moon had been high when she last closed her eyes, but now she felt herself already being baked by the morning sun that poured through the open window above her legs.

Before Dr. Reising could respond, Cara heard footsteps approach from outside the hut. They were slow and sloppy, not one of the Nacana. Sure enough, Dr. Michael shuffled through the open doorway. His clothes hung off him like a big brother's hand-me-downs and there was sorrow in his saggy face.

"Is he dead?" Cara asked.

Dr. Michael sank down beside her. "No, but he's getting worse. I'm running out of options that I never really had to begin with. And before you ask, yes. I was able to convince the chief to bring Peak today, but it's getting quite difficult to make that happen."

Almost three months had passed since her team arrived at the village. Peak had remained as comfortable as possible, thanks to Dr. Michael doing his best to mask the boy's symptoms through medication, administering it strategically before Cara's sermons—to help further the belief that the words of the Bible were key to Peak's healing process.

"And Quando?" Cara asked. The shaman came to the sermons as well, speaking softly into the chief's ear while Cara spoke. Quando's eyes stole distrusting glances at Cara while he whispered, though she never knew what was said.

"No doubt he will be tagging along," said Dr. Michael, using a hairy arm to wipe sweat from his brow—a habit that he repeated so often that his forehead displayed a constant rash. It looked particularly bright this morning and touching it made the doctor wince. He combed through his messenger bag then frowned. "Anyone have any aloe left?"

"I gave you the last of mine a *hurak* ago," said Cara, looking at Dr. Reising. "Is that right?"

Dr. Reising shook his head. "You meant Hu-*rat*: moon cycle. Month. Hu-*rak* is vagina."

"Well, that's pretty close actually," said Cara.

"Why don't you see if Quando has anything for it," Dr. Reising suggested.

"Ha," said Dr. Michael, "that would give him satisfaction wouldn't it? As much as he cares for me, he'd treat it with an actual bowl of menstrual blood."

"You mean that *doesn't* work?" Dr. Reising replied and the three of them managed to share a tired laugh.

"If it gets worse, maybe I *will* ask the shaman," Dr. Michael said. "Anyway, that's it for my report. Everyone is waiting for you at Pride Rock."

"Are you coming, Michael?" Cara asked.

"Not today," Dr. Michael replied. "I would like time to myself. You've been a lot drearier lately, more than I prefer."

"You've told me enough times," Cara responded coldly. "I hope I can have your support again soon—not your criticism."

Cara stood up, pushing off the doctor's knee, then walked out the door without saying goodbye. Dr. Reising followed and kept pace with her until they reached the outskirts of the near-empty village, then stopped.

"What?" Cara asked him.

"I'm afraid this stalemate is making for unexciting research." Cara stared at him to go on, and he did. "Oxford gives me the discretion to pull this mission whenever I want—not that I'm ready to. I'm just reminding you that I have that power."

Cara didn't need reminding; she knew all that. Hearing it, however, still managed to rattle her. It wasn't like him to play that card.

"You're saying that at only three months—you're *bored* because a completely isolated society hasn't come to accept the truth about Christ?"

Dr. Reising scoffed when she said *the truth*, but did not fight her on it. "Don't twist my words. What I'm saying is, you're the missionary expert. I just need to know that if you hit a dead end—and you realize this has become a lost cause—you'll tell me, so I don't waste my time. The longer we wait, the more disappointing it will be to go home with nothing."

"Disappointing? We are talking about their salvation."

"I'm not," said Dr. Reising. "I'm talking about my research."

"Right. You don't care about anything but that."

"How can you judge me?" Dr. Reising asked. "You've been lying to this boy's father since the beginning. Your sermons won't heal him. The boy is dying and you're giving everyone false hope."

"I know," said Cara. "I just don't have a better option."

"Do you think you can save him?"

"Yes, Peter. I feel the breakthrough coming."

"OK," Dr. Reising said, solemnly. "I believe you."

"Then *support* me! Feel my passion and carry it to them. Make my words bore holes through their hearts!"

"I'm doing everything you've asked."

"Well, now I'm asking you to step it up, because what you're doing is not good enough."

Dr. Reising gave a dismissive nod and headed up the hill.

Cara followed, but the rest of the walk was silent—between the two of them at least. The jungle continued to sing.

†

"Witnessing is useless if the witness is not trustworthy," Cara had told the members of her missionary group again and again—even before their trip began. She had made sure that the majority of their time in the Nacana village was spent building that trust and, much to Cara's satisfaction, a lot of progress had been made.

In the past three months, Cara and her group upgraded a man-made well, resulting in better filtration for healthier and tastier water. Then, they moved on to constructing additional homes for the village, which were also sturdier than the preexisting ones. Every improvement, fortification, and science lesson they gave the Nacana seemed to be received with genuine appreciation.

They managed to have fun together, too. Cara's favorite story so far was when Dr. Michael tried to teach football to the tribe's children. None of them could hold still at the line of scrimmage and they quickly lost interest in the sport. It was Dr. Michael who ended up learning a Nacana game: *Mu'intum*. It was essentially like tag—but with sticks.

They ran out of Band-Aids after the first week.

Eventually, between work and play, Cara began incorporating religious lessons. She invited the entire tribe to daily meetings she held outside of the village. There was a natural rock formation that protruded over a small, slow-flowing river. Dr. Michael called the stony overhang Pride Rock, after its resemblance to the one in the Disney movie *Lion King*.

Sitting along the river beneath Pride Rock, the Nacana partnered up with the missionaries to practice each other's languages. At some point during each pow-wow, Cara would stand and speak atop the cliff about God and His son, Jesus, who had saved her and was here to save them all.

Cara had her system down pat: she would give her sermon in English—very slowly and very basic, like speaking to a pre-K Sunday School class—while Dr. Reising would interpret. The two worked together, meticulously preparing each lecture to maximize its clarity.

Thanks to Peak and the chief's attendance, the majority of the tribe came as well. They all seemed genuinely intrigued by her stories, especially Peak, whose eyes never left Cara's, although it was Dr. Reising that spoke the boy's language. The only one to ask questions, however, was the chief. They were the right questions too: *Why does Jesus love us? Where is Jesus now?* and—most encouraging—*how do we get to Heaven?*

Cara felt she answered each one concisely, especially the last. "Mark, one of the first of Jesus's tribe, tells us all we need is to believe and be baptized, then we are taken there."

"*Qut?*" the chief said. "So easy?"

"Yes. So are you ready to be baptized?" Cara asked.

"No," he said.

Cara turned to his son. "Peak?" she asked.

The boy opened his mouth, about to speak, but the chief answered instead. "No, he is not."

And so it went. Cara never got to speak alone with Peak. She didn't even know what the boy felt about anything. That had been acceptable for Cara, at first. The reverend knew it took time to come to Christ; pressuring anyone was the least effective thing to do. When the chief refused for himself and his son, Cara would end her teachings for the day and try again next time. However, no matter how many times she spoke of God's love and desire to save them, the chief was never willing to accept Him. And as it turned out, if the chief said no, everyone said no, too. No one from the Nacana tribe ever came forward to convert.

As Peak's condition worsened, Cara had no choice but to push harder. If God's love did not sway the chief, she thought perhaps the fear of God would. Her sermons became grim. She preached about the end of days, those left behind in the rapture, and the power of the devil. She introduced the concept of eternal damnation, the price paid for not accepting Jesus Christ.

Still, the chief rejected her. Cara knew she had presented all the evidence, but couldn't figure out why they resisted. She began to question Dr. Reising's effectiveness. Although he spoke confidently and energetically enough when he interpreted for her, Cara often could not keep up with what he was saying. Perhaps he had misinterpreted her words, failing to convey the power she felt. Or maybe he was mistranslating on purpose. Cara wondered if she gave the agnostic too much responsibility for the village's redemption.

On one particularly humid morning, the day before Cara awoke to find the ants on her feet, she told the Nacana the story about Legion. With conviction, she described Jesus as he cast the impure spirits out of the innocent man and into a herd of pigs before drowning them in the lake. Like always, she asked if they were ready to be baptized. Seeing the chief shaking his head "no" in the already dizzying heat, Cara could resist no longer.

"Peter," she said. "Ask him why not."

Dr. Reising nodded, then turned to the chief and conveyed the question.

The chief's response was calm and succinct. Peter interpreted, "He is waiting for Jesus to heal his son."

The answer scared Cara. It was the only concern she could not alleviate. It rendered her helpless. She needed a plan and swore to herself she would find one.

But then Peter let her sleep.

†

As Cara approached Pride Rock, with the ant bites pulsing between her toes, she was struck with an idea.

The meet and greet between the two peoples of different worlds had already begun. The tribesmen and women sat cross-legged in clusters, each group containing one of the missionaries. Cara heard the pleasant murmurs of basic phrases as each side stretched the limits of their new languages, like children trying to have adult conversations.

From atop Pride Rock, Cara watched and listened for a few minutes. Finally, the anticipation overtook her.

"*Geh-geh,*" she called out, gesturing everyone to gather around. "Come, come."

The broken conversations stopped and everyone gathered into a loose semi-circle around the shadow she cast over the earth.

"People of Nacana," Cara began, and Dr. Reising hurried up the incline to interpret. "You are not just Nacana. You are not just people of this jungle. You are people of God, and that is a tribe far bigger than you can imagine. I told you about Heaven, then I told you about Hell. I told you about the paths to each place and that you decide which one to take.

"I taught you the Ten Commandments and the Golden rule. Then I taught you that being good is not good enough. There is still sin that must be washed away. Sin is doing bad things, but it is also *not* doing good.

"When you see a snake behind your friend and you do not tell him, you are sinning. When you see a starving child, but do not feed it, you are sinning. When you allow others to keep someone away from God, you are sinning. When you sin *that* sin, you are punished and they are punished, too."

When the chief perked up, Cara knew she had his attention.

"There is a little boy here," she pointed to the chief's son and Dr. Reising repeated the gesture. Everyone turned and stared at Peak. "A little boy who is very sick. You cry out for him to be healed because Jesus heals the innocent? Though he *is* a child, he is not innocent."

Her adrenaline made her words fly. Dr. Reising could not keep up. She heard him stumbling in his translation, but she could not slow down. She felt the spirit move her.

"No one in this village is saved! There is sin everywhere among you. God punished you by making Peak sick. He will make all your children sick! Only through prayer, repentance, and baptism will God make him better! If you do not convert and come to God...Peak will die! And it will be because of you!" Cara pointed directly at the chief.

"Bloody hell, Cara," Dr. Reising said, turning to her. "I'm not translating that!"

"*Cha-rot*," the chief said. *Stop*. He stood from his place in the circle, pointing back to Cara. "*Cha-rot!*"

Then, the chief lowered his arm and began to move forward. He continued to shout as he crossed the shallow river below Cara. She tried, but couldn't keep up with what he was saying; he was now the one speaking too fast.

Cara took a step back and looked to Dr. Reising.

"He says that he has heard enough," Dr. Reising said, speaking in fragments as he quickly alternated between listening to the chief and translating his words for Cara. "He let us stay for this long...because he wanted to heal his boy...with any medicine or any words."

The chief continued around to the base of Pride Rock, his posture was stern, imposing though he was below Cara.

He was still shouting and Peter continued to interpret. "He says we are doing nothing...but dividing the beliefs of these people...but Peak remains sick. Jesus heals a...cripple. He heals the blind...raises a man from death...but he will not save an innocent boy?"

The chief was now scaling Pride Rock.

"Peak is not innocent!" Cara shouted.

The chief came to a complete halt.

He understood, Cara thought, and continued. "He is not

217

innocent so he must be saved."

"Peak *is* innocent," the chief said. He spoke in broken English. "My boy is most innocent!" Then, he returned to his native tongue with a soft, angry tone.

Dr. Reising's mouth dropped. "He says he wants us gone. Tomorrow."

"Let me take Peak," Cara said in broken Nacana. "Let me take him. I will get him help." At least that's what she had intended to say. The look on Dr. Reising's face suggested that she may have gotten the words wrong.

"In God's name," Dr. Reising said. "Cara, you just threatened to kidnap his son."

The chief drew his spear from his belt.

"No," Cara said. "Tell him what I meant!"

Dr. Reising approached the chief, speaking frantically. The chief pushed him to the ground and Dr. Reising rolled down the rocky incline.

Cara was desperate. She grabbed the chief by his arm. "Please. I will *save* him."

The chief swung an open hand and Cara fell backwards, her head over the edge of Pride Rock. She felt her nose bleeding. Below, she could see the Nacana surrounding the group of missionaries, knives and spears drawn.

Cara turned around to see the chief coming towards her, but both Dr. Reising and Quando stepped in his way, each pleading in their own language for him to stop. The chief, though face red in fury, complied. He took a few steps back, then spoke again.

Dr. Reising interpreted, his words shaky and his eyes full of fear and blame. "If we are not gone by sunrise tomorrow, we will die."

Will 1:9

Whereas Will had over a decade to spend with his mother, Danny barely got a year.

Will never forgot this fact so he shared stories of her any time his little brother asked. Danny had his favorites, like the one about Will's high school dance, when Rita chaperoned and ended up scaring away his bratty date, or the time Will tried to play a prank on his mom by sneaking a duck inside the house while he *thought* she was sleeping. Danny would listen intently to the tales and laugh at all the right moments as Will artificially built the boy's relationship with his mother through words and fading photographs.

When it came to the days surrounding Rita's death, however, Will's memories were few. They had—through some combination of time and subconscious suppression—eroded to the vagueness of a dream. Will was OK with that, though. He never tried too hard to recall that period of his life—never wanted to—and eventually Danny stopped asking. Nevertheless, a few select moments of that afternoon were unable to be shaken away.

Will remembered that his parents had been overdue for a date. They arranged to have Griff come over to babysit while they went out for lunch and ice skating at Mirror Lake. Will remembered seeing his father's truck pull into the drive, much later than expected and with only Richard inside it. It was a long time before he cut the engine. Will remembered lying in his bed, ordered there by his father without explanation. It was Griff who had eventually come in to talk about what had happened. Will's mother had an accident. She had fallen and broken her neck.

Will remembered crying.

That night, Will found himself riding in his grandfather's white Grand Marquis and listening to its chain-wrapped tires grind down the frozen road.

"Your dad appreciates you giving him some time to himself," Griff explained, though Will was old enough to know that he was too young to have a choice.

Will was only away from his father for a few days, but it felt like weeks. The only thing he remembered from his stay at Griff's house was the sleepless nights, helplessly replaying the same one scene. When Griff had tried to usher him past his parents' bedroom, Will caught a glimpse inside. There, he saw his father, hunched over the corner of the bed, sobbing, with his face in his hands.

The first funeral Will attended was his own mother's and the thought of being there so filled him with dread that he almost refused to go. It wasn't about saying goodbye—he was ready for that. He needed that. The fear lay in seeing his father again: the once strong Deacon Battese reduced to the pitiable figure that cried on the bedside.

Will's anxiety only increased as he entered the church that day. St. Andrew's was packed as full as any Easter or Christmas mass. Through handshakes, hugs, and the pianist's gentle hymns, Will walked down the aisle. He felt all eyes on him as he slumped into the reserved front pew, between Griff and baby Danny. Will intertwined his sweaty fingers and tried to think of scenarios in which his father would not show up.

As it turned out, none of those situations came true—but neither did his fears. When his father did appear, there was no sign of that broken man from the bedroom. Richard entered in the procession with the priest and the altar boys, then stood tall over Rita's open casket. Later, when it was time for the priest's sermon, Richard rose from his seat to give it instead. With his large hands grasped peacefully in front of him, Richard made eye contact with Will, gave a quick, gentle smile, then began.

"If God is good," Richard said, while he projected his voice throughout the church, "why does He allow bad things to happen? It is the question we as Christians face every day. There *is* an answer, though it may be hard to find satisfaction in its truth."

Richard gestured to the front row. "My stepfather, Griff, here, once took me to adopt a rescue dog. It was a five- or six-year-old Beagle, and we named him Miracle—I'd like to say I chose the name for biblical reasons, but in actuality it was just to honor the Olympic hockey team.

"Griff and I often took Miracle out into the woods for hikes, and the dog loved it—couldn't get enough of the outdoors. He would run up and down the paths, explore through the bushes and, on this one unfortunate occasion, decided to leap into a giant puddle of mud just *minutes* before we were to load back into the car.

"Griff uttered some choice words, unsuitable for me to repeat here in the house of the Lord," Richard paused while the audience laughed, with Griff possibly the loudest, then continued. "What you don't realize is that Griff did not curse because his car was going to get a little muddy, he cursed because our Miracle would be needing a bath.

"Now, I do not believe that animals have the capacity for hate, but if any came close, it would have been Miracle and his aversion to our cast iron tub. Miracle loathed the confinement, he shook with fear at the roar of the shower and the rough, foreign textures scrubbing against his body. This particular day seemed the worst of all; we could barely hold him still as he squirmed and yelped and growled. And then, when I came forward with the sponge...Miracle lunged and bit me.

"I was in shock. I looked down at my bleeding hand as Miracle bolted down the hallway, leaving behind a trail of suds. My hand turned out fine—the bite didn't even leave a scar—but I couldn't get over the question of 'why?' *Why would he do that?* Despite the fact that we rescued him from the shelter, despite the fun hikes we took him on, despite the fact that his food and water bowls were never empty, despite all of the attention and the petting and the treats, all the love we gave him, all Miracle could believe during that bath was that *I* was the enemy.

"There was no way that I could explain to Miracle: I am cleaning you, detangling you, freeing you of fleas and ticks that would otherwise bring you pain and disease. I am trying to help you, protect you—please trust me."

Richard paused again. "Do you see the connection? Jesus tells us the same thing in John, Chapter 14, Verse 1: 'Do not let your hearts be troubled. Trust in God; trust also in me.' As Christians, we confess that God is almighty and that He is eternally wise, yet we often pride ourselves to believe that His intentions should conform to our logic. When it can't, it hurts us, angers us. It *offends* us and we begin to resent Him, but we are *wrong* for that. We are wrong because the truth is that our minds simply cannot grasp His plan for us, the same way Miracle could never grasp mine for him.

"And I cannot grasp," Richard's mouth quivered for a moment, but he steadied it with a deep breath, "why He took my Rita away from me—from my sons—but I remember that God's plan for us comes from a love so strong that we should take comfort—and not offense—in its mysteries. As the prophet Isaiah says in Chapter 40, Verse 8: 'the grass withers, the flower fades, but the word of our God will stand forever.' I ask you all to forever trust in it."

The sermon resonated with Will from that day forward, and he applied it not only to the death of his mother, but even to the smallest crevices of his life. If he was late for class or if a girl he liked stood him up at the movies, it was where God wanted him to be.

Will was God's Miracle.

But there was a difference between giving your dog a bath and breaking all of its legs.

Will no longer accepted God's plan. How could he? He hung from his wrists in the darkness, betrayed by at least three people he trusted. They had kidnapped his son, committed unspeakable acts of violence, and tried to use his family as meat in a Satanic ritual. In the wake of it all, good people were murdered: Gustavo, Leigha, Kavi, Griff, and Jessi...or Shannon.

What kind of plan is that? Will wondered in the pitch black auditorium. *We were the wrong people for their ritual but you let them take us anyway. All the people that died are dead for nothing! The rest of us are just a bunch of dud fireworks, waiting to be doused and swept away.*

And what kind of people are you letting roam free? Ones that make pacts with demons? Will believed evil people existed, though until now they were just names and faces on the television, no more real to him than a killer in one of his slasher films. But *demons?* Will supposed they existed, too. They were specifically mentioned in the Bible. If God said they exist, then Will guessed it wasn't really a question.

What perplexed Will, however, was the Eden's idea of a voluntary demonic possession. All four gospels mentioned evil spirits forcing themselves into human hosts, but Degas claimed he could do it willingly. Will didn't want to believe it. He didn't want to believe the devil's minions had anything to do with the Edens, yet he could not explain the blood running down Degas's arm, the scorching wind, or the mysterious scream. *Nothing a small-time special effects studio couldn't do*, Will reasoned, *but then...what if it was real? Maybe we needed to be the wrong people for the ritual. What if it had* actually *succeeded?*

No! Stop defending God. He doesn't get excused for what He's done!

Will heard a door open on the far side of the auditorium.

A flashlight swept faintly in the darkness, like a lighthouse at the edge of a moonless night's sea. It was a perverse beacon, however, for it led Will away from the thoughts of the failed ritual to one even worse: *They're coming for us.*

Shadows formed and hurried down the aisle with heavy

footsteps—two figures were approaching. The one that held the light arrived at the stage first and directed the beam upwards.

Will was face to face with his wife.

"No," Will sputtered. "No, not you, too." He felt the tears surge up again. Nothing could hurt him more than this.

Shannon froze for a moment, then her eyebrows shot down in anger.

She slapped him across the face.

"You think I'm with them?" She smacked him again, harder. The sound of the impact echoed in the darkness.

Will felt his face flush and the tears swell anew.

"I'm here to rescue you, you *idiot!*"

As she shouted, Will saw the gap in her teeth and the bluish purple bruise that had formed over her cheek. There was dried blood caked on one of her ears and along her front hairline. *What had she gone through to get here?* Will wondered. Feverishly, he searched for the words to apologize, but nothing came out.

"How about a thank you?" Shannon said, still sounding angry, but no longer yelling.

"I'm so sorry, Shannon," said Will. "I mean, thank you. And I'm sorry." When his wife didn't reply, he continued. "I didn't know what to think, OK? Haynes, the Benteras, they were all in on it—"

"What? *Abe and Sara*?" Shannon asked, raising her voice again.

"They planned it all, to *take* us," Will continued. "They wanted a sacrifice..."

"Enough!" said the other cloaked figure, coming up onto the stage. His voice was a stern whisper; one Will did not recognize. "Here," the stranger said to Shannon. "I need the light to free them. Move. Here, point it at his wrists." Shannon obeyed, stepping to the side. When she redirected the light, her face disappeared into the darkness.

The stranger bent forward and squinted for a better look. In the low light, his deep-set eyes appeared void of emotion—a portrait of a skeleton's gaze. "Thick ropes," he said, "this will take a minute." He removed a tactical switchblade knife from somewhere and flipped it open. "I've never seen handcuffs like these, the inside is lined with *what*? Some type of padding?" He looked up at Will. "They sure wanted to make you comfortable, huh?"

"Who are you?" Will asked, which to Will was the more pressing question.

"Just let me work," the man snapped.

"He calls himself Bass," Shannon said. "He's working undercover."

"Does that mean he'll help us find Giddy?"

"Wait. Where the fuck is Giddy?"

"Abe and Sara. They wanted him…so they took him."

Shannon jerked her head towards Bass. "Well we need to get him *back*!"

"Not a priority now," Bass said without looking up. "I never met your neighbors, but I eavesdropped on their conversation with Degas. It seems they genuinely care for the baby. It's unlikely that he'll be harmed."

"And that makes it OK?" Shannon responded, then turned her attention back to Will. "You thought I joined a cult so I could let those old fucks steal my own baby?"

"No," Will responded. "I don't know—*oof!*" He grunted as his right arm fell free. Bass had succeeded in sawing through the first rope; Will was able to drop down off his tiptoes. The relief was immense.

"Pull tight," Bass ordered, referring to the rope securing Will's other arm. Will yanked back, getting rid of the slack, but before Bass even raised his blade, the rope snapped from behind the backdrop.

"What the…" Bass said, stepping forward to examine the rope. "That was pretty sloppy. It must have already had a tear in it..."

Are you kidding me? Will thought. *I thought I was pulling as hard as I could before.*

But the sight of his wife overshadowed his self-pity. "Shannon..." Will started, but didn't finish. His legs were half-asleep and tingling, but he forced himself to waddle over to her and wrapped her in his arms. "I'm sorry."

"It's OK, I get it," Shannon said, and she returned the hug.

"Light *please*," Bass reminded her unsympathetically, "there's two more people hanging here."

"Three," Shannon corrected.

"No..." Will said. "There's just two."

"But I saw—" Shannon cut herself off and ran the beam of light over the bodies on stage. When it landed on Griff, she dropped the flashlight. There was a loud crack, but the bulb stayed lit.

"Dammit!" Bass said. He picked it up and shoved it forcefully back into her hands. "I need you to focus."

"You knew?" Shannon snapped.

"I did. I saw it happen. Now do what I tell you to do or else we're all going to have our throats slashed."

Shannon wiped away her tears with her sleeve then went over to Danny. She stepped forward to pull away Danny's gag, but Bass stepped in front of her. "Leave it in," he snarled. "I'm tired of all the talk."

Shannon stared at Bass for a second, then removed the gag anyway.

"I'll be quiet," said Danny to Bass.

"You *all* better," he replied, shaking his head.

In the silence, Bass worked through Danny's ropes quickly. When the little boy dropped, he thanked Bass and Bass ignored him. Shannon pulled Danny over to her for a hug as well.

Richard was the last to be freed. When he dropped, he removed his own gag and gave Bass a firm nod. "What now?"

"Now, everyone follows me," said Bass, one foot already on the steps. "I'll get you to the surface. Shannon has a car ready." Then he abruptly stopped and turned around. "Do *not* go after the baby; Degas will alert your neighbors as soon as he realizes you escaped. They'll be gone, but other Edens will be watching the house. You'll be caught and killed. So again, it's best that you just consider your son safe for now. I give you my word that once things stabilize, I will find a way to get him back to you."

"And then what?" Shannon asked. "Our home is full of dead bodies. We have to explain that!" She turned towards Will. "He says we can't contact the police."

"Aren't you with the police?" Will asked.

"No," Bass replied fiercely. "And if you send them here, you won't get your revenge. The Edens will be tipped off and they'll scatter. They'll regroup and come at you stronger than you can imagine. These are evil people—goddammit, I know—but people with *reach*. I'm here to learn more about them. If you sound the alarm, the Vatican loses everything they've worked for."

"What?" asked Richard? "You're with the Vatican?"

After a brief hesitation, Bass seemed to be choosing his words carefully. "You heard me right. Just know that I have a lot more authority than you, deacon. So stop asking questions."

At that point, Bass pulled out a pen and a worn Polaroid picture of a large ranch-style home. Resting it on his knee, he wrote quickly. "Drive to this address and follow these instructions," he said, then handed it to Richard who studied the handwriting on the back. "You'll be safe there until my people arrive," Bass continued. "When they do—and if they're not welcoming—show them this photo. Tell them what happened and that I'm alright."

Richard nodded, then slipped his hand around his robe, searching for a pocket.

"Inside your right breast," said Bass. "Now let's go."

Richard found the pocket and slipped the photograph inside.

"Wait," said Will. "Bass, you watched...the entire ritual?"

"Yeah."

"Pia...is she still alive?"

"...Yeah," Bass answered reluctantly. He understood Will's implication. "Forget it. I barely have time to get your family out."

"Pia?" Shannon asked. "The cleaner from your restaurant? She's here?"

"And she's staying here," said Bass.

"Please," Will urged. "She's a good person."

Shannon grabbed her husband's hand. "For God's sake, Will. You don't owe that woman *anything*!"

"She doesn't have anyone to come for her," Will argued back.

"I already said *no*!" Bass shouted.

There was a brief silence in the auditorium, then Danny stepped in from the shadows. "What are they going to do to her?"

"Bad things, kid," said Bass. And almost on cue, the flashlight flickered.

"Bass," said Richard, coming to Will's side. "Is there *any* way you can get her out? What if Will takes Shannon and Danny to the car. I can stay to help you."

"We are not splitting up," Shannon argued.

"That's right," said Bass.

"Please," said Will with pleading eyes. "I don't know you— and I know we'd have ended up dead or worse if you hadn't come along, but I can't leave knowing we abandoned her. Even if we fail, we would know we tried, we—"

"You think I give a shit about your goddamn conscience?" Bass snapped. The reply was so fast it sounded like one long word. "Degas says you're a devout Catholic, that you trust in God's plan." He got nose to nose with Will. "Do you know what's going to happen to Pia? As soon as her stump stops bleeding, she's going to be passed off to the Mongrels—they're the 'less sophisticated' Devil worshippers in this social circle. She'll be tortured, raped, mutilated, and, if she's still young enough,

228

she'll be used to breed little Mongrel babies. *That's* God's plan. He wants Pia to *suffer* and *die*. Who are you to question Him?" He left a stunned Will at the top of the stairs.

"I'll scream," said Shannon, running down towards him. "I'll scream right now and tell everyone you're a traitor." She looked back up to Will with a frown. He could practically feel Shannon's regret. *Somehow she found me,* he thought, *and found someone that can break us out. Escape is right in front of us, and here I am gambling it all away.*

Bass's shoulders tensed and he turned his body around almost robotically towards Shannon. Will believed that the threat had worked; Bass's cover was too important to him, he was giving in.

But Bass didn't give in. Instead, he struck Shannon in the neck with the side of his open hand. She fell to her knees, holding her throat and croaking like some sort of bullfrog.

"Threaten me again," said Bass, "and I'll tear out your tongue."

"No!" Will cried out in surprise and rage, but it was Richard who shot down the stairs in Shannon's defense. Will refused to let himself freeze up this time and followed in his father's footsteps.

Bass drew his knife, releasing the blade and holding it out, ready to strike. Will and Richard stopped in their tracks.

"You guys think you're helping!" Bass seemed to forget his own no yelling rule. The shouting caused him to clutch his side with his free hand. "You think you're being *heroic*? What I'm doing has *worldwide* ramifications!"

Bass held the knife as his face twisted with conflicting emotions. "Goddammit," Bass said. "Goddammit, OK. We'll try to save her." He lowered his weapon. "But you all listen good. If we get into a position that compromises my cover, I will kill you myself."

Shannon 1:8

Intense claustrophobia swept over Shannon when Bass locked her in the control room. It took tremendous effort for her not to scream or hammer her fists against the door. She knew that Bass was already gone and her commotion would serve only to draw the non-friendly cultists to her location.

Be patient, Shannon told herself. *And calm down.* She leaned back against the door and combed her fingers through her disheveled hair. The gesture used to relax her, but now it just aggravated her existing injuries. It was a type of helplessness akin to Will never being able to itch the bottom of his feet without tickling himself.

But even more frustrating for Shannon was her inability to be mad at Bass. *He's rude and a liar,* she thought. *He tricked me and abandoned me...but at least I'm still alive. He's still helping me, right? Out there somewhere, hatching a plan?*

Yes, she believed. *I just wish he'd left the fucking lights on.*

Although her faith in Bass remained, Shannon had no plans to remain idle. *Find another light source,* she commanded herself. *Bass ducked out of here so quick—there has to be something he forgot about. A circuit breaker? A backup generator? A laptop?*

Despite her degree in interior design, Shannon found that she was unable to recall much about the layout or the details of the room. She resorted to using the wall-hugger approach instead: placing her palms against the wall next to the door, then sliding them up and down as she strafed along in search of illumination.

Within seconds, she came across a light switch. She flicked it a few times, but nothing happened. *Yeah...that would have been too easy,* she told herself. *What else we got?* She continued forward, feeling around for anything useful when...*WHAM!*

Shannon's forehead slammed against an object mounted to the wall. The impact gave off a thin, metallic ring sounding very much like the large, hanging cabinet she now remembered had been there. She touched her forehead with her fingers. Blood was already trickling from the new wound—surely another scar in the making. *Put it on my tab*, she thought, and felt a nutty grin possess her.

"Oh...I'm going insane," she said aloud, but her missing tooth made it into "insthane." It was too much for Shannon to handle and she exploded into both laughter and tears. It took a minute for the maniacal episode to clear. When it did, Shannon took the time to investigate the object and realized it was actually a large, hanging, *locked* cabinet.

She had no choice but to continue on past it, though slower now, and with wider, almost theatrical sweeps of her arms to prevent further injuries or breakdowns of sanity. The technique proved successful in evading a few more obstacles, but failed to produce a light source, and ultimately brought her full circle back to the door.

One more idea, she thought, and detached herself from the wall. Shuffling towards what she believed to be the center of the room, she managed to find the computer chair she had sat in earlier. From there, she reached out to the security terminal. Like an unsupervised toddler, she pressed through all the buttons, trying to get the screen to light up. She never really believed that it would. And it didn't.

Defeated, she slouched in the chair and found it to be quite comfortable. It wasn't long before her eyelids fell and her mind drifted away.

†

Somewhere there was music and Shannon was dancing.

A dusty, wooden clock above a turntable revealed a familiar location: The Cuckoo's Nest. Shannon had been a regular at this Santa Monica nightclub throughout high school, particularly because the doormen had never noticed—or perhaps didn't care—that her ID was fake.

The Nest's DJ wore green plastic sunglasses with a four-leaf clover molded around each lens. Strobe lights flashed over a crowd of college kids decorated with cheap beads, hats, and t-shirts that advertised them as Irish for the night. The house music was steady, but Shannon's sways began to lose rhythm. Eventually, it reached the point where her movements couldn't be considered dancing at all, but merely her body's instinctive efforts not to fall over. Shannon had lost count of how many pints of Guinness were in her system, but she still wanted another.

After the break-up she had just been through, Shannon welcomed the escape that the alcohol provided. She knew that escape would be temporary, but as she headed towards the bar, she realized that now it was already over.

Shannon didn't need to see straight to see that it was him. He had found her. He always did, her ex-boyfriend, though he never agreed to that title. It just made him more possessive. Shannon watched helplessly as he charged towards her. The floor swayed like a catamaran in the bay, though the only balance it seemed to affect was her own.

He got to her. He grabbed her and he shook her. The music kept playing; it didn't care about them. He shouted something, but Shannon couldn't focus on the words. She hated him. He raised a fist and it shot towards her. She didn't feel it, but the force sent her to the floor. She wanted Will. Will would never hit her. But she wouldn't meet him for another year. Not until she had decided to escape from California for good. It wasn't time yet and she wasn't ready.

Shannon shot awake from the nightmare. This time, it was Bass who shook her.

"Wake up," he said with some urgency in his voice. Shannon looked around. She was still in the security room, though it was illuminated now by a trail of soft, white LEDs along the baseboards, like the kind of lights used in movie theater or airplane aisles. "Come on, girl. Wake up."

"My name is *Sthannon*," she slurred.

"Right," he said, but did not repeat it. "We have an opportunity to save your family now. Are you ready?" The look in his eyes was different somehow; Shannon couldn't place it. It seemed distant and tired.

"Are you ready?" he asked again.

Shannon nodded groggily. It wasn't enough to convince him.

"Collect yourself for a minute," he instructed, and walked over to the mounted cabinet—the same one that Shannon had unwittingly head-butted earlier. From his tiptoes, he reached to the top of the unit and grabbed a key. With it, he unlocked the cabinet door and pulled out a flashlight.

"You're kidding me," Shannon said, causing Bass to glance back.

"What?"

"I came real close to finding that," she said, tapping her forehead.

Expressionless, Bass turned back towards the cabinet and grabbed a first aid kit.

"Yes, please," Shannon smiled.

"Do it yourself," Bass said, handing over the kit. "I need a minute." He wheeled Shannon away from the terminal, then hunched over it himself. "I may have been a bit overzealous when I cut off the power in here. It disabled the cameras, but I forgot to delete the earlier footage of me—you know—killing two men that Degas personally recruited. I'm rebooting so I can take care of that now."

"That's a big thing to forget, huh?"

"I've got a lot on my mind."

"Risking your life and your cover for strangers. I get it," she said, peeling open a Band-Aid. The strip folded back onto itself in her shaky hands. She picked at it with her nails while Bass punched away on the computer.

Bass finished first. "Done. Ready?"

Fuck it, Shannon thought, and tossed the Band-Aid to the floor. "Let's go."

†

It did strike Shannon that she had never thanked Bass for anything, not when he rescued her from the guards nor when he agreed to sneak her inside the complex. Now, he had just freed her family from the auditorium. As Bass led the exodus of Batteses, barefoot and robes flowing, through the Satanic halls, Shannon felt yet another thanks was due. She also felt, however, that Bass deserved a hearty *fuck you* for chopping her throat, so she considered the whole thing a draw and said nothing.

Pia was being held in the infirmary..."*probably*," Bass had said before they left the stage. He explained that because she was to be kept alive, the Edens would have to stop the bleeding, and the infirmary was the most likely place to do it. Shannon thought it was impressive that there even *was* such a place and she wondered how large this complex really was. Regardless, if Pia wasn't in the infirmary, Bass said that she could be anywhere. If that turned out to be the case, his deal with Will to save her would be off.

Bass did not explain where exactly the infirmary was, but instead revealed the path step by step. He was consistently a few strides ahead, which made Shannon a bit nervous. He also remained silent, save for answering three radio check-ins (once as himself and twice more with very convincing Irish and maybe-African accents). He assured Gregos that everything was in order and, in essence, that none of the guards were dead and buried in the snow outside.

At one intersection, Bass raised a closed fist just above his shoulder. He had never trained the group on any hand signals, but they all seemed to understand the meaning: *freeze*. Shannon heard footsteps, then saw Bass slowly drawing his switchblade. She remembered his promise: *if my position is compromised, I will kill you myself*. She took a step backward, her eyes trained on Bass. But the footsteps faded and Bass sheathed his weapon. He waved the group forward, then continued on through a door and up a narrow flight of stairs, finally stopping at the top.

"Out this door and at the end of the hall is the infirmary," Bass explained. "Everyone stay here. Except you," he pointed at Shannon. "You'll come with me. We'll enter together," Bass spoke slower. "We'll enter *calmly*. I don't think many Edens will be inside. Tell them that you've been injured. I'll likely kill them before they figure out you're not one of us—them."

"Likely?" asked Will. "No. Take me instead."

"Use your head," Bass shot back. "Look at yourself. You're still in sacrificial robes."

"He's right," said Richard.

"Your wife can handle this," said Bass.

"I got this, babe," Shannon said to Will, and redressed her uniform's face wrap.

"Then let's go," Bass said, and pulled her away before the family could say another word.

Together, the two walked briskly down the hall, but before they reached the door which led to the infirmary, a man in a charcoal suit and dark green tie strolled around the corner from another hallway ahead of them. He, Shannon, and Bass all came to a sudden halt in front of each other.

The man smiled. He had an aging, but handsome, tanned face and a dark-blond Caesar haircut. "In a hurry there, brother? Sister?" The man asked, his voice deep, smooth, and friendly enough.

"The name's Bass. Security."

"And I'm Jan Barnard, a guest." The man answered, but did not attempt a handshake, nor did he move any closer. "And you,

Miss?"

The last thing Shannon wanted to do is butcher her name with her recent speech impediment and sore throat, but Bass gave her an uncomfortable glance that said "answer him."

"Beck-ky," she said, grossly over-articulating. She followed it up with an awkward wave that included a wiggling of her fingers. *Jesus*, she thought, fighting the urge to cringe. *I'm going to get us killed.*

But Jan held his smile and stepped closer. He was now within a couple feet of them. "Nice to meet you, Becky. And Bass, security. *Is* everything secure?"

"It is, but we're looking for the widow," Bass answered. "Why are you still here? Missek ordered everyone to clear out."

"I'm hailing all the way from Johannesburg, brother. And I have the archbishop's permission to tour the legendary St. Herodias while I wait to speak with Degas."

"After the Sentencing, Degas may not be in the mood for chatting. His failure has tarnished the reputation—the *legend*—of this place."

Jan's voice became solemn. "Don't be so harsh on your brother, *young brother*. St. Herodias has reaped two successful *bar yetzer haras* in its history, more than any other parish."

"That was before my time," said Bass.

"You're still old enough to understand that simply having a member chosen to attempt the ritual is worthy of praise."

"Perhaps," Bass responded.

"And don't forget the wedding!" Jan's smiled returned. "Though a bit of a spectacle for my tastes, surely the symbolic division of Catholic marriage is always enjoyable?" Jan looked at Shannon and she nodded agreeably, though she wasn't sure what symbolism he was referring to. Truthfully, she didn't want to know.

"Speaking of which," Jan continued, "the widow is no longer in the infirmary. Not long ago, I paid a visit to the Mamertine—

another one of your parish's landmarks worthy of coveting. I saw her being transported inside. You'll be pleased to know she is fully distraught." Jan spoke the last sentence with a large smile.

"Good," Shannon said, trying to sound gruff. Jan stepped forward again. Shannon could smell him now, a mix of salt water and scotch.

"Do either of you know her fate by the way?"

"As of now," Bass answered, "she's still property of Biana and Pavel, but I believe the Mongrels will be receiving her."

"A shame." Jan sighed. "There is no imagination in *physical* torture." He looked at Shannon again, holding his gaze longer now. He lowered his voice to what was nearly a whisper. "Perhaps Degas would give her to me instead. I would make her *truly* suffer."

"It's worth a try," Bass said. "But we need to be on our—"

"You know, Becky," Jan said, cutting Bass off without even looking in his direction. "It was Becky, right?" Shannon nodded again and her unease grew. "I met him once before—Victor Degas. He visited us at St. Cain's in South Africa, back when he first claimed to be courting Decaar. At the top of his agenda was to cage dive with the great white sharks, of all things. I was the one tasked with arranging the private charter. When the time came, I was honored enough to have him invite me, and me alone, to accompany him on his voyage. We spent an entire day at sea and although we saw over a dozen dorsal fins on the horizon, not a single shark ventured close to the boat."

"Not much of a story," Shannon said. Bass shot her a look, then regained his composure.

"Oh, but it is!" Jan smiled warmly. "You see, the captain of the ship had a homemade chum that practically *guaranteed* encounters with the sharks—not just a glimpse through binoculars. The captain told us that the recipe had worked for the last seven years, but that day, for the first time ever, the sharks avoided the boat like the plague. We never even dropped our cage into the water. There was no point.

"I later found Degas standing at the front of the boat, hands clasped behind his back. I approached him to apologize, but when he turned to me, he was smiling. He said that this had been a test. When I admitted that I did not understand, he told me to read the Bible! *Ha!* Particularly the story of Daniel and the Lions. After I did, I believed in Victor Degas. What I *never* believed, however, was that he would fail his final test tonight."

"Nor did I," Bass agreed. "It saddens me greatly. More than you know."

But Jan continued on as if he didn't hear him. "Degas *would* have summoned the demon successfully...if only he had memorized his lines correctly, kneeling at the altar. Isn't that correct, Becky?"

Shannon started to nod, but before her chin completed the gesture, Jan was already reaching for the large blade in his belt.

But Bass drew quicker. He grabbed Jan's wrist with one hand and stuck the switchblade into his heart with the other. Jan had a look of disbelief that Shannon almost fully understood. She had had her share of near-death experiences today and knew how surreal it felt: the sensation that this really could be it—the end of *me*. She watched Jan's face as his life faded out of him and he collapsed to the floor in Bass's arms.

When the last of Jan's spasms ended, Bass removed the knife from his chest. Very little blood spilled out and Shannon bet that that was skill—not luck—on Bass's part.

"How did he know?" Shannon asked.

"Memorizing lines wasn't part of the ritual. He was suspicious of you, but hid it well. He tricked you. I almost didn't see it coming." Bass stood up. "Hurry, let's get him back to the stairwell." He bent over the body, gripping under Jan's armpits. Shannon grabbed his feet.

This was the third body Shannon had helped Bass dispose of

so far this night, and by her lack of hesitation she wondered if she was already becoming desensitized to death.

"What is the Mamertine?" she asked as they dragged the body down the hall.

"It's the Eden's prison, at the lowest level of this building."

"Why the *schtoopid*—why the weird name? Why not just...the prison?"

If three kills were enough to desensitize Shannon and make conversation come easy, Bass spoke as if he had killed thousands. "The Mamertine *was* a prison, in ancient Rome. Saint Peter was incarcerated there and said to have performed a miracle by summoning a river inside. He used its water for baptisms. Edens like to tarnish good names—irreverence is their inspiration—so the intent was that this time, the *Mamertine* would be miracle-free."

"Until tonight," Shannon corrected. "When we bust Pia out."

Bass didn't answer, but used his back to push open the door to the stairwell. Shannon looked up and exchanged looks of relief with her family. Danny stepped forward, staring silently at the body.

"Goddammit," Bass cursed, "Eh...cover your eyes, little boy."

"I don't think I need to anymore," Danny answered.

Nobody objected.

Degas 1:4

The archbishop of St. Herodias sat slumped behind his crooked desk. Books were all around him, covering every inch of wall. They contrasted with the wilted man, the books, standing tall and orderly on antique wooden shelves that rose to meet the twenty-foot-high ceiling. The impressive sight led parishioners to nickname Lawrence Missek's oversized office "The Library."

And Missek treated it accordingly. It was a place of knowledge and of study. Not once had Degas entered without finding the archbishop poring over a volume, scribbling notes, or operating (quite adeptly) the rolling ladder in search of the next item on his agenda. He believed that every book in the room served a specific purpose in the Edens' war against God. There were volumes on psychology, medicine, and linguistics—and just as many on witchcraft and alchemy. *Understand the body and understand the mind*, Missek taught. *You must twist both to warp the soul.*

Also among the shelves were Holy Bibles of every translation. Missek knew both testaments better than most believers and encouraged all Edens to strive for the same. *The* Word *is the truth and, like Satan, we must mix it with lies.* Texts of other religions were available as well, including multiple copies of the Torah, Qur'an, Bhagavad-Gita, and Guru Granth Sahib. Any form of monotheistic belief was to be understood and discouraged, as Missek believed it was dangerously easy for those followers to convert to Christianity.

In his visits to The Library, Degas spent the most of his time in Demonology. This vast section contained the more commonly available titles like the *Clavicula Salomonis* as well as one-of-a-kind scrolls and manuscripts describing entities whose names had not been spoken for centuries. Those texts were only available for study with Missek's express permission and supervision. It took years for Degas to earn it.

Only two items were off limits: a pair of ancient books, each as thick as his flexed bicep, that sat in separate corners of The Library. Their tattered, leather bindings were brown and maroon, but lacked any text or inscriptions, leaving Degas to only guess at the contents. They were sealed inside tempered glass displays with Missek being rumored to have the only key, though no one could recall ever seeing it.

Too much knowledge destroys, Missek claimed, the first and only time Degas inquired about them. *We'd be wise to learn from the mistakes of Adam.* Though the archbishop had spoken that warning with a smile, it was clear that the conversation was over. He had gone on to pour them both a cup of blooming tea from a transparent tea pot. Degas had pointed out that the unfurled bundle of jasmine resembled a tentacled monster emerging from a murky sea.

"Who *is* like the beast?" Missek replied with his always quick wit. "Who is able to make war with him?" The reference to Revelation made the two men laugh.

But that was then. The atmosphere in The Library was much different now.

After Degas's failed ritual, Missek was neither speaking nor smiling. Degas watched from the opposite side of a slanted desk as his longtime mentor and friend refused to make eye contact with him. The old man hung his head, his eyes shifting beneath ptotic lids, searching for the right words to begin the inevitable.

Degas could feel Missek's pity—something he had never experienced from the archbishop before. Quite the opposite, while Degas's colobomas often elicited pity from others, Missek had always encouraged him to embrace the deformity, letting it serve as a constant reminder of God's flaws.

Degas could no longer bear the silence and spoke first. "Whose *bones* are those?" he asked. The question had been gnawing at him since he first entered The Library tonight. Missek had gotten a new desk and it seemed to be made entirely of human skeletons.

The piece was structurally simple—and with the absence of drawers and cabinets, more resembled a table. The only decoration was an array of phalanges along the perimeter of the writing surface, sticking diagonally outward like the spikes of medieval cheavaux-de-frise. For support, a combination of femurs, tibias, and fibulas were fused together to form the legs, which then connected to small skulls (bottom jaws removed) that served as each foot. Their sizes all varied slightly, resulting in the desk's innate tilt.

"These were once orphans from New Delhi, I'm told," Missek answered with a sigh. "There are pieces from at least forty children, anywhere from newborns to ten years old."

Degas nodded slowly. He didn't like it. The whole thing seemed cartoony and out of place in such a noble room. "We used to share a distaste for killing innocent children. Now you showcase it?"

That seemed to jolt Missek from his spell. His eyes shot up at Degas. "I'm not *proud* of this," he stated, though with patience, not anger. "But it was a gift from St. Putna's."

"And you accepted it? Doesn't that send the wrong message?"

Degas, like most Edens, believed the act of murdering a child was wasteful. It did little more than give the young soul a free pass to Heaven. There was no chance of corruption. To truly hurt God, children must be spared; allow them to grow out of their innocence, lead them into a life of sin, and *then* kill them, while their backs are turned to God, so that His own laws forbid Him from calling them home.

Missek shook his head. "My views haven't changed, Victor, but taking an immoral high ground isn't worth insulting India's archbishop."

"Even if he's acting like a Mongrel?"

"Yes," Missek said sternly. "Some prefer sacrificing their

lambs, others prefer feasting upon them. Satan understands the occasional indulgence."

"But *forty*? That's beyond gluttony. Not to mention the huge risk he took." It was the other disadvantage of killing children: the risk of spiritual rebound it brought. Massacres of children rarely resulted in a net loss of faith. Instead, every priest, reverend, and religious leader came rushing in to rally their congregations. They banded together for love and support, prayers and donations, and reassurances of God's mysterious ways. A small number of believers might question their faith and lose their way, but as a whole, tragedy rekindled Christianity's torch.

"It was a dangerous thing, yes," Missek agreed. "But used sparingly, used delicately—have you forgotten how pleasurable it is to torture children? To watch their undeveloped mind attempt to comprehend the senseless violence against them? I was assured each piece from this desk came from a boy or girl that suffered for *weeks*."

"I haven't forgotten," Degas replied, realizing he was being hypocritical. "I agree that there are situations where killing a child is acceptable, necessary even. I did not mean to start an argument."

"It's quite alright," Missek said, and leaned forward to rest an elbow on the desk, making the whole thing wobble. "If I'm going to be upset at anything, it would be that this thing provides *zero* functionality! Look here at the desktop. They made it by gluing the little ones' sternums and scapulas together, but the carpentry work is sloppy. There are so many imperfections that I can barely sign my name! Not to mention these kids' bones wouldn't fully develop for another ten years. I can hear them start to crack when more than one book rests atop it."

"You mean they're more fragile than yours?" Degas asked, managing to lead Missek into an honest laugh. The archbishop quickly caught himself and cut it off with another sigh. Degas could tell that his friend had clung to the small talk for as long as possible.

It was time for the Sentencing. Any demon that presents itself for a *bar yetzer hara* is one that has enormous faith in their chosen Eden. If the ritual fails, that demon is deeply shamed and seeks vengeance. It is the role of an archbishop to make it happen. Following a failure, the archbishop meets alone with the participant and channels the demon in order to convey its wishes. Sentences in the past had varied, depending on the demon's mercy, and had most commonly included imprisonment, banishment, castration, and death.

The impending Sentencing weighed visibly on Missek. Despite the friendship between him and Degas, the archbishop must carry out the demon's orders or else face the wrath of Satan himself. Finally, Missek lifted his eyes from his desktop. "What happened tonight, Victor?"

"I can't give you a satisfying answer," said Degas, and the response was truthful.

Missek nodded and sat still for a few moments. His slow, congested breathing was the only sound in the room other than a single pop from one of the candles in the brass chandelier above them.

After a few moments, Missek cleared his throat. "Before I begin, I want you to know that I am proud of you. With my initial shock at your failure came disappointment—how could it not? But my pride in you remains. Just being chosen for a *bar yetzer hara* is an honor beyond words. For the decades that I've led the parish, I've never been approached for one. I must admit I harbored a degree of jealousy after you were chosen—though I never doubted your worthiness.

"Nor did I ever expect you to fail. If anything, I thought the challenge was too easy, too simple for someone with your intelligence. Ending a Catholic bloodline? I felt as if any Mongrel could do that—but I never questioned you. It wasn't my place. I thought perhaps with Decaar's unusual affinity for you, the *bar yetzer hara* was merely a formality. I'm truly surprised that what went wrong, went wrong.

"Nonetheless, please know that if it were up to me, there would be no punishment. I believe that Decaar leaving you—taking with him all the perks you've no doubt grown accustomed to, all the power—would be punishment enough."

Degas opened his mouth to speak, but was then quiet.

Missek picked up on the hesitation. "Decaar *has* left you, Victor...hasn't he?"

Degas could no longer maintain his composure. He smiled widely.

Missek's eyes widened, then he squeezed them shut. He was channeling Decaar, listening for his whispers as he would for the Sentencing.

"Yes!" the archbishop cried, opening his eyes again. He was gleaming. "Yes, it's true! I've never witnessed this—never *heard* of this. Remarkable that he would give you this type of faith. He is allowing you to try again? No, that can't be right—"

"He says you will know in due time," Degas interrupted.

"Ah *ha*! I knew you two were keeping something from me. It is rare for me to be humbled so. It's refreshing." Missek stood up with a decrepit grin, something that to Degas was a pleasurable sight.

"Well," said Missek, "I shall not hinder whatever else must be done. Do you still need the rest of the Battese family? Is that why they are still alive?"

"I gave the baby away, but the rest are still in the auditorium. I will see to them soon."

"Splendid."

Degas stood as well; it was time to go. "Anything else I can do for you, archbishop?"

"No, Victor," Missek reached out and gave Degas a vigorous handshake. "Is there anything I can do for *you*?"

Degas 1:5

Haynes stood, arms crossed, outside the arched double doors of The Library as Degas emerged from them. Degas knew immediately that there was a problem.

"I was about to interrupt you," Haynes said shakily.

"What happened?"

"We don't know exactly," Haynes answered. Degas could see a hint of moisture near Haynes's hairline. "I went to the control room to monitor the family, but the cameras were disabled." He began to speak faster. "I checked the night's recordings and they were *all* erased. I don't know who could have done this."

"Decaar is present, Haynes. Watch your anxiety."

Haynes nodded with a grunted laugh. "It's so easy to get lost in his aura."

"He only amplifies what is already inside you. Steady your emotions and come this way." Degas lead Haynes away from The Library doors, stopping a few yards away at a human-sized statue of Belaal. "I don't want the archbishop overhearing us."

"You didn't tell him?"

"Not everything. He knows Decaar is still with me and he has given me free reign. Now, what happened to our security team?"

"They're nowhere to be found," Haynes answered, sounding more composed. "Kokayi, Bass, Quinn…they are all answering their radio check-ins. 'Aware of the problem,' they say. 'Making rounds, heading back to control now,' but they don't come. And none of us have physically seen them. Something didn't feel right, though I did not want to broadcast my concern over the radio. I rushed to the auditorium instead. Will was already gone…but so were Richard and Daniel."

That was not the plan, Degas felt an inner twinge of panic. "Have they escaped St. Herodias?"

"I don't know. I sent Dullahan to the front gate. He says

Gregos is still there, claiming he never left his post. He says most of the attendees have left—the lot is nearly empty. Nothing out of place. Let me call him again." Haynes tapped his phone's screen a couple times, then brought it to his ear. "Dull, I'm with him." Haynes then activated the speakerphone and gave the phone to Degas.

"Anything?" Degas asked.

"You're caught up on the situation? Gregos is working to getting the cameras back online here at the gate. Should only take a few more minutes and I'll be able to access all the feeds. Problem is, this station only has one monitor, so—"

The rest of his sentence was lost to static.

"Say that again," Degas replied. The reception underground was spotty despite the signal boosters equipped throughout the property, but Degas could make out most of what Dullahan was saying.

"This station...one monitor, we can only...one camera at a time. Finding...could take some time...don't know if they're even on the premises."

Degas thought about it. St. Herodias had a large, complex design—easy enough for a stranger to become disoriented in, but it was not a deliberate labyrinth. If the family searched for an exit, they could find one soon enough. They would, however, have to wait for the halls to empty. Even if they found disguises, the little boy would give them away as there were no juvenile Edens. *But how would the Batteses know that?* Degas wondered. *How would they know where to hide, or manage to get* everyone *out of their restraints in the first place? That would require outside assistance.*

"I believe they are still here," Degas concluded. "Dull, did anyone enter the facility after the ceremony began?"

"No," Dullahan responded, "but get this: I pressed Gregos hard for anything out of the ordinary. He admitted...woman who forgot the password, but was vouched for. She was about five foot ni...disheveled redhead."

Degas did not believe in this much coincidence. He was both frustrated and impressed.

The look on Haynes's face showed only concern. "If it is the wife," he said, "could she have brought the police?"

"Doubtful," Degas answered. "She's been here a long time. They would have moved in on us by now."

"...no reports on the scanner," Dullahan added over the speaker.

Not the police, Degas thought. *But she did find someone.* "Who vouched for her, Dull?"

"Bass."

That didn't make sense to Degas. He had known Bass for almost five years and he had even been involved in some of the recruits' security training. It was designed specifically to excavate any remaining Godliness inside them and shatter it. Gregos had passed, but Bass had done so with flying colors. In fact, Degas had almost chosen Bass for his *bar yetzer hara* team, but went with Dullahan last minute for his experience living on the streets that would come in handy when monitoring the Batteses.

As such, Degas wasn't ready to believe Bass was lying, or Gregos for that matter. *Is there a third party at play here? What if Bass is already dead?* Degas couldn't worry about that now, locating the Batteses was the highest priority.

"Degas, are you there?" Dullahan asked.

"Yes."

"What do you want me to do?"

"Let Gregos continue working on the cameras. If you find anything, let's go back to using the radio, but change yours over to channel six. Gregos is not to communicate to anyone. He is to report to you alone. He is not to leave the outpost. If he tries to slip away, slit his throat."

Degas hung up and turned to Haynes. "Where are Fen and

Lamia?"

"Lam is almost back now. Fen is rounding up any Edens he can find—my orders—to search for the family. There aren't many, but Jan from St. Cain's is still here. The Mamertine guards, too. Fen will make sure they do not spill a drop of Battese blood, but is telling them nothing else. Missek can help, too."

"No, leave him out of it. This whole point is for this to be done with minimal numbers. There's already too many. If I fail with this, I fail." Degas sighed. "Let's accept these developments as an added challenge. Find the rest of the family. Nothing else changes."

Richard 1:8

He heard his son, but did not understand.

Was Danny truly unfazed by the presence of a dead body? How could that be? Richard thought. *He should be scared and repulsed— not indifferent. Where was the Danny who giggled after he honked the truck horn? The boy whose biggest challenge was wiping snow off the couch with his sock? How could he change so fast?*

How do I change him back?

Bass propped the corpse up against the wall while Danny stared at it with vacant blue eyes.

Can I change him back?

Richard stepped forward and put a hand on Danny's shoulder. Will was in reach, so Richard did the same to him. Neither of his sons looked at him, but they didn't resist his touch.

They stood together, as a family, waiting for Bass's next move.

Bass, meanwhile, acted as if none of them existed. He looked back and forth between the dead Eden and the small, square window of the stairwell. Then, with his knee, he pushed the body further into the corner, out of the window's line of sight. A shiny buck knife sat in the dead man's belt. Bass took it and turned, finally acknowledging Richard by holding out the knife's brown wooden handle towards him.

"Do you want it?" Bass asked.

Richard didn't think it was the best idea. He felt proficient enough with his body. He could punch, grapple, and tackle opponents. On the other hand, Will knew none of those things.

"Give it to Will," Richard answered.

"No," said Will. "I...I'd be no good with it. You take it, Dad."

"Goddammit," Bass said. "Never mind." He placed it on his own belt loop, next to his switchblade. Richard opened his mouth to ask for the weapon after all—better in his hand than on Bass's belt—but Bass spoke first.

"Here's the situation, everyone," he said, his gaze now on Will. "We found out that your friend is no longer in the infirmary. She's been moved to the Mamertine—that's our—I mean, *their*—prison here. That will be my last detour for you. My *last* favor. Do you understand?"

They all nodded, though Richard began to wonder if he could really trust this man. He didn't think Bass was lying to them—he had already reunited their family, risked his life for them, even killed for them. Richard knew that Bass wanted to see this through, get this over with, and get back to whatever routine was normal to him. What Richard *had* begun to doubt was Bass's ability to succeed in doing all these things. Bass's instability seemed to be growing at a rapid pace. At one moment, he had the poise of a drill sergeant, but at another, a heroin junkie. Even now, as Bass stood explaining his next move to the group, Richard noticed the sweating, the small shuffles in place, and the hands fidgeting at his sides. It reminded him of someone.

Back in Lake Placid, St. Andrew's Parish sponsored a twelve-step program for alcohol and drug abuse. As deacon, Richard attended regularly for prayer and support. One morning, Richard was reunited with Percy Johnson, one of Griff's old colleagues on the force. Percy worked for the Lake Placid Narcotics Unit and had gone undercover for a time. How Percy had ended up in St. Andrew's rec hall that Tuesday morning was not an original story for someone in his line of work. In his pursuit to uphold the law, he had immersed himself in the drug world and, as a result, succumbed to the substances he had sworn to combat.

Bass was immersed in something much worse—a world of pure evil. Richard could only imagine the inner demons—figurative or literal—that Bass carried for cementing himself this deeply within the Edens. *What acts of worship and violence did he have to commit for them to call him one of their own?* The unflinching way Bass handled the dead body in the stairwell all but announced that this wasn't his first victim. *How many deaths did Bass have under his belt? How many of them were innocent?*

Richard was no psychologist, but he could recognize a man who was battling with his conscience. If there was good left inside Bass—and Richard believed there was, or else there would be no battle at all—it was steadily collapsing under this spiritual weight. Bass's mission for the Vatican was secret. Richard had no idea what its goals were or the time allotted to meet them, but that time was surely running out—maybe not for the organization, but for Bass.

A man cannot serve two masters.

Richard felt it was time for a prayer, something they all could use before the last leg of their journey. He would remind them all of Psalm 34:17: *When the righteous cry for help, the Lord hears and delivers them out of all their troubles.* It was simple and couldn't be more relevant.

He grabbed Danny's hand on his left and Will's on the right, but before *Dear God* even left his mouth, Bass charged out of the stairwell with Shannon right behind him. Will and Danny broke free of Richard's grip and headed through the door themselves.

Richard was the last to leave and hoped his intention of prayer was good enough.

†

The halls of St. Herodias, and its juxtaposition of rich, Renaissance design and Satanic imagery were no less unnerving the second time around. This particularly long corridor had men with wings painted all along the ceiling—fallen angels with bloodstained swords. Flying over an unbroken background of flame, they smiled brightly, as if none regretted their allegiance.

At the end of the hall, Richard and his group arrived at a giant iron gate that stretched from the floor to the ceiling, which looked to be about ten feet high. The gate was open, like a private estate expecting visitors.

Bass led the family through. On the other side, the décor took a sudden transformation. Instead of tiles, the walls were composed of jagged rocks and there were no longer lamps mounted to the wall—or lighting of any kind. The hall quickly grew dark ahead of them, resembling the mouth of a deep cave. A faint sound of running water came from within.

"Stay here," Bass said, his voice echoing from the path ahead. He took the flashlight from Shannon and hurried forward. His footsteps faded and soon Bass was absorbed by the darkness. Everyone else stood waiting in the hall's remaining light. No one spoke, but Richard took his sons' hands again. This time, just for comfort.

After a few minutes, a dim light appeared in the distance, then focused into a beam. Richard heard rapid footsteps approaching. He felt his sons' grips on his hands tighten, but he broke free, straightening his posture and readying his stance, wary of who was coming.

Thankfully, it was Bass that emerged, though he didn't seem happy to see them.

"There are no guards down here," he said. "There are *always* supposed to be guards down here. This means that they've been pulled to look for us. Come with me, it's best not to stand out in the open."

He led the group into the darkness.

"Watch your step," Bass said, shining the light at the floor. "We're going down."

Sure enough, the ground gave way to a wide spiral staircase, descending in tight circles on sturdy, wooden steps. The temperature seemed to sink along with them.

When they reached the bottom, the ground became moist and Richard felt clumps of cold dirt between his toes. There was light again. Two torches burned vigorously, one on each side of a large metal door, though they did not rid the air of its chill. A set of wooden chairs sat against the wall next to a grid of footlockers. On the opposite wall, a faucet protruded from the rocky surface at about waist level. It was silver with laurel leaves molded around its neck and sat above a short, rectangular stone basin. The faucet was off—it was not the source of water Richard heard.

Without speaking, Bass unlocked the door between the torches by swinging up a large, wooden plank, then pushed it open. Everyone followed him inside.

They entered a room that was about the size of a small church. It had a high ceiling and was perfectly round. Its walls were comprised of more jagged rocks, as if the space was chiseled from inside a mountain. Torches were bolted into the stone at evenly-spaced intervals, their flames playing a convoluted tug of war with each other's shadows. It was warmer inside, but not at all pleasant as Richard caught the scent of urine and feces.

"Ew," Danny said. The little boy covered his nose.

Richard did the same while he continued to survey the room. At the far side stood a golden statue on a pedestal. It resembled a bull, though almost double the size and Richard counted at least six horns on its head. The creature was lurched forward, vomiting a murky stream that flowed noisily out into the center of the room along a path carved into the ground. From there, it formed small tributaries that branched off in all directions before each eventually drained into the floor.

But that was not the worst thing he saw.

"There's no one here," said Will in disbelief.

There sure isn't, Richard thought. *My son's conscience may have just cost us our lives.*

"No," Bass said. "Your friend is here somewhere." He pointed to the floor. "Look."

Richard hadn't noticed before, but there were small, perforated hatches—like manhole covers—maybe fifteen or twenty of them, spread out along the perimeter of the room. They served as the drains for their own dark little river.

"She'll be in one of those cells."

"Which one?" Will asked.

"I'm not sure, but let's find her quickly." Bass cupped his hands over his mouth. "Pia," he called out. "Pia, can you hear me? We're here to help you." Richard thought his voice sounded weak and insincere, like the rescue was a chore. By now, Richard assumed it was.

When there was no answer, Richard shouted as well. "Pia!" Bass jerked his head towards Richard as if he were going to scold him. *Maybe that was too loud.*

But there was a response from somewhere down below. "Hello?"

"Pia!" all five of them responded disjointedly, almost comically.

"Help! I'm down here!"

Bass rushed over to the far side of the room. "Say again," he commanded.

"Help!" the voice repeated, enough for Bass to pinpoint the correct hatch.

He knelt down beside it. "Give me a hand with this, deacon." Richard knelt down along with him. There, the smell of feces intensified. "And watch out for the water. It's sewage."

Jesus. Richard felt the guilt take over, hating himself for the thoughts he had projected at Will just a few moments ago. Pia was locked away in this God-awful prison with an unending stream of shit being poured onto her.

Bass seemed familiar with the locking mechanism of the hatch and gestured for Richard to follow his lead. Together, they turned a heavy crank that released the lock. The two men grunted as they lifted up the metal cover and slid it aside and away from the stream of sewage. Underneath it was a ladder that quickly disappeared into a dark pit. The ladder was speckled with feces and moist from the stream.

"Bring the light," Bass called to Shannon. "Hold it here—

down the rungs."

Shannon dropped to her knees and aimed the light where she was told. The beam made it to the bottom—maybe twelve feet—where a pool below rippled and splashed from the seepage of tainted water.

Richard couldn't tell how deep it was, nor did he see anyone at the bottom. He moved aside for Bass.

"Pia," Bass called, leaning over the hole. "I don't see you. Come over to the—shit!" He shot back and fell onto his butt. "Close it!" He shouted, fumbling for the lid to the cell. "Close it! Close it!"

Richard couldn't help himself, he peered again into the hole.

What scurried up the rungs was not Pia, but a slender, bald man with eyes so bloodshot no white remained. He was laser-focused on the exit above.

The man let out a snarl that startled Shannon away, taking the light with her. Richard watched the man get reabsorbed into the darkness. All he could hear now was the *clang, clang, clang,* of the man's hurried ascent.

"I'm here," the man cackled in a woman's voice, before taking on a much deeper tone. "I'm here!" Then, laughter rose from the pit.

"Goddammit, everyone. Help!" Bass called out.

Richard snapped out of his trance, embarrassed at the prioritizing of curiosity over safety. He turned to see Bass and Will struggling with the lid then rushed over to help them from the other side. The laughter continued, intensifying as it came closer to the surface.

Danny took a step towards them to help. "Stay back!" Richard cried. "Will, we got this! Get your brother out of here!" Will let go and took hold of Danny, but they did not run.

As Richard and Bass began moving the cover back, the prisoner's head popped above the surface. In the light of the torch fire, Richard could see details that he did not want to see.

This man's entire face and head were laced with slash marks—some scarred over—some fresh and bleeding. Whether they were a form of punishment or self-mutilation, the man did not seem fazed by them. He was smiling so widely that the skin around his mouth and cheek wrinkled together, squeezing blood from his more recent wounds.

In unspoken unison, Richard and Bass heaved the lid down on the prisoner, but the man swung at it with his ghoulish arm and knocked it away with a strength that seemed almost unbelievable. The deflection gave the man time to get his entire torso above the ladder. His red gaze snapped towards the closest body, which was Shannon's. She tried to back away, but the man's hand caught her ankle.

That was enough for Will to let go of his brother. He took his wife's hand and tried frantically to pull her free, but the man's grip held tight.

Richard realized that the only thing Will was going to do was pull the prisoner right up out of his cell. Richard jumped to his feet, and, with the same technique he had used to score a field goal, kicked the man in the temple. The prisoner's laughter immediately stopped. He let go of Shannon and held one hand in the air, groggily, and placed the other on the ground for support. Richard went for that one. He stomped down on it with his heel. The prisoner released an almost canine yelp and retracted his arm to his chest.

Richard retreated slightly to wind up for another kick. He had every intention of taking this man's head clean off this time. But, perhaps sensing that intention, the prisoner ducked back into his cell.

With a visceral groan, Bass muscled the lid back into place over the ladder. Quickly, he resealed the latch, locking the man inside for good.

"It wasn't my time, yet, Edens!" The prisoner shouted from below. "I can wait, brothers. I can wait!"

Then, like a switch was flipped, not another sound emerged from the cell.

Richard bent over, hands on his knees. From that position, he looked up at Danny. The boy was shaking. *Good*, Richard thought. *That* should *have scared the hell out of him. It did to me.*

Shannon was still lying on her stomach. Will sat down beside her, still holding onto his wife's hand. He turned towards Bass.

"Who *was* that?" Will asked.

"A very bad man," Bass replied. "This prison is for innocents and guilty alike." Bass stared at the ground in front of him. "It was...careless of me to be so hasty. I'm going to try this one more time." He stood up at an angle that allowed the torches to illuminate the lines of exhaustion on his face. "Last fucking chance, Pia. If you don't answer us, we're leaving!"

"Yes," a voice responded from another cell.

Bass rushed over to it. "If you're Pia, tell me your dead husband's name."

"*Jesus*, Bass," said Shannon.

There was a pause, but the voice responded. "Gustavo."

Bass looked to Will. "Is that right?"

Will nodded.

"Why didn't you answer me the first time?" Bass asked.

"Do you really need to ask that?" Richard snapped back. "Cut her some slack."

"She almost got us killed," Bass responded, but Richard stared fiercely at him. "OK, let's just get her out."

"We're here to help you," said Will.

"Who are you?" Pia asked.

"It's me, Will."

"*Who?*"

"Will Battese, I work at Cosmic Ocean. The restaurant where you clean. I'm one of the cooks."

"Oh, yes. Yes...I remember."

"Let's go!" Bass shouted.

"I...I don't think I can make it up," Pia said once the latch was removed and the ladder illuminated. She stood below, knee-deep in the sewage, with bandages haphazardly covering her stump. Indeed, it seemed this was something no one had considered. Pia was a large woman to begin with. That fact combined with a newly severed hand made for a hard time to climb a ladder.

"I'll help her," Will said.

"No," said Richard. "I'm the strongest. I'll do it." He started down the ladder before anyone could object. When he came close to the bottom, he jumped off of the rungs, making a splash in the sewage. The smell was overwhelming.

Without speaking, Richard helped Pia up the ladder, supported her from the bottom so she could ascend with her intact hand. He held his breath as much as he could and tried to ignore the wet, brown chunks that dripped off Pia's legs and onto his face.

When she was high enough, Bass and Will reached down and pulled her the rest of the way. Richard emerged behind her, breathing heavily and wiping his face with his sleeve.

"Thank you," Pia said weakly.

"Here," said Will, taking her arm and draping it over his shoulder. "There are some stairs ahead."

"Let me take her, Will," Richard said, feeling like he could better carry her.

"I got it, Dad. I got it."

"Alright," said Richard, sure that Bass didn't want to hear them argue.

"Let's get out of here," Bass affirmed.

No one had to be told twice.

†

Before ascending the stairs out of the Mamertine, Bass stopped everyone in the guard room. He turned on the faucet and clear, odorless water flowed from it.

"Clean yourselves as best you can," Bass said. "We don't need to be leaving a trail of dirt and shit and stink behind us. And be quick, Goddammit."

The family did as they were told, rinsing off the muck from their feet and hands (and for Richard, his face and neck and ears). They got as much out of their clothes as they could as well. Meanwhile, Bass broke off the locks from the footlockers and passed around towels. Some lockers held shoes and spare clothes, but none fit those who needed them, so they moved on.

As Richard climbed the spiral staircase, he suddenly found himself overcome with hope. He was surprised at how foreign the sensation felt. He knew they weren't yet out of this man-made hell, and that they were actively being hunted, but he genuinely believed they were going to escape.

After reaching the halls, the pace became hurried. Shannon kept up with Bass effortlessly, even jogging in place as he checked the corners. Will and Pia shuffled behind at the rear, with Danny never more than a step or two away from his brother's side. Richard was in the middle of the group, exhausted.

His primary doctor was always impressed with how great his health was, but never forgot to add "for someone your age." The years made their presence known now more than ever. After the fight back in the kitchen, the way he was strung up on stage, and the barefooted kicks to a man's skull back in the Mamertine, Richard's body demanded rest.

When they crossed a large hallway intersection, Richard heard a cry from behind and two loud thumps. He turned around to see Will had fallen on the tile with Pia right beside him, both of them groaning. Will hurried to his knees and tried to pull her up, but couldn't muster the strength.

Richard raced back to them, feeling a piece of hope chipped away with each step back.

"Dad," Will began. "She tripped, I—"

"Just move, Will," Richard grunted, pushing Will out of the way with more force than he had intended. Will fell back onto his butt, but Richard, possessed by his frustration, didn't apologize. "If you were too weak to carry her, then you shouldn't have volunteered!"

"I'm sorry," Will said.

"Come on, Pia," Richard said. "You need to stand." He looked up to see Bass and Shannon watching from down the hall. He waved to them and nodded in an *I got it* gesture, though he wasn't sure he did. The pitiful woman on the floor was almost dead weight. Richard decided to squat down beside her so she could wrap her arms around his neck. From there, with a huge grunt and lifting from the legs, he managed to get Pia back on her feet. "Get your brother up, Danny. And let's go."

"Are you alright, Will?" Danny asked.

Richard didn't wait around to hear the answer and shuffled with Pia back out into the intersection.

"Here!" someone screamed. "I found them!"

Richard looked and saw Fen rushing towards him with two other guards.

Richard's mind split between three choices: head back to Will and Danny, head forward to Bass and Shannon, or stay right where he was and buy everyone else some time to get away.

Richard needed only a moment to decide. He had prepared himself for this sacrifice. His only regret was that he forced Pia to make it as well.

"I'm sorry," he said to Pia, "but I'll need both my hands."

Then, Richard let her go.

Instead of dropping to the floor, however, Pia fell into Bass's arms. He had come back for her.

"I have her, deacon!" Bass shouted. "Keep going!"

Richard wasn't sure if Bass had realized his intentions, but if Richard resisted now, all three of them would be caught.

No, all four of them.

Shannon ran into the intersection and grabbed onto Pia as well.

The next thing she did sent chills through Richard's body.

"Run, Will! Run, Danny!" Shannon yelled, but faced the empty hallway she had just come from.

She gestured that way with her arm, waving it as if she were directing someone away from her—pretending that Will and Danny stood there, in front of her, rather than behind her like they actually were.

Richard realized what she was doing and added to the act.

"Go, boys! We're right behind you!" Richard hoped he sounded convincing enough. He took Pia back from Bass and they all ran forward, in an attempt to lead the Edens away from Will and Danny. "Don't look back!" Richard added, though it was difficult to follow his own advice.

Will 1:10

Will's arm snapped straight out to the side, stopping Danny beside him. Their father's reaction to the hostile scream made it clear that he had been spotted.

No, God, Will thought. *No, no, no. We just needed a few more seconds to get clear of that sightline.* If he hadn't fallen with Pia, they all would have made it.

"Run, Will!" Shannon shouted. "Run, Danny!"

For a moment, Will was confused.

"Go boys! We're right behind you!" Richard added. They were both shouting in the opposite direction of where he was standing, but Will realized what they were doing: leading the danger away from him. *This is wrong,* Will thought initially. *After all the delays I've caused, I don't deserve this sacrifice.*

But Danny does.

Will looked down and saw that he had his little brother's sleeve bunched up in his fist. He loosened his grip a bit, but kept hold. Even though Shannon's command was for them to run, Will worried that he'd be seen or heard doing so. Instead, he guided Danny so that their backs were flush against the wall behind a massive red cauldron. The exhibit would hardly obscure them from anyone's gaze for more than a few seconds, but Will hoped it was enough. With his free hand, he mimicked a librarian's shush at his brother. Danny had not been making any sounds, but he nodded nonetheless.

A split second later, Fen stormed into the intersection. He was no longer in his wedding attire, but wore jeans and a white t-shirt with prominent pit stains. Fen spun halfway around and called out to someone behind him. "Go back! Cut them off at the other exit!" Fen's once calm face was now red with strain and sweat as he barked his orders. It was unclear to whom he was talking or how many of them there were, but no one else appeared in the intersection.

Alone, Fen bolted off in the direction Shannon had led him. There was no more of the slow-paced, taunting giant—he was now a Thoroughbred on the final stretch.

And he never looked back.

Will closed his eyes in deep relief. When he opened them, he found his little brother staring up at him.

Danny is my responsibility now, Will thought. *My only responsibility.*

"We need to move," said Will, weakly.

"Which way?" Danny asked.

Good question. Will considered the three options available. Two for sure had Edens—whether it be Fen or an unknown number of henchmen. "The way we came," Will answered. "Let's retrace our steps back to the stairs and up to the auditorium. There *has* to be a way out nearby. What do you think?"

"Good idea," Danny said.

With that, the two brothers grabbed hands and took off. Navigation was easier than expected. If Will saw a painting or a statue that found a new way to disturb him, he knew it was a hallway they hadn't been down before and chose another path. Likewise, he used familiar landmarks—blasphemous idols he had originally hoped to never see again—as a trail of breadcrumbs to guide him back through the maze.

The strategy worked, and they soon managed to find the stairwell that held the dead man. The body appeared undisturbed, slumped over in the corner as they had left it earlier. From there, they retraced their steps to the auditorium without any unwanted encounters. Will reasoned there would be a prominent exit in the vicinity, but he did not see one. There were many doors, but Will hesitated to open any of them for fear of barging in on a group of cultists.

Will led Danny slowly around yet another corner. Further ahead, they came to a set of wooden double doors, etched beautifully with sheep. It looked like the most inviting of all the options. Will told Danny to stay in place next to a pillar a few feet away. Not too far, but enough to have a running start in case Will was about to stir up a nest of Edens.

Will pulled down the handle and pushed one of the doors open with a grunt.

Inside was a dining hall, roughly the size of a school cafeteria. Fortunately, it was not in use. Large metal tables were folded up against the wall next to a number of stacked chairs. On the far side of the room was a serving counter and commercial-sized restaurant appliances: stoves, ovens, refrigeration units, and the like. There were also two doors, one near each corner, flanking the appliances. Will recognized one as a freezer swing door, but the other could very well be a service entrance that led to the outside, similar to the one in Cosmic Ocean.

Will stuck his head back out into the hall and waved Danny towards him. The two held hands again and they trotted towards the exit door. Will went to open it, but found it was locked. "You're kidding me!" he yelled, banging his fist on the door.

"Will..." Danny said softly.

Will ignored him, continuing to face the door, searching for a latch or a switch—something to unlock it, but there was nothing except a keyhole.

"Will," Danny repeated.

How can you not unlock this from the inside? Unless...

"That's not an exit, Will."

That time, it wasn't his brother's voice.

Will snapped around and saw Haynes standing under the arch of frolicking sheep. The door swung shut behind him. Haynes wore light-blue jeans and a black polo shirt and in his right hand was a familiar bloodstained hammer.

Will felt his entire body go cold.

Haynes took a step forward and Will immediately stepped in front of Danny. Will had meant the act to be brave, but it seemed ultimately inconsequential. He could not come up with an option that would give him and his brother the advantage.

If the tables were set up, Will thought maybe he could have gotten Haynes to chase him around a bit, then somehow maneuvered his way to the exit. Except the tables *weren't* set up. There were no knives or other potential weapons out in the open either and Will knew he didn't have the time to search for anything. *I wish I had taken the knife Bass offered me when I had the chance.* Will thought about taking Danny into the freezer and barricading themselves inside, but they'd be cornered and wouldn't last long in that frigid temperature.

The best I can do is charge Haynes, distract him long enough for Danny to slip by. But even that scenario seemed beyond the scope of Will's abilities. *The first swing of that hammer could probably take me out. Haynes will get Danny before he's even made it to the door.* Will was hit with a sad reality: *I might not take long enough to die.*

However, just as Will believed he had eliminated every possible scenario, Haynes tossed the hammer to the floor.

"I can't believe I just did that," Haynes said, looking at his own hands as if they had acted independently.

Will couldn't believe it either. "Why...why did you?"

Haynes's expression was piercing, yet somehow soft. "Because you were my friend, Will," he said, and moved forward. Will took a step back, bringing his brother with him. Haynes seemed to sense Will's unease and held his position. "I never wanted any of this to happen to you," he continued, "or to your family. They *forced* me to do it. It would have been *my* family on that stage if I refused. It doesn't excuse my sins—I know this—but I still feel compelled to confess them. Who *wouldn't* do anything to save the ones they love?"

Will said nothing. He had never met Haynes's family— Haynes hadn't even spoken about them. It never crossed Will's mind that Haynes could be fighting his own fight.

"I'm supposed to kill both of you," Haynes said, then he

shrugged. "But I can't do it."

"So, what?" Will asked. "You're just letting us go?"

"No," Haynes said. "I can do better than that. I'm going to help you get your son back."

The statement shook Will to his core. Just the mention of Giddy brought him back to the verge of tears. Even though Haynes's apparent change of heart came unexpectedly, Will's hope of seeing his child again outweighed any skepticism. "Where is he?"

"Abe and Sara took him. They intend to raise him as their own."

Will already knew this. "A phone. I need a phone. I need the police."

"You can't," Haynes said sternly, pressing the fingers of his hands together in a prayer formation. "That's *not* an option. There are Edens in the NYPD. If you alert the authorities, Abe and Sara *will* find out. They will disappear with him before the first squad car flips on their siren."

"Then...what? What do I do?"

"You do what *has* to be done." Haynes pulled out a handgun from the nape of his back and held it by the barrel so that the grip faced Will. "You kill them."

Will looked at the weapon in complete shock. "I'm not...I can't..."

Haynes took a step forward. "What's happening to you isn't fair, Will. I know it. And I'm sorry for the role I played in it—"

"Then *you* kill them!" Will interrupted. "It doesn't seem that hard for you."

"I would, my friend, I would, but there are things I must do here to cover your escape. There are others looking for you. I need to make sure they don't find you." He took the pistol in both hands and rotated it sideways, presenting it like a prize on a gameshow. "This is a .45 Sig Sauer."

Will wasn't sure what that meant, and stared blankly at

Haynes.

"Do you know how to use this?" Haynes asked.

"My grandpa took me shooting. Once."

"Good. That's all you need. A .45 has a heavy recoil—be prepared for that. Like most guns, it's normally quite loud, but I've equipped it with a silencer, so no one will be alerted to the premises and interrupt your heroic act. The gun is loaded and there's no manual safety, so be careful. You point, you shoot, you get your son back." Haynes spoke as if it were as simple as picking up a child from daycare.

"The Benteras are old," Haynes added, "but they are evil. Do not hesitate to kill them because they will not hesitate to kill you. Do you understand?"

Will knew all too well the consequences of his inaction. A flashback of Kavi's skull splitting open hit him as hard as cannon fire.

Will couldn't let that happen again, especially not when it came to his son's life—his son's *soul*. Will knew he had to act this time. He remembered the rage he felt when he was bound and gagged on stage, how ready he was to kill every last one of the Edens in attendance. But now that Will actually had an opportunity for retribution, his fury had dissipated. He wished for there to be another way.

"Do you understand, Will?" Haynes repeated. He had stepped right in front of him, within striking distance, but all the Eden did was place his hand on Will's shoulder. Haynes's eyes bored into Will's with a bizarre look of calm intensity. Haynes asked the question one more time, but it occurred to Will that it was Haynes that didn't understand.

"I don't think I can do it," Will answered softly.

"They will turn your son into a murderer!"

"It feels *wrong*...like God doesn't want me to kill."

"God doesn't want you to, or *you* don't want to?"

Will didn't know.

Haynes gave him a look of pity. "Answer me this: when David killed Goliath, was he going against God's wishes?" Haynes didn't wait for Will to answer. "Of course not. He wasn't punished for it either. God made him a king. And what about Joshua? He slaughtered countless pagan armies with God's blessing."

Will understood the point he was making, but Haynes's words only picked up speed and intensity. "Moses raised his hand and God swept the Red Sea over the Egyptians. Elijah called for fireballs from Heaven and God immediately rained them down."

"OK," Will said, looking downwards with a new sense of shame, but Haynes wasn't finished. He leaned forward, right in Will's face. His breath smelled faintly of peppermint.

"When evil people make God angry, good people carry out His vengeance. Moses, Joshua, David, Elijah...now you, Will Battese. Some were chosen to take out legions. You're only called to bring justice to two. You have it easier than any of them, yet you deny Him!"

"OK!" Will shouted, unable to bear the increasing weight of his self-loathing. "OK, here. *Give* it to me!" He snatched the gun from Haynes. It shook so violently in his hand he feared it would go off. Evidently, so did Haynes, who took a couple steps backwards.

Will looked at Haynes. "How do I get out of this hellhole?"

"Yes," Haynes said spiritedly, though he still kept an eye on the gun in Will's quivering hand. Haynes gave him directions to the parking lot outside the front entrance of the building. "I have a black Dodge Charger parked there," Haynes continued. "The lot is virtually empty—you should have no problem finding it. The keys are inside, as well as my aviator jacket, sunglasses, and spare boots. Put them on so Abe and Sara don't immediately realize who is coming up to their door. Got it?"

"...Yes." Will said.

"Repeat the directions back to me."

Will recited them to Haynes who nodded in approval.

Haynes then took Danny by the hand. "Go now, Will. I can keep your brother safe."

"No," Danny said, pulling away. He wrapped his arms around Will's waist.

Haynes frowned. "It'll be too dangerous—"

"We're not splitting up," Will said, even though he thought that Haynes was probably right. "We're just not."

"OK, then...I understand. Just make sure he stays away from...what will happen. Keep him in the car."

Will nodded.

"Is there anything else we need to go over?" Haynes said with a wide-eyed urgency. "If not let's—"

"Wait," Will cut him off. "Shannon and my father. We were separated. Can you find them? Tell them we're OK? Get them out, too?"

Haynes's excited expression immediately collapsed into a frown. "I...I was hoping you wouldn't ask me that."

"Why? What do you mean?" Will asked, all but knowing the answer.

"They're dead, Will."

Hearing those words was unlike anything Will had ever experienced. He thought they would bring another cascade of guilt and shame, but those feelings were surprisingly distant, as if they were too worn out and calloused to be effective any longer.

Haynes dropped his head and shook it furiously. "It was moments before I found you. Fen announced it over the radio. He killed them. There was nothing I could do."

Danny began to cry. It came out in quick, sharp sobs that should have all but stabbed Will in the chest yet he was able to keep his own tears inside. Will's hands continued shaking, but it was anger now—not fear—that vibrated through them.

"Will…" Haynes began again.

"No! Shut up!" Will shouted, raising the gun and pointing it unsteadily at Haynes. "You destroyed my family!"

"Please *don't* shoot me," pleaded Haynes. "You have every right to, but you need me to make sure your way out is clear."

Will kept the gun aimed at Haynes, but considered his options.

"I'm so sorry, Will. You must decide quickly. But if it's any consolation, I did not destroy your *entire* family. You have Daniel, and you *can* have Gideon—there's still time to save him. Your anger…it is God's anger. He's given it to you to carry. Accept it and make it your strength."

"God…" Will wanted so badly to pull the trigger, but the bullets belonged in someone else.

Will lowered the gun. "I can't forgive you, Haynes. But thank you. Thank you for helping us now."

Haynes smiled, as if a burden was lifted. "You're a good man, Will. Your family would be proud. Let me go now to do what I have promised."

Will gave a dismissive nod and Haynes hurried out the door.

Danny grabbed Will's hand and began pulling him towards the exit, but Will wasn't quite ready and held his brother back. Danny eyed the gun in Will's hand, which was still trembling slightly.

"Are you going to do it?" Danny asked. His eyes were moist, but he was no longer crying.

"I don't know."

Danny sniffled. "I think they deserve it."

"I think they do, too."

"I can do it, Will. If you can't."

Will shook his head. This was his task.

And finally, the gun stood still.

Shannon 1:9

Shannon and Richard were human crutches, moving forward in sync as they supported Pia and propelled her down the hallway. The overweight woman did her best to run, to contribute to her own escape, but through some combination of blood loss and poor cardiovascular conditioning, her stride was weak and unsteady, no more effective than a child treading water in high class rapids.

"Puedes hacerlo," Pia repeated frantically under her breath. "Puedes hacerlo."

Shannon didn't speak Spanish nor did she care what the words meant—she was too busy regretting her latest kneejerk act of selflessness. Shannon's trick had worked—Fen was charging after her, not Will and Danny. That had been the plan, but she found little satisfaction in it now as she sprinted for her life. She wondered if she would have made the same choice had she been given more time to debate it.

A jolt of pain shot through Shannon's ankle from a misstep that caused her to roll it. She shrieked and stumbled forward, almost bringing Pia down with her—and she would have, if it weren't for Richard's swift reflexes. The deacon leaned back and pulled, mustering up enough force to keep them all standing. Shannon recovered and was able to regain her previous pace, though she had to grit her teeth through the pain with every step.

If Bass had looked back when she tripped, Shannon had missed it. He was racing forward, leading the trio faster and more carelessly than even through the ornate maze. There was an unspoken understanding that it didn't matter what was ahead of them if Fen was coming from behind.

Shannon lost sight of Bass when he turned the corner ahead of them. When she finally made it there herself with Richard and

Pia, she saw Bass in mid-air, arms fully extended above him, hanging from the ceiling. After a second, he began to lower, pulling some contraption down with him. Shannon recognized it immediately. It was a steel grated security gate, similar to those seen in the mall after the stores had closed for the night.

When Bass's feet hit the floor, he continued to hold the gate above his shoulders allowing Shannon, Pia, and Richard to pass under. Only then did Bass let the gate drop. He squatted and latched it. Without speaking, he waved everyone to continue running and again led the way.

Shannon heard the crash, but did not turn back.

"Fuck!" Fen shouted. Shannon could hear him shaking the metal gate; she had no idea if it would hold. Fen shouted again, though this time there were no words. It sounded like a roar.

Bass did not stop until they reached a familiar looking door. He opened it to reveal yet another stairwell and all four of them entered. Shannon cringed at the idea of dragging Pia up a story or two, but she helped Richard steer her towards the ascending steps nonetheless.

"Stop," Bass said, and everyone obeyed. "Another change of plans. They found us—as you might have figured out."

Shannon could not suppress the smirk that emerged from what she could have sworn was Bass's attempt at humor.

"Let's take a quick breather, then it's time to go our separate ways," Bass continued.

Shannon's smile disappeared as quickly as it came. "What do you mean?" she asked. "You haven't gotten us out yet!"

"Your husband and brother need my help now."

Shannon was thrown off by the gallantry of his answer, but could only bring herself to yell at him. "What about us!"

"You three will be on your own from this point," Bass replied, "but you'll be OK. Come on, let me show you where to go."

Bass led them back out of the stairwell. He pointed in a direction that they hadn't gone yet. "This passage connects underground to Manufacturing. Just keep heading straight and you'll end up in what looks like a factory. All production has been halted for the ceremony, so it should be empty. Make your way through it; the exit is on the opposite side. We have vans sitting outside with the keys in them."

"We can handle that," said Richard.

"I hope so," Bass replied. "Do you still have the safe house address?"

Richard tapped his chest and nodded.

"I'll try and get your family there. But no guarantees. I've already been way more involved in this than I should have been."

"And Gideon?" Shannon asked.

"I remember my promise."

Pia's head darted back and forth with a furrowed brow throughout the entire conversation, clearly struggling to follow it.

Richard seemed to notice her confusion as well. "You'll come with us, Pia," he said. "Stay with us until it's safe to go home. We can get a message to your family that you're alright."

"Don't communicate with *anyone* outside the house!" Bass snapped.

"Someone has to get the message out," Shannon shot back. "If we can't, then will you?"

"Fine, dammit," said Bass. "I'll try. Will you all just *go* already?"

Pia smiled softly. "Thank you, mister."

"Yes, thank you, Bass," said Richard. "For everything. I understand the risks — "

"Yeah, I get it," Bass cut him off.

"You did the right thing," Shannon added.

"I haven't decided that yet," Bass replied, then he ran off without another word.

Shannon 1:10

The group found Manufacturing just as Bass had described. The tight corridors of St. Herodias had given birth to an expansive industrial warehouse that was eerily silent and lifeless. A variety of assembly lines and conveyor belts were powered down and bare, devoid of any hint as to what they were used to produce. Shelves were constructed along the walls, filled with cardboard boxes and neatly-organized but unidentifiable pieces of machinery. Most of the illumination came from powerful fluorescent strip lights attached to the two-story high ceilings, not from the windows—though there were many. Their panes were all painted black, yet exhibited a dull glow from sunlight that refused to be shut out completely.

"Are you OK, Rich?" Shannon asked, peering over at her father-in-law. He still held onto Pia, but seemed more winded than before. It looked like he needed another break. Shannon asked if that was the case.

Richard nodded. "Just give me a few seconds."

When they stopped, Pia slowly stepped free of them both. "I think I'm OK on my own," she said, "if we're not running. Thank you both, for not leaving me."

"You're welcome," Richard said, sounding earnest. Shannon just nodded.

When Richard signaled that he was ready, the three walked together at as fast of a pace as Pia could handle—much slower than Shannon would have liked. It did, however, give her time to further process her surroundings, which filled her with equal parts intrigue and dread. They passed a row of factory grade furnaces, each one large enough to fit all three of them inside. Further on were a series of workbenches, perhaps fifteen or twenty, each consisting of a powered off computer terminal and an identical set of tools.

Richard stopped briefly to examine the selection, then grabbed a pipe wrench that was hanging on a pegboard. "Just in case," he said.

Shannon wanted a "just in case" as well. She took the same model of pipe wrench off of the next workbench, but thought it was a little too heavy for her to swing effectively and put it back down. She considered some of the other options: small screwdrivers, vice grips, and various drills, but none of them seemed effective. There was a hammer, but just the sight of it put a bad taste in Shannon's mouth. So did the box cutters.

"Come on," Richard urged.

Shannon settled for a monkey wrench, somewhere in the middle of all the sizes available, and grabbed the next smallest one for Pia. She accepted it with her remaining hand.

The group continued beyond the workbenches to an area that seemed dedicated to repair. A fourth furnace was partially dissembled, its body suspended in the air by a bright-yellow hoist attached to an overhead crane. Other mechanical operations appeared to have been underway, but were now paused, with their components, big and small, spread out along the floor. There were more shelves that contained larger, more specialized tools as well as a solid metal rack draped with a mass of spare chains and hooks that hung from it like beaded curtains.

Across the room from the repair zone was an even more curious arrangement. Rectangular wooden crates, half the size of coffins, were stacked five and six high and in total must have numbered over a hundred. They appeared to be sealed and were located near a heavy, metal garage door, likely that they were either ready to be shipped out or had just arrived. As she passed closer by them, Shannon noticed each one was labeled "Tefé" in handwritten red text.

"What does that word mean, Pia?" she asked.

Pia paused briefly for a look. "That's not a word. Not in Spanish."

Shannon ran her fingers across the wood, then faced forward. As interested as she was in the contents of the crates, she was more interested in the exit. On the wall beside the garage door was a round button that gave off a dim, green glow. Shannon slapped it and the door whirred awake. It rose an inch—just enough to let the sunlight pierce through—and stopped. Then, it reversed its direction and lowered back to the floor. Shannon hit the button again, but the same thing happened.

"You've got to be shitting me," she said. "What's wrong with this thing, Rich?"

"I don't know," he said, looking up to the gears above the door. "It seems to be working fine, I'm not—"

A woman shouted from the outside, cutting him off. "Whoever's in there, can we please not open the door at the same time!? It's cold out here!"

Shannon and Richard turned to each other with matching expressions of surprise.

"*Hide*," they whispered in unison.

Richard 1:9

The conditions on Mirror Lake did not justify the lack of activity atop its surface. An occasional breeze delivered a few unexpected chills, but overall the afternoon sun was warm and pleasant. Richard had no idea why the frozen lake and the wooden benches spread out along its perimeter were almost entirely deserted.

Nonetheless, he and Rita fastened up their ice skates and took advantage of the open space, gliding and weaving around each other, even breaking out into a two-person game of tag. They were both proficient enough skaters, but Richard was no match for his wife's speed. Even if he was given a head start, Rita would close the distance on him in little time. She would never slow down, either, instead allowing herself to crash into Richard, whose lack of speed was made up for by strength and balance. She would laugh as they collided, fully confident that he would catch her and keep them both from falling. He always did.

"You're 'it' again," Rita said, as the sun ducked behind a cloud.

"Great," said Richard unenthusiastically. He let go of her and she skated a few feet away from him. "Go easy on me?" Richard asked.

"*Pssh*, no. But maybe I can inspire you."

"Oh yeah?" Richard asked. "How's that?" He moved towards Rita, but she quickly doubled the distance between them.

She looked in both directions around the lake to make sure no one was watching, then giggled. "You can touch these," she said, then shook her chest.

"While I like the idea of that, I'm still not gonna be able to catch you."

"Fine. Here," said Rita, "I'll stay like this. I'll skate backwards. But then you only get ten seconds."

"In that case..." Richard said, stroking his chin and pretending

278

to consider the deal, "I can do it in *five!*" He charged her before even finishing the sentence.

Rita squealed in surprise, bent her legs and pushed off backwards away from him.

"Four!" Richard shouted.

"Three!" He was gaining on her.

"Two!" He was so close. He was actually going to catch her.

"No!" she cried out, still laughing.

"One!" Richard reached out his arm and pushed for one final burst.

But Richard had come in too fast, too hard. His open palm slammed into Rita's sternum. The force sent her straight back into the edge of the lake, where the ice met a thick curb of snow. Her feet came to a sudden halt but her upper body kept its momentum. She fell backwards so fast that her arms weren't ready to catch her.

Rita's head landed on the seat of a wooden bench at just the right angle to break her neck.

†

There were no witnesses to corroborate Richard's story, but he told it honestly and Sheriff Joe Blackburn believed him.

By chance or fate, Blackburn turned out to be the first officer on the scene. He was a short, fit man in his late forties and listened to Richard retell the events without interruption. The entire time, Blackburn had a distant expression, not that he seemed uninterested, but that he was rolling everything over in his head.

By that time, the paramedics had arrived. The few people that were in the vicinity were now crowding behind the police tape, watching the men in uniform zip up Rita's body in the long, black bag.

"Come this way," said Blackburn, beckoning Richard to

follow him. They moved a bit further from the scene. Richard was now facing away from it, though he could still see the lights of the ambulance shimmer over the surface of the lake.

"I want you to listen to me," said Blackburn, looking up at Richard. "I knew your stepfather, a little bit. And I know you enough, too. I listen to you at church, the times I manage to come. I like your homilies. Can never sleep through them because you talk too damn loud." Blackburn gave a feeble attempt at a smile, but did not hold onto it. His face was serious once again as he continued. "I know you got yourself two boys—one of them young enough that he might not be able to understand how his daddy accidently hurt his mommy. Do you see where I'm going with this?"

Richard did not respond.

Blackburn dropped his voice as he lost all subtlety. "Right now you have a confession that doesn't have to be confessed to anyone other than me. No one is going to doubt that this was an accident, but no one needs to know who caused it. Especially your boys. I've seen families disintegrate from less."

Richard couldn't believe what he was hearing. "You're asking me to *lie*?"

"This ain't anywhere *close* to lying. You told the truth. You know it. I know it. Your lovely wife and God know it. Far as I'm concerned, it can end there, with a free conscience."

Blackburn gave Richard until the next morning to think about it. The Sheriff was going to leave Richard and Rita's game of tag out of the report unless Richard called back to insist it be put in.

Richard never did.

†

Richard watched from his hiding place as the garage door now rose uninterrupted. Inch by inch, it unveiled the woman on the other side. Knee-high, leather, winter boots gave way to tightfitting pants, gloves, then a jacket, all black, followed by long stands of blonde hair and oversized movie star sunglasses. The woman stood still, waiting patiently for the door to open, one hand on her hip while the other held onto the strap of a black and pink backpack slipped over her shoulder.

Once the door was over her head, she stepped inside, limping slightly, and removed her shades.

"Hello?" Lamia called out.

Richard quickly squatted behind his cover—something that resembled a giant refrigerator with multiple exhaust valves. Shannon and Pia were seated with their backs against the same machine, flanking Richard, but with no view of the garage door nor the killer who just walked through it. Their wide eyes were on Richard, waiting for direction.

Richard peeked out again. Lamia was now examining the switch to the door. She tapped it and carefully watched the door as it shut.

We could kill her, Richard thought. *The three of us could probably do it, right now, if we caught her off-guard. Or even just me; one swing of this wrench would put her down for good.* Still, Richard hesitated. It somehow felt beneath him to attack an unarmed woman— even one who would likely cut him into pieces if she had the chance. The ambush wouldn't quite be self-defense. Plus, if he unsuccessfully snuck up on her, he would risk a fight, which could cause a commotion and draw in other Edens—or Lamia could simply outrun him and return with reinforcements. In the end, Richard decided it would be best to just let her get to where she was going as she did not seem to be looking for them.

He flattened his hands perpendicular to his side, signaling for Shannon and Pia to wait.

When Lamia finished her investigation of the garage door panel, she turned around and began to walk forward, but only made it three steps before the sound of a slamming door stopped her once again. Fast, heavy footsteps echoed throughout the warehouse. Lamia looked with concern at the rapidly approaching sounds.

"Where the hell have you been?" Fen shouted. "Have you not been checking your phone?"

"I was dropping off the baby—I don't text and drive."

Fen just stared back at her, panting. She took a step closer to him. "Why are you out of breath? What happened?"

"They've escaped."

"They?"

"*All* of them."

Lamia's shoulders dropped, letting her bag fall to the floor. "How?"

"They had help, Lam. We have a traitor. Someone on security, we think. We don't know."

"Shit."

"But this just happened, Lam! I saw them minutes ago, but lost them. Has anyone come this way?"

"I don't know, I literally just walked through the..." Her voice dropped down to a whisper. "They're here. Someone was trying to get out while I was coming in. They've got to be hiding—and listening. *Shit.*"

Fen spun around full circle. "Did I say anything that could give away...?"

"No," Lamia said. "Did I?"

"If we fucked this up, Lam..."

"Stop! Let's spread out and find them. Degas prepared us in case this happened." Then she leaned closer to Fen and said: "It will take some finessing, but we can still herd Will." This last sentence was spoken so softly that Richard wasn't sure if he had heard her correctly.

Richard watched the two Edens split off into different directions. Lamia walked further away from where he hid, while Fen moved closer. Fortunately, he was staying towards the center of the room, searching crudely, not yet looking behind the equipment closer to the wall. The thought of killing Fen brought about absolutely zero moral conflict. This was the man that had killed Jessi. Richard's grip tightened on his pipe wrench and he waited for Fen to pass by completely.

Richard rose slowly and took a step out from behind his cover. Pia's eyes shot open, wide with fright, while Shannon looked at him and furiously shook her head. Richard gestured once more for them to stay put, then looked away before their fear became contagious.

For the first time, Richard's bare feet were a blessing, as they allowed him to move silently over the concrete floor. He maneuvered around the rack of chains and emerged behind Fen. Quickly but cautiously, he tiptoed up to within an arm's length of the lumbering Eden. In his days of physical competition, Richard was not often the smaller of his opponents. Now he was smaller, older, *and* weaker.

But I have a pipe wrench. With both hands, Richard lifted the weapon above his head, then swung down hard.

The forged steel connected with Fen's skull with a wince-worthy crack that sent the giant to his knees. Blood trickled from the crown of Fen's head. Richard wasted no time going forward with his next attack and wound the wrench up like a baseball bat. Before he could swing, however, Fen shot himself backwards, driving his bleeding head into Richard's chin.

The impact caused Richard's teeth to clamp down over the tip of his tongue. The pain was immense and he could already taste the blood, but Richard knew he had to ignore it. With a hand on each end of the wrench, he brought it down around Fen's neck, but Fen managed to get one hand between the wrench and his throat.

"Lam!" Fen called out with a raspy voice, but didn't wait for his partner to arrive before bowing forward with such intensity that he flipped Richard over the top of him. Richard tumbled and landed hard on his back.

The pipe wrench escaped Richard's grip. It clanged as it hit the concrete floor and slid out of reach.

Richard looked up to see that Fen had already risen to his feet. "You're dead, deacon."

Still dazed, Richard looked up at the man towering over him and realized that prediction was probably accurate.

Suddenly, there was another crack. Fen let out a guttural groan as he bent over, clutching his head with one hand.

"How do you like that, you big piece of shit?" Shannon shouted, standing with her own wrench. She struck him with it again, smashing his fingers. He moved his hand to his chest, leaving his bleeding head exposed once more. Shannon wound up for another swing but it did not have time to connect.

"Watch out!" Richard tried to warn her, but it happened too fast. Lamia rammed Shannon against the stack of crates and they both crashed through them and fell out of sight.

Richard began to crawl after them, but then looked back to Fen. The giant was still buckled over, letting out weak moans. Richard willed himself to his feet while he might still have the upper hand, but Fen noticed. Somehow, he also mustered the strength to stand upright.

Richard raised his fists to his temples. He spit out a mouthful of blood and began circling Fen. The giant tried to keep square, but was unsteady on his feet and took noticeable effort in holding his arms up.

Richard threw a jab that was too short, but Fen instinctively shot his arms together to block his face. It was precisely the reaction Richard had wanted.

With his vision obscured by his own defense, Fen did not see Richard come forward with a thrust kick. The ball of Richard's right foot connected hard with Fen's stomach. The Eden let out a surprised grunt and hunched forward. Richard drove his knee into Fen's nose and heard it break.

The impact sent Fen stumbling backwards into the sea of

hanging chains. Fen reached out for them dizzily for support, but ended up getting his arms tangled inside them instead. He twisted and squirmed like an insect stuck in a spider's web.

Richard seized the moment. He rushed behind Fen, whose struggling had knocked a few chains to the floor. Richard snatched one up and strung it around Fen's neck.

The giant screamed in rage. Richard ignored him and wrapped the chain around a second time before twisting the ends around his own wrists. Then, he planted his heels on the floor and allowed himself to fall backwards, adding his bodyweight to the pull as he choked the life out of Fen. Fen continued to struggle, but it seemed to only make the chain dig in deeper. Richard closed his eyes, drawing strength from the sounds of gagging and spit.

"Help!" Shannon screamed from somewhere in the distance.

As urgent as it sounded, Richard could not bring himself to let go.

He has to die.

The giant's struggle weakened. Richard only pulled harder. His knuckles grew white as the chains around his wrists pinched and tore open his skin. Even when Fen fell limp and silent, Richard held strong.

Shannon cried out again. "Richard, *help!*"

Just *a few more seconds*, Richard told himself. *Fen could be faking it. I have to make sure he's not faking it.*

After those few seconds, Richard heard screams in the distance. He came to the horrible realization that he had denied his daughter-in-law three times.

Though he let go of the chains, Richard's fingers refused to fully uncurl. They were numb and Richard shook them as he ran away from Fen's body, feeling shame, not pride.

"Shannon!" he called out, racing around the collapsed crates.

When he arrived on the other side, however, he saw that it was too late.

Shannon 1:11

Lamia had knocked Shannon through the section of piled crates and now both women lay dazed, sprawled out on their backs a few feet away from each other. Shannon watched as the crate atop the nearest still-standing stack tipped over and fell to the floor, missing Lamia's head by inches.

The wooden container shattered and hundreds of metal rods the size of small rolling pins spilled across the warehouse floor. The crash seemed to breathe life into Lamia, who rotated her head towards Shannon.

Shannon shot up to a sitting position, but when she began to stand, the pain in her ankle caught her off guard. She crumpled back to the floor with a cry.

Lamia got to her feet without issue and began a slow approach toward Shannon.

"Help!" Shannon cried, scooting backwards on her butt. Lamia reached out for her, close enough to touch. Shannon attempted a kick to the chest, but Lamia easily slapped the foot away. Shannon tried again with her other leg, but Lamia grabbed her ankle with both hands. The pain that ripped through Shannon's lower body was dizzying.

In a last ditch effort to break free, Shannon shot her knee to her own chest which pulled Lamia forward with it, throwing the Eden off balance. With her good leg, Shannon kicked Lamia square in the nose. Lamia cried out in agony.

"Richard, *help!*" Shannon shouted again, wondering where he was. She heard the rattling of chains in the distance, but no one responded.

With Lamia still staggering, Shannon rolled to the side and began crawling away as fast as she could. In the midst of her scramble, her right hand hit one of the rods that had spilled out from the broken crate and it shot open like a push-button umbrella. Instead of releasing a nylon canopy, however, the device extended in both directions to form a three-foot-long double-sided spear.

Shannon's eyes widened in disbelief. *Holy shit.*

Shannon scooped up the spear. She couldn't believe how it felt in her hand: sturdy and strong, yet weightless, as if it were made of nothing more than imagination. Shannon spun back towards Lamia, but the Eden had a gun pointed at her chest. The miracle of the spear was neutralized.

"Put it down or I put a bullet in your kneecap," Lamia ordered, with a newly nasal tone to her voice. "You'll never run again." Blood dripped steadily from her nostrils and she appeared to have difficulty holding the weapon steady. A thick silencer mounted to the barrel drew small, irregular circles in the air.

Shannon did as she was told. The spear hit the floor without a sound.

"Where's your husband?" Lamia asked.

Shannon shrugged.

"Last chance or I aim just below the gut. You might live, but no more babies."

The threat hit Shannon with surprising effectiveness, but she still did not reply.

"*Where* is Will?" Lamia repeated. The look in her eyes all but promised she was going to shoot either way.

"I think...he's off fucking your mother," Shannon said with a smile.

"Wrong answer," Lamia said, and pulled the trigger.

But the shot went low—a section of concrete burst in front of Shannon's feet as the ricocheted bullet flew past her ear.

Pia had come from behind, slamming Lamia's arm with the wrench. The impact redirected the shot, but Lamia held onto the gun. Then, Pia took her intact hand, wrapped it around Lamia's waist and grabbed her own stump, trapping Lamia inside an aggressive bear hug with her arms pinned to her sides. The Eden struggled to get free.

"Get her!" Pia yelled.

"Keep holding her!" Shannon spat as she returned to her feet, despite the fresh pain in her ankle.

"I'm trying!" Pia shouted back. Judging by the reddening hue of her face, she could lose her grip at any time.

Shannon picked up the spear again. *Let me have this one, God.*

Everything Shannon had been through in the last twenty-four hours boiled over into a scream of such rage that she didn't even recognize it as her own. She charged forward and drove the spear straight into Lamia's heart. There was zero resistance as the blade penetrated through skin, muscle, and bone, not stopping until the side of Shannon's fist hit the Eden's breast.

Lamia let out a scream that was louder than Shannon's. After a moment, Lamia's voice dropped off completely, replaced by a soft gurgling sound as blood poured from her mouth.

She went limp in Pia's arms.

A wave of accomplishment crashed over Shannon. She smiled as she let go of the spear still protruding from Lamia's chest.

Pia did not seem to share the enthusiasm. She simply lost her grip and dropped her arms to her sides.

In unison, Pia and Lamia tipped over and fell to the floor.

Shannon immediately saw why. The spear had not only impaled Lamia, but went straight through Pia as well. The two dead bodies were skewered together like a human shish kabob.

Shannon cupped her palm over her mouth as tears filled her eyes. She stood there, staring blankly through watery, blurred vision as a large figure appeared in her periphery.

"Oh, God. Shannon," Richard gasped.

Shannon blinked, allowing the full clarity of her father-in-law's face to come through. Richard came forward and hugged her tightly.

"Jesus!" Shannon began to sob. "I didn't mean to, Rich. I'm sorry. I didn't mean to."

She felt his lips press into her forehead.

He whispered to her that it wasn't her fault, that it would be OK, and a host of other things she wanted desperately to believe, but knew she never could.

Richard 1:10

Richard's hands were coated with an invisible stain of wrath. As he embraced Shannon, he could feel the sin spreading like blight, branching upwards through his arms, his chest, his neck, and ultimately into his tongue. It lingered there for a moment, then mutated into pride. Richard could not admit to his daughter-in-law that his desire to kill Fen had been stronger than her cries for help. The most he could bring himself to confess was that Pia's death was not Shannon's fault. The promises that came after were completely unfounded: that it would be OK, that Degas would pay for what he'd done, and that every innocent that suffered today would be avenged. Richard had no right to make those promises.

He pulled away from Shannon as his empty words began to overwhelm him. He looked at her while she stared down at the floor. Her face was as red as her hair and another bruise had formed under her left eye, but her sobs were diminishing. Richard placed his hands on her shoulders. "This is not your fault," he repeated, more sternly this time.

Shannon tilted her chin up, making eye contact. "It sure feels like it," she said, letting out a shaky, uneven sigh. "I did that to Pia. I didn't even know her, but now I can't even look at her."

"You don't have to. We can go. We *need* to go."

"Just leave her like this?"

Richard paused for a moment. "Yeah."

Shannon nodded, no longer crying. She turned to leave, but immediately snapped back. "Wait. Lamia had a gun."

"Where is it?" Richard asked.

"By...them," Shannon said, gesturing to the bodies by swiveling her torso towards them with her arms crossed. Richard understood that she wasn't going to get the gun. He nodded to himself and went over to the two dead women. The gun was on the floor beside them. He picked it up and examined it. A Glock 17 9mm. It was equipped with a silencer. While he knew that the attachment was illegal in the state of New York, he had no plans to remove it—silence could save their lives. He checked the magazine: seven rounds left—almost full. Even so, Richard decided to check Lamia for any spare clips.

"We should take some of those capsules," Shannon said, having decided to follow him over to the bodies.

Richard had noticed the floor near the broken crate was covered with the strange things, but was in too much of a hurry to care. "Why?"

"They're spears."

Richard's eyes jumped to the long blade that stuck out from Lamia. "That came from one of those?"

Shannon nodded. "The boxes were full of them. It could be what they were making here."

"OK," Richard said. He had never encountered this type of device, but agreed that taking some would be a good idea, figuring that they could serve as a surprise weapon and perhaps even evidence if they ever made it to the authorities. "Grab Lamia's backpack then, will you? It's in front of the garage door."

"Sure," she said, hurrying away, the assignment seeming to breathe some life back into her. A moment later she returned, dropping the bag in front of him. Richard unzipped the main compartment and found it already quite full.

Inside was a half-empty baby bottle, an unopened can of formula, two more clips for the pistol, a few articles of clothing, and something else at the bottom. Richard dug it out.

It was a gray and pink wig.

"What?" Richard muttered to himself. It appeared to be the same hairstyle that Sara had onstage when she asked Degas if she could take Gideon. *Why does Lamia have it?*

He looked over at Shannon, who was kneeling nearby, cautiously gathering some of the capsules. She picked one up slowly, pinching it with her index finger and thumb like an arcade crane machine. With her other hand, she pressed somewhere in the center of the device and it shot open in her hand. Richard was impressed with the sight.

"I don't know how to close it," Shannon said, turning the spear around in the air.

"Well, just put it down and let's take some unopened ones," Richard said. "Hey, by the way, did your babysitter wear a wig?"

"I don't think so," Shannon answered without turning around. "Why?"

"There's one in here," Richard said.

"Weird," Shannon said, still collecting the capsules.

Richard put the wig back into the bag, but ran his fingers through the strands, as if caressing it would reveal why it was here. When it didn't, he stuffed it back down to the bottom.

Richard was frustrated. His mind—already muddled from the fight with Fen—now searched for an answer to a question that hadn't fully formed. He rested on his knees, staring at Lamia's body. His eyes came across the rose tattoo on her wrist, facing up over a congealing pool of blood. Richard had seen the tattoo on Degas as well, in the Primordial Room, right before Degas pushed his head under the water.

Shannon came back with an armful of collapsed spears and began placing them gingerly into the backpack.

"Sara had one of these, too? On her arm?" Richard asked.

Shannon turned to see what he was referring to. "Yeah."

"Do you know what it is? A sign of membership?"

"I guess," Shannon answered. "Sara said it was something she and Abe got—something to remind them of their love for each other." She gestured towards Lamia's tattoo. "Same thing, though that one's a little different. It's brighter. Sara and Abe's flowers were faded. Guess they've been members a lot longer."

That sounded plausible to Richard, except he remembered Degas's to be quite bright as well. *Wasn't he a high ranking Eden?*

That must require years. His rose should have been faded as well.

Faded. Suddenly, his mind jumped to Rita's funeral.

The grass withers, the flower fades, but the word of our God will stand forever.

There's no way, Richard thought, but he was already licking his thumb. Once it was moist, he pressed it down on Lamia's wrist and began to rub. Sure enough, the bright colors began to break apart and smear. A few more seconds and the entire rose disintegrated.

Richard jumped to his feet.

"What?" Shannon asked, startled.

"We need to get to your babysitters. Right now."

"But the safe house..." Shannon began.

"We need to go now!" This time, Richard didn't wait for a response. He swung the backpack over his shoulder, raced to the garage door, and punched the switch. As soon as the door rose to reach his waist, he ducked under. The morning sun swept over his face, but Richard felt colder than the snow beneath his feet.

Will 1:11

In the deserted Eden parking lot, the Dodge Charger's engine roared to life. It was 7:15 a.m. according to the dashboard display. As Will approached the security booth, he saw that it was unmanned—it seemed that Haynes had kept his promise of ensuring safe passage.

Will blasted through the arm of the security gate and the hunt was on.

He did not know the exact route from St. Herodias to his neighborhood, but the Manhattan skyline across the East River told him that he was still in Queens, somewhere southwest of Woodside. It was enough to find his way. Will drove slowly at first, but once he began to recognize the streets, it took constant effort not to flatten the chrome pedal to the floor. He knew that he could not afford to be pulled over with a pistol sitting in his lap.

As it turned out, speeding wasn't necessary. Every traffic light was green, every intersection with a stop sign was clear of traffic, and anytime Will got behind a sluggish driver, they immediately changed lanes. It was as if God was clearing the path just as He had parted the Red Sea.

Danny rested in the backseat. He was slumped over against the passenger side door, but his eyes were still open. Will and his brother did not speak during the drive and, in a way, Will was glad. The silence kindled Will's hatred. It became a burning, white-hot hatred aimed at everyone in the city: waiters, police officers, neighbors. *Everyone*. The hatred gave Will strength and conviction.

Are there even ten righteous people in this Godforsaken place, Will wondered? *If not, it deserves worse than Sodom and Gomorrah.*

Will never realized when it happened, but his mind had gone blank with fury. When his senses returned, he was parked half a block away from the Benteras' house.

7:27a.m. It was the closest Will had ever come to time travel.

He grabbed the gun. "Wait here," he said to Danny.

"I know," he said, though the boy was sitting up and alert, as if ready to go along had Will only asked.

Will slid the Sig .45 into the breast pocket of Haynes's jacket and stepped out of the car. As subtly as he could, he looked up and down the street. It was empty, but Will hurried down the sidewalk anyway, fighting the urge to look back at his brother. He slowed down when he got to the cement pathway that led to Abe and Sara's front door. Twice, he patted his chest to check that the pistol was still there. And both times, it was.

He rang the doorbell. A familiar soft melody chimed from inside the house, followed by the sounds of shuffling. Will kept his head down until the door cracked open. Strands of pink and gray hair filled the inch-wide gap, along with a slice of Sara's face, her one visible eye squinted beneath the thin, gold-chained door lock.

"I didn't—" The babysitter started to say.

Will kicked the door as hard as he could, cutting her off and sending a shockwave of pain through his skinny leg and into his spine. The chain broke off from the frame and Will could hear Sara tumble to the floor. Will charged in.

The impact seemed to have dazed Sara. She shook feverously, but didn't speak. Tears had already formed around her eyes. She gave Will a look of confusion that filled him with his first bits of satisfaction. *She had no idea I would survive. No idea that I would come back for my son.* Will pulled out his pistol and pointed it at his neighbor.

"Where is he? Where's Gideon?"

Sara held up her hands in vain defense. "He's...he's asleep. I don't—"

Do not hesitate. Because they will not hesitate.

Will pulled the trigger before he could change his mind. Sara's face exploded and the back of her head emptied over the white carpet. Will stood over her, shaking, his body simultaneously hot and cold. There were specks of her blood everywhere, including on Will. He wiped his face with his leather sleeve. Part of him regretted the kill, but a greater part regretted doing it too quickly. *Sara deserved to suffer,* Will believed.

There was flash of movement from the side.

Will turned to see Abe darting towards him with a fire poker. Will raised his gun, but Abe smacked it with the poker before he could shoot. Will lost his grip of the pistol—more from the surprise of the pain than the amount of it—and it dropped to the floor.

Abe swung the poker again, but this time Will was able to dodge it with ease, stepping to the side. From there, Will reached out and grabbed the poker by the shaft. He and Abe struggled for it for a moment before Will ripped it away from the old man.

With his free hand, Will threw the first punch of his life. It hit Abe's temple, throwing the glasses from his face and causing him to stagger backwards. Will had never felt so powerful in his life.

Behind him, the fireplace was alive with flames. Will lunged forward and drove his shoulder into Abe's chest. The old man fell right in front of the burning logs. Before Abe could scramble away, Will stuck the poker between the old man's chest and shoulder, then put all his weight on the weapon, pushing Abe laterally until his head was in the flames.

"No!" Abe cried out. "Please! Stop! *Stop!*"

Will was tempted by the plea, but another voice—a new voice—told him to press even harder. There were a few moments where time appeared to stand still and Will worried that the cultists were immune to fire, but then, in a swift gulp of the flames, the old man's head ignited.

Abe's scream was haunting. It didn't seem to end despite the fire engulfing him and bursting forth from his mouth. Will squeezed his eyes shut.

The scream stopped, morphing into a series of steaming gargles. When those subsided, so did the last of Abe's struggle. Only the tranquil crackling of the fire remained. Will's eyes were still closed.

Until he heard a baby crying somewhere in the house.

Gideon.

Will dropped the poker and rushed to search for his son.

Besides an aching wrist, Will was not physically harmed, yet as he moved through the back hallway, he suddenly felt weak. He stumbled and fell against the doorframe of the guest bedroom that held the crib. Gideon was inside.

"Daddy's here," Will said. He had almost made it to the crib when he heard footsteps behind him. Will spun around to a fist hitting him square in the face. He fell unconscious before he saw who it belonged to or even registered the pain.

Will 1:12

Will woke to the taste of blood. It lingered faintly on his tongue in an otherwise dry mouth. Swallowing was difficult—his tongue felt tender, maybe swollen—and it did nothing more than alert him to the fresh pain throughout his jaw.

Will saw that he was back in the Benteras' living room. The fire was out, though a few remaining tendrils of smoke still rose from the ashes. The bodies of Abe and Sara were right where he had left them. Will felt nauseous and did not want to be there a moment longer.

It quickly became clear, however, that he did not have a choice. He was bound in a sitting position in one of Sara's self-upholstered dining room chairs. Unlike the soft cuffs he remembered in the Primordial Room, the material used to bind Will's wrists behind the chair was sharp, like thin wire. He had the same feeling around his ankles. Anytime he squirmed, the binds sliced into his skin.

Will was still unsure of what had happened. *Another Eden must have been here*, he reasoned. *Got the drop on me and tied me up—holding me until someone brings me back to St. Herodias. Or maybe they called the police to arrest me for the murders.* Will wasn't sure which scenario was worse.

Then, Will's thoughts went back to his son. He no longer heard the baby crying, just silence. "Gideon!" *Please don't be gone.*

There was a rustling sound from just outside the room. Will's heart raced in his chest.

Degas entered. He cradled Gideon in his arm while the baby stirred softly.

"No!" Will shouted, regretting his wish that Gideon was still in the house.

"Look," Degas said to Gideon. "Your father is awake. I'll need a few minutes with him now. For grown up talk." He set the baby down gently on the Benteras' couch. Gideon laid on his back, completely calm—oblivious to the death around him. A small wave of relief swept over Will, seeing that his son was safe, though the feeling was immediately lost as Degas turned towards him. The Eden smiled bigger and brighter than Will had ever seen him smile before.

"The ritual worked," Degas said.

Will shook his head, though he could already feel a lump forming in his throat. "It failed. *You* failed. In front of everyone."

"No," said Degas, still smiling, "but you weren't the only one fooled. The act was meant to be convincing; I left all but a select few out of the loop."

Will said nothing.

"You're confused," Degas said. "But that's why I'm here: to walk you through it. You need to truly appreciate what I have done." He sat down on the couch and ran his fingers through Gideon's wispy hair, causing Will to shudder.

"The ritual was never to erase your family's bloodline," Degas explained smugly. "Bloodlines end every day from natural circumstances: women miscarry, or are barren, couples adopt or simply choose not to have children at all. Tragedies strike: a car crash, a house fire, a random mass murder. Who cares? Do you think a demon of Hell would be impressed if all I did to court him was slit your family's throats? It wouldn't earn me a second glance.

"Here's what I wanted on stage: I wanted it to 'fail' due to something I appeared to overlook. Ending five generations of untainted Catholic blood—there were so many *innate* errors in that proposal. The biggest was that Griffin was not your biological grandfather. That makes the whole bloodline thing invalid. I hoped you would call me out on it—but Richard did instead. It's what saved his life, at the time. Your father was a clever man, I wasn't surprised he caught it.

"Another potential error someone could have pointed out

was that Richard's maternal grandparents were Jewish. You may or may not have known that, but it would have nullified the pure Catholic angle. Oh, and there were only four generations of Batteses present—not five like I said I needed—you and Danny are, of course, the same generation."

Degas paused and seemed to study Will with delight.

"And then," Degas continued, "if you or your family didn't come up with any of those *oversights*, Haynes was ready to come forward and 'confess' to Missek before my knife got to your throat—for not even the archbishop knew that I meant for the entire ceremony to end with my embarrassment."

Will didn't understand and no longer cared if Degas knew it. "Why?"

"Yes! *Why*?" Degas shot up and held out his arms as if to embrace Will. "The act on stage served as a spiritual waypoint if you will—the second of three—that brought you to where you are right now.

"The first was the attack at your home. Masked intruders raining down brutal, unforgiving violence to the likes you have never seen. The experience was designed to shock you, disgust you, and turn your world upside down. I wanted to make you weep and ask God *why*. Why was this happening to you?

"As you found out soon enough, the *bar yetzer hara* was the answer. It *is* a real ritual, the rarest and the highest honor an Eden can achieve. You were made to think I needed you to complete it. I *did*, just not the way I described on stage. Instead, I convinced you that I failed. Why? That's the second waypoint. *Bitter senselessness*. I wanted to enrage you. I wanted you to blame God, despise Him and His plan because all the violence and all the murder He subjected you to ended up being for *nothing*.

"Which led to the final waypoint: losing your baby. The ultimate violation. I wanted it to transform you. With the seeds of fear and doubt sown in the fertile soil of rage, a new Will was born. One of blind fury that I could mold in my hand. A Will that would guide himself into sin.

"After the ritual 'failed,' I came back into the auditorium. From behind, I loosened your bindings. Any eventual pull on your part would result in you breaking free. Not Richard or Daniel, however. Their restraints would hold. And with them unable to follow you, you would go off alone in search of help. As you know, that didn't happen exactly the way I wanted it to. I did not account for the traitor that helped the rest of your family escape from the stage. Who was it, by the way? Who helped you?"

Will pursed his lips.

Degas chuckled. "It was worth a try. It doesn't matter ultimately, though it gave us a scare. It just makes this victory even sweeter as my plan was able to come back together. The guards throughout St. Herodias had already been reduced to a skeleton crew; those remaining were instructed to avoid you and let you escape. One person *would* find you, however. I didn't see it, but I'm sure Haynes put on quite a show. Did he ever tell you he takes acting lessons? Another reason why I love recruiting in New York. His performance filled you with the desire, the confidence, and the conviction to do what you did here today. He gave you the last push that you needed to complete the ritual."

Will was still having trouble following. "What *is* the ritual?"

"Look around you!" Degas shouted. "Corruption!

"The *bar yetzer hara* is never the same thing twice. Think of it like a college thesis, my final project. It was up to me to create something devious enough to impress Decaar—to prove to him that I had the creativity, the devotion, and the ability to crush the Godliness in men.

"After Haynes discovered you in Cosmic Ocean, I knew you were the perfect victim. Innocent, kind, trusting. At first, my proposal to Decaar was to take that heart of yours and defile it with vengeance and direct it, lethally, towards those that did not deserve it. Decaar liked the idea, but it wasn't enough for him.

He added some challenges. I had to accomplish this feat without physically harming you. Not a scratch. And I was very careful about that. I made sure no one carried knives around you and no guns were loaded until Haynes gave you his. Even the handcuffs that held you in the Primordial Room and on stage were as soft and gentle as your first *blankey*. Again, not a drop of your blood was to be spilled until you spilled that of innocents."

The mention of blood made Will taste his own again. "I didn't kill anyone who didn't deserve it."

"No?" Degas lifted up his sleeve, showing Will the same rose tattoo that Abe and Sara had. Then, Degas brought his arm to his mouth and gave it a long, slow lick before rubbing it with his thumb. Will watched in disbelief as the rose and its petals disintegrated. Will felt a tingling of horror.

Degas smiled again. "You never saw her face, did you? When Sara asked for your baby after the ceremony? Of course not. If you did, you'd have seen Lamia in a wig. And if you had put a little saliva on her wrist, the same thing would have happened."

"No," said Will, but it was empty.

Still smiling, Degas stepped backwards to Sara's corpse, grabbed her arm, then dragged the body closer to Will. Degas kneeled and spit on Sara's tattoo, then rubbed furiously. The flower remained unblemished. Degas looked up to Will and shrugged, then pulled out a serrated blade from his belt holster.

Will could not turn away as he watched Degas slice off the area of skin housing the tattoo.

"There we go," said Degas, standing and holding up the tuft of flesh. "Safe to say this one was real. Its origin appears to be true. In fact, everything Sara and Abe have ever told you was true—as far as I know. I've never met them before."

"But they had Gideon..." Will was wishing it all away, talking out loud to find a rational explanation.

"They were innocent, Will! Don't you get it? I had Lamia bring your baby to the Benteras. She said she was a friend of yours and told them you needed him watched for the day while you got called into work. I'm sure they were happy to help." Degas picked Gideon back up from the couch, making Will flinch more than when Degas cut off Sara's tattoo.

Will felt his eyes swell with tears unable to be wiped away.

Degas bounced Gideon roughly in his arms. The baby began to fidget, narrowing his eyes and frowning as if he were about to cry, but he didn't.

"Edens would never want to raise one of these," Degas continued. "We are above parenthood. We know how pathetic it is to brainwash a child. Christianity has yet to realize how a family's bias leads only to empty beliefs and secret resentment." Degas's grip on the baby tightened and the bouncing stopped. "Only *adults* are invited to join our church. Only *adults* can be made into Edens. They must come to hate God on their own terms, for their own reasons, and there is *never* any shortage. Let me show you how worthless children are to us."

Degas palmed the top of Gideon's head, his fingers digging into the baby's face and cheeks. Then he twisted.

There was a soft pop, no louder than a cracked knuckle.

Gideon went limp.

"No!" Will screamed. "No! Giddy! Oh, God! Oh, God!"

Degas tossed Gideon into the corner of the room as if he were a piece of dirty laundry. The baby landed behind the far side of the couch with a thud.

"I'm sorry! I'm so sorry, Giddy!" Will screamed, shaking the chair as hard as he could.

"Yes!" cried Degas. "Show me that raw emotion, the shame, the rage. Don't forget—this is all your fault! You know it's from the sins you committed. The sins I created in you!" Degas closed his eyes and lifted his chin into the air. "Decaar wants your blood. He wants to taste the guilt of its corruption!"

Degas ripped open Will's robe, revealing his bare chest. Once again, Degas drew his blade. Will shook as hard as he could but could not break free. Degas slid the blade across Will's surging chest, but Will barely felt the pain. He looked down to see blood slowly running down his abdomen like dripping paint. Degas cupped his hands and collected it into a little, red pool within his palms. He brought it to his mouth and sipped, then tipped his head back, taking the rest in one unbroken slurp. He dropped his hands to reveal a red goatee as he began to speak. "And that—"

Degas was cut off by a small blip and something bursting through his shoulder and the fabric of his shirt. The impact spun Degas around, spraying blood over Will's face and chest. Will could see his father in the entrance, aiming a pistol in Will's direction.

Degas was wavering from the first shot, but was still on his feet. Richard pulled the trigger again. A piece of Degas's head plastered the painting behind him. Degas spit up blood—some combination of Will's and his own—yet somehow, still remained standing.

Degas turned towards Will. He could see Degas's pupils widen so fully that the iris deformity was barely visible. Finally, Degas collapsed.

Richard stepped closer and without looking at Will, shot Degas three more times in the chest. The muffled *blip blip blip* sounded as glorious to Will as Gabriel's trumpet. Richard kept the gun pointed at Degas for a bit longer, either savoring the moment or making sure Degas stayed dead. Seemingly satisfied, he turned towards Will.

"Are you OK?" Richard asked gently.

Will shook his head no.

Richard came forward, examining the gash on Will's chest. "It's alright," Richard said. "This is nothing."

Will had no way to explain how wrong that statement was.

"What *happened* here?" Richard asked, working at untying Will's restraints. Will wondered how he could begin to explain. He didn't want to—not to mention he was overcome with his own questions. *How did Richard find him? Wasn't he dead? Shannon...?*

"It's OK, you can tell me later. Let's get the hell out of here. Where's Gideon?"

Will felt the wind taken from his lungs all over again. The tears spilled anew. He shook his head at Richard, who only stared back confused. He hadn't seen Gideon yet. All Will could do was use his eyes to convey the answer.

Richard followed Will's gaze and he saw Gideon's corpse, crumpled in the corner of the living room. "Oh, God," he whispered. "Oh, God." Will had never seen his father tremble the way he did, not even the day his mother died. Richard's entire body seemed to be shivering, like he was out in a snowstorm. Then, suddenly it stopped. Richard turned back to Will.

"Let's go. *Now.*" The strength in his voice had returned.

"I can't..." Will started, but Richard yanked him off the chair by his shoulders.

"Yes, you can," Richard said, almost pushing Will towards the door. Will was convinced the anger was directed towards him—as if his father already knew somehow that Will was to blame for this.

"Not a word of this to Danny or Shannon."

"...Shannon's alive?" Will felt a small burst of joy despite the horror he had just been through.

"Yes. And she doesn't need to hear about this. Not now. Do you understand?"

Will shook his head. "I need to tell her."

"No," said Richard.

"I can't ask you to keep this a secret."

"Trust me, Will. I can do it. No more news of tragedy today. We keep this between us. Not to the grave, just until we are *all* ready."

"When will that be?"

Richard didn't answer, just turned and opened the front door. Will followed. He saw a white van parked across the street.

Its driver's side door slid open and Shannon rushed out. She hobbled towards him, almost comically.

"I thought you were dead," Will said, breaking down into tears once again.

Shannon hugged him, stronger than he would have liked. Her chest pressed against his, reminding Will of the pain in his open wound. Then, she kissed him. That hurt as well.

"What happened in there?" she asked, gesturing towards the cut across his chest. Before Will could answer, Shannon spoke again. "And where's Giddy?"

Will could not find the words, so Shannon looked to Richard. "Someone answer me."

"He's not here," Richard said.

"What do you mean he's not here? We heard Lamia say he was."

"We don't know what we heard," Richard answered again.

"If not here, then fucking *where*?"

"I don't know," said Will, "but we'll find him."

"That's right," said Richard, frowning, "so both of you get in the van. Danny's already inside, Will. I caught him on his way to the house carrying a tire iron."

Will and Shannon both made their way to the vehicle, though twice Shannon slowed and looked back at the house. Will went ahead and took the front passenger seat.

As soon as they all were inside, Danny leaned forward between the center console. "Where's Giddy?"

"We're still looking, buddy," said Will.

Danny had another question. "Did you kill them?"

Will stared blankly ahead through the windshield. "Yes."

Danny sat back. "Good."

There was a moment of silence as everyone seemed to absorb the boy's sentiment, then it was broken when Richard started the engine.

"Where are we going?" asked Will.

"Saratoga Springs," Richard answered, handing over the photograph that Bass had given to him. Will looked at it more closely than before. Three men stood in front of the house. One of them was Bass. He was almost unrecognizable in a blue t-shirt, white shorts, and sandals, but the hair and the eyes were surely his. Bass stood in the middle of the trio with his arms around the others. All three were smiling—and it seemed that Bass's smile was widest of all.

Will envied them. He placed the photograph down on the center console.

In the rearview, Will watched the Benteras' house recede. His son would be found by strangers, buried by strangers, never know how much his father loved him, nor how badly his father failed him.

The van turned a corner and the house disappeared. Will closed his eyes. In the darkness there was nothing but hate. No longer towards the city or for the Edens, this hatred was newer, more intense and more unadulterated than any Will could have imagined. And it was directed entirely at himself.

End of Act 3

Kirchheimer 1:1

Detective Bryan Kirchheimer got the case.

He didn't recognize the address when the call came in, though one look at the house and he remembered who lived there.

When Kirchheimer was a uniformed officer, he had patrolled the neighborhood quite often, even off duty. It was a habit he learned from his late father, the celebrated sheriff of a small Oklahoma town.

His father believed the role of the police was not only to respond to crimes, but to be a symbol of security among the people. For this, an officer needed more than just his presence. One had to immerse himself in the community, attend events, and volunteer their time. Know the neighbors, shopkeepers, and crossing guards. Learn their names, their spouse's names, and their children's names. Remember them and greet them, so they are comfortable greeting back, and that will make them feel safe. Be available and be approachable.

But New York City wasn't the easiest place to follow in his father's footsteps. A lot of people didn't like cops, but Abraham and Sara Bentera did. And though many considered Kirchheimer's friendly and conversational attitude as suspicious or even unprofessional, the Benteras never fell into that category either. Abe always greeted him with a handshake and a comment about the weather and Sara never lacked some pastry or baked good to send him home with. Their interactions, however brief or cliché, always felt genuine to Kirchheimer.

Since his promotion, however, Kirchheimer could not remember the last time he had seen them. Two, three years maybe? There had been little need for a homicide detective to visit that street.

The Benteras had always been childless, and that, Kirchheimer believed, was why he could remember their first names after so long: they shared theirs with arguably the most famous childless couple in all of history—though the Benteras' biblical counterparts eventually received one. The Benteras, now, never would.

Kirchheimer arrived at their home only ten minutes after the first responders. He smacked his size twelve boots against the side of the door frame before he entered, knocking free the muddy slush, then ducked under the yellow tape. He nodded to the officers in uniform while showing his badge. They nodded back.

For a murder of an elderly couple like the Benteras, Kirchheimer figured it was a robbery gone wrong. Intruders didn't usually kill unless they had to—in other words, when someone put up a fight. From what Kirchheimer remembered of Abe's military history, that could have been a possibility.

"Jesus Christ," said Kirchheimer as he took in the scene. *This was more than a fight.* In fact, he couldn't be sure that the bodies even belonged to the elderly couple he once knew. The female's face was half blown away and the male's was charred so badly that Kirchheimer could make out the contours of a skull. A third body, male and possibly early forties, had multiple gunshot wounds and a mostly intact face, but Kirchheimer did not recognize him.

"What do we have?" Kirchheimer asked.

"A mystery," said Blair, a female officer and the first on the scene. She was young and bulky, with black hair and a pixie cut. "The door was kicked in," she continued as Kirchheimer paced around the bodies.

"Does anything look stolen?"

"Nothing. This seems to be the only room that saw any action. Everywhere else is pristine. If our John Doe was the burglar," she said, gesturing towards the unidentified body, "he never made it far enough to swipe anything."

Kirchheimer nodded, though he had already entertained that

thought and moved onto other possibilities. "Someone else was here at some point. And look at this chair, it belongs at the dining room table. These wires on the floor—they're bloody. Someone was tied up, but no one has any abrasions around their wrists or ankles."

"Mrs. Benteras?" Blair asked.

"No. Look, her laceration is different. Skinned by a knife, maybe."

"You're right," Blair replied mechanically. Kirchheimer didn't mind the officer's oversight. *Incompetence is a rite of passage*, his father believed. *But get through it as fast as you can.*

"I see the results of two different calibers," Kirchheimer said, comparing Sara's wounds to John Doe's. "But where are the guns?"

"Had to be taken by our missing person," Blair responded, now scribbling in her notepad.

On the wall behind the couch was a large framed photograph of Abe and Sara. Kirchheimer made his way to it, to remind himself how the faces of the couple used to look. "Did you know," he said to Blair, "that I knew these folks—just casually— way back when. The old man had the sturdiest handshake and always commented about the—oh, my *Jesus.*"

"What?" Blair rushed over. "Oh my *God*! Is that a baby?"

Before Kirchheimer could respond, he heard a hacking cough from behind. He spun around, swiftly drawing his gun. John Doe was sitting up, spitting out mouthfuls of blood.

"Lord!" Kirchheimer called out. "You said that man was dead!"

"He had no pulse. I know he didn't—"

"Get the paramedics back in here *now!*"

Blair rushed outside. Kirchheimer watched through the window as the two young paramedics tossed their cigarettes to the ground and sprinted towards the house.

Kirchheimer knelt beside the John Doe. "You're going to

be alright. We're going to get you to the hospital." The victim responded with a stare that chilled Kirchheimer to the bone. It wasn't just the look of contempt—it was the eyes. They were a deep, bright red as if composed solely of broken blood vessels. And his pupils, each lopsidedly spilling over into the iris, filled him with fear. But he knew this man was clinging to life, surely feeling more fear than anyone. "We're going to get you help, brother."

John Doe's face grew tight with anger. He opened his mouth like he was about to speak, but just hacked up more blood—all over Kirchheimer's shirt and tie—then fell unconscious.

Degas 1:6

You are not my brother, he thought. He tasted blood. He felt it spew from his mouth. Then, he felt nothing.

Degas awoke in a hospital bed with his head slightly elevated. Two familiar faces stood at the foot of the mattress.

"You are one!" Missek proclaimed. Haynes said nothing, just flashed a toothy smile.

"It worked?" Degas asked weakly, but then he felt it, the power inside him.

"Not only did you survive five gunshots," Missek responded, "but your Aura now is overwhelming. If you don't want to start a riot in the hospital, you may want to dial it back. Control will become easier with time."

Degas was not in the mood for a lesson, nor did he share their smiling sentiments. "I want Richard!" he rasped, his voice already growing stronger. "I want Will! They think they *beat* me!"

"I'm afraid they're gone," replied Missek, "with Shannon and Daniel as well. Not everything went—"

"I will track them. I will catch them and kill them."

"No," Missek said gently, "you won't. I have no doubt you would be successful, but there is a more important task that neither you nor Decaar were aware of. One that cannot wait." Missek's decrepit teeth seemed to come alive, dancing as he smiled. "One assigned by Satan himself."

Degas could not respond, this was the honor he had always lusted for, yet it meant no revenge. Not now. Maybe not ever.

It was Haynes that broke the silence. "I have been tasked with finding Will and the others. I hope you know how motivated I will be. I also have Dullahan, Pavel, and Biana to assist me."

"Why not Fen and Lamia?" Degas asked.

Haynes turned to Missek, who answered that question. "They

were killed trying to stop the rest of the family from escaping."

Degas closed his eyes, surprised by the sting of the words. He had been unsure how much of his humanity would remain after the *bar yetzer hara*. As it seemed, there was quite a bit. Degas refused to let it overtake him.

Degas opened his eyes. "Listen closely," he said, focused on Haynes. "Make them suffer in my name. Get as much joy out of it as you can, for after their last breath they will be taken to Heaven and any pain you caused them will be forgotten."

Degas sat up in his bed. "Except Will. I do not know if he will recover from this. I believe his sins may have overwhelmed him. If he has not repented, *do not* let him. Find him quickly, kill him quickly. Send him to Hell."

Haynes listened intently without once breaking eye contact. "Well, I shall waste no more time." He reached forward and shook Degas's hand. Degas squeezed back. With a final nod to Degas, then to Missek, Haynes left the room.

Missek stepped forward. "Let me get that bandage off you. We should leave as well."

"Tell me," said Degas. "What of the traitor?"

"Unknown at this point, though finding him or her or them is my top priority. I've narrowed it down to a few—" Missek stopped short.

"What is it?"

"Your wounds are *completely* healed. The reports said an eighth of your skull was blown off, but here I see it, fully intact! As if it never happened! The strength of this *bar yetzer hara* is remarkable. I've never seen healing this fast—except for your eyes, Victor. Each coloboma is still there. Could you not fuse them back together?"

"We chose not to," Degas responded, with a deeper voice than was his own. "They are no longer physical deformities but a symbol of what we represent."

Missek smiled again. "Of course. Then arise, Lord Degas. Do

me the honor of escorting me out of this place. I cannot wait to give you your assignment."

State of Amazonas, Brazil

Peak opened his eyes, but could not see. Like every time, the boy wondered if he had gone blind for good. He rubbed his eyes vigorously then tried again. Some vision returned.

Peak was not alone. His father, as always, was by his side, but the man next to him was new. Another white man. Peak thought they had all left. He was sad when they did. They had been nice to him, taught him new things, and tried to help him feel better—but the adults in the village had not felt the same way.

Peak knew he was sick. A tumor, Dr. Michael had called it. *Kunnok*, according to Quando. *Darkness*. The two never agreed on anything, and neither of their medicines had worked. The headaches, the dizziness, the slurring speech, the loss of sight and hearing—they always came back.

Except this morning. Right now, Peak actually felt healthy. Kind of like he did before the problems started. His vision had even improved from what it had been just minutes before. He saw his father's face clearly; he was smiling.

"Glorious," the chief said, almost in tears. "My son looks better already."

"And that was just from the touch of my hand," replied the stranger, speaking the language of the Nacana. Peak had never heard an outsider speak it so fluently.

"Truly, you are who you say you are," said the chief.

The stranger nodded. "You shall always receive the truth from me. But now, as we agreed, it's time to clear out those who do not belong. Those who tried to hurt your child."

Peak listened intently, wondering who the stranger meant. *Who had tried to hurt me*, he wondered? But the question was quickly washed away when he heard his father's reply.

"Let us burn our enemies."

"Who are our enemies?" Peak asked, startled by the severity

of the punishment. The Nacana had never burned a human before.

His father shushed him.

"No," said the stranger politely, glancing briefly at Peak, then back to his father. "Not all of them will be burned. I know how painful fire can be, but the suffering it causes is too short. For those responsible, we need to send a *stronger* message."

"What do you propose?" The chief asked.

The stranger touched his forehead to the chief's. "I want to teach you how to *crucify*."

The last word was spoken in English, but Peak recognized it. Reverend Cara had used it in one of her speeches.

"Show me," his father said.

The stranger nodded. "Summon your best builders. Have them gather wood and the nails the visitors left behind. We need to build four big crosses."

Then, he squatted next to Peak, reached out, and stroked the boy's face. The touch made him feel sick—not in the way the tumor had, but somehow worse.

"Put your son back to sleep," the stranger continued instructing the chief. "And make sure the other children in the village remain in their homes." He looked directly at Peak. His eyes were unlike the other white men's—or any man Peak had ever seen. Part of each blue ring was missing, as if an animal had taken a bite out of them. "This is not something for you to see."

Then, the stranger left, followed closely by his father.

Peak remained in his bed, uneasy and confused. *Why crucifixion?* He remembered that by crucifixion Jesus had saved the world. *The white visitors wore crosses around their necks. Held them while they prayed. Said it gave them strength. Crucifixion couldn't be a punishment. It couldn't be worse than fire.*

But it was.

It began with hammering. Familiar sounds that had filled the village ever since the white people came, ones that represented building and growth, even comfort. But then it stopped and there was pleading—cries for help from voices he recognized, in both English and Nacana. He heard Dr. Reising, Dr. Michael, Cara, and Quando. All of them shouting desperately for whatever was happening to stop, but their pleas were met with only the sounds of beatings.

Shortly, the hammering resumed and the pleas of the four became screams of agony.

From among the cries, the voice of Pastor Cara stood out. "Jesus!" she called out. "Jesus, save me!"

Peak wanted it all to stop more than he had ever wanted anything. But guards were stationed outside the hut. He was not allowed out. There was nothing he could do. Or was there?

For where two or three are gathered in my name, there am I among them. Cara taught Peak that lesson, the power of prayer. Jesus did not come because Cara alone shouted to him.

So Peak prayed. He prayed wholeheartedly. He begged Jesus to make it all stop. And as he did, his vision dimmed, then went black. A ringing began in his ears, then faded until he could hear nothing at all. Though it seemed like the tumor was roaring back to life, Peak felt no pain—only that his senses had been taken away. All evidence of the tortures around him were gone.

And there, in his sanctuary, silent and dark, Peak met another stranger, one whose touch brought warmth and peace.

From somewhere in the darkness above, a dove descended.

End of Book One

Acknowledgments

I must thank God first and foremost. Faith and doubt come hand-in-hand and while I tried to approach both sides fairly in this novel, albeit from some extreme angles, I believe everything I have comes from Him.

Secondly, I have to thank my wife. I started writing this novel before I even met her, but I don't know how I could have completed it without her. She gave me the space and encouragement I needed. The back massages, too. When I wanted to work less days at my real job so that I could focus on my writing, she was cool with that. We made the finances work. When I needed a set of eyes to proofread yet another rewrite, she was there as well. Ali, thank you for your pure support. I love you.

Thank you to Jeff Gore, my longtime friend, who provided the often harsh feedback that shaped the Cult of Eden into (what I believe is) the smart and solid story it came out to be.

A big thanks to Uncle Richie and Grandma. You have both been with me from the beginning, reading and discussing each new chapter with excitement and, in Grandma's case, absolute bias. You believed my first draft was good enough to publish (it certainly wasn't).

Thank you to my dad, who dislikes any story darker than an Andy Griffith episode. Still, you encouraged me every time I lost momentum and guaranteed that I'd have at least one sale through you—even if you might not read it.

My mom, on the other hand, loves horror, so she didn't like it when I refused to show her any early work. I made her wait until official publication so that I could give her the best version I had to offer. Thanks for your patience and I hope I made you proud.

To every early reader that provided feedback, not only did you improve the quality of the book, you maintained my morale throughout the process. Thank you Lindi (one love), Andy, Dina,

Jenn, Jenny, Alwin, and Kelly.

To the staff at Cosmic Egg, thank you for seeing potential in my submission and taking my project to where it is today.

Thanks to Aimee and Alan...I'm sure for something.

And lastly, thanks to everyone who bought, borrowed, downloaded, burned for sustenance, or otherwise consumed this book. Thank you for giving a debut author a chance. I hope I gave you a group of characters to care about.

Their story is not over.

About Bill Halpin

Bill Halpin was born and raised in Orlando, Florida, where the seeds of horror were planted at an early age. As a kid, he often slept over at his grandparents' house. Much to his parents' dismay, he stayed up late with Grandpa to watch all of the monster movies Blockbuster and afterhours TV had to offer. To this day, his love for all that is scary has never left him. After graduating from the University of Central Florida, he moved on to New York City and earned a degree in Optometry from SUNY. Now he practices in Saratoga Springs, NY and writes in between his appointments. He has been blessed with a beautiful wife, Ali, and their daughter, Finley. Outside of horror, he enjoys Muay Thai, crane machines, beer, escape rooms, the Marvel Universe, and in-depth board games.

THE CULT OF EDEN is his debut novel.

Visit Bill at:
www.BillHalpinBooks.com
Follow him on Facebook at:
www.facebook.com/BillHalpinBooks/
Or reach out by Email to:
authorbillhalpin@gmail.com

Thank you again for reading The Cult of Eden. If you have a few moments, please add a short review on Amazon, Goodreads, or Apple iTunes Store. I would be grateful. Reviews are very important for authors, especially those early in their careers. They help us, big time, and I truly appreciate every one.

The Gawain Legacy
Jon Mackley
If you try to control every secret, secrets may end up controlling
you.
Paperback: 978-1-78279-485-1 ebook: 978-1-78279-484-4

Readers of ebooks can buy or view any of these bestsellers by
clicking on the live link in the title. Most titles are published
in paperback and as an ebook. Paperbacks are available in
traditional bookshops. Both print and ebook formats are
available online.
Find more titles and sign up to our readers' newsletter at
http://www.johnhuntpublishing.com/fiction
Follow us on Facebook at https://www.facebook.com/JHPfiction
and Twitter at https://twitter.com/JHPFiction